WANTON WOMEN

ANONYMOUS

CARROLL & GRAF PUBLISHERS, INC.
NEW YORK

Copyright © 1994 by Carroll & Graf Publishers, Inc.

First Carroll & Graf edition 1994
Second Carroll & Graf edition 1999

Carroll & Graf Publishers, Inc.
19 West 21st Street
New York, NY 10010-6805

ISBN: 0-7867-0673-2

Contents

Rosa Fielding:
Victim Of Lust

Chapter One

It was a fine morning in May, and the dull, little frequented High Street of the small country town called Rutshole seemed absolutely cheerful, as if inspired by the exhilarating atmosphere.

So at least thought Mr Bonham, a portly widower of fifty or thereabouts, as having left his carriage at the inn, he proceeded down High Street leisurely, but with the usual solemnity on his countenance, (which he considered dignified and respectable) much lightened by the cheering weather. He stopped at the door of a small shop, on which was inscribed, 'Trabb, Hosier and Glover'. Here he entered.

Now that capital woman of business, the widow Trabb, was engaged in suiting a stiff-necked old maid with a pair of mittens; but even if she had not been so occupied, we very much doubt if she would herself have attended to a gentleman customer. The worthy woman knew that there are other means of making a shop attractive besides the excellence and cheapness of the wares therein sold: and she had enlisted in her services a pretty girl of sixteen, whose remarkable grace and modesty had already attracted numerous young squires, young farmers, and officers from the neighbouring garrison town, as real or pretended customers, to the manifest advantage of Mrs Trabb's till.

When therefore, she saw the rich and respectable Mr Bonham enter her shop, she summoned her aide-de-camp with 'Rosa, attend to the gentleman!' and continued her attention to her customer. Now Mr

Bonham, though nearly fifty as we have said, and of a very staid and even strict outward demeanour, was by no means so elderly in his feelings and capabilities as would have been judged from outward appearances. He had been early left a widower, and the very fact of his having to keep up the said outward appearances and his ambition to have a saintly character among his neighbours and friends, had forced him to restrain his indulgences within very narrow bounds, and to be circumspect and moderate in the enjoyment thereof. So that this self denial was of a double benefit to him; among the saints of his acquaintance he was esteemed as 'one of the elect and a babe of grace', while he himself was pleasingly conscious that, thanks to his regular but very generous diet, and his habit of self control (not abstinence) as to the softer sex, he was enjoying what is called a green old age; and was when on the verge of fifty, pretty confident that his latent powers when called into action would be found quite equal to those of many a worn out young roué of five and twenty.

He was remarkably struck with Rosa's beauty, and well he might be. Long, flowing, golden hair; deep blue eyes, a sweet but by no means insipid expression of face, combined with a graceful figure, and manners very attractive even in her humble occupation; all detained Mr Bonham in purchasing a pair of gloves, longer than he had ever been in his life before. Certainly he was very difficult to suit; and Rosa had to take the measurements of his hand more than once. At last he was suited – as far as gloves were concerned – and was about to leave the shop when a bright idea struck him. He turned back to where Mrs Trabb was standing, that estimable woman had just got rid of her Low Church-looking customer triumphantly, she had clapped two pence extra onto the price of the mitts, and then after some bargaining submitted to rebate a penny. So both parties were satisfied, and Mrs T felt not only 'at peace with all men' (that she generally was) but with all women too (which was not so frequently the case).

'Mrs Trabb,' began the respectable gentleman, 'I would like to consult you about a little matter of business that may be a source of gain to a trades woman in your line; besides being conducive to the moral benefit of a tribe of benighted heathens.'

'Dear me, Mr Bonham,' exclaimed the gratified hosier, 'step this way – very kind of you I'm sure – a glass of cherry brandy? – do now – and sit down and rest yourself.'

So saying, she ushered the artful old gentleman into her snug back parlour; and producing the refreshment alluded to, awaited further disclosures.

We will not weary the reader with a full account of the proposed mercantile transaction. Suffice it to say that Mr Bonham disclosed a case of soulharrowing destitution among the Fukkumite Islanders recently converted to Christianity.

The interesting females had not the wherewithal to cover their bare bottoms, but used to display those well rounded features to the unhallowed gaze of the unregenerate sailors of whale ships calling at the islands. Now the missionaries considered that if any bottoms were to be displayed by their precious converts, the exhibition should be made in private to their spiritual advisers. And to end the story, the benevolent gentleman, by way of advancing the moral and physical comforts of the Fukkumite ladies (to say nothing of the missionaries) asked Mrs Trabb if she would like to contract for the supply of say to begin with, one thousand pairs of frilled pantalettes.

'Really very kind of you, Mr Bonham, to give me such a chance,' said the gratified shopkeeper, 'but may I ask you, sir, if the creatures, or converts, or whatever is most proper to call them, are to wear nothing else but those trousers?'

'No, I believe not,' was the answer. 'Why?'

'Because sir,' replied the experienced widow, 'a woman's pants are made, to speak plainly, with openings at the front and rear, corresponding to her natural openings; so really, though I shall be very glad to undertake the contract, I must tell you before hand, for fear of having my goods thrown back on my hands, that the garments proposed are no obstruction whatever to a man who is determined to violate a woman.'

'Very proper of you to make the remark, Mrs Trabb, very business-like and fair; but then of course the women should have opportunities for performing their natural functions conveniently; and then our self-sacrificing brethren, the missionaries, they must have facilities for their comforts.'

'Oh, of course, sir,' was the response.

'Then send in your estimate, Mrs Trabb, I'll see that you have a good chance. By the bye, Mrs Trabb, who is that modest looking and rather attractive young person who attended to my requirements in your shop just now?'

Aha! thought the sharp widow, that's it, eh? (Rather caught I should think.)

'That young woman, sir, is a daughter of the Fieldings. You know, sir, farmers about three miles from here. Rosa her name is – a very nice girl and as good as she looks. Take another glass, sir!'

'No, thank you, Mrs Trabb, send in those estimates as soon as you can and good luck to you.'

Exit Bonham.

The very next morning he mounted his fine weight-carrying cob and riding out leisurely, as if for exercise, had no sooner got out of sight and hearing of Rutsden Lodge, as his residence was termed, and out of the ken of his sharp daughter Eliza, than he spurred his good hackney into a smart trot, which pace being occasionally varied by a canter, very soon brought him to Elm Tree Farm.

Farmer Fielding was out, which his visitor was not altogether very sorry for, as he thought it would be better in every way to begin his tactics by talking the old lady over. She received him very kindly and hospitably, though evidently puzzled to know the object of his visit. Mr Bonham was not long in breaking ground, for he knew the farmer might return in five minutes. He recounted to the gratified mother how he had been struck by the elegant yet modest and quiet appearance of Rosa, and how he was pleased to learn from Mrs Trabb, that she was as good as she looked; that notwithstanding the great respectability of Mrs T and her establishment, and the high opinion he had of her moral worth, still he could not but be aware that a position behind her counter was pernicious, if not absolutely dangerous, to a girl of Rosa's attractive personal qualities.

'Why my dear Madam,' urged the moralist, 'I am informed that the young squires and farmers will ride a couple miles out of their way to deal in Mrs Trabb's shop; and then those dragoon officers come all the way from Baboonfield Barracks. I know that man of Moab, their Colonel, Earl Phuckum the first, gets all his clothes from London, and I'd like to know what he wants in Mrs Trabb's in High Street.'

'Perhaps dear Rosy will make a good marriage,' simpered the fond and foolish mother.

'Perhaps, madam,' interposed Mr Bonham sternly, 'she may learn something what ought to come after marriage but never before. How would you like to hear of her bolting off to London with one of those swells who perhaps is married already, and her returning to you in about twelve months, neglected, sick and heartbroken, with a baby in her arms? Now listen to me, Mrs Fielding,' continued Mr Bonham, gazing attentively into the good dame's horror-stricken face, 'I am not too old to have my fancies. Moreover, my daughter will soon be married and off my hands, and I have no one else to interfere with me.'

With this introduction, the model gentleman proposed a scheme of his own, namely that Rosa should be placed in a first-rate school in the neighbourhood of London; that all the expenses, including her equipment, should be borne by him; and that in twelve or eighteen months, if Rosa had been well behaved and steady, and had improved in body and mind, as there was every reason to suppose she would, he, the speaker, would make her Mrs Bonham, and mistress of Rutsden Lodge.

This grand proposition fairly took away the good old lady's breath, and there is no doubt her reply would have been a ready acceptance of Mr Bonham's proposition but then there appeared old Fielding and the whole story had to be commenced over again.

He did not receive Mr Bonham's offer as enthusiastically as his wife had done; but he owned at the same time the risk that Rosa ran in her present situation; and in plain blunt speech detailed how Susan Shufflebum had been seen behind a hayrick with her legs over young Squire Rootlepole's back.

'And I suppose, missus,' continued the worthy man, 'I needn't tell ye what he was a-doing to her; and Harriette Heavely went a-walking in Snugcroft woods with one of the danged soger officers, and when she got home her white petticoats was all green with damp grass, and she was so sore between her thighs that she has not been able to walk rightly since. But still, Master Bonham, although your proposal would take our Rosa out of the way of danger; leastways out of a good deal, for a young good-looking lass is never to stay quite out of danger; yet I don't quite like the girl brought up above her station. She'll maybe look down on her old father and mother, and maybe she'll be looked down upon and made to feel the difference by them that's born of better families.'

This sensible speech of Farmer Fielding's was combated pretty sharply by the other two parties to the conversation; the old woman being anxious to see her daughter made a rich lady, and loth to miss the present chance; and Mr Bonham continuing to urge that his being almost entirely without relations and that his daughter being about to be married, would place Rosa in a far different and much more pleasant situation than is usually the case under such circumstances. He even went on to say that although Fielding had a right to deal as he liked with regards to his own daughter, yet he considered it would be almost sinful for him to throw away such a good chance to have her well educated and married, and that too in the fear of the Lord. Half badgered to death between the pair of them – the old farmer yielded a reluctant consent, upon which Mr Bonham and Mrs Fielding went at once into matters of detail with regard to preparation of outfit and so on.

One thing was determined upon, that the matter might not be talked about more than was absolutely necessary; Mr Bonham in particular to conceal his philanthropic schemes from his daughter Eliza, lest peradventure she had been addicted to wrath. And Farmer Fielding thought that the less said about Rosa until she appeared as Mrs Bonham the better.

We do not intend to weary our readers as to matters of outfit, suffice it to say that Mrs Trabb was in high glee and began to think that Mr Bonham, what with his missionary zeal on behalf of the sweet Fukkumite savages, and his philanthropic intentions regarding Rosa's welfare was going to make her fortune. Certainly she never had had two such orders in one twelvemonth, much less in one week. One remark of hers to Mr Bonham is worthy of notice.

With the natural sharpness of a woman and a widow to boot, she took it for granted that Mr B would like to know some particulars about the undergarments she had been furnishing for his pretty protegee, and after expatiating for about an hour or so about silk stockings, cotton stockings, chemises, night-dresses, petticoats, and the Lord only knows what besides, she concluded with:

'And I quite remember your sensible remarks Mr Bonham, about those trousers made for those converted cannibals. Miss Rosa's are much finer of course, and prettier altogether, but they are equally convenient, they are quite open back and front.'

This remark was made with a good deal of emphasis and meaning; but the venerable philanthropist merely replied, without moving a muscle of his face:

'You are quite right, Mrs Trabb, and have acted very judiciously; one never knows what may be required in case of emergency!'

It was reported to a few friends and neighbours that Rosa was offered a situation in London as a nursery governess and that as Mr Bonham was going to town on business he had kindly offered to convey the young lady thither in his own carriage; being, as he said, altogether safer and pleasanter for a young unprotected girl than the public conveyance. This excuse passed currently enough, and if some of the envious or captious neighbours shook their heads and said Old Bonham was a sly fox, what business was it of theirs, after all?

Rosa enjoyed the ride immensely. Her guardian, as she took to calling him, was so kind and so affectionate (the fact was that he kept kissing her a great many times, and much more warmly than there was any occasion for) that she considered herself a very fortunate girl. And then he took such an interest in minor matters, he wanted to know how Mrs Trabb had executed his orders – with regard to her wardrobe – and in his anxiety to know if everything was nice and proper, actually commenced to investigate Rosa's underclothing. He expressed his opinion that the petticoats would do; but that the outer one was hardly fine enough, but that defect could be repaired in London; his researches became more interesting when the chemise was put upon its trial.

'And now, Rosa darling,' said the ancient voluptuary, 'let me see if Mrs Trabb has obeyed my orders about your trousers, I told her to have them made a certain way or you were to wear none at all.'

'Oh, dear me, Mr Bonham,' exclaimed Rosa, who all this time had been dutifully holding up her clothes to facilitate her guardian's exploration, 'you will make me ashamed of myself!'

'Not at all, my dear girl,' was the reassuring reply, 'it is my duty to see that you have everything nice and proper, and your duty to submit to the inquiry; so put your graceful right leg over my left shoulder.'

Trembling and blushing, the innocent girl, fancying that it was not quite right and yet not knowing very well how to refuse, did as she was requested and made a splendid exposure of her secret parts immediately.

'Ha!' exclaimed Bonham, 'I see that Mrs Trabb has not neglected her duty; your trousers are well open in front certainly, though for the sake of seeing your thighs I would have preferred no trousers at all. But your cunt shows very nicely – golden hair, I see – not quite as much as you will have in twelve months, but a very fair show for a young girl of sixteen, – and very nice lips.'

Here the moral gentleman inserted the first two fingers of his right hand in Rosa's tender orifice, at which the poor girl could not help an exclamation and making some slight appearance of resistance. On this her companion remarked:

'As you are going to be married to me in twelve or eighteen months, my lovely Rosa, I regard you already as my wife, morally speaking, and if the jolting of this carriage will allow, I will give you a practical proof of it.'

'A practical proof sir?' stammered Rosa.

'Yes, my beloved child, look here!' So saying, he unfastened his trousers and brought to view his cock, and a very good, useful, stiff-standing, domestic piece of machinery it was.

'Take hold of it, my little pet, do not be afraid, it won't hurt you.'

'What is it?' asked Rosa, who had never seen anything like it before, but who was clasping it as she was told, in a way that was increasing the weapon materially in size and stiffness.

'How hot it is,' she remarked.

'Yes love,' said her guardian, 'he is rather feverish, and there is considerable irritation, but you have a little warm bath between those lovely thighs of yours; and he will be quite cured after I have plunged him in and let him soak a couple of minutes.'

'I shall be very glad, my dear guardian, to do anything to contribute to your comfort or to show my gratitude for the kindness you have done me; but I do, I certainly do think that this thing, this part of your person, (I hardly know what to call it) is far too large to go into the slit between my thighs – which just now you called my cunt. Of course, you have a right to do as you please with me, and are perfectly welcome; but I fear you will hurt me dreadfully, even if you do not actually split my belly open, or extend my little orifice as far back as my bottom hole.'

'No fear, my sweet charmer,' replied her guide, philosopher and friend, 'your sweet orifice is destined by Providence for these assaults, and is wonderfully elastic; there is no risk therefore of my splitting your belly up or knocking your two holes into one – I should be very sorry to destroy such an elegant specimen of nature's handiwork, especially as I hope to live and to enjoy you for fifteen years to come – so open your thighs as wide as you can possibly stretch them, with your feet placed upon the opposite seat.'

Trembling, but obedient, the girl did as she was required, producing, as any of our readers will find, if they choose to try the experiment, a very favourable position.

(NB Should the seat on which the lady's bottom is situated be too high, a small carpet bag, a folded cloak, or an extra cushion under the gentleman's knees will raise him to the desired height.)

After this slight digression, let us proceed. However confidently Mr Bonham might have expressed himself as to his facilities of entrance into Rosa's virgin sanctuary he still did not neglect the only precautions which were at hand. It had never been his intention, until stimulated by the girl's outward graces and secret charms, to violate Rosa in his carriage, and therefore he had not provided himself with any cold cream or pomade, so the only lubricant he possessed was his mouth, and of that he proceeded to make such good use, that his pretty friend, who at first shrank nervously from the operation, as he proceeded, found it endurable, and at last actually began to like it, at least if her leaning complacently back with a half-smile upon her face, and endeavouring to stretch her thighs beyond their present extension could be interpreted as signs of such a feeling. We think so, and it is quite evident that her guardian thought so too, for murmuring to himself: 'Now's the time!' shifted his posture so as to bring his priapus and appendages into the situation just previously occupied by his mouth. The lips of Rosa's cunt were still open, and Mr Bonham had a fair chance and greatly to his credit he availed himself of it manfully. In he went about an inch and a half, and – there he stuck. Now had he attempted Rosa's maidenhood when first his prick came to full stand, we do not know what he might not have effected, but he had retained his member's tension too long, and had excited himself too much; consequently after getting

in a short way as we have described, and making Rosa
cry with his efforts against her barrier, his eager
pushes were brought to a close in the most natural
manner possible; viz – by the arrival of the moment
of delight, which certainly in this instance was a one-
sided pleasure, and indeed hardly that, for we hold
that even to give the man his proper share of transport, the injection must be performed when he is
fairly within his companion, for spunking about the
lips and mossy hair, or even an inch or so into the
passage, as Mr Bonham did on this occasion, can
hardly be called a satisfactory termination to a fuck.
On this occasion it was not quite as bad as it might
have been; for Rosa, who had gathered from some
expressions of disappointment on the part of her
friend, and a sort of intuitive feeling that all girls
possess, that all was not right, was spared for the
moment the pain of a burst maidenhood, and if her
guardian was not quite satisfied, he was at least quieted, and that did quite as well, particularly as by this
time the carriage was entering the suburbs of London
– to say nothing of the risk of Thomas the coachman,
or John the footman, becoming accidental spectators
of his little game, and reporting him at home accordingly. So by his advice, Rosa wiped herself dry, and
he looked as fatherly and demure as he could; and
from his long practice in what we hardly choose to
call hypocrisy but something very like it, succeeded
very well. And by the time the carriage arrived at the
gate of Mrs Moreen's Seminary for young ladies
in Clapham nobody could have guessed from his
manner that anything had transpired during the short
journey irreconcilable with the fatherly manner he
exhibited toward Rosa.

Mrs Moreen was most favourably impressed with
his manner, and indeed was prepared to welcome
him cordially, in consequence of the liberal
arrangements entered into in the correspondence

that had already passed between them.

She was also much interested in Rosa, being quite judge enough to see that, country bred and uneducated though she might be, she had all the capabilities of making a very elegant and showy young lady.

Leaving Rosa then thus happily situated; and her protector sitting down to a late dinner at a hotel in Covent Garden, for the old sinner made an excuse to himself for passing the night in London, being that his carriage horses would be knocked up by the return journey on the same day – besides, had he not business of some kind next morning? – leaving then these friends of ours so comfortable, we will return to Rutsden Lodge, and entering a small room where a tall, dashing-looking young lady with dark eyes and raven hair is writing a letter, we will take the privilege of narrators who are ex-officio, invisible, and ubiquitous, and peep over a round white shoulder.

The letter began: 'My dearest Alfred,' and after a few ordinary remarks, got business-like and even warm.

'I am afraid,' the letter ran, 'that my father is going to make a fearful fool of himself. There was a baby-faced girl in a shop here and the old idiot, I fear, has seen her and fancied her. If he would only give her a fucking and a five pound note,' (this was the style the young lady wrote in,) 'there would be no harm done, but I believe, though don't know anything for certain, that she has got a governess's place in London, and he had conveyed her there in his carriage. He had to go up to town on business.

'Now I no more believe in his business than in her governess's situation – for she is not fit for one; and I believe the whole thing is a blind. And, what's more, her stupid old mother has been talking nonsense about her Rosa being a lady, all which, without being absolute proofs, make up a strong case against the old gentleman. Just fancy me with a mother-in-law! – a vulgar, uneducated country girl, about sixteen or seventeen years old. Of course, my dear Alfred, I know that you will marry me as soon as you can; indeed I think that in gratitude for the numerous privileges I have granted you, you should make a point of doing so – not that I regret that I allowed you to fuck me for I have enjoyed it very much, and trust entirely to your honour. But, then you see my dearest cousin, that somebody else can fuck besides you, and as sure as that stupid old party, my respected father, marries a young fresh country girl, he'll get her with child – just you see if he doesn't! And then my inheritance will be lessened at his death, or perhaps cut away altogether. And as for you, my dear cousin, you will come in simply for nothing at all. But you had better get a few days leave and come here on some pretext or other and we will have a consultation on the subject. You see if you or some of your brother officers could get access to this girl, give her a good rogering and get her with child, or turn her upon the town, it would settle the question at once. And I think it might be done. I will try to find out her address from that foolish old mother of hers. But do you come here at any rate, my dearest Alfred; for I rather think that I want something else besides a consultation; indeed the night before last I had a dream about you, awoke with a wet night-gown; so if you do come you had better take the precaution of bringing a dozen preventatives in the shape of French letters in your pocket. For I suppose you will be wanting as usual to make the best use of your privileges both as a cousin and an engaged lover; and I know how those affectionate liberties usually terminate.'

This was in effect the termination of the young lady's letter, with the exception of a few strong and passionate expressions of enduring attachment.

It was addressed to Captain Alfred Torrant, 51st

Dragoons, Baboonfield Barracks, where it was duly received by that meritorious officer. He read it over twice, so as to read, mark, learn and digest the contents; then prudently and properly burnt it.

Then he relieved his feelings by swearing a good deal; having by this precaution blown off any surplus steam, he at once applied to his commanding officer for a few days leave of absence, which was forthwith granted; then he took his departure for Rutsden Lodge, travelling in a dashing tandem, as a gentleman holding a commission in HM's Dragoons ought to travel.

Chapter Two

As the gallant Captain Torrant alighted from his dashing equipage, he was met at the hall door by Miss Bonham's attendant, a pretty, impudent girl, always ready to be kissed or pulled about by any handsome young gentleman, though habitually reserved and discreet with young men of her own station in life. She received the commander smiling, as he, as a matter of course gave her a kiss and a squeeze, together with his 'Good morning Lucy, how blooming you look today!'

'You had better keep all that sort of nonsense for my young lady, Captain Torrant!' was the reply, 'for I know she is expecting you!'

'How do you know that, my dear?' enquired the dragoon.

'Easy enough,' replied the lady's maid, 'as I helped her to dress, she made me take out her prettiest morning frock, and moreover put on white stockings and her nice little bronze slippers. And I pretty well know what that means,' added the soubrette, archly nodding her head, as she tripped upstairs, leading the way to her young mistress's sitting room.

There the young captain was neither unexpected nor unwelcome. We need not retire, as did the discreet Lucy after ushering in the guest, but remain witnesses to the affection, not to say transport, with which he was received by Miss Eliza Bonham.

'My own darling Alfred,' she exclaimed as she flung herself into his arms, kissing him most rapturously, 'how good of you to answer my note so quickly!'

Nor was the young gentleman one whit behind hand in reciprocating her profession of love. He glued his mouth to hers, pressed her to his breast, and even began with his right hand, which he purposely disengaged, to make a demonstration towards the lower part of her person. But this performance Eliza eluded, not from any dislike to the proceeding – oh, no! but from prudential motives.

'Stop, stop sir!' she laughingly exclaimed, 'not so fast, if you please – I understood you came here to talk over a disagreeable business matter; and besides, Alfred dear, you really must cover your beautiful instrument with that sheath, or condom, or whatever you call it. I have no notion of having a pretty white belly bow-windowed before marriage! – indeed I shan't particularly care about it after marriage!'

But the gallant young officer had not driven over from the barracks for nothing, and begged to assure his beautiful cousin that in his present state of mind and body, it would be quite impossible for him to give proper attention to any serious business, until his burning love for her received some temporary gratification, (the plain English of this being that he had a tremendous cock-stand, and felt that if it was not allayed pretty quickly that he must burst), and that as for the sheath, she might set her mind quite at rest, for he had brought a dozen with him.

'A dozen!' exclaimed Eliza, lifting up her eyes and hands in pretended astonishment, 'what on earth does the man mean by bringing a dozen? You are not going to fuck me a dozen times, I can tell you that, sir! And I don't want my waiting maid spoilt, mind that, and who else you intend to favour, of course I don't know—'

Here her speech was brought to an abrupt termination by her cousin covering her mouth with kisses and begging her to seat herself in a low easy chair, while he prepared himself for the promised treat. Fastening the door was a precaution taken as a matter of course, for Lucy knew that it was as much as her place was worth, to permit any intrusion in the neighbourhood, and Mr Bonham was not to arrive until the following day.

Coat off and trousers down, Alfred produced a bundle of safeguards, and selecting one of the filmy looking coverings, besought his lovely cousin to put it on for him. Of course he could have put it on himself perfectly well, but he was too great an epicure to miss any piquant delicacy in the approaching banquet. Accordingly, Eliza's delicate fingers as she performed the required office, added new fire to his already terribly inflamed prick, so that the scarlet knob absolutely turned purple and the whole nine inches, from the hardened balls to the orifice at the end, throbbed with excited lust. This was heightened by Eliza's appearance for, (being almost as eager as her gallant cousin, and that's saying a great deal), as she seated herself she drew up her clothes, and put one of her splendid legs over the chair on which she sat. Consequently, her rump being advanced quite to the extreme edge of the cushions, she made a most admirable display; her excitement and her lover's embraces had produced the usual result, and the lips of her cunt were slightly opened, temptingly inviting an entrance; while her bushy black hair showed off to advantage the creamy whiteness of her belly and thighs.

No wonder that as soon as the condom was securely put on, Captain Torrant fell down on his knees, and expressed his adoration of the shrine he was going to enter by covering it with amorous kisses. Under this treatment, the pink-lined portals expanded more and more and as Eliza flung back her head with a smile and a sigh, the young officer saw that the auspicious moment had arrived – not that he was an unwelcome visitor at any time in the mossy retreat, so getting his charger well in hand, he put his head straight for the gap and rushed in. It was indeed a short-lived pleasure as may be conceived: the fact being that the gentleman was in that state of lust that two or three judicious rubs from the hand of his fair cousin would have released his evacuation; and as for the lady, if her hot lover had continued on his knees before her, kissing her cunt one half minute longer, he would have had some warm cream over his moustache, of a kind not generally sold by Rose or Gillingwater. So three good shoves, actually only three, did the business most effectually, and, no doubt to their great mutual satisfaction. But there was no mistake as to Miss Bonham's prudent regard to the sheath, or the Captain's good sense in acceding to her wishes.

For his beautiful antagonist met his attack so grandly and discharged her battery so promptly in reply to his, that if the latter had not been retained by the discreet covering, very serious consequences to the lady would have almost inevitably made themselves apparent in nine months' time or thereabouts.

And in our humble opinion gratification is not increased by running any risk. On the present occasion both Miss Bonham and her lover congratulated themselves on having enjoyed each other thoroughly, and without any fear of the result.

Their extreme transports being over for the present, the young gentleman applied himself to putting his dress in order, while Eliza rang the bell and desired Lucy to send up the lunch.

While this acceptable refreshment was being done justice to, the loving pair proceeded to consider what was to be done in regard to Mr Bonham's infatuation. Captain Torrant's first step was prompt and business like. He told his man Robert, a smart soldier, to take a walk through the fields in the neighbourhood of the Fieldings' farm, and, by getting into conversation with some of the farm lasses, he would most likely find out something as to Miss Rosa, the great probability being that the old dame would not be able to keep her mouth shut, but would have been dropping boastful hints as to her daughter's great prospects, being made a grand lady of, and so on.

'Find out this for me if you can Bob,' said his generous master, 'and I will give you free liberty to do what you like by way of amusing yourself with any of the girls.'

'Cert'nly sir, thank you sir,' replied that valuable domestic, saluting as he marched away on his errand.

Leaving him for a while to enjoy his country walk, we will attend at the consultation between the lovers.

'You see, my darling Alfred,' began Eliza, 'I fear there is considerable truth in these reports that are going about. I don't believe all I hear about the girl's beauty.'

'Oh, of course not,' said the Captain, inwardly chuckling.

'I dare say she is a pretty, dowdy doll; but when a man of my father's age makes a fool of himself, he does it with a vengeance. And if you were to speak to him seriously on the subject, he would ask you what business it was of yours, quarrel with you, and perhaps cut you out of his will, or turn you out of the house and forbid our marriage.'

'That would never do,' interposed the young gentleman warmly.

'No indeed, dearest Alfred,' replied the lady looking at him warmly and lovingly.

'What plan would you propose then my pet?' asked he, 'supposing that your governor does contemplate making a jolly jackass out of himself in his old age?'

'Well, Alfred, if he could be put out of conceit with the girl in some way – if he found anything against her character – something to disgust him in short—'

'I perceive,' replied Captain Torrant reflectively,

'but there is some danger. In the first place, proof may be very difficult to get to support the accusation; and in the second place any one setting such reports on foot would be liable to heavy damages.'

'Pooh, pooh,' replied Eliza, 'you have plenty of young scamps among your brother officers who would be delighted with the chance of taking a pretty girl's maidenhood. Only let me find out her address, and then you can give one of your friends the information, and let him make her acquaintance and seduce her; fuck her well, get her with child – anything – so that she is quite ruined and spoilt as to any purpose of becoming a stepmother to me.'

To this hopeful scheme, the gentleman assented, merely remarking that it would never do 'to trust any of our fellows with such a delicate business.'

'I see how it is sir,' exclaimed Eliza, 'you think that if there is any maidenhood taking to be done, you can do it pretty well yourself. And so you can, I can testify; only I think that your regard for me, that you profess so largely about, might keep you from straying after such a nonsensical baby-faced doll.'

'My darling Eliza, I did not propose to do anything of the kind,' replied the aggrieved dragoon, 'I merely said that I would not venture to entrust such a piece of business to any of our youngsters.'

'Ah well,' said the lady, 'I would rather have avoided this part of the business; but I suppose what must be, must; and if the girl is to be seduced and rogered, you will have to do it. Of course, it is all fun for you, but I can't help but feel a little bit jealous. You don't care for her I know, as you care for me, but still all you young reprobates like a little change, and I am told that she is fresh and rosy-looking, with golden brown hair; while as for poor me, I am sallow and colourless, and my black hair looks dismal – I know it does.'

We may presume that Miss Bonham made these

remarks in full consciousness of her charms; for she really was a splendid woman. And of course her lover judiciously lost no time in informing her of the fact, accompanying his protestations with the warmest caresses. So that at last the young lady, fairly vanquished, promised to be no more jealous – than she could help; that she supposed Alfred would have to like Rosa a little – just a little bit – or he would not be able to seduce her; and that when that nice little bit of business was done, he must leave her in some gay house, or in keeping with one of his friends, or somewhere or other; Miss Bonham was not particular, only that Alfred must never see the girl again; and must marry her – Eliza – as soon as it could be managed, and then they would live happy forever afterwards, as the story book says. On this there followed more kisses and caresses, and the lovers went out for a walk in the garden.

Leaving them in their happiness we will follow Master Robert on his excursion to the Fieldings' farm; an excursion taken on his master's account as far as business was concerned, but not without an eye to his own amusement should opportunity occur. The day was fine, and he walked leisurely along, thoroughly enjoying the feeling of having got away from the barracks, and of having nothing to do; not that Master Robert was particularly over-burdened in that respect at any time. He had asked directions as to his road from one or two country louts, and was following a side path which bordered a wood, when he caught sight of some chimneys in the distance; this he thought might be the farm he sought; and while he was considering the matter he perceived in the adjoining wood a girl and a boy gathering fallen sticks. He spoke to the couple, desiring to know whereabouts Farmer Fielding's might happen to be. On this, the girl said her brother should show him the way, while she went home with the sticks.

But Master Robert, who had his eyes about him, and perceived that the girl, though coarsely dressed was a stout, buxom, fresh-looking lass of about seventeen, proposed that she should show him the way, and that her little brother should take the sticks home. The girl seemed to hesitate; but the boy being presented with a penny, cut the matter short by running off to spend it, and thus left Robert, as he wished, alone with the nice-looking girl guide.

She was for going to the farm by the path, from which indeed, as she said, the house was easily to be seen; but Robert knew better than that, and said he was sure the wood must be a shorter way, and putting his arm around the girl's waist, led her along to where the bushes appeared to grow tolerably close. She laughingly declared that the way he was taking did not lead to anywhere; but did not seem to object nevertheless, even when Robert, spying a mossy bank, pretty well sheltered from observation, proposed that they should sit down there and rest awhile.

Finding that the girl was not at all ill-disposed for a little love-making, though she might be a little shy, the jolly dragoon proceeded to seat her on his knee, taking the precaution in the first instance of raising her petticoats, so that he might have facilities for exploring her bare rump. And of course, when he had got her great fat arse thus comfortably established, he lost no time in shoving a couple of fingers up her cunt. As he found no maidenhead, he asked his rustic friend if she had any sweethearts among the country lads, to which she replied, smiling and shaking her head:

'No, no, Susan Flipper she had a sweetheart and she let him shove his cock into her, and she had a child and it gave her a great deal of trouble, – no, no sweethearts for me, thank you!'

'But what do you do, my precious, for something instead of a cock, and how do you happen to have lost your maidenhead?'

'Well, I don't know much about a maidenhead,' was the reply, 'but when I feel queer like, I get a carrot and ram it into me, into the slit between my thighs, that you've got your fingers in; and it makes me feel so nice – only one day I did it rather too hard, and burst through something and hurt myself.'

'Let's see,' said the astute Robert, as he turned the damsel over on her hands and knees, and pulling open the lips of her cunt, took a deliberate inspection, 'I can manage to give you a deal more pleasure than you can get from a carrot, Nelly (if that's your name) and without any risk of getting you with child.'

'Could you really now,' said the simple country girl. 'Is your cock quite harmless, then?' she asked.

'Certainly,' replied Robert, uncovering about nine inches of a wholesome looking and decidedly thickish prick, 'you perceive my dear, that if you go down on your hands and knees and I just shove in the red end of this machine, no harm can possibly happen to you; it is only when a girl is laid down on her back – with her thighs open, and her sweetheart gets atop of her and shoves the whole length of his tool up her that she gets big with child.'

'Ah, I know that's true enough,' replied Nelly, 'for Susan Flipper told me, that was the way her John got her down in the cow house, one day when she was milking, and what's more, she said he nearly split her arse up.'

'There's no fear of that with me, my pretty Nelly,' said Robert coaxingly. 'If you'll just go down on your hands and knees – on that soft mossy bank, I'll fuck you very gently, and will neither split your arse nor get you with child.'

'Well, you are a nice-looking civil young gentleman,' replied the rustic lass, 'and your cock is certainly an uncommon nice one, and a big one, – I only hope it is not too big, and so—'

'And so, I may! Isn't that what you mean to say,

my pet?' interrupted Robert.

Then, taking consent for granted, he placed the strong well-shaped girl on all fours, with her jolly rump prominently stuck out, and the whole of her regalia completely displayed. As she was pretty tight, he at first kept tolerably well to his promise about not going further into her than the knob, but every shove made a difference, and by the time he had got to the fifth push, he was in up to the hilt, simply as far as his weapon would go.

Nelly did not reproach him greatly for his perfidy, on the contrary, she wriggled her bottom about, and even shoved it out to meet his furious lunges so that Master Robert enjoyed himself even more than he expected to do. That Nelly did the same may be pretty well inferred from the fact that when he was spunking into her, she was actually sinking under him with pleasurable emotion.

The young woman's first remark upon getting up was: 'Well now, I must get home to mother, or she'll wonder where I am. I don't know, young man, whether you kept very strictly to your word as to the amount of prick you just put into me, but I felt as if you put a deuce of a length! Howsome ever, it was all very nice; and if you should happen to be passing this way, some other time, I am generally somewhere about, and if you don't see me, any of the lads or lasses working hereabouts will be able to tell you where to find me. That is if you want to do so, because perhaps you think one go is enough, and you are tired of me already.'

Robert gallantly assured her that this was far from being the case, and took a most affectionate leave of her; at least, if giving her a crown piece to buy a new bonnet, while his fingers were groping about her rump, is a fair proof of affection on the part of the young man.

Then he pursued his way towards the farm house,

which he never would have had the slightest difficulty in finding without any guidance; secretly congratulating himself that whether he succeeded or not, in doing any business for his master, he had managed a very nice little bit of amusement for himself. So far so good. Entering the farm house, he at once accosted a jolly looking dame, whom he correctly enough supposed to be Mother Fielding, asked permission to sit down and the favour of a drink of milk.

The old lady perceiving at once, from his neat plain groom's dress, and the cockade in his hat, that he was some superior gentleman's servant, and propitiated probably by his good looks, not only asked him to rest himself, but put before him a tankard of strong ale, and some bread and cheese, remarking that it would be hard if Fielding's Farm could not afford a tired stranger a mouthful of beer.

'Then this is Fielding's Farm, is it?' said the apparently astonished Robert, 'and you are the Mrs Fielding, mother of that beautiful young lady the officers at the barracks are always talking about.'

Mrs Fielding acknowledged that she was the mother of the young lady in question, not without a deal of conscious pride at hearing Rosa so described, remarking however that it was like the officers' impudence, to be so free in talking about her daughter.

'But I suppose,' concluded the old lady, 'it is all the same to them, my daughter or somebody else's.'

'Truly madam, I fear you are not far wrong,' said the moral Robert, 'our young gentlemen are rather too free both in their conversation and manners, but in the case of so very distinguished a beauty, as I hear Miss Fielding is, little talk comes natural. Besides, madam, in this case it is quite excusable, as report does say that your daughter is going to make a high marriage.'

'People should mind their own business and not tell

lies about other folk's affairs,' said Mrs Fielding, remembering Mr Bonham's admonitions on the subject of silence and secrecy.

'Ah, well, if it is a lie,' replied the astute Robert, making his point at once, 'I'll correct it – whenever I hear it – and mention my authority.'

'Not but what Rosa could be if she choose,' interposed the old dame, 'of course such things are generally unlikely.'

'Very unlikely,' here interrupted Robert, in order to interrupt her, irritate her and lead her on.

'But there are exceptions to every rule, and my girl Rosa, who is as good as she is pretty, may be an exception in this case. Mind, I don't say she is!'

'Oh, of course not!' interposed the military groom, 'and that's exactly the reason she has gone to London, I suppose!'

'Why, not exactly to be married,' replied Mrs Fielding, forgetting all about concealment in her own satisfaction, and drawn on by her guest's confident manner, 'not to be married just yet. You see, though Rosa has been well brought up, yet a little London polish is desirable to fit her for the high station she will occupy.'

'Oh, of course,' replied Robert, in a matter-of-fact way, as if he knew all about it, and highly approved, but thinking to himself all the while:

'You are a nice soft old lady, and if you let out this secret to every one as easily as you let it out to me, it will very soon be parish news. But your ale is good at any rate, so here's your good health, ma'am.'

This last remark was uttered aloud and acknowledged.

'Oh, I am afraid that you are a dreadful set up at the barracks, young man. You are in service to one of the gentlemen, I see. Pray, who may he be?'

'Only acting as officer's servant, madam,' replied her guest, 'you know the officers are at liberty to choose the smartest and best looking-ahem-of the men, to act as servants for them.'

'Certainly,' said the farmer's wife, 'why not? And who are you with at present?'

All this interlude gave Robert time for invention, so accordingly out he came with one of the biggest lies he had ever told in his life, – and that is saying a good deal.

'Major Ringtail, madam, of the 51st Dragoons, is the gentleman I am with. He drove over to Rutshole this morning, and as he did not want me to assist him in the business he was after, he gave me a holiday; which I thought I could not employ more innocently than by a walk in the country.'

'Quite right, young man,' replied the old lady, 'and what sort of a man is the Major?'

'Oh, he's a very nice quiet sort of a gentlemanly man,' was the reply, 'he's rather addicted to drinking and gambling, but then you know, Mrs Fielding, that officers at country quarters must amuse themselves somehow – and he may be said by strict people to be damnably given to cursing and swearing and fighting. Indeed, the Reverend Brother Stiggins said so the other day, when the Major kicked him out of the barracks yard. But then, you know, madam, men will be stupid and aggravating; and fools like Stiggins will interfere where they have no business. And people do say of my respected master, – people will talk you know – that he spends too much of his time in fornication; and that he is over much given to rogering any of the pretty country lasses, or any other girls that he may happen to fall in with. But I suppose that he considers that proceeding to be part of his duty, as an officer of HM's 51st Dragoons. And,' said Robert in conclusion, 'considering that he is a Dragoon officer, I think he behaves himself on the whole as well as can be expected.'

'On the whole,' said Mrs Fielding to herself, 'well

perhaps he does, I wonder how he behaves off the whole?' But she only said, 'Pray young man, what did the respectable gentleman, your master, kick the sainted Brother Stiggins out of the barracks for? I think that holy man was terribly indiscreet in venturing to trust his sainted body in such a den of iniquity. But I beg your pardon, young man, I did not mean to hurt your feelings, the words slipped out unaware.'

'Well, madam,' said Robert gravely, 'we don't generally call the barracks a den of iniquity. You see, perhaps our gentlemen might not understand what that meant, but it's commonly known by the name of Hell's Blazes; and Mrs Mantrap, the Colonel's lady, – his wife's at Cheltenham – calls it Little Sodom. But that's neither here nor there,' continued the narrator, with a side glance at his hostess's horror-stricken countenance, 'you were asking me about that little unpleasantness between the Major and that apostle, Stiggins. I know all about it; for you see the Major had got me with him in case of Stiggins, or any of the congregation turning nasty.'

'What, were you in the chapel?' asked the old lady, in great surprise. 'And what were you doing there?'

'We were in Little Bethel Chapel, madam, to offer up our devotions to the best of our ability,' replied Robert demurely. 'You see in the tenth pew from the pulpit, on the left hand side, a deuced nice girl used to sit, and in the afternoon, generally by herself. I told my master, as in duty bound, and he was taken with a pious fit. So he found out who the girl was, and after speaking to her two or three times in the street, in the most impudent way, he pretends that she has converted him, – ha, ha! and says that he should like to be gathered into the fold, the only fold he was thinking of being the folds of her petticoats. Well ma'am, I don't think she could be quite such a fool as to believe all he said, but what with having her brain softened with Stiggins' nonsensical saintly trash, and what with the pride of showing off a Dragoon Officer as a brand: saved from the burning, in her own pew: and perhaps a little feeling of another kind besides, – you know what I mean, Mrs F – all combined together to induce her to make a fool of herself, and she made an appointment with the Major to meet her in her pew one Sunday afternoon, when her mother would be asleep at home and her father smoking his pipe. All this my master told me of course, for I was to stick to him, and what's more I got a special chum of mine, Tom, Lieutenant Larkyn's man, to come with me and sit pretty close, for you see madam, there was no telling how the congregation, to say nothing of the deacons and elders, and that bad lot, might take it.'

'Take it! Take what?' exclaimed Mrs Fielding.

'Patience, madam, and you shall hear,' replied Robert with drunken gravity, for the strong ale was beginning to take effect upon him. 'During the first part of Stiggins' mountebanking, his prayers and howlings, and damning everybody except himself, up hill and down dale, my master behaved himself tolerably quiet, merely kissing Miss Larcher, (that's her name) every now and then, giving her an occasional squeeze, and putting his hand up her petticoats in a devotional manner, when they knelt down together.'

'Good Lord!' interrupted the farmer's wife, 'do you call that behaving quietly?'

'Very much so indeed, madam,' was the reply, 'not a sound was to be heard in the pig-market – I beg pardon – chapel – except the bawling of that Stiggins who bawled enough for sixty. His bawling had one good effect at any rate, it sent half his disciples to sleep before he got to tenthly and when he arrived and called thirteenthly, half the congregation were snoring comfortably. Not so my master and his fair friend. I had noticed him getting on very favourably. Once he laid her backward, on the seat, and took a regular good, long, groping feel at her privates. On another occasion he took out his standing prick and showed it to her; I suppose she wanted to convert that too, for she took hold of it admiringly. All this was very pleasant, and I suppose the Major had been keeping a pretty bright look-out on the state of the congregation, for when he perceived what I noticed, that one half of them were happily out of hearing of Stiggins' howls; he thought it a good opportunity to go to work in earnest. I had been stooping down below the level of the door of the pew to get a good suck at a flask of brandy and water, which I had brought with me to enable me to bear up against the fatigue and to bring myself into a devotional frame of mind, when on raising my eyes, the first thing I saw, was a pair of remarkably good legs, nicely set off by clean white stockings, and neat little shoes, showing over the side of the adjoining pew. Of course I knew what such an apparition as this meant, and if I couldn't guess, I was very soon enlightened, for on peeping over the edge, – as was my duty, in order to see that all was straight-forward and pleasant, there I saw my respected and gallant master fucking, as the common people call it, Miss Larcher in a most splendid style. The seat of the pew was not much of a rest for her fine broad rump, but in spite of her heavings and wrigglings, he pinned her hard and fast; and did not leave off until he had completely enjoyed her beautiful body. As for her, I only hope she enjoyed herself in proportion to her sufferings, for when the Major got off her, before she closed her thighs or put her clothes down, I noticed that her chemise was stained with blood, as she must have smarted a little.'

'But do you mean to tell me, young man,' interrupted Mrs Fielding, 'that none of the congregation noticed what was going on?'

'One of them did, Mrs Fielding,' coolly replied the narrator, 'but, as he came towards the pew, I told him it was the case of a female in a spiritual conflict with Satan, and that if he didn't go back to his seat, I'd make him and that damn quick. So, he went, apparently quite convinced. And as for the rest of the congregation, they were either asleep or stupid, as of course they naturally must be, to come to such a stinking hole at all! So my master buttoned his trousers in peace, and his pretty friend adjusted her dress, and they marched out, before Stiggins had nearly finished his yelling. But the brute from the top of his sentry-box, which he calls his watch-tower, had the advantage of overlooking the sleeping pens of his flock, and great was his disgust, as you may imagine, on perceiving a fine young ram like master, getting into the mutton of a pretty ewe lamb, like Miss Larcher. And he came to the barracks, firstly to threaten the Major with hell-fire, which he seems to know a good deal about, secondly to endeavour on finding the Major did not seem to care very much about the flames, to get a ten-pound note out of him, by way of a bribe for holding his tongue. Then, on finding the Major did not care one damn whether he held his tongue or not, and did not propose to give him any money: he changed his tone once more, and told the Major that if he did not give him ten or fifteen pounds, he would tell Miss Larcher's father and mother, and would have her turned out of the congregation of the saints, completely disgraced. Upon this the Major informed him, that he, the saintly Stiggins, had been discovered in a pig-pen, rogering a young sow, that he, the Major, had half a dozen witnesses quite ready to prove it, and that if he annoyed him, or Miss Larcher with his blackguard lies, he would have him up before the magistrates for bestiality. And before the horror-stricken Stiggins could recover his presence of mind on hearing this intelligence, he found himself being kicked out of the barracks with speed and dexterity; and I have no doubt it did him a power of good.

'And now, Mrs Fielding, with many thanks for your

kind hospitality, I must say goodbye. If you had
another daughter at home I would ask for an introduction, but as it is, I must do without. Duty calls,
madam, farewell!'

So saying the half-drunken Robert took his departure to report progress to his master, leaving Mrs
Fielding lifting up her hands and eyes, as she
exclaimed:

'Good Lord – a – mussy me!'

Chapter Three

Considerable amusement was excited by Robert's recital of his conversation with Mrs Fielding. This, he lost no time in reporting to his master immediately upon his return; finding him in the garden, gracefully and agreeably employed in tossing his beautiful cousin about in a swing hung between two trees. The most important part of his story was relating to what the communicative old lady said about her daughter, and her journey to London, which at once confirmed Miss Bonham in her suspicions.

'Depend upon it, Alfred, the old goose has placed her in some good first-class finishing school, so that the future Mrs Bonham, confound her! may have a little surface polish.' (This was hitting the right nail on the head with a vengeance.) 'But,' continued Eliza, 'the deuce is in it if I don't find out either from her mother, or my respected father's correspondence, what her address is, and once found, I'll leave the rest to you, dear Alfred.'

As a further allusion to their plans before Robert, might be indiscreet, they changed the conversation; the Captain asking his servant if Mrs Fielding's ale was pretty good, and whether she had asked him who his master was. To the first question the hopeful young man returned a most unqualified assent; to the latter, he replied by giving his master an account of a certain Major Ringtail, to the Captain's intense amusement.

'And, upon my word, sir,' said Robert, 'it's just as well there is no such officer in the regiment; for while professing the greatest regard and attachment for him, I've given him a character that would damn a whole brigade, officers and men. The old lady's hair stood on end, so that it actually lifted her mobcap off her venerable head.'

'Why – what in the name of wonder, did you tell her, Robert?' asked Captain Torrant, who perceived his valet's half-tipsy predicament and anticipated some funny disclosures.

'Faith, sir, I could not tell you half what I said to her – not in Miss Bonham's presence, sir.'

'Oh, never mind Miss Bonham,' replied the Captain giving that lady a push to set her swinging, so that the colour of her garters was no particular mystery, 'she knows what soldiers are, and will excuse a little loose talk, so out with it!'

Thus adjured, Robert, who in his excited state wished for nothing better, started at once into his description of the gallant Major, while crediting him with every vice under the sun, or nearly so, and ending with giving him a character for high respectability, tickled Alfred's fancy amazingly.

Both he and his cousin Eliza were delighted with Robert's description of the scene in the chapel; and although the young lady actually did blush, and pretended to look confused, she swallowed every incident of the story with great gusto, from the appearance of the pretty legs over the side of the pew, to the mythical Major's withdrawal of his prick from its bleeding sheath.

'How can Robert invent such a pack of nonsense, my dear?' appealing to her lover in pretended indignation.

'Indeed, my love, I think it is very natural and clever. I only hope that it is all invention. I say, sir,' (turning to his man) 'how did you come by Miss Larcher's name? Was that a name out of your own head, like the Major's?'

Here Robert, evidently a little confused, scratched the article referred to, as he said very slowly:

'Why, no, sir, not exactly. I was hard up for a name, and I noticed one as we came through Rutshole: Mary Larcher, sir, Temperance Hotel, sir. Little disreputable hole, left-hand side, High Street, sir.'

'My good gracious Heavens, Alfred!' almost shrieked Eliza, 'she is a most respectable woman, a regular prim, starched, old maid; and what's more, she's acquainted with Papa, and her being a regular member of Mr Stiggins' congregation will make the story seem as if it had some truth in it! And that abominable chattering old goose will go telling the story everywhere! Oh! how can you laugh so? It is very serious!'

This was addressed to her cousin, who seemed to think that this description of the maligned Miss Larcher, gave point to the joke; for he absolutely roared with delight, and went about stamping his feet in perfect ecstasies of enjoyment. It must have been contagious, for in spite of Eliza's vexation, knowing that the scandal must reach her father's ears, she began to laugh merrily, and even Robert, finding that his bringing forward a respectable woman's name was not going to bring punishment on him by his master – he cared for nobody else – indulged in a respectful snigger.

'It's all the same, sir, I suppose it don't matter much what I said about such rubbish as that there Stiggins?'

'Why sir?' replied the Captain.

'Only sir, that he went to the barracks next day.'

'You mean, you rascal, that you told Mrs Fielding that he went to the barracks,' interrupted his master. 'It's all the same, sir,' remarked Robert, coolly; and then proceeded to give his hearers an account of the Reverent party attempting to extort a bribe from the

Fabulous Major; and that personage retorting upon the apostle with an accusation of his having been detected in the act of copulating with a pig. All this Robert related as he had told it to Mrs Fielding, with as much preciseness and gravity, as if he had been an eye-witness to the whole affair; copulating, kicking out of the barracks, and all.

Captain Torrant fairly shrieked and yelled with laughter.

'You'll be the death of me, you lying rascal!' he gasped out, 'you will, by Jove! Do you mean to tell me that Mrs Fielding swallowed this enormous bucketful of lies?'

'Well, I think she took it nearly all in,' was the deliberate reply. 'At any rate sir,' continued Robert, more cheerfully, 'if she did not believe it quite altogether, she is certain to repeat it all!'

'Your remark, Robert, is perfectly correct, and shows a knowledge of human nature, for which I did not give you credit. And now you can go and look after the horses; you have done more mischief during this forenoon than any other man could do in a month and I am perfectly satisfied.'

On this, Robert raised his hand to his hat, and turned to go, Miss Bonham calling out to him:

'And Robert, I'll trouble you to leave my maid Lucy alone, she is a nice girl, and I don't want her pulled about!'

Robert silently saluted, and took his departure.

'What a jolly row there will be all over Rutshole, won't there, my beauty? I can fancy I see Stiggins and Miss Larcher, instructing their lawyers to bring actions against Major Ringtail or his man, or both for defamation of character! There is one good thing, the fact of Mrs Fielding being instrumental in spreading these reports won't raise her in the estimation of her future son-in-law!'

'That it won't,' replied Eliza, emphatically, 'and I

think that Robert has done us a very great service this morning, both in raising these reports, absurd as they are, and getting us the information about Rosa.'

'Yes, he's a useful, clever fellow, but a dreadful scamp among the girls.'

'Takes after his master, I suppose!' archly interrupted Eliza, for which she was rewarded by almost being pulled off the swing to be kissed, while her lover thrust his hand between her thighs into her moistened cunt. Still keeping her in this pleasant position the Captain continued:

'What on earth did you tell him to keep off your maid for? Don't you know that it was the very thing to make him attempt her person?'

'Certainly not,' replied the lady, 'he dare not after my forbidding him, besides Lucy would not let him.'

'Oh, nonsense!' replied the experienced dragoon, 'if his prick begins to stand, he won't care for your forbidding him, or anybody else, and as for Lucy – to pay you off, my beauty, I dare say she takes after her young mistress!'

'Catch that for your impudence, sir!' said Eliza, giving him a slap on the face but not a very hard one, that's the truth.

'Well, dearest,' said the Captain, 'I'll bet you anything you like that Robert fucks your maid within the present half hour!'

'Done, sir,' was the ready reply.

And it was thereupon agreed that they should return to the house to keep an eye on the interesting pair; Alfred lifting Eliza from the swing in such a way as to expose all the secret charms that young lady had to show, both to his delighted eyes and his searching hands.

'There, that'll do, dear,' said the lady reprovingly, 'no more at present, thank you! What shall our bet be?'

'Well,' replied her cousin, 'a younger lover than myself would bet twenty kisses, or a delicious fuck, but I am so blessed as to be favoured with those exquisite treats, nearly as often as is good for me. I'll tell you what your penalty shall be.'

Here he whispered in his cousin's ear something or other which the lady appeared at first to receive with high disdain.

'Nonsense, sir,' was her reply, 'you shan't do anything of the sort! My bottom indeed! most disgustingly indecent; and what's more, I do not see what pleasure I shall have in the matter. You will gratify your lust, of course, and very sensual lust it is in this instance; but I should think I shall be more hurt than gratified. Oh yes, I dare say my bottom is very white and pretty, but you are not going to enjoy it as you propose, Master Alfred, for all that.'

Now it was the Captain's turn and very eloquent he was. He represented that it would not hurt her at all, only tickle her; and as he would not have to use a condom, he should enjoy the unusual felicity of spunking into her.

'A special delight, dearest Eliza, from which in justice to you, I debar myself!'

'Well,' said the lady, rather relenting – 'you are a very good boy in that respect; and as you say you are quite sure you will not hurt me – to be sure, it is a horribly indelicate proceeding! But you are pretty sure to lose your bet, so the chances are that I shall not have to submit my posterior to any such indignity after all. And mind, sir, if you lose your bet, you are to bring me half-a-dozen pairs of silk stockings.'

'That I shall do – whether I win or lose,' replied the enraptured lover, squeezing his cousin's graceful waist, as they proceeded towards the house. As they went, they argued the point, as to where their faithful domestics were likely to be found; Alfred suggesting the stable or the hay loft as a likely place for a find, but as this involved the fact of Lucy going there to look after Robert, Miss Bonham repudiated the idea on behalf of her sex, and suggested a spare bedroom on the same floor as her chamber, as a likely place. Finally they came to the determination of visiting the stables in the first instance, and if unsuccessful there, of trying the bedroom.

On entering the stables, certainly there was no Robert. His horses were there, and all right, as the Captain at once perceived. Before leaving the stables however, he noticed an intelligent looking stable helper, busy with a broom, about nothing particular. To him the Captain presented a half-crown, asking him at the same time if the horses were all right, and if his man Robert, had been in the stable lately.

'Oh, dear, no sir,' said the lad, 'not for a quarter of an hour at least,' quite loudly, as if for the benefit of some third party hearing him; but at the same time he winked knowingly, and pointed with his thumb over his shoulder to an iron grating, which, as Captain Torrant well knew, divided the stable from the unoccupied loose box.

Unoccupied however, on the present occasion it was not, as the gentleman and his cousin very soon discovered. Proceeding very quietly in the direction indicated, while the stable lad made as much noise with his broom as he conveniently could, in order to drown any possible sound of their footsteps, the pair of lovers peeped through the grating and then their eyes were greeted with the prospect of another pair of lovers; and this was the position in which they were discovered.

On a loose truss of hay the elegant lady's maid, Lucy, was kneeling, with her thighs tolerably opened, while Robert, crouching down behind her, was imprinting lascivious kisses on her thighs, her rump and her cunt. Finally, confining his attention to the last feature, he divided the orifice with his tongue, working it about in such a way which must have inflamed Miss Lucy's amatory organs considerably. Then as he proceeded to take down his breeches, Alfred whispered to Eliza:

'Now, love, you see as he has ploughed up the furrow he is very properly going to put his seed into it – aye! there he goes – devilish nice legs, your little girl has got! Fine bottom too, very fine!'

'Surely, Alfred dear,' whispered his cousin, 'he cannot be going to shove his cock into her button hole!'

'No, dearest, I think not,' returned the gentleman, 'if he had intended to do so, he would have moistened that orifice and not her cunt.'

Captain Torrant was partly wrong and partly right. Robert certainly began in what is generally considered the legitimate sphere of action, but as Lucy was very much excited, and he had had already a very first rate fuck that morning, it so happened that the hand maiden arrived at the crisis of her enjoyment before the amiable young man had affected his share of the business. No doubt, in feeling her elixir bathing his cock, a bright idea struck him: he withdrew his weapon, and Lucy no doubt, fancied that he, like her, had finished his performance; so she made a slight movement, as if about to rise. But no such thing, mademoiselle! Robert put his hand to the orifice he had so lately occupied, and covering his fingers with her warm, oily liquor, dexterously lubricated her small rump-hole with it, inserting one of his fingers morever, as a light advanced courier, to prepare the way for that grandee – his prick. That noble plenipotentiary followed in due course, the only objection made by Lucy being such as may be expressed by a small exclamation of 'oh!' and a slight shrinking of her buttocks, as Robert's inflamed end forced its way into her small but elastic hole. And then the rogue seemed to enjoy himself thoroughly: his face absolutely glowed with lustful delight; and at every fresh thrust he gave, he made a low grunt, as a paviour does when using his rammer in the street. At last with one grand shove, he went right in up to the balls, and stayed in for about half-a-minute, motionless.

'Does that not look nice, my sweet Eliza,' whispered her lover. Eliza said nothing, but we suppose thought the more, and not altogether in a hostile spirit, it is to be presumed since, when her cousin again said, 'Now darling, while they recover themselves, suppose you come and pay me your debts,' she made no objection, but smiling and blushing, put her arm within Alfred's and allowed him to lead her out of the stable. The gentleman as he passed the stable boy, put his finger on his lips, which signal the discreet functionary well understood.

Then the lovers walked silently into the house, where however, a disagreeable surprise awaited them, being no less than the unexpected arrival of Mr Bonham!

'Oh, bother take him!' his dutiful daughter remarked, 'I did not expect him until tomorrow, or late tonight at the earliest. What can have induced him to return so soon?'

'Confound him!' muttered Alfred, apostrophizing his future father-in-law, 'what's to be done now?'

'Oh, perhaps now I shall get off paying my bet!' said Eliza, glancing wickedly at her cousin, then seeing the look of deep vexation that came over his face, she continued, 'never mind, dearest, he will perhaps want some refreshment, as it is still a good three hours till dinner-time, and while he is taking it, we can have another short stroll in the garden. There is a convenient little house of retreat, you know, among the bushes at the end of the serpentine walk, and there you know, although it is not a very genteel place for the purpose, you can—'

'Of course I can, darling,' interrupting her with a graceful kiss, 'what a capital manager you are!'

'Then mind, sir, that you are a good manager too,' replied the young lady. 'And don't hurt me any more than Robert did Lucy.'

'I shan't hurt you at all, pet,' was the reply. 'Robert was rather rough and piercing, I shall be very gentlemanly, only mind you bring a small pot of cold cream with you. A privy or a water closet is a capital place for such an encounter, as my injection might produce all the effect of a warm clyster.'

'Upon my word sir, this must be a nice treat that you have in store for me,' said Eliza, pretending to pout, 'but I have a little curiosity to find out a new sensation, and I suppose I must submit. Do you go back up to the stables, and warn the interesting pair whom we have just left, that our coachman will be coming in with horses, and I'll tell Papa that you have gone for yours, to be got ready for your return after dinner. Of course you have called here accidentally.'

So saying she slipped away.

Captain Torrant, going into the stables, called to the stable-boy, saying in a loud voice that his master had returned. This piece of intelligence produced Robert and Lucy pretty quickly out of the loose box, while the boy hurried out to open the stable yard gates, to admit the carriage. Lucy looked blushing and self-conscious, while Robert received his master's orders to prepare his tandem for their return at eight in the evening, with a most imperturbable expression of countenance.

'Please don't tell Miss Eliza, sir, that you found me with Robert in the stable,' pleaded Lucy.

'Oh, of course not,' was the officer's reply, thinking how unnecessary it was for him to say anything about it. 'I hope you have been enjoying yourself,' said he with a meaning look, and as she, covered with blushes, attempted to run past him, he caught hold of her and lifting her petticoats, exclaimed as he put his hand in her cunt. 'What a devilish nice pair of legs and thighs, and – ha! just as I expected, your nice little cunt open and moist! Did she make a good fuck, Robert?'

'Most lovely, sir,' with praiseworthy solemnity.

'Do let me go sir,' entreated Lucy, 'I hear the carriage coming into the yard.'

'Well, get along with you,' he said, 'I won't tell any tales, you may depend.'

'Thank you sir!' and off she ran blushing deeply.

'Governor come home, sir?' said Robert interrogatively.

'Yes, Robert, he has, and it's rather a bore, for he don't approve of my staying here all night – and if he does not invite me specially, I must go away at eight, but if it comes on to be a wet evening, I shall only drive as far as the Red Lion, in Rutshole, and go on to the barracks tomorrow. But you do be ready with the horses at eight, unless you hear to the contrary.'

Robert said, 'Certainly sir,' and his master walked into the house.

Here he met with a most gracious reception from Mr Bonham, – a couple of glasses of madeira after his drive, having put that gentleman into a rare good humour. He even bantered Alfred on his seizing the opportunity of his absence as a favourable occasion for calling upon his daughter Eliza; and he little knew – poor, innocent old gentleman – how near he was to the truth, when he affected to suppose that the young lady had given her lover notice of the house being clear. But Captain Torrant declared, with every appearance of virtuous innocence, that he came to consult his revered uncle in supplying part of the purchase money.

This was so plausibly put, that, after some humming and ha-ing, Mr Bonham promised to take the matter into consideration. Then his fair daughter remarked, that as her Papa did not seem to have brought home any London news worth hearing, she would go and take a walk in the garden and of course Captain Torrant offered her his company.

'I'll join you in half an hour or so, my dear,' said her obliging Papa.

'Thank you, Papa,' said his grateful daughter, who could have dispensed with his company remarkably well.

'Have you got the cold cream, dear Eliza?' asked her lover, as soon as they were fairly in the garden.

'Of course I have, sir,' she replied, 'I don't want to run the risk of being split up more than is absolutely necessary, and although it is not becoming in me to be eager for such an abominable performance, still I should humbly recommend your getting your share of it over, before my respectful parent makes his appearance, for he might not seem to see it in the same light, and might even consider it somewhat remarkable, if he found us both coming out of the privy together.'

'You are quite right, as usual, my darling,' replied Alfred gallantly. 'And here we are, arrived at our little city of refuge – snug enough and not much fear of being interrupted. There is a bolt to the door I see. There now,' suiting the action to the word, – 'we are all snug, and you'll allow me to put you in the most convenient position.'

With this he raised one of Eliza's long graceful legs upon the closet seat, and instructing her to bend her head downwards, he turned her clothes over her shoulders. Then taking the cold cream from her, he not only lubricated her small orifice, but bestowed a plentiful supply of the emollient, over his eager cock, this time unsheathed and erect, in all the pride of naked beauty.

'And now, my lovely pet,' said he, laying the end of his cock upon the orifice.

But no sooner did Miss Bonham feel the rounded

end, than a sense of great disproportion between his instrument and her hole became apparent to her mind, and she exclaimed:

'My dear Alfred, I do not wish to disappoint you, but I am afraid we have attempted an impossibility, you never can get into my body by this road!'

But the lustful young officer thought differently; he knew that if he could get one good inch well in – the rest was easy; and so, firmly but gently, urged his point; and was rewarded for his pains, by going into his darling's arse, with an easy gliding motion; the tight india-rubber-like elasticity of the passage being partially conquered by the copious application of the cream.

All that the young lady did was to mutter in broken sentences: 'So you have managed – it! dearest – I thought – you never would – be able! It does not hurt – me – as – I feared it – would – it only – rather tickles me. My good gracious! What a flood of hot oil you have injected into my bowels! Why Alfred dear, fond as you are of me, I think you never paid me such a lot of compliments at once, since we fell in love with each other!'

This last remark on the lady's part, was occasioned by the enthusiastic praises, lavished by her delighted lover on her various charms, as he was ramming his belly against the fine soft cheeks of her rump.

He seemed half mad with sensual rapture, and as well as his physical efforts would permit, kept up a running fire of expressions of admiration; in which his blind adoration mingled with good qualities of his mistress's mind and body together, in a most incongruous manner. He went on, in what would have been under any other circumstances, a most ridiculous way about her loving nature and her plump thighs, about her loving disposition and her delicious cunt; about her perfect taste in dress and her glorious buttocks, and finally referring to the delicious operation he was performing, declared that in all his experience he had never known such exquisite and complete enjoyment.

A good deal of this pleasure was, doubtless to be attributed to his lovely friend, who naturally flattered at hearing such enthusiasm exhibited with regard to her person, endeavoured to return the compliment by exerting herself as well as she could under what, to her, were rather unusual circumstances. All she could do was to straddle her legs as far apart as she was conveniently able, and to shove her rump out to meet her lover's long shoves. This she was the better able to do, as he did not perform nearly as quickly as she had been accustomed to be fucked when lying on her back, or in any posture with her belly up. On the contrary, he worked his prick in and out, as if he were desirous of protracting his treat, as there is no reason to doubt he really was. But he could not continue forever; and at last the interesting incident occurred, which called forth the remark from Eliza, about her 'bowels' and 'warm oil', and etc., etc. Nor was this all, for when he withdrew his comely weapon from its charming sheath, and prepared to stow the much subdued implement away in the sanctuary of his trousers, Eliza remarked:

'Be quick, dearest Alfred, and get away with you, for to speak plain English, I want to make use of this little house in a necessary point of view.'

Indeed, before the gallant Captain could get himself buttoned up, nature compelled Miss Bonham, greatly against her ideas of delicacy, to lift the seat she had just been stooping over and again baring her beautiful bottom, to put the temple of refuge to its legitimate use.

All this the Captain viewed with the utmost complacency; in fact, he rather expected it, as a natural consequence, and was cool enough about the matter to hand his cousin some soft paper which he happened to have in his pocket. And there is not the slightest doubt that he would have waited in attendance on his fair lady, until she had finished her business, had not the prudent Eliza suggested the propriety of his absenting himself, for fear Mr Bonham should find him in or near the temple, which with Eliza inside, must have looked very suspicious.

So the gallant commander, lighting a cigar, took himself off and paraded a neighbouring walk, until such time as Mr Bonham should make his appearance, or his daughter should emerge from her lurking place. The former event took place first, and Mr Bonham's approach was made known by his heavy footsteps, and his blowing his nose after the manner of a trumpet, heralding his advent.

'Ha! Alfred my boy, all by yourself! What have you done with Eliza?'

'Miss Bonham, Uncle, left me a few minutes ago, I don't know exactly where she has gone but I have no doubt she will return directly.'

The answer was made with the greatest coolness and most commendable gravity, and certainly without leaving the elderly gentleman room to suppose that anything uncommon had taken place during the last twenty minutes or thereabouts.

'Eliza is a charming girl, though I am her father and perhaps should not say so,' remarked the old gentleman, as they walked along. To this, the younger one gave ready assent.

'And as good as she looks,' continued Mr Bonham.

'You should be no stranger to my opinion of my cousin Eliza's charms, by this time sir,' replied the young officer. 'I consider her to be all perfection, both in her mind and person (I wonder what the old boy would say if he knew how intimately I am acquainted with all parts of her beautiful body, both back and front.)'

This last remark, as may be imagined, he made to himself.

'Well, Alfred,' his uncle resumed, 'as soon as you get your step, I do not see any particular objection to your being married. What with your private property, your pay and Eliza's money – ahem! – you ought to be able to do very well, and I'll look and see what cash on hand I have at my bankers. I am not sorry to hear that your Major is about to leave your corps. I have heard a very bad character of him.'

'Indeed sir!' was the reply, 'I am surprised to hear that. Major Pobjoy is considered a very respectable man, rather pious indeed, and very discreet.'

'Pobjoy wasn't the name mentioned to me, but I heard of the affair this day, as I passed through Rutshole, and very hurriedly. A respectable tenant of mine, or rather the wife of a tenant,' (Mrs Fielding, I'll bet a sovereign, muttered Alfred) – 'told me some hardly credible stories about a certain Major named Ringdove, or Stifftail or some such name as that.'

'By Gad, she's very sharp about it!' muttered Torrant, and then said out aloud:

'I don't know any officer of that name, sir, but pray, what has the culprit been doing?'

'Why my dear boy, I hardly like mentioning such indecent subjects; but I believe he had connection with a young lady of the Reverend Stiggins' congregation, in the chapel, under that faithful shepherd's very nose!'

'Pray, uncle, did the lady enjoy being fucked?'

'Why no, I can't say that I understood she did,' replied Mr Bonham, completely taken back both by the question and the straightforward way in which it was asked. 'But the scandal does not stop there, for on the sainted pastor proceeding to the barracks next day to reprove the man of sin, and entreat him to flee from the wrath to come, Major Dovetail, or whatever his name is, accused the apostle of having been detected in the criminal action of having connection with a swine, and kicked him out of the barracks.'

'Had Mr Stiggins been discovered poking a pig?' asked Captain Torrant, with an air of great interest, not as if the incident was at all unlikely.

'Great Providence, nephew, no! Why Stiggins is next door but one to one of the holy apostles and—'

'But he may have buggered the pig for all that,' stubbornly insisted Captain Torrant, 'at least it is as likely as any part of the story. There is no Major Ringdove or Stifftail, or any such name in our regiment. One of the lambs of the fold may have got rogered, in the fear of the Lord, and in the middle of the sermon – very likely – and Stiggins may have been kicked out of the barracks, and may be again, if he goes there on any of his stinking errands. The pig copulation I know nothing about – I wasn't there so didn't see it. But here comes my fair cousin, so perhaps we had better defer our discussion until some other time.'

'I think so, indeed, Alfred,' was the reply, 'but I see that I have been imposed upon, and I should like to hear a little more from you on the subject, so instead of returning tonight, suppose you stay here and we will talk over matters in general, and your future prospects, matrimonial and otherwise. Here comes Eliza; let us walk together to the stables, and countermand your horses . . .'

So saying the trio walked off in the direction of the yard, Miss Bonham not at all displeased to hear her dear cousin's consent to pass the night at Rutsden Lodge.

Chapter Four

If Mr Bonham fancied when he asked Captain Torrant to pass the night in his hospitable mansion, that this gallant officer would content himself with the solitary wretchedness of what was generally known as the bachelor's room, we believe him to have been very considerably mistaken. Indeed Miss Bonham, by virtue of her position as mistress of the establishment, took the first step with regard to her cousin's comfort in ordering the best bedroom to be prepared for him. This the reader will recollect our noticing as being adjacent to her room.

The kind, thoughtful girl considered that if her dear Alfred were taken ill in the middle of the night, he would be so far away from any assistance she could render him, and, worse still, he might be afflicted with that terrible complaint known in the medical vocabulary as 'prickstand', in which case he would be inconveniently far from her bed and a great deal too near Lucy's.

The result of this prudent arrangement was that the young dragoon did not occupy the luxurious bed allotted to him at all, but partially undressed, devoted half-an-hour to a fascinating book of a decidedly lascivious character. When that space of time elapsed, he made pretty certain of two matters; first, that his respected uncle was in bed and sleeping the first sleep of the just, and secondly, that notwithstanding his delightful encounters with his lovely cousin, in the course of the day, he was perfectly able to do her as much justice as she could possibly desire in the fucking department. Under this impression, he noiselessly glided from his room to Eliza's, the door of which, he quietly opened.

'Is that you, dear Alfred?' asked the young lady, neither surprised nor frightened; indeed the probability was that she had been expecting him, for she was wide awake and a dim lamp was burning in her room.

'Bolt the door gently,' she continued, 'and come to bed. You know after what Papa said this evening, I consider you as good as my husband now. But my goodness, Alfred, you have not got your sheath on, and how awfully stiff you are!'

To this the young gentleman made reply to the effect that he supposed the painful stiffness would be cured in a couple of minutes, and that with regard to the condom, as he expected his darling Eliza would become his wife in less than a month, that useful precaution was no longer necessary. The young lady assented, as indeed she would have assented to anything her lover proposed, and as he entered her luxurious couch, folded him in something more luxurious still, throwing her soft white arms around him, and placing one of her beautiful legs over him as he lay. We shall not detain our reader long in the lady's bedroom, as the lovers, being calmer than usual after the day's enjoyments, were disposed to be rational, somewhat in the manner of married couples after the honeymoon; so that the proceedings comprised a judicious amount of straightforward fucking, variegated by alternations of refreshing slumber, enjoyed in each other's arms. But this quiet domestic sort of rogering, as it may be termed, is singularly effective in its results, though not as full of incident and excitement as more impromptu and passionate licentiousness – at any rate, one thing is pretty certain: that when Captain Torrant crept quietly back to his room about five o'clock in the morning, he had planted something in his cousin's garden, which bore fruit nine months afterwards in the shape of a fine boy.

After breakfast, the young gentleman mounted his tandem-cart, attended by his faithful Robert. On the sly he had taken the most loving farewell of Eliza, and without that secrecy, a most affectionate one of his uncle, who promised everything that was good natured, both with regard to his promotion in the service and his marriage to Eliza. All this was very agreeable to Alfred, although he certainly considered that his uncle's ready regard for his interest was partially attributed to his desire to get his daughter married and out of his house, before introducing a new Mrs Bonham as mistress thereof. But whatever the cause, the experienced commander sensibly reflected that it was his duty to take advantage of his uncle's liberality while he could. Serenely turning these matters over in his mind, he arrived at the barracks, where he was welcomed by his brother officers, with whom he was a decided favourite, each in his own peculiar way. The Colonel, in a polite, man-of-the-world style, hoped that he had had a pleasant visit, and wanted to know when he might be presented to Mrs Alfred Torrant. The Colonel did not like his officers to marry except with wealthy and handsome women; money of course was an advantage in the regiment, whoever it belonged to, and the Colonel liked pretty women – maids, wives and widows; so as Alfred bade fair to acquire both advantages united, the Colonel wished all success to his suit. Major Pobjoy remarked that it was not always that a young man had a prospect of so many worldly advantages, together with the blessing of a regenerate father-in-law. To which Alfred – who did not care much about the Major, as he was leaving the corps, – replied that he did not know what a 'regenerate' meant, but if it meant religious, his venerated relative was a devilish good fellow, but rather too strong on that point.

'He read us an epistle, or a chapter, or something last night, Colonel. He did, I assure you,' said Alfred, addressing his superior officer. 'The first epistle of Saint Jeroboam to the Rechabites, or some such people, and it was all I could do to live through it, thought I should have yawned my head off – upon my word I did.'

Thus saying, the Captain toddled off to his quarters, out of hearing of the irreverent comments of divers of his younger comrades, some of whom opined that if Torrant was not married to Miss Bonham, the sooner he was the better, while one of the lot, Julius Larkyns, gave it as his opinion that Alfred looked as if he were married already.

A shrewd remark – founded upon Alfred's subdued appearance – for which our readers who have borne that young gentleman company during the past twenty-four hours, will feel disposed to give Captain Larkyns credit. This gentleman with one or two others of the same kidney, were speedily summoned to a conference by Alfred, he being suddenly smitten with an idea that a messenger might be very shortly expected at the barracks enquiring for Major Ringtail, in order to serve him either a summons before a magistrate, or to deliver him a lawyer's letter, threatening an action of damages for defamation of character.

And as Captain Torrant had nothing to do until he received Rosa's address from Eliza, it struck him that it would be a pleasant and profitable method of spending his leisure time, if he and his companions in arms were to get somebody to impersonate the Major, and thereby get some fun out of the victimized Stiggins, and the unfortunate Miss Larcher. Words are faint to describe the delights expressed by the young officers of HM's 51st Dragoons on hearing such an agreeable game proposed to them; and their respect for their friend's henchman, Robert, as a mischief-maker, liar and blackguard generally, amounted to something very like reverence. But it would never do to let him personate the Major, for he might be brought into contact with Mrs Fielding and be recognized, but as one of the lieutenants piously remarked:

'Thank God there are plenty more scamps in the corps, and we shall find one clever enough to impersonate the Major or anyone else for that matter.'

The first thing to do was to warn the sentry on duty not to refuse anyone admittance who came asking for Major Ringtail, the second thing to do was to dress up Julius Larkyns' man in a shooting coat belonging to that gentleman, and arranging that he should occupy his master's quarters, as soon as Stiggins or any of his missionaries made their appearance.

This was not very long in happening, for Larkyns, who was smoking a cigar, with his head out of the window, suddenly exclaimed:

'Here he is! That must be him, I'll go and direct him up here. You stay here you fellows!' addressing Torrant and three or four more, 'you are only keeping the Major company in weed, you know!'

So saying off he went, and his friends followed the idea, saw him accosting a fat, bloated, palefaced unwholesome looking man, who seemed staring about half-bewildered in the barracks yard. Under the kind pilotage of Captain Larkyns the doubt was soon solved, and the hapless Stiggins entered the room of the so-called Major Ringtail. On entering, Captain Larkyns gravely addressed his man Tom with:

'Sorry to intrude upon you Major, but this party was looking for you, and I thought it was well to bring him up to your quarters.'

'Quite right, my boy, as long as he isn't a dun,' readily replied the soi-disant Major.

'I am no dun, sir,' answered Stiggins, intending to be majestic, but rather taken aback upon seeing what a knot of daredevil looking youngsters he had intruded among. 'I am a minister of the word, sir, an 'umble apostle of the truth sir, and my name is Stiggins!'

'Oh, indeed!' was the cool reply, 'sit down, Mr Stiggins, glad to see you – you're the man that buggered the pig, ain't you? Interesting zoological pursuit, I should imagine! Julius, mix a little refreshment for Mr Stiggins, he must be thirsty after his walk.'

The pious man half rose from his seat and essayed to speak, but he could not. He stuttered and gasped, and his eyes rolled in his head, while his pasty looking face became purple. While he was thus endeavouring to give vent to his indignation, Captain Larkyns adopted the hint of his quick-witted man, made him some 'refreshing' drink. He got hold of a rum bottle and half filled a tumbler, then he was going to administer a trifling modicum of water, but Torrant took the jug away and gave him in its place a bottle of gin. A portion of this added to the rum made a cool wholesome mixture; the flavour being slightly modified by a lump of ice, three or four bits of sugar, a piece of lemon and some nutmeg. To this fearful compound, Larkyns gave the impromptu title of 'The Prince's Mixture'.

Gravely addressing the almost convulsed preacher, the young officer said:

'You seem rather unwell, reverend sir, wearied in body and somewhat troubled in spirit, perchance? Pray allow me to adopt our worthy Major's suggestion, and offer you a slight refreshment. It was considered a valuable stomachic by that model of all the monarchs – the late George the Fourth – named Prince's Mixture, in his honour when Regent.'

'Under those circumstances, young man,' replied Stiggins, majestically, 'I shall lay aside the conscientious scruples which I entertain against drinking anything but the water of the brook; but being in duty bound to reverence the powers that be, I feel myself called upon to follow the example of the august monarch you have named.'

Hereupon, reducing his features to something like a human expression, he took a pretty fair pull of the dangerous compound; remarking, as he placed the half emptied tumbler on the table, that it was somewhat potent.

'Not at all,' replied Larkyns, 'it is only your Reverence's water drinking habits that make you fancy everything else strong in taste.'

'Truly it may be so, but my business here is with Major Ringtail,' replied Stiggins, turning to address that individual. 'There is a terrible story spread abroad sir, to the effect of my having been seen in an unseemly position with a swine, and that you have been heard to accuse me of that indiscretion without any consequences resulting on my part, and I have come here not only to put a stop to such abominable reports, but also to demand satisfaction in some shape or other. Indeed, I consider it due to myself as a preacher of the word, to have amends made to me in a pecuniary sense, for the damage my character has sustained.'

To this exordium the so-called Major made no reply, but Larkyns quietly slipped a wine glass full of Scotch whisky into his reverence's tumbler, while Torrant coolly said:

'I presume Major, that your friend here is the party who was accused of fucking the old sow, in Farmer Codson's pig-stye?'

'Nothing of the sort sir! It's an infamous falsehood!' shrieked Stiggins, rising from his chair and stamping in high wrath.

'Take it easy, my friend, take it easy,' continued Alfred, 'anybody may be mistaken.'

'Oh certainly!' interrupted the mollified pastor, taking a big drink.

'And if you preferred buggering a pig to fucking a sow, I don't see that it is anybody's business!'

Here there was another outbreak on the part of Stiggins, drowned however by the roars of laughter following Alfred's peace-making amendment. All that could be distinguished was a heap of broken sentences, such as:

'Go to magistrates – bring action – defamation c'racter – spectable lady member cong-g-ration, Miss Larcher, thousand pounds damages!'

'Silence, gentlemen, if you please, a lady's name is mentioned! Let us be cool and hear all about it!'

This was from Captain Torrant.

'And take your drink, Mr Stiggins,' said Julius, 'have another lump of ice in it?'

'Not because you tell me, young man,' replied the holy man in an offensive tone, 'but because I am a free agent and shall do as I like.'

So saying, to the unconcealed delight of the young scapegraces, he took a little more rum and another lump of ice. Then being anxiously pressed by the Major to know if he had any fresh accusation to make regarding Miss Larcher, he began such a rigmarole about the Major having fucked that much injured lady, and not having done so, and only spreading a lying report to that effect, and that he had never been kicked out of the barracks – not he indeed! – he would like to see the pig that would fuck him out of barracks; and he would bring an action against Miss Larcher, that he would.

'I presume the long and short of the story, Mr Stiggins, is that you fucked Miss Larcher,' said Captain Larkyns, continuing with an appearance of great interest. 'Well, I never did roger a girl in chapel myself, during divine service, but I have no doubt there is a certain piquancy in it. Did she make a pretty good fuck, Stiggins? Had she a fat arse?'

There is no telling what answer that sainted man might have made in return, for drink and indignation had made him half mad. But the question was immediately started whether it was not the pig who committed himself with Miss Larcher in the chapel, and one of the young sinners bawled out one thing and one another, till the whole question of the pig, Miss Larcher, the chapel, Major Ringtail and the barracks was involved in chaos. One thing was plain enough, Stiggins was drunk.

Then arose the question: what was to be done with him? Finally, it was resolved to adopt Captain Larkyns' views. He suggested that their respected victim would be in a state of total unconsciousness, and that a strong solution of gum, if glue or tar could not be had, should be applied to the sainted countenance, and that some feathers, taken from the pillow of Cornet Periwinkle, as the officer who had joined last was known, should be distributed, so as to give the holy man the appearance, as nearly as possible of an owl. That being the bird of wisdom, was hailed as combining amusement with compliment, if the Reverend Stiggins could only be brought to view it in the same light. Then the apostle should be placed on a wheelbarrow, with his saintly mug enveloped in a sack, lest peradventure, the eyes of carnal men being cast upon him, scandal might be the result; or what the young dragoons were much more afraid of, the order of the procession might be interrupted in some way.

Major Ringtail, divested of his master's shooting jacket, was ordered forthwith to go and find a wheelbarrow, and a country lout game enough to wheel a load to the Temperance Hotel in Rutshole. Yes, dear reader, that was where the Reverend Stiggins was going, to the much-maligned Miss Larcher's Temperance Coffee-House; he, her much revered visitor and pastor, being in three predicaments – in drink, in a wheelbarrow, and in the semblance of an owl!

During Tom's absence, his master and his master's companions betook themselves to adorn Stiggins, with as much earnestness and business-like gravity as if they were doing the most praiseworthy act in the world. One of them concocted a note purporting to be from his Reverence to Miss Larcher, containing expressions of attachment and an offer of marriage. This, neatly folded and addressed, was placed between his right thumb and forefinger, these articles being lashed tight together, greatly to his Reverence's comfort no doubt.

Towards dusk, according to orders a wheelbarrow and a grinning country lad were in attendance outside the barracks gates; the youngster being promised half-a-sovereign if he performed his errand satisfactorily, and one shilling and a licking if he mismanaged matters, readily undertook to convey the apostle to the private door of Miss Larcher's hostelry, there empty him out, and ring the bell as if the place was on fire.

Moreover three or four of the gentlemen present undertook to walk in the same direction, in small but separate parties, so as to watch the result; and also to give aid to the countryman, in case of his conveyance or its interesting freight being interfered with by impertinently curious people, or any such disagreeable interlopers.

Then Stiggins was borne forth and deposited in his chariot: the conductor thereof upon being questioned as to whether the load of sanctity would not be rather too much for him, replied in the negative, asserting that he had barrowed many a heap of 'mook' as doubtless he had, and in the same barrow too – very lately.

'So,' as Mrs Hermans says, 'the stately march went on.'

Torrant and Larkyns were about twenty yards ahead on the side path; then, in the middle of the road came the body of their victim, watched by Tom, walking carelessly along the path abreast the barrow; then two more officers.

Robert begged his master to let him take part in the procession, but it was considered dangerous.

When Rutshole was reached, these precautions showed the wisdom of the prudent young men who had adopted them. For the vedettes, if we may use the expression, encountered a policeman, who was staring with some curiosity at the conveyance moving slowly along the High Street. He was immediately collared by Larkyns and Torrant, humbugged by an impromptu story of a lost pocketbook by Larkyns, and escorted to the Red Lion to talk about the matter, over a glass of brandy and water. So the coast was clear, and the two gentlemen of the rear guard arriving immediately reported that the barrow was in the act of depositing its precious freight.

Immediately there was a rush made for the door, when the conductor was seen bowling his empty machine down the street on his homeward journey at a devil of a rate.

Simultaneously there arose from the opposite side of the street a shrill scream. The policeman and the officers immediately hurried across to render what assistance they could, most probably – and also perhaps to see the fun.

There they found Miss Larcher, her waiter and two housemaids in agonies of screaming at a prostrate figure, the upper half of which was enveloped in a sack, which the animal inside whatever it might be, was endeavouring to get rid of – but in vain. We are bound to say that the two young officers upon arriving at the scene of action, did not devote their first attention to the writhing tenant of the sack. They knew all about that kind of thing – but Julius nudged Torrant, saying:

'I say, Al, is that Miss Larcher? I thought she was an elderly piece of goods.'

'Well,' said his friend, critically, 'so she is, certainly, one of the has-beens! I should say: forty or nearly so, but still I agree with you, she is a fine well-made sort of an old girl, well kept too, I shouldn't wonder. Devilish good fetlocks, she has got!'

This interesting comment referred, as the reader will perceive, to the general appearance of Miss Larcher, who was by no means the starched old maid that Miss Bonham, in her conversation with her cousin implied her to be. She had decided remains of former good looks, and, as Alfred's acute eye had remarked, very neat ankles, judiciously clothed in neat kid slippers and black silk stockings.

'Toss you up for her, Alfred!' suggested Captain Larkyns, in as commonplace a sort of way as if it was a bottle of wine that was in question.

'Oh, no, my dear fellow,' replied his friend, 'you are quite welcome to try your luck.'

'Then don't you interfere,' said Julius.

'On the contrary, my dear fellow, I shall be happy to assist your virtuous endeavours in any way that I possibly can. Shall I curry favour with the lady by ordering a couple of gallons of coffee, and a bushel of buttered muffins? That's the sort of thing to do her I suppose?'

'Ha, ha,' laughed Julius, 'in half-an-hour's time, if I have any luck, you may have either a buttered muffin or bun if you like!'

While this confidential interlude was going on, the policeman, assisted by the waiter, had been dragging at the sack. This was removed at last with some difficulty to the operators, and more pain to the patient, as some of his glued-on plumage came off in the operation. Still there remained enough to make him look 'a thing of beauty,' which one of our poets remarked, 'is a joy forever.'

We presume that it was from some deficiency of poetical temperament that none of the spectators, always excepting our military friends, could see the adornment of the Stiggins mug in this light. At any rate, Miss Larcher screamed, and her maids yelled. The little waiter stood in speechless awe, and the policeman remarked in a musing tone:

'Well, I've seen a good many rummy stares but this beats all I ever did see. Suppose 'e must a been an' got drunk, an' slept in a 'en roost.'

'Drunk, the disgusting brute is certainly,' interposed Captain Larkyns, who was a three-bottle man.

'But he must not lie here, disgracing a respectable lady's house,' said Alfred, backing up his friend.

'Then I shall get a stretcher,' said Bobby, 'and have him taken to the station.'

'No, don't do that,' said the considerate Julius, 'or else Miss Larcher will have to appear – as a witness before the magistrate – most disagreeable position for a young lady to be placed in.'

'You are always right, Larkyns,' replied his faithful friend. 'I say, Officer, never mind saying anything at the station. Take the degraded beast across the street to the Red Lion and tell the boots from me to find some sort of a bed somewhere. I'll pay for it. He can be turned out when he's sober, you know, and there'll be no trouble to you, and no nuisance to Miss Larcher.'

That lady simpered and smiled, and expressed her sense of the polite consideration of the two gentlemen, and finally asked them to step in and refresh themselves. This being exactly what Julius wanted, the two friends were preparing to enter, when all of a sudden Captain Torrant pretended to discover that the object of their united disgust had a folded paper in his hand. This he extricated from between his finger and thumb, not dreaming however of severing the ligature that bound them together. And then gravely addressing Miss Larcher he remarked:

'By an extraordinary coincidence, this note seems to be addressed to you.'

'To me!' exclaimed the lady in great surprise, tearing it open, and in the first instance looking at the signature:

'Seth Stiggins! Why it can never be! Yes, but it is though – oh my, what a state for a babe of grace, a minister of the word!' Then, looking into the contents, she continued: 'Oh, the nasty, filthy wretch, take him away – out of my sight – such an insult! Into the nearest horse-pond with him,' and so on, in a high state of wrathful excitement.

Here the policeman returned with a couple of men and a stretcher; and Captain Torrant paid them all three for their trouble, while reiterating his commands to have the culprit conveyed to the Red Lion.

In the meantime, Julius was accompanying Miss Larcher to the house, begging her most earnestly and affectionately not to agitate herself.

'Indeed sir, you are very kind and polite,' replied the lady, 'but to think of that wretch, whom I have so long considered one of the elect, coming to my house in a filthy state of intoxication, and with a face like a badly stuffed owl, and to deliver me such a note – oh, I shall die of shame and horror!!'

'Not at all, my dear Miss Larcher,' replied Julius tenderly, 'we cannot afford to lose you on account of any such a wretch as that. Pray what is in his vile scrawl that should agitate you so deeply?'

'Indeed sir, I am almost ashamed to show it to you, but here it is. It would have been bad enough if he had written it while tipsy, but he had been sober enough when he wrote it, and that makes it more insulting, I know his handwriting.'

Here Julius could hardly keep his countenance, for the note had been written, partly under his direction, by Cornet Periwinkle. It stated in effect, that as she, Miss Larcher, was tolerably well provided in the world's goods and he Stiggins was not, he would have no objections to save her character by marrying her. That his friend, Major Ringtail, had told him that she made a most delicious fuck; as indeed he himself partly guessed from seeing the way in which she tossed up her pretty white legs and doubled them over that gallant officer's back, when he was rogering her in the pew last Sunday; but as he, Stiggins, considered that locality too much exposed, he suggested the vestry, after divine service, or indeed the sofa in her own private apartment, as a more suitable spot for the consummation of their mutual affection. Concluding with a philosophical remark that she needn't be shy, for he had ascertained that the dimensions of the Major's cock were so huge that she needn't be afraid of one of a milder description.

Upon reading this precious production, Julius rose with a grave face, went to the door and locked it, glad of the opportunity of turning his back upon the lady, to conceal a triumphant grin that would come upon his features. When he returned, his face had resumed its gravity as he remarked:

'My name, dear Miss, is Larkyns, a Captain in the same regiment as this Major Ringtail, and I assure you I shall call him to account for his abominable slander.'

'And then he'll shoot you, Captain Larkyns,' exclaimed the lady, clasping her hands together in an agonized way, for the young gentleman's handsome face and figure had begun to produce a great effect upon her.

'Perhaps he may, dear Miss Larcher, but in the cause of injured beauty and innocence, I can dare anything, and if I fail you can drop a tear to my memory.'

On this artful speech, Miss Larcher (who had not been made love to for some years) turned on the Captain a look so full of love and gratitude, that the young gentleman who was by no means troubled with bashfulness, passed his arms around the lady's waist and pressed his lips to hers, murmuring as he did so:

'Make me your champion, my darling, and I will dispel this vile slander or perish in the attempt.'

To this magnificent speech, Miss Larcher could only mutter something about bloodshed, and never seeing him again. Then Julius, as if a bright idea had struck him said:

'Perhaps this villian of a Major will retract and confess it is all a lie. It is a lie, I suppose, my darling girl, is it not?'

'Oh, Captain Larkyns!' she exclaimed, in a tone of reproof.

'Nay,' said he, hastily, 'I believe it is a lie, but to make other people believe; that's the thing. There is one proof of the incorrectness of the story – that the wretched Stiggins talked about your white stockinged legs over the side of the pew. Now that part of the story is evidently false as I perceive you wear black silk.'

'Certainly,' said she very readily, 'of course, I always do,' and at the time displaying more of her legs in corroborating her statement than in prudence she ought to have done.

'Oh what exquisite legs!' said the artful dragoon, kneeling down and commencing to kiss them.

'Do you think so, Captain,' replied the lady smiling and blushing.

To this there was no verbal response, but there was more extensive kissing, in both senses of the word, higher up (he had got to her thighs by this time) and stronger in quality. And then Julius, as quietly and slyly as the operation would permit, insinuated his hand between the lady's thighs, and his finger inside her cunt.

'Oh, Captain Larkyns,' she sighed, 'I am learning to love you. Do not destroy my self-respect.'

'My sweet friend,' Julius astutely replied to this, 'I am your champion for life and death; permit me to assure myself that when I give the slanderer the lie to his teeth, I shall be speaking truly and conscientiously.'

To this the lady made no reply, but a heavy sigh. Perhaps she was soft enough to believe the seductive Larkyns; perhaps she had a longing for something, she knew not what. At any rate she was fairly in for it by this time, and made no resistance when Julius laid her back on the sofa, with one of her legs over the back of it, and the other supported by a neighbouring chair.

'This is the sofa, I suppose, on which that brute Stiggins proposed to violate you, my darling, but from henceforth it shall be kept sacred as the altar on which you sacrificed your sweet person to your devoted lover Julius!'

'Ah, Julius,' said Miss Larcher, as the dragoon was raising her clothes and opening her thighs, 'be gentle with me, indeed, I am inviolated and free from the lust of man, do not hurt me.'

'I respect you as much as I love you,' replied the lying scamp, taking out his long stiff prick, and saying to himself as he did so, 'what a jolly tight fuck the old girl will make! Here goes for her maidenhead the very first shove!'

And indeed it was so, or very nearly. Before making the shove, he took care to have himself very well established, and then when he did make it, there was a scream, not that Julius cared, for he knew that his faithful friend, Alfred, would keep intruders out of the room. He persevered in his vigorous shoves, until Miss Larcher, reassured by his passionate words and burning kisses, forgot the smart of the pain, and tasted something very like pleasure – and when Julius injected his spunk into her, and sank into her arms, she experienced a feeling of satisfaction from the sentiment that he belonged to her now and would come and ride her again. She was right there, and not far wrong in believing Julius – she would believe anything he said – when he assured her that he would have Major Ringtail turned out of the regiment next day. She little thought how easy it was to turn a man out of the regiment who was never in it.

Leaving Captain Larkyns to congratulate himself upon knowing where to go for some fresh cunt, when the spirit moved him, and Miss Larcher to take what pride she could in the idea that if she were not a married woman, she was at any rate no longer an old maid, we will follow Rosa to her finishing school at Mrs Moreen's.

Here, as may be expected, a parlour boarder like Rosa, met with a good deal of consideration. A few showy accomplishments, and a fashionable deportment, were all that she was required to learn, and naturally lady-like and clever, their acquisition did not cost her much trouble. But she was destined to learn some other accomplishments at Mrs Moreen's establishment, such as that worthy lady probably knew nothing about, and which she certainly never charged for in her half-yearly bills. For instance, it is usual among young ladies of Rosa's age when thrown a good deal into each other's society to form close alliances, bonds of everlasting affection and so on. Then ensue confidential communications about lovers, cousins and brothers, revelations as to secret longings, and the liberties which the dear little creatures have permitted to that naughty boy, Harry, or that darling Frederick, and so on. And in the young ladies' bedrooms the descriptions were sometimes illustrated, particularly as when in Rosa's case her bedfellow was her most intimate friend and confidante, Miss Harriet Lovit. This young lady, who was a few months younger than Rosa, was a thorough adept in all sorts of licentious practices. On the very first night of their sleeping together, she clasped Rosa in her arms and tried by getting between her thighs to excite her lust, and produce something that a young gentleman in the same position would not have failed to produce. But though Rosa had no objection to the proceeding, and stretched her thighs as wide as she could, and kissed her newly-found friend affectionately in acknowledgement of her well-meant efforts, the only effect produced by their two tender young cunts rubbing together, was to make the pretty pair long for something else, something which was not at hand.

'What are you two girls doing there?' asked Charlotte Arden, one of the occupants of the other bed, in a sleepy voice.

'I am trying to fuck dear Rosa,' said Harriet plaintively, 'and I can't manage it so as to make her spunk.'

'Of course you can't,' was Charlotte's prompt reply, 'it is only one woman in fifty who has her clitoris prominent enough to produce the desired effect upon another woman's cunt, and for a girl like you the thing is a sheer impossibility. Shove one of your fingers into her and frig her well. She is very ungrateful indeed if she does not perform the same kind offices afterwards, for you.'

That Harriet immediately acted upon this sensible advice, may be inferred from the fact of Rosa beginning very shortly afterwards to sigh, to spread her thighs open right across the bed, and finally to clasp and kiss her bed fellow in a transport of delight, murmuring broken sentences expressive of gratitude, and finally covering her two fingers and her knuckles with warm spunk.

'Have you done her business, Harriet? And has she

a maidenhead?' asked the young lady from the other bed.

'That I have nicely,' was the reply, 'and she has a maidenhead, really and truly.'

'Oh, upon my honour,' exclaimed Charlotte, 'that state of things will never do. I'll take it for her with a candle; we can't have any maidenheads among girls of our age, in this establishment,' continued she laughing.

'You shan't do anything to her tonight, Charlotte, I can tell you that!' said Harriet, 'she is very well frigged and does not want anymore at present. Besides you goose, if Miss Downey' (the second governess) 'were to find, on her inspection of the rooms tomorrow morning, our candle, stained with blood, there would be a pretty to do.'

'Miss Downey is not a bit better than any of the rest of us,' replied the other young lady. 'When she was in the garden privy the other day, I peeped through the keyhole and saw her ramming a huge carrot into herself until I thought she was going to have a fit, and I know that Signor Loretti, the Italian Master kissed her and felt her, on the stairs a day or two ago.'

'That is all very well, and likely enough,' responded the prudent Harriet, 'but it would not prevent her from reporting us to Mrs Moreen, if she found any suspicious signs and tokens. Besides how do you know whether Rosa would like to have her sweet little virgin treasure violated by you and your candle? I should think that she would very much prefer me to take it.'

'Oh, yes, dear Miss Harriet,' exclaimed Rosa affectionately, 'I don't think you would do anything to hurt me, and if you were a young man, I would allow you to shove your cock into me as much as you pleased.'

'What is the child talking about?' interrupted Charlotte. 'What does she know about cocks?'

'I have seen my guardian's – Mr Bonham—' replied Rosa, simply, as if it were the most commonplace affair in the world, and her guardian had only been doing his duty in displaying his jolly tool, and attempting to roger her in the carriage.

'Good gracious, your guardian's prick? How was that? How did it happen? Tell us all about it.'

Such was the chorus of exclamations that broke forth, and Rosa promising that it was a great secret, delighted her room companions by relating the trifling circumstances that took place during her journey to London in her respected guardian's carriage.

Then came a running fire of cross examination, something as follows:

'Wasn't it delicious when he put his tongue in and licked your cunt? Was his prick a large one? Did you take hold of it? Did he hurt you when he shoved it into you? How much did he spend in you? Wouldn't you like it again?' and so on; all of which Rosa Fielding answered to the best of her ability, and apparently to the satisfaction of her friends, who showed their sympathy with the proceedings by a certain degree of restlessness in bed and sundry long drawn sighs and 'Ahs' just as if they were tasting or fancied they were tasting something very nice.

Indeed Miss Lovit gave a practical proof of the excitement the short story had raised in her bottom, (and private parts) by altering her position in the bed, and placing her lovely bottom over Rosa's face, so that her cunt rested on the sweet girl's mouth, and her face, by this manoeuvre, of course brought upon Rosa's lately moistened orifice.

As she did this she begged Rosa in a most coaxing tone to thrust her tongue into her feverish cunt, and to lick it, and roll it about therein, just as Mr Bonham had done to her. The good-natured girl at once complied, and really, for a novice, managed this difficult office to perfection, as the lascivious Harriet, already

excited by frigging her new friend, was brought to the
verge of spunking by Rosa's simple narrative, and the
latter had not licked and sucked the gaping orifice for
more than a minute and a half, before Miss Lovit
began to interrupt the grateful licking she was administering to Rosa's quim, by various licentious and
pleasurable exclamations, such as:

'Oh, you sweet girl – you darling! That's right!
Suck my clitoris! I wish your tongue was twice as big!
Oh that's it! Go on,' etc. etc., concluding by a long
drawn sigh, as she covered our heroine's face and half
filled her mouth, with a delicious ejection of warm
spunk. Of course with such capabilities and loving
inclinations to accommodate themselves to each other's wishes, the two young ladies fast became friends.

Rosa had very little more to tell, but her more
experienced friend found great pleasure in dispelling
her ignorance and charmed Rosa, particularly by
describing with great gusto, her first experience in the
fucking line, and the loss of her maidenhead.

'We had a large Christmas party, last year, my dear
Rosa, and my mother requested my brothers, who
were then at home, to bring as guests, two or three
handsome young eligible men of their acquaintance.
This they had very little difficulty in doing, as one of
them being at college, and the other in the army, they
knew plenty of handsome young men, capital partners in a waltz.

'Or,' added Harriet, consciously, 'in any other
amusement. I really believe, vanity apart, I was looking very well and my brother John who is intended to
be a clergyman, and who is the naughtiest fellow I
ever saw or heard of, seemed to take some pride in
introducing his particular friend, Mr Melville, to me.
He also, it appears, was destined for the church, and
conducted himself accordingly. I suppose there is
something in the prospect of wearing black, and
preserving an outward appearance of respectability,

that induces young gentlemen similarly circum-
stanced, to conduct themselves like young bulls, or
lively rams; at any rate they generally do so. On the
present occasion, my brother John, introducing his
friend to me, said in a whisper, which he hardly cared
to make inaudible:

'Stunning girl, I can tell you, Harry, she has the
finest and longest legs of any girl of her age you ever
saw!'

'For shame, John, hold your tongue,' I exclaimed,
blushing scarlet.

'All right!' said he, laughing, as he went away,
leaving me with Mr Melville.

'Now I must acknowledge that I had permitted
Master John to take sundry improper liberties with
me. I considered at first it was very wrong in any
young man, unless he were an engaged lover, to take
up a lady's petticoats and feel her cunt and bottom,
but John assured me that it was quite a family matter,
and further demanded, if a brother could not take
liberties with his own sister, who was he to take
liberties with? This line of argument might not have
been altogether approved of by my Mother and Papa,
but we carefully concealed our little interviews from
other eyes than our own. He it was who initiated me
into the mystery of frigging. He really gave me a great
deal of pleasure and I used to do my best to show my
gratitude by chafing his white cock until the spunk
used to fly off in a jet nearly a yard from him. And he
used to do even worse than this.'

'Why surely,' interrupted Rosa, 'you never allowed
him to get into you? That would be very wrong I
know.'

'Not in the way you mean, my dear,' replied her
friend, 'though, really, if he had attempted it on some
occasion when he had excited me with his finger I do
not know how I should have been able to resist him.
But however, he had too much prudence, whether I

had or not, and confined his devotions to my small orifice.'

'Do you mean your bottom-hole?' asked the wondering Rosa, 'I should have thought it was too small altogether!'

'So I should have thought at first,' was her friend's reply, 'but it really is not so. A little ointment , or hair oil, and gentle shoving for the first minute, and then it becomes a very nice operation, delightful to the gentleman and not at all objectionable to the lady. There is nothing so bad but what some good comes of it; and these proceedings of my favourite brother, though I must consider them improper, had the good result of making me very particular in my person and dress, especially in regard to my underclothing.

'John used to say that he used to detest a girl who wore her hair bedecked in the height of fashion, and wore necklaces and jewels, and had a dirty cunt and bottom. Next to this, one abomination, he declared, was a twenty-guinea silk dress, concealing a dirty chemise and drawers and slovenly gartered stockings. It's a pity that girls more generally speaking, are not aware of the very strong opinion held upon this subject by the opposite sex; at any rate on this occasion I had reason to congratulate myself upon being particular. How many waltzes Harry Melville danced with me I cannot remember, but I have good reason to remember breaking my sandal towards the latter part of the evening. This dreadful accident had to be paid immediate attention to, and we withdrew from the dancing room to the stairs for this purpose, but, Heaven help us, whether any other ladies had been breaking sandals, or loosening their garters, I could not tell, but the first flight of stairs was thickly populated. Harry proposed that we should adjourn to the second flight, but I hardly liked this, as it seemed rather too brazen an operation. As I hesitated, John came up and addressing Melville suggested the

propriety, with some cheerful slang, of an adjourn-
ment for bitter beer purposes. But my gallant partner
would not have it so, for the present, at all events, and
put the fracture that had taken place in such a terrible
point to view, that John, who knew that a couple of
minutes' attention from one of the servant girls would
set all to rights, pretended to take the calamity in the
light that his friend did, and suggested his study and
smoking room – chiefly the latter – as a harbour of
refuge. As he said this he chuckled to himself, but did
not offer to accompany us, as we both, knowing the
way perfectly well, proceeded to the sanctum in question. Here I seated myself in John's lounging chair,
while Harry turned up the gas and bolted the door.
These proceedings I pretended not to notice, as
demurely stretching out my silk-clad foot, I awaited
Master Melville's proceedings. These were at first
simple enough, he drew off my satin slipper, took out
his penknife and deliberately cut away the broken
parts of my sandal. These he coolly pocketed,
remarking that he would retain them – as a keepsake.
But his next proceedings were not so cool, before
putting on my shoe, he covered my foot with kisses,
from my feet he proceeded to the calves of my legs,
and even higher, and as he had taken care to locate
himself between my legs, he was favourably situated
for making further researches.

'Even with your very slight experience, my dear
Rosa, you can imagine the exciting nature of my situation. I knew that my handsome admirer was doing
what is commonly called wrong, and that I was to say
the least of it, guilty of indiscretion, but still when he
began kissing my legs and shoving his hand under my
petticoats; with his fingers gently separating the tender lips of my cunt, I could not help stretching my
thighs open, no, not for the life of me. The consequences may be easily imagined. He altered his situation a little, taking up my clothes with him as he arose

and dropping his trousers to his heels, he imprinted hot, lustful kisses on my lips. Then standing a little way off me, he raised his shirt and taking one of my hands, laid it upon his Lordly priapus. I eagerly clasped the great, stiff, throbbing machine and felt so eager for its insertion, that I had neither fear of the operation nor dread of the possible consequences. You see, Rosa dear, that I have a sensibly sized mouth, not a little bit of a rosebud as you and some of the other girls have, and it is almost always the case that when a girl has a useful-sized mouth, that her cunt corresponds to it in dimensions. Besides I have had the advantage of many a luscious fingering and licking from Master John; so that when Harry guided the end of his mossy tool in between my mossy portals, I felt no pain until the hot plum-shaped knob came against my virgin barrier and then I exclaimed, "Oh, my dear Mr Melville, you are hurting me!" But instead of drawing back, he pushed into me with renewed energy, laying his hot lips to mine and murmuring. "Will you not try and bear one minute's pain for my sake? My darling girl, do not drive me out of Paradise!".

'This was said so lovingly and enthusiastically, that I did my best to reciprocate his ardour; so, raising his shirt, I clasped my silk-clad legs, which John had recommended, over his naked back, and shoving forward his rump, did my best to meet his thrusts half way. Between our joint efforts, my maidenhead, as you may guess, vanished like a cobweb, Harry ejecting his semen well up me, almost at the very moment of his successful penetration. Very fortunately for me, the pain of the operation checked my inclination to spend at the same time, or the consequences might have been serious. Nothing less than a swelled belly, I am convinced, would have been the result!!

'You have never been properly fucked, yet, my dear Rosa, but let me give you a little bit of advice.

However good and kind your guardian may be to you, you will never have the same intense pleasure in yielding to him your virginity as if he were a handsome young lover. I cannot convey to you an idea of the kisses, the embraces, the vows of eternal affection, which were lavished on me by the enamoured young man, as, still retaining his position, but without exerting himself, he lay with his cock still soaking in its lacerated orifice. He specially recommended the purity of my skin, and the great taste and care bestowed upon my underclothing.

'Even when he drew out of me his limp and dripping, but still swollen cock, he did not cease his praises, but bestowed bountiful kisses upon my bottom, body, legs and thighs. I must confess that I was sorry to see him begin to button up, because the first momentary pang having been got over, and the passage having been well lubricated by his spending, I thought that a second edition of his proceedings might let me have my share of delight. How reckless a girl is, Rosa, when once she gets her animal passion fairly inflamed! The men are held chiefly to blame in most cases of rape and seduction, but upon my word, I think they have generally more consideration for our sex than we have for ourselves.

'I mentioned to you the precautions taken by naughty brother Jack with regard to my rump, when I declare that I could have hardly refused him entrance into the other orifice if he had attempted it, and now on this occasion, when my endearing expressions, lingering kisses and sighs, told Harry Melville all too plainly that I wanted him, in plain English, to fuck me again, the dear self-denying fellow told me that he must take proper precautions or I should certainly find myself in the family way. He proposed to visit me on the following day, and to provide himself with certain sheaths, made, as he described them, of some very delicate fabric, so delicate indeed as to be imperceptible to me, which would however prevent any serious consequences, even if he fucked me a dozen times a day. The dear fellow smiled joyously as he announced this fact, and I blushed, but more with pleasure than shame. The next thing was to arrange where to meet, and we finally settled that if we found it impossible to have a few quiet minutes to ourselves at my home, I should walk out to the library, or some other equally eligible spot, and meet him, at the residence of a highly respectable old lady, who professed to keep lodgers, but who had a kind and feeling heart for young people in distress and want – of each other.

'But we did not immediately feel the necessity of this hospitable arrangement; for instance, two days after our ball Mr Melville called, and after a little ordinary polite conversation with my mother, said he would take the liberty of waiting for my brother John in the study, as that young gentleman had made an appointment to meet him at that time. My mother was going out for a drive in the park, and I announced my intention of putting on my bonnet and going out for a short walk. To this my mother assented and shortly afterwards took her departure, when I went upstairs. But I did not reach my bedroom, as passing the door of John's study the door partially opened and I saw my lover peeping out.

'Time was precious, so that he murmured my name in appealing tones and I lost no time in entering the room; where I was instantly clasped in his arms, and he forthwith bolted the door. After a few kissing preliminaries, he forthwith took out of his pocket-book a semi-transparent sheath, with which he covered his beautiful standing prick. This being done, he applied a little ointment procured from one of my brother's drawers, and really at a little distance it was impossible to tell that he had any safeguard on at all, then placing myself against the wall as he requested, I put one of my feet upon a chair, while he took my petticoats up. My inspection of his cock and the sheathing process, had raised my expectations and my clitoris, to a remarkable extent, and the position I was in, though rather hard to sustain, is certainly one where the lady gets the full extent of the gentleman's powers. In this instance, though I did not feel the pain of a lost maidenhead, I was nearly lifted off my legs. Still the inconvenience of this proceeding did not prevent my experiencing the most exquisite pleasure, and I bathed my admirer's hair at the root of his weapon, before he arrived at the crisis of his enjoyment. This was but the prelude to numberless encounters of a similar description, always more or less ecstatic, both in my brother's study and at the respectable and convenient lodgings, kept by Mrs Boss. But pleasure cannot last forever, and I had to return to school while Harry had to go back to college. Before we parted however, we renewed vows of mutual affection; he, on his part, declaring his intention of marrying me as soon as he could see his way clear towards anything like a settlement in life, and I faithfully promising that however good my offers might be, received in the meantime, I would wait for him.

'Now, whether anything will come of the matter, I know not,' exclaimed Miss Lovit, in an amusing tone. 'He may fancy somebody else better than me; or circumstances may compel me to marry for money, but at any rate Rosa, to finish my story, I can tell you that I have enjoyed myself very much, and without any harm being done.'

This narrative pleased Miss Fielding very much, the prospects of enjoying the ecstasies described by Miss Harriet without running any risk of becoming big with child, on any favourable or tempting opportunity, was very delightful. Then Mr Bonham's attachment was a certainty, whether he made her his wife, or kept her as his mistress, he would not have taken the trouble and expense of placing her at Mrs Moreen's for no purpose.

Consequently, she was very much pleased upon receiving a letter from Mr Bonham about a week afterwards, in which he announced his intention of visiting her to see if she was happy and comfortable. He had, he said, informed Mrs Moreen of his intended visit. That lady, on the day indicated, gravely recommended Rosa to go upstairs and change her dress, and to make herself look as becoming as possible. The good old lady had not lived sixty years in this world for nothing, and knew that the better Rosa looked, the better her self-made guardian would be pleased, and the more Rosa was indulged, the better account she would give of her situation, and the more likely she would be to stay out the year, or two years, whatever Mr Bonham designed. Consequently when Rosa was sent for into the drawing-room to see Mr Bonham, with whom Mrs Moreen had already had some interesting points of conversation, she was looking so very blooming and handsome that the older lady evidently considered her a credit to herself and her school. And then she withdrew politely, considering that the guardian and his ward might have some interesting family matters to talk over. And Rosa did commence the conversation, by enquiring as in duty bound, how her father and mother were. This question being answered satisfactorily, her worthy guardian proceeded to take her upon his knee, which proceeding Rosa rewarded by giving him an affectionate kiss. Thanks to the conversation and fingerings of Miss Lovit, and one or two other young ladies, our heroine was not nearly so bashful as she had been during the incidents in the carriage, and thought that if Mr Bonham was a little encouraged, she would be mistress of an establishment of her own, and no longer a schoolgirl all the sooner. So when Mr Bonham began gently to raise her clothes, instead of remonstrating with him, or offering to prevent him doing so, she said in a coaxing tone:

'I hope my dear guardian, you are pleased with my appearance, Mrs Moreen told me to dress myself as well as possible and to make myself look nice, and I hope – oh, if you want to inspect my silk stockings and underlinen, you are quite welcome. You ought to, for it is due to your great kindness that I look so well. Had you not better bolt the door?'

This last speech was produced by her respectable lover beginning to show signs of virility. He had got the forefinger of his right hand in his protégée's cunt, while with his left hand he was trying to free his manly weapon from its imprisonment, but he was in too great a hurry to have taken any such precautions as bolting the door. If he thought at all on the subject, he no doubt considered that Mrs Moreen knew better than to come into the drawing-room again. If so he was right.

But whatever he considered, it is quite certain what he did, that was to shove Rosa backwards upon the sofa, requesting her to pull her clothes up and stretch her legs wide, while he let his trousers slip down to his knees and tucked up his shirt. As he carefully inserted the purple end of his respectable tool into the young girl's little quim, she said in whispering tones:

'Oh, my dear Mr Bonham, recollect that I am still a maid, no one but you has so much as even attempted my virginity, and if to give you this pleasure, I suffer pain at present and loss of reputation in future, you will keep your promise, won't you, and make me your wife?'

By this time the worthy gentleman had got well into her, and she was so deliciously tight, so sweet in all her private parts, and her face was so blushing and beautiful – that if she had asked him to make her Empress of China, he would have sworn to use his best endeavours in that direction. As it was, he stuttered out as well as he could, for he was ramming through her virgin barrier, that she should be his wife in twelve months, if he could wait so long for the full enjoyment of her lovely person. It must not be supposed that he made this honestly intended purpose coherently, for it was much interrupted by his gallant efforts to penetrate into his ward's sweet sanctuary, and also by soothing her, and stopping her mouth with kisses to prevent the half-uttered exclamations which Rosa could not entirely repress. At last, he managed to get in, up to his balls; and in two or three more shoves experienced the delight and relief of spunking into a virgin womb. He sighed with satisfied pleasure, as he sank with his whole inert weight upon Rosa's belly and breasts, telling her that she had charmed him beyond anything that he had imagined possible, and that he would come to see her again as soon as prudence for her sake would possibly permit.

All this was very pleasant for Rosa to hear and made up in some degree for the smart caused by her burst maidenhead. This however her experienced protector assured her could easily be alleviated by the use of a little lukewarm milk and water. And so making her a present of a pretty purse containing a sum for pocket money, and complimenting Mrs Moreen upon the improved manners and appearance of his ward, he took his departure.

That very afternoon, however, as he was strolling towards his club in Pall Mall, somewhat to his surprise, he met with Captain Alfred Torrant, of the 51st Dragoons. That young swell attributed his presence in London to having some business at his army agents; and as this was natural enough after the conversation he had had with his uncle, the pretext passed without challenge; the facts of the case, however, being that Captain Torrant had treacherous designs against his worthy uncle, intending if possible to find through this means, some opportunity of introducing himself to Rosa, and also not adverse, upon a suitable occasion, to offering to lead his relative's elderly boy-hood into snares.

This trap the good Mr Bonham did not fall into at once, as he announced that he was going to dine at his club, so Alfred declared, prompted by a bright invention, that he and a brother officer were going to dine at Greenwich, and proposed that they should call for him at the Fag and Famish Club, and go down the river and dine together.

This suggestion was at once adopted by Mr Bonham, as being a very good one, and the three carried out their project. Mr Bonham brought with him a country appetite, and perhaps felt the want of a stimulus to supply the natural exhaustion caused by his exertions that morning. He ate heartily and drank deeply, more deeply indeed than he was aware of.

Such stuff as champagne and Moselle and claret, could not take effect on such a port-wine drinker as he was, he thought.

Couldn't they though? More especially when consumed upon top of cold punch, pale ale, Madeira, all of which beverages he had partaken since dinner began. So that when a return to London was proposed, the worthy gentleman felt quite regenerated, physically speaking, and 'up to' any species of amusement proposed by the young officers.

After a little consultation with his friend, Captain Torrant confidentially informed Mr Bonham, that if he would promise not to tell Eliza, he would show him a scene or two of London life known only to a few of the initiated.

'All right, Alfred my boy, I'm game for anything,' was the reply.

So upon arriving at London Bridge, two hansom cabs were chartered for the friendly trio. One four-wheeler would have held them all - but catch Captain Torrant riding in a four-wheeler except with a pretty girl inside, and even then with the blinds down, so his fashionable friends could not witness his degradation.

We did not hear the direction given to the drivers, and so cannot specify the exact locality of the establishment to which their course was directed; suffice it to say that at the end of about a half hour, Mr Bonham found himself at the door of a respectable looking but rather dingy house, in a quite out of the way street.

On the young officers presenting their cards, the party was instantly, and most graciously received by a stout, smiling and gorgeously dressed lady, who did the honours of a gorgeously and handsomely furnished room, provided with what Mr Bonham considered a superabundance of luxurious sofas.

More champagne was immediately the order of the evening, and Mr B having been introduced to the hostess as a gentleman of high standing in the country, that lady politely enquired of him if he would like to see some of the handsomest girls in London, completely stripped, or only in partial deshabille, as with the semi-transparent skirt of the ballet dancer, and nothing else.

Captain Torrant immediately proposed that the young ladies should exhibit themselves in a state of nudity, all but slippers and silk stockings; but his friend, Lieutenant Archer, declared himself for a short, a very short skirt. There was a certain charm, the gallant officer averred, in taking up a girl's dress, however scant it might be, and perhaps he is right.

The prudent Mr Bonham, agreed to leave the matter in the hands of his more experienced young friends, and fancied he had done quite right in doing so, when six very handsome girls were introduced; three being dressed, if their skirts can be described under such an appellation, according to Mr Archer's idea, and the rest delighted Captain Torrant's ideas and eyes, with the exhibition of their beautiful forms, perfectly nude.

There was every variety too, tall and short, plump and slender, brunette and blonde vying with each other in the display of their ravishing limbs, buttocks, bosoms and private parts.

Our readers will probably be astonished at Mr Bonham's apathy when he saw his daughter's accepted suitor, his future son-in-law, take one of the naked girls up in his arms, seat her on the edge of the table, open her thighs, and the lips of her cunt, and then, with her legs supported over his shoulders, begin to ram into her, as if the great object of his existence had been to shove his cock through her up to the roof of her mouth. Nor was Lieutenant Archer one whit behind his friend in taking advantage of the delights by which he was surrounded. True to his creed, he knelt down behind a tall, lithe, dark-haired ballet-dancer, and alternately kissed her milk-white rump and her well preserved and scrupulously clean orifice. Then placing her on her hands and knees on the floor, he dog-fucked her, to the intense admiration of Mr Bonham, whose middle-aged prick began to glow and stiffen, as it had not done for many a year.

We can easily imagine that every movement of his person and every glance of his eye, was eagerly watched by the four disengaged girls. At length a plump little one, a ballet dancer, impudent as little people are wont to be, came and perched herself upon his knee, and commenced kissing him with admiration, genuine admiration too, no doubt, for she had been told that he was rich, and was a jolly-looking bird enough. But one of the sisterhood was bolder still. She was a tall, brown-haired girl, good-looking enough, but not strikingly handsome as the other girls were. Perhaps on this account, her mossy sanctum had been less worshipped, and she felt the want of a few inches, or yards – as the case may be – of wholesome cock. Be this as it may, she knelt down before Mr Bonham, and, no doubt; to the disgust of the little lady who had taken possession of his knee, deliberately opened the front of his trousers, and released his cock: stiff and swollen up to the bursting point, from its irksome confinement. Determined to carry out her idea successfully, she not only chafed the interesting stranger, but sucked him gently; this established her advantage over Maria, – the little girl on his knee – for the effect on the excited gentleman was such that he hastily called out:

'For God's sake, don't do that! or I shall spunk into your mouth!'

And arising from his seat, he kissed Maria, whispering:

'You next, my little pet!' and laid the tall brown-haired Emily on one of the purple, velvet-covered spring sofas.

Short-lived indeed was his joy. Emily held the lips of her mossy treasure open: at one single thrust he was in her up to the balls, two more shoves on his part, two upward heaves and a convulsive wriggle of the rump of the highly-accomplished Emily, and it was all over, for the time being, at any rate, and the highly respected Mr Bonham, of Rutsden Lodge, lay with bare rump and soaking prick, exhausted in the arms of his lascivious enchantress, in the presence of eight much edified spectators, male and female.

Chapter Five

The two remaining girls and Mrs Goater, the mistress of the establishment, were not entirely idle spectators of this delightful proceeding. They began to take advantage of the champagne and cold supper, oysters and other provocative delicacies, displayed on the side board; and while enjoying these, they passed laughing comments on the pretty tableaux, which were being performed around them.

One of the lasses indeed, a French girl, called Coralie, had been a special favourite with Captain Torrant, and probably only missed being first fucked on this occasion from the circumstances of her being arranged in about five and twenty inches of skirt and silk stockings up to her rump, whereas, as we have seen, the gallant commander's tendencies on this occasion were in favour of nakedness.

This girl, we say, exhibited her attachment towards her former admirer by slapping his buttocks, kissing and rubbing his balls, inserting her finger into his hole, and making use of other little endearments, which clever girls, and French girls particularly, consider serviceable in raising and renovating a man's lusts.

We hardly suppose, by the way, that the young gentleman required any such stimulant, but however, he was duly grateful, and when he drew out his drooping and dripping prick, he rewarded the lady with a lascivious kiss, and a groping feel which explored her secret recesses in most effectual style. An adjoining bedroom supplied the means of ablution to the participants in the luscious games, and then they all set down to supper. We might prolong this chapter ad infinitum were we to describe the eating and drinking, and the lascivious conversation that went on, but we must confine ourselves to the most striking incidents. One of these was that Maria, who no doubt considered that it was high time for her to have something to do, collared Mr Bonham's cock and by frigging it gently, endeavoured to induce it to regain its perpendicular station. But notwithstanding the oysters and wine, and other more direct incentives to lust, Mr Bonham was not able as yet to stiffen so as to be serviceable. Our readers will readily understand what we mean, when we say that a middle-aged gentleman as he was, may have the desire for an immediate repetition of his joys, but be unable to raise his virile member up to the altitude which ladies consider as their due. On this occasion, he begged Maria to wait a little, but the young lady was evidently afraid lest someone else should cut in before her, as Emily had done, and deprive her again of the benefit, not only of Mr Bonham's prick, but of his pocket. So she fondly whispered to him that if he would allow her, she would raise a prick stand for him in two minutes.

Mrs Goater, who only partially heard this conversation, but who, (experienced soul!) guessed what was going on, proposed the operation of a birch rod, but Maria rejected the idea, for the present at any rate, but that the rod might be serviceable at a later period of the night. So saying she made the moral Mr Bonham lie down on his back, on one of the luxurious couches; then taking his shirt up and breeches down, she put his virile member in her pretty, soft mouth, as Emily had done. The effect was almost immediate: the gentleman's dormant powers were raised, his tool slowly lifted its head and began to fill Maria's mouth. When the clever girl perceived that her operations were successful, she requested her lover to remain in the position he then occupied, and placed herself astride of him, à la St George. In this way she certainly saved him every trouble, for she grasped his tool, inserted it, settled her weight down upon him, thereby admitting the whole length of it into her pretty little person, and began to work up and down in the most effectual and delightful way. And Mr Bonham was just about to spunk, when he was temporarily stopped by a proceeding which astonished him a good deal more than Maria, who had probably seen the same operation performed more than once.

His surprise was due to Lieutenant Archer, who had been contemplating the movements of Maria's lovely bum with evident pleasure, and at last could not resist the tempting object any longer. He made his advances very cautiously, both for fear of startling and disturbing Maria, and from a charitable dislike of disturbing the interesting rite which was being celebrated.

But he did it – yes, he did! Administering some saliva upon the girl's small, yet not altogether maiden orifice, he gradually, and with gentle pushes, insinuated the head of his instrument and then the rest was easy. He slid in – up to the root of his plant.

Looking over Maria's shoulder, he cheerfully addressed the prostrate Bonham with:

'How are you going on, old fellow? Jolly, eh! I'll take all the trouble off your hands, and Maria's too. I'll shove her down upon you! You like having two pair of balls banging against your arse, don't you, Maria?'

But Maria was speechless. Whether she thought the more, or whether her attention was so completely absorbed, by a duplicate application of prick, she knew best herself, but this was certain: she exerted herself to the utmost, and earned well deserved praise from both her admirers, who injected their copious jets of warm cream into her as nearly as possible at the same time. On the conclusion of the operation Mr Bonham exhibited some curiosity to know how his pretty partner liked the bum-hole part of the entertainment, remarking that it was quite a novelty to him.

'What, my dear sir, and you a lusty widower!' exclaimed his dutiful nephew, Alfred Torrant, 'I should have thought that when you were the husband of such a splendid woman as my late Aunt, that you would not have neglected making trial of such a luscious performance.'

'Well, I must own,' responded the elder gentleman, for wine and lasciviousness made him speak out, 'that I did try on the little game more than once, but then I never took proper precautions. Had I gone deliberately to work and anointed my weapon properly, I might have succeeded, but the only occasions when I dared venture upon it, were when Mrs B was asleep, or pretended to be so, and then it took such immense shoving and exertion to get the knob of my tool in, that she awoke, if indeed she were ever asleep, which I rather doubt, and then she was angry, and declared it was the sin of Sodom, and a lot more nonsense of the same kind, for she was a very pious woman, so that I was obliged to turn her over and give her a jolly good fucking, only for the sake of peace and quietness. Though it is my belief,' continued the worthy gentleman, in a musing tone, 'that if I had got fairly into her, I should have had no scolding, or heard any balderdash about Sodom, or any other place.'

'Dear me!' exclaimed the graceful Emily, 'I am quite surprised! I thought that married men knew everything, – that they were up to every move, as the saying is.'

'It just depends upon what sort of a bachelor life they have spent, my darling,' replied Captain Torrant, 'if they have spent a "good boy" humdrum sort of existence, the chances are they make but stupid companions for their young brides, who I am sure, must have either the trouble frequently of enticing them, and instructing them in their duties (which I have no doubt plenty of them are able to do, by the bye) or else go without their lawful gratification. And as for any married ladies calling any such innocent little gambols as we have just been carrying on, "unchaste" why, it is all nonsense! A pretty thing it would be indeed,' continued the young officer in a state of righteous indignation, 'if a husband could not get into his wife, how, when, and where he liked.'

'Certainly, Alfred,' responded Mr Bonham, nodding, 'I quite agree with you.'

And in his present frame of mind he was quite sincere, and if he had seen his son-in-law in prospect fucking his beloved daughter Eliza into fits, ar administering a hot clyster of spunk up her arse-hole, he would have looked at the scene with delightful eyes, and given the performers his fatherly benediction.

'Well, sir,' remarked Mrs Goater, 'if you like to sleep here tonight, as no doubt you will choose to do, you shall be made very comfortable – and you can pick out any one or two of the young ladies here as your bedfellow. They will show you some delicious little performances between themselves that will make your prick stand whether you like it or not, and when it does so, they will treat you with such voluptuous lubricity as you would never have experienced if you had been married a hundred years.'

This matronly advice being warmly seconded by Captain Torrant, who added a recommendation to the effect that one of the girls should be French, and Mrs Goater having recommended an experienced demoiselle called Juliette, and one named Maria, as her companion, the delighted Bonham was shown into a most luxurious chamber, feeling more like a he-goat or a young bull than a sanctimonious elder of the chapel which he patronized.

We have quite enough to do to follow his fortunes, so shall not at present trouble ourselves about Messrs Archer and Torrant. Indeed we may safely leave those inexperienced gentlemen to take care of themselves.

In the morning, however, Mr Bonham was exhausted and no mistake. Never since his honeymoon had he felt so thoroughly fucked out, and not even then, for the late Mrs Bonham was a model of propriety; strong in her own person, strenuously resisted such lover-like, not to say sensual proceedings, as fucking upon the sofa, easy chair, up against the wall, in an arbour in the garden, and so forth; so it was rarely that the bridegroom was able to satisfy his longings, except in the legitimate place, namely, bed, and then, in the dark. So that when his handsome companions had retired to make their toilettes, desiring him to ring for anything he required, he was agreeably surprised upon doing so to find the bell answered by his dutiful nephew, who was accompanied by a slavey bearing a large dish of opened oysters and two or three bottles and tumblers.

The experienced young soldier insisted on his uncle immediately swallowing a half a tumbler of brandy and soda-water which was exceedingly grateful to his heated palate. Then he urged upon him the advisability of devouring as many oysters as he could possibly stow away.

They would, he said, give tone to his stomach, strength to his nerves and fresh vigour to his physical capabilities.

'Ha, hum!' said the elderly gentleman, in an assenting tone, 'that I think will be rather needful. I have taken more than one maidenhead in my times, I have fucked your aunt of blessed memory, for nearly a month at a time hand-running, but never, never have I experienced such a night as I have just passed. Those girls are perfect devils for fucking. Why, Alfred, my dear boy, if you will believe me, they fucked each other!'

'Oh, I know,' replied Alfred, 'that was Juliette's performance, I suppose.'

'Yes,' said his uncle, 'that tall, black-haired girl, when she saw I was temporarily used up, laid Maria down pulled her thighs open and got into her as if she herself had been a man. At first I thought that was all make-believe but seeing Maria beginning to wriggle her rump, I looked carefully at the process, and I'll be damned,' continued Mr Bonham, forgetting his sanctity in his surprise and lust, 'if her clitoris was not sticking out of the lips of her cunt – more than an inch-and-a-half and was working into Maria like a cock, a small one certainly, but effective. Well this excited me so greatly that I got new vigour, and taking advantage of Juliette's prostrate position, I made my first successful attempt at getting into a girl's bumhole. Dear me,' said the worthy country gentleman, 'what a novice I have been, and what a number of delightful and comparatively innocent pleasures, I have in my ignorance debarred myself from. Much allowance must be made of course, for the novelty in my case, but I don't think I ever enjoyed myself so much in my whole life before; and what's more, the girl liked it too! or if she did not, she is a most accomplished actress, and it does her a good deal of credit. And my honest old cock has hardly had ten minutes peace all night; but I must say that these oysters and brandy have refreshed me extremely, and I am much obliged to you, Alfred, for your forethought.'

'Well sir,' replied the promising youth, meekly, 'you know where to come now. Of course you never intend to get married again at this time of day.' (Which was an artful speech of Master Alfred's and his uncle felt rather conscious.) 'And you are very fresh and vigorous, better than many a younger man, and it is a pity that you cannot enjoy yourself in a comfortable, bachelorlike, legitimate way. Why should you bury yourself and Eliza in that dismal hole at Rutsden? Excuse me sir but it is rather a dreary place, when you might have a pretty villa at Richmond or Twickenham, with a pretty mistress keeping house for you, and you, yourself at liberty to visit your club, take dinners at Greenwich, or pay a visit to our esteemed hostess, Mrs Goater, or to inspect her cabinet of choice curiosities by way of a change, whenever you felt disposed.'

That idea seemed to strike Mr Bonham very favourably. A new vista in his career was opening to him. He had a very strong notion to partake of a pretty linnet (at present at Mrs Moreen's) that would exactly suit such a cage as Alfred suggested at Richmond, or elsewhere.

As for marriage, or any such moral proceeding, that faded from before his eyes, his excuse to himself was that in a married man promiscuous fucking would be objectionable, and he foretold that he had not paid his last visit to Mrs Goater's by many a one.

By this time it was eleven o'clock, the Lieutenant had taken himself out of the way, thinking that very probably the uncle and nephew would have some business affairs to arrange which might turn to the advantage of his chosen friend and comrade Torrant. And indeed the affair seemed likely to turn out in this way. For the first thing Mr Bonham did was to call Mrs Goater and request her to summon the young girls who had given him such unqualified pleasure.

Among them he distributed all the loose cash he had about him, and it was no inconsiderable amount either, while Mrs Goater was remunerated by a handsome cheque on his London bankers, for which she professed herself, and no doubt sincerely felt, very much obliged.

As for the girls, their gratitude knew no bounds. They half smothered the two gentlemen with lascivious kisses, and treated them to sundry exhibitions of their shapes and private parts, which brought on sundry fingerings and feelings. These farewell proceedings the young ladies doubtless considered would preserve their charms in the memory of the gentlemen, and probably they were right enough.

On leaving the hospitable mansion, Alfred proposed adjourning to his hotel, where they could have an early lunch on broiled bones, stewed oysters and sundry restoratives of that nature. But his businesslike uncle affirmed that he must first of all visit his banker, both to replenish his exhausted purse and make other arrangements.

We may imagine that Alfred was by no means indifferent to taking a ride with his honoured relative in the direction of the bank. He fancied that somehow or other, especially after the evening they had spent, something to his advantage was pretty certain to turn up. Nor was this idea of his without foundation; for Mr Bonham had been considering that to get rid of his daughter was absolutely necessary, before entering upon any of his newly hatched schemes of felicity. Therefore after the elderly gentleman had drawn the pretty heavy cheque on his own account, he agreeably surprised the young gentleman by asking what amount would be absolutely required for the Majority which would immediately become vacant upon the retirement of the piously disposed Major Pobjoy. Alfred specified the amount with a small margin, and to his delight it was immediately transferred to his credit by the orders of his generous uncle. Nor was this all, for when the uncle and nephew were parting that afternoon, the elder gentleman pressed into the hand of the younger a bank note of pleasant amount, accompanying the gift by saying:

'I think Alf, that it would be as well to consider my

visit to London had been specially made to arrange
this little business of yours. Such an account of my
London excursion will shut Eliza's mouth, of course
and she is devilish curious, and saucy too, when she
thinks that I have been doing something that she does
not approve of; for I daresay you know her as well as
I do.'

'A deuced sight better, old boy,' thought Alfred to
himself.

'And at any rate, you will agree with me that it
won't do to tell tales out of school.'

'Certainly not, sir,' gravely replied the Captain,
'and both for your sake and my own, I will take care
to represent this visit of yours to London as only on
matters referring to your own business and partly on
mine. I can easily show that it is so by your kindness
to me. I presume sir,' he continued, 'that upon my
obtaining my step, there will be no objection on your
part to my urging Miss Bonham to fix an early date to
our marriage?'

'As early as you like, my boy,' responded the other,
whose heart was considerably warmed and enlarged
by the rakish proceedings he had just been initiated
into. 'As soon as the young lady can ascertain from
her milliner what is the latest fucking fashion – I
mean the newest fashionable carriage dress – and get
together a new assortment of drawers, chemises, and
silk stockings, though heaven knows she ought to
have plenty. She has cost me enough for such things in
the last few years, but of course she must have them
entirely new. It is a part of the sacred rite of marriage,
I suppose. And then there is a little money to be made
over to her, but that won't take the lawyers very long,
I should think. You ought to be pretty comfortable,
Alfred,' concluded the old buck, as he shook hands
with his nephew.

Alfred, after seeing him fairly off on his road
home, went to his club, and before ordering his

dinner, on the principle of 'business before pleasure', we suppose, indited a note to his beloved Eliza, which contained among the usual expressions of fond affection, compliments to her charms delicate or indelicate (as may happen), allusions to the happy two days they had recently spent (the garden privy scene was referred to with so much enthusiasm that Eliza fairly blushed which was somewhat unusual for her), and so on to the following passage:

'I have not seen the young lady you recommended to my notice as yet; but shall make a point of doing so tomorrow if possible. Of course, with the remembrance of your delicious person and lovely private parts, before my eyes and enshrined in my heart, it is mere blasphemy for me to think of being fond of any other girl; and if I fuck your young acquaintance, Miss Fielding, it is entirely as a matter of business. Of course, I don't wish to do anything of the sort; but it seems to be necessary for our mutual happiness – and it is enough that my Eliza requests me to do so. I sacrifice myself to do her behests! Duty calls and I obey!'

What a fine soldierly feeling young Captain Torrant had, even where fucking was concerned.

But this letter, wherein he so nobly announced his determination to do his duty under all circumstances, was not the only bit of correspondence which he achieved before sitting down to his dinner. The next day Mrs Moreen received the following note:

Dear Madam,

Instead of leaving town as I expected today, I have yielded to the solicitations of my deceased wife's sister, Mrs Smith, to dine at her house. She particularly wishes to see my ward, Miss

Fielding, and though my request may appear to be somewhat out of rule, perhaps you will indulge me so far as to let Rosa be dressed by four in the afternoon, when either myself, or my nephew, Captain Torrant, who is a steady and amiable young man, will call for the young lady to escort her to Mrs Smith's.

This letter with the usual polite formulary, was signed 'H Bonham' and after signing and addressing it, and transmitting it to the post, Captain Torrant was conscious of having performed his duty, at the cost of considerable exertion and self denial, and sat down to his dinner with healthy appetite. We can easily imagine the glee with which Rosa received Mrs Moreen's announcement that she was to dress herself to go out to dinner with her guardian, and of course her chosen friends and room-mates were not long unacquainted with the happiness in store for her. Charlotte affected to pooh-pooh, the whole affair, saying that Rosa had never been 'Brought out' and had no business to be going to a dinner party.

But Harriet Lovit sympathized with her pleasure, and impressed upon her mind that she was to bring back an exact account of the ladies' dresses, and especially of the appearance of the gentlemen.

'I wonder dear,' she said, 'if your guardian's nephew, Captain what's-his-name, will call for you instead of the old gentleman! That would be fine! If he does – and from what you say it seems likely enough – mind you don't let him feel your cunt, or fuck you in the carriage. It will rumple your dress and make your hair untidy!'

'My goodness Harriet, you cannot imagine a young gentleman being alone with a young lady ten minutes without feeling her or fucking her, or something else of the kind.'

'Well my dear, I only speak from my own experience, and I should not wonder, if, after taking a short drive with a young officer, you will not be able to talk about your experience also.'

In due time a neat brougham brought not Mr Bonham, but Captain Torrant, who behaved himself most demurely towards Mrs Moreen. Not that his affection of a staid and precise demeanour was at all necessary, for after receiving Mr Bonham's note, she would have entrusted one of her pupils to old Nick himself, and washed her hands of the consequences.

'It is rather a long way to Great Poke-hole Place,' remarked Captain Torrant to his lovely companion, when they had started on their ride. 'Would you like to have the blinds down – the glare of the sun is rather strong?'

With this, without waiting for Rosa's consent, he suited the action to the word. Rosa might have objected, wishing not only to see but be seen, but then the young dragoon was a particularly handsome young fellow, and there was something fascinating in the fact of taking a long drive with him, quite in private as it were.

'I understand, beautiful Miss Fielding,' began Alfred in a tone of respectful admiration, 'that there is some chance of you becoming my aunt. I am sure I admire my Uncle Bonham's good taste; and I shall be very proud of having such a lovely young aunt, and I hope you will be very cruel and severe to his daughter Eliza and me.'

'Oh, sir, how can you talk in such a way?' replied the blushing Rosa, 'I am sure I shall hardly know how to conduct myself properly as Mrs Bonham, and as an aunt to such a – a – young gentleman as you are.'

'Never mind, Miss Fielding, I am going to marry Miss Bonham,' was the encouraging reply, 'and I'll ask her to love you for my sake, she can refuse me nothing.'

'Ah, I don't wonder at that,' replied Rosa, quite off her guard.

'Don't you indeed?' said the gentleman, 'then perhaps you will grant me a kiss upon the strength of our approaching relationship.'

Rosa smiled, and turned up her sweet face and ripe lips towards her nephew-that-was-to-be, who immediately took advantage of the opportunity. She kissed him once and in return he kissed her about half a dozen times, and then began to roll his tongue into her mouth. This second performance surprised Rosa not a little, for it had never been part of Mr Bonham's proceedings. Still, she felt the indescribable excitement and voluptuous titilation which the operation inevitably induced, and never thought of preventing him from doing as he liked, until he, and perhaps she too, began to think of some further proceedings. Captain Torrant knelt by her side and holding one of her hands while with the other he was gently and cautiously feeling her ankles:

'What a happy man my uncle must be!' he remarked, 'he has told me how deliciously pure and beautiful you are in your concealed limbs and those delicate parts, which no mortal eye has ever beheld, except his, I suppose.'

And here the young gentleman paused, astutely wishing to entrap Rosa into some acknowledgement as to whether his esteemed uncle had managed to get into her or not. She certainly felt rather confused and blushed a good deal, but managed to carry the matter off pretty well by saying:

'Pray sir, if it is usual for gentlemen when they are about to marry ladies to know as much about them as you would seem to imply; perhaps, as you seem to know so much about it, Miss Bonham has permitted you the extraordinary favour of peeping into her charms? I should think they must be something most magnificent.'

'Ah, my beautiful relative!' exclaimed the lively Captain, 'you thought you could catch me, did you?

No, no, one secret for another if you please! If you'll betray my uncle's secrets, I'll betray his daughter's – that is only fair.'

'But,' said Rosa, laughing, 'in betraying Mr Bonham's secrets I should betray my own, and it is hardly fair to make me do that, is it?'

'No, it is not,' replied Alfred, in a high state of excitement, 'and so I shall find it out for myself. Now sweet Rosa, it is of no use for you to struggle or resist, I mean to have a peep and a feel, so be kind enough to put your pretty little feet upon the opposite seat. There now,' (as she did so) 'that will be snug and comfortable. Bless us, what darling little white kid boots and silk stockings! The old governor has more taste in young ladies' dress than I gave him credit for. And now for the inspection of your young thighs and precious little cunt.'

'Oh, no, Captain Torrant, you must not,' exclaimed Rosa, 'indeed I could not allow it!'

At the same time she was gradually stretching her thighs open while the handsome young fellow felt and opened the lips of her all but virgin cunt, whose aspect, however, evidently betrayed that the invader and destroyer had been there.

'You have been fucked,' exclaimed the delighted Alfred, 'a slice from a cut loaf can never be missed, and as it is all in the family, as the saying goes, I shall—'

Here he interrupted himself by shoving his tongue into the lady's sore and somewhat inflamed parts, while he unfastened his braces and unbuttoned his trousers.

'Oh dear Captain Torrant, how indelicate! and the carriage will be stopping directly, I know it will, and you will rumple my silk dress so.'

We hope our readers admire the force of the young lady's objections to being fucked in a carriage. The gallant dragoon set them at naught, requesting her to take up her dresses – as completely and as carefully as she could – he would take care of her petticoats and chemise; as for the carriage stopping, he affirmed that it was a long way from Clapham to Great Poke-hole Place, and they would not arrive there for half-an-hour.

'So, now dearest Rosa,' he continued directing his charger towards the gap in her pretty hedge.

'But you have not kept faith with me,' she cried in a pretty affectation of pretending not to know what he was doing. 'You have not told me whether you ever got into your beautiful cousin's private parts – Oh!'

The last exclamation was produced by the effectual insertion of the gentleman's cock; the milk and water, recommended by Mr Bonham had been effectual but not altogether so – hence the slight involuntary scream. But now her companion was well in and quite comfortable, as kneeling upon one of the carriage cushions, he was ramming into the young girl, immensely to his own satisfaction, while he stimulated her lusts and reconciled her to the proceedings, by repeating in broken sentences and somewhat exaggerated terms, some of his adventures with Miss Bonham, interspersed with the episodes of Bob fucking and buggering Lucy in the stables, and Major Ringtail fucking Miss Larcher in the chapel, to the great satisfaction and edification of the minister of the word, as Stiggins called himself, and to such of the congregation as were fortunate enough to catch a glimpse of the lady's legs over the side of the pew. This last apocryphal adventure, Captain Torrant related as an actual fact, thinking that as Rosa probably knew the principal actress in the scene, she would not only be interested and instructed, but consider her present predicament an innocent one in comparison.

And he was quite right, Rosa richly enjoyed the description of her future stepdaughter's black-haired cunt and long white legs and snowy rump. She began to wriggle her bottom with delight at the vivid description given by Alfred of his man's laudable endeavours to split up Lucy's arse hole, and when it came to the chapel scene, she murmured:

'Miss Susan Larcher! - so respectable - in chapel! Her legs over the pew - and one of the officers right into her in broad daylight! - and her revered pastor watching the performance! - Oh! - oh - h - h Captain Torrant.'

This was the crisis of the performance, and silence reigned in the carriage, unbroken except by a still, small sound, as of kissing. Then, after a few minutes calm, Captain Torrant arose, and buttoning his trousers told Rosa there would never be any reason for making the most distant allusion to anyone as to what had taken place, or what their conversation had been about which, as may be imagined, Rosa promised for her own sake, readily enough. Then drawing up the blinds, as Rosa pulled down her clothes, Her Majesty's officer put his head out of the window and told Thomas he might drive as fast as he liked - now. A very significant proof that his proceedings had been premeditated. Then turning to his lovely companion, he told her not to be startled by anything she saw at Mrs Smith's house, and particularly not to be frightened if she did not find her guardian there. At this Rosa stared at first, but by degrees a light seemed to break in upon her, and she exclaimed laughing:

'Oh! I see now! How wicked of you Captain Torrant, deceiving my venerable schoolmistress, taking advantage of my unprotected innocence, and forging your uncle's name! Don't you know what a crime forgery is, sir? - and that you deserve to be hung?'

'Hung around your neck, if you like, you sweet, saucy witch!' exclaimed the Captain, clasping the young beauty in his arms, and imprinting a dozen luscious kisses on her lips.

In fact his proceedings were becoming so very forcible that Rosa was obliged to tell him the blinds were up, and that they must be getting near their destination, if it was in London at all; and finally that she did not want her hair and her mauve silk dress more tumbled than it was. Captain Torrant assured her that this was a matter of no consequence, and that it would not be noticed; that even if it were, the good-natured ladies and gentlemen to whom he would introduce her would take it all as a matter of course, and promised that she would have an elegant dinner and a merry evening.

To these allurements Rosa made no sort of objection, merely striking a bargain with Captain Torrant that she should be sent back to Mrs Moreen's in good time, for as the girl very sensibly observed, a night's pleasure was all very well. She was duly sensible of Captain Torrant's admiration, and the loving affection he had shown to her, but still it would never do to run the risk of losing Mr Bonham's favour and protection, which would be inevitably the case, if she were reported absent from the Academy all night.

Now with a different kind of girl, Captain Torrant would have felt disposed to treat an interloper between him and his uncle's favour by fucking her as hard as he could, and allowing any of his dissipated companions, who they were about to meet, to do what they liked with her. A little sodomy might be the prescription suitable to the development of her faculties and rump-hole – and then having given her as much wine (and a trifle more) than was good for her – leave her to find her way to Clapham as best she could or go to the devil, if this proceeding suited her better. But Rosa was such a sweet, pretty girl, and she surrendered her delicious young charms to him with such a tender grace, that the Captain, moved by emotions of gratitude for the luscious fuck he had just enjoyed, and with a lively sense of expectation of fucks to come, not only during the present evening, but when Miss Fielding became his uncle's mistress, vowed and declared with all sincerity, that she should be delivered safe and sound at Clapham Academy.

He reflected that the money for his Majority was deposited; that his cousin's hand was promised to him; and he knew his uncle better than to suppose he would not give his daughter a handsome dowry, which with the money she had inherited from her mother, and his pay and private means, would make them very well off indeed.

'And I am sure,' mused Torrant to himself, 'that after the conversation I had the other morning with the old boy, he will not think of getting married at all, and Rosa, and two or three natural children of his or my begetting, will not stand in the way of Eliza's succession: so I will not ruin the dear little chit. I will only fuck her dreadfully and send her back to Mrs Moreen's with a sore cunt, to set her two or three bedroom confidantes longing for prick, by the interesting adventures she will have to relate to them.'

Having come to this virtuous resolution, the young officer relaxed his thoughtful features, calling a playful remonstrance from Rosa as to what he could possibly be thinking of, with so grave a face, and whether he considered it polite to leave a young lady, whom he had been professing so much regard for, all by herself? This produced a playful and affectionate rejoinder, and indeed Rosa was in danger of displaying to the eyes of the outer world the colour of her elastic garters, and other little private matters in those directions, when the carriage drew up at the door of an oldish looking house, but evidently well built and in a state of high preservation.

'This, my sweet little pet,' observed her conductor, 'is one of the houses of the Earl of Longbowles. I think,' he added, laughing, 'that your dear friend, Mrs Moreen, will be rather puzzled to discover the address of Mr Bonham's widowed sister by turning up the list of "Smiths" in either the Court or Trade directory. And if you are cross questioned on the subject, my beauty, you can mention any jumble of street names that occur to you first (you have such a bad head for streets, you know) and you can mention having met Mrs Smith, and your guardian, and the Earl of Longbowles. Allow me to assist you to alight.'

So saying, with great courtesy, he handed Rosa out of the carriage, saying to the coachman as he did so:

'Half past eleven, sharp – mind Thomas!'

So it certainly looked as if he meant to keep his promise to Rosa.

As our friends were uncloaking in the hall, the Earl of Longbowles emerged from his study, which was on the ground floor. He was a fine looking middle-aged man with a bearing about him that showed in some degree the marks of the fast life he had led from an early age. He greeted Torrant cordially, exclaiming:

'Ah, Alfred my boy, how are you? Very glad to see you and your fair friend. And what a pretty girl!' continued he, surveying Rosa with the air of a connoisseur. 'Is she as good as she looks, Alf?' he asked, with an expression that brought the colour into Rosa's face.

'I assure your Lordship that she is a sweet creature in every respect,' was Torrant's reply, as he pressed Rosa's arm to reassure her.

'Well,' said the Earl, 'you had better go upstairs to the drawing room. You will find a select party of our friends there – fine men and fair women! I will follow you directly.'

And his Lordship was as good as his word, indeed a good deal better, for instead of following them after the delay of a minute or two, as any one might have supposed from his speech, he followed them instantly, being rather curious to have a more intimate inspection of Rosa. Accordingly, when the young lady was half upstairs, leaning on her protector's arm, she was not a little startled by feeling her clothes gently, but effectually raised from behind, and a hot kiss pressed upon one of the cheeks of her bum. At the same time a half-smothered voice remarked:

'Delicious indeed! Very fine legs, too!' And then his Lordship, emerging from her graceful drapery, remarked in a business way: 'She'll do, Alfred, she'll do very well! She is fit to show up with the finest in the room!'

Rosa was indignant, and disposed to be very angry, but Torrant whispered to her not to mind it, that one must do at Rome as Rome does, and that his Lordship submitted to a similar inspection almost every lady that entered his house – at any rate, this particular house.

His Lordship, he also informed her, had some peculiar tastes and lusts; and she should see some curious scenes, but he told her not to be frightened, but to eat a good dinner, and to enjoy herself as much as she possibly could.

And Rosa, who now felt she was 'in for it', as the saying is, wisely determined to follow his advice and make the best of her situation.

Chapter Six

Rosa was of course a little fluttered by the exciting nature of the incident produced by her noble host's behaviour on the staircase, but she still possessed enough presence of mind to walk into the drawing room of the Earl's mansion, hanging on Captain Torrant's arm, with as good a grace, and as cool an aspect, (or nearly so) as if nothing particular had taken place during her transit between the hall door and the top of the staircase. In the drawing room, she was both astonished and delighted, delighted by the brilliant appearance of the room, and astonished at the magnificent display of beautiful women and handsome men; such as the Earl of Longbowles usually invited to join his circle. Indeed his Lordship, who could afford to suit his own fancies, invariably declared that he liked to have good-looking people about him – small blame to him for that! and displayed his taste, not only with regard to his judgement in hiring chambermaids and waiting maids, but also in respect to the young gentlemen and ladies he invited to his entertainments. And on this occasion, Rosa was quite bewitched by the galaxy of beauty exhibited by the women she saw; some of them kept-mistresses; some of them young demoiselles from a fashionable house of a certain repute, and some neglected wives, who in the unpleasant predicament of having married old men for the sake of money and a fine establishment, had found out later in the day, that jewellery and coaches and horses, were not the only luxuries that a young bride required, and were glad to make their appearance at Lord Longbowles' evening parties, to obtain what every young lady – aye and a good many elderly ladies too – consider the indispensable requisite: prick! and a downright good fucking.

And to show how cleverly his Lordship had forseen the wants of his guests in this particular, there were certain curtained recesses established, furnished with well-cushioned ottomans; wherein gentlemen and ladies, who felt all excited by their delightful proximity in the waltz, or their companionship during the luxurious supper, might relieve the inevitable tendency, which such luxurious proceedings might create in their minds and bodies.

Our readers can understand that Captain Torrant was not very long in making Rosa understand the meaning of these little accommodation recesses, nor did she, on her part, blush more than a charming girl should do, at being made to understand the purpose for which they were intended, and being shown the deliciously licentious pictures that decorated their walls. But she did colour up prettily, when the Earl of Longbowles, who had by this time entered the apartment, begged to be introduced to Captain Torrant's pretty partner, (just as if he had never seen her before) and after making some outrageously complimentary remarks about her beautiful face said:

'I say Alfred, you have such very good taste in girls' shapes and general capabilities, that I have no doubt that Miss Fielding's hidden charms are quite equal to those she openly displays. Permit me the luxury of kissing her thighs and bottom, – you have a right to her other choice delicacies.'

To this announcement, Rosa was going to offer a feeble protest, saying something about so many ladies and gentlemen being present; but instead of the ladies being shocked, a good many of the couples present, who no doubt were pretty well initiated into his Lordship's proceedings, came up and declared, that as a young stranger, she must, of course, 'pay her footing', and that they would like nothing better than to see the charms of a young novice exposed, as they certainly would be during his Lordship's intended proceedings.

Captain Torrant, moreover, began to loosen his trouser's front, as if he on his part did not intend to be an idle spectator of the bottom-kissing operation; nor, to tell the truth, did Rosa wish that he should be. She had been a good deal excited by witnessing sundry performances among the well-paired couples present, and felt proportionately kindly disposed; much more apparently than did the beautiful Mrs Courville, who, wedded to an old and worn out husband, had up to this time amused herself with encouraging young men, almost but not quite to the point of opening her thighs. But a lady who encourages young men up to a certain point finds out sooner or later that her passions may betray her, and on this occasion the virtuous Mrs Courville betrayed herself. She was leaning on the arm of Mr Harcourt, who had long been a suitor for her favours, and who had probably had more wet dreams and frigged himself oftener in the nightly contemplations of her charms than anyone else of her thousand admirers. And so it came to pass, that when she saw Captain Torrant deliberately raise up Rosa's dress in front, while Lord Longbowles did the young lady the same kind of office behind, her feelings so long restrained, broke forth with a vengeance. And no wonder, for Rosa's exhibition was splendid. She was dressed for a ball, and as graceful and delicate as a young lady of taste is, as a matter of course, upon such an occasion. Consequently when, under the impulse of the behind and front pressure, she began to open her thighs, she provoked the admiration of all the company present.

Lord Longbowles, as we may easily imagine, was not satisfied with kissing her rump, but as Alfred Torrant got into her cunt, he performed the same kind office for her bum-hole; a part which his Lordship had a peculiar fancy for, and for which he had capability; his cock being one of the long and slender description and rather more easily inserted.

In Rosa's case this was rather fortunate as she was enabled to enjoy her lover's operation without feeling any irksome effects from doing double duty. Of the effects produced we may judge from Mrs Courville's remarks, who exclaimed to the enraptured young man who held her on her arm:

'Oh, Arthur, only look at that sweet girl's thighs! – and see how Captain Torrant is ramming it into her! How she does seem to enjoy it! I wonder if she appreciates his Lordship's performance at any rate as much as he does? There's no mistake about that! Just look at him driving into her! There – he has done now!'

Those interesting observations were made as the crisis was taking place, and all three of the actors arrived at the desired goal and spunked together. Naturally Rosa contributed to give Captain Torrant his share of the delight which he had been giving her, but it is doubtful if even under that delightful reciprocity, whether the handsome dragoon experienced more pleasure than did his partner, the Earl.

Every man to his taste, say we, and on this occasion, if his Lordship did not gratify his taste, it's a pity!

He had inspected Rosa's beautiful legs and milk-white rump during her ascent of the stairs, he had acquired by so doing a tremendous prick-stand; and he had been able to quench that raging fire in the bowels of the loveliest and sweetest girl in the world; and if he was not pleased, he ought to have been – that's all!

Now the effect upon the Earl we shall describe presently; in the meantime we have to refer to the case of Mrs Courville.

'What are you doing, Arthur?' was the first thing she said. 'You should not do that, you know!'

But this we must inform our readers was very feebly and hesitatingly said after all.

'Good heavens, Arthur,' she continued, 'what a colour has got into your cheeks, what a fire in your eyes! Ah, you are doing wrong to a married woman, you know you are, and I shouldn't allow you, but – but – somehow I can't stop it. Oh, pray, pray don't hurt me!'

The reader can readily understand from our illustration that this broken form of words (we can hardly call it conversation) was being carried on while Mr Harcourt was lifting up her silk robes and under-clothing and inspecting and feeling too – what he had for so many years longed for. And who can blame him! He had been thinking of Blanche Courville's legs, her cunt, her bottom, all her charms, in fact for many and many a long day; and now when he caught the lady, a little excited and disposed to be compliant, would he not be a dreadful idiot not to take advantage of the delicious feast offered him?

Well he did, and the company present, some of whom, the gentlemen at least, had thought Mrs Courville unapproachable were surprised and delighted by seeing her well clad legs, alternately lifted into the air and laid over a gentleman's back, as she exclaimed:

'Arthur dear, do please recollect, that it is almost a maidenhead that you are taking! – do pray be merciful!'

But Mr Harcourt had been hungry for his feast for a long time and had no mercy; and indeed we hold with the doctors, that in cases where the patient requires operation, quick performance is best.

Whether or no on this occasion the beautiful and virtuous Mrs Courville, found out what was meant by a fine, handsome man's prick stuck up her, somewhere near her kidneys, as she fancied, the said gentleman's finger being rammed up her arsehole, with the idea apparently of finding out how her digestion was.

The appreciation of his Lordship and his guests was something wonderful to witness.

Both the young gentlemen and young ladies seemed to unite in their approbation of Mrs Courville's pride being taken down. They said they did not understand what pride meant, by encouraging young fellows to band about her, and again to come to the notorious Earl of Longbowles' evening parties.

But Rosa was more gentle-hearted. As Mr Harcourt withdrew his prick out of its beautiful sheath, and began to button himself up, leaving his charming friend partially exhausted on the couch, Rosa came to her, remarking:

'If you would excuse the liberty from an entire stranger, Mrs Courville, and permit me to wipe you, I shall be very happy I assure you.'

So saying, and without waiting for assent, she produced her lawn pocket handkerchief, and proceeded to wipe the besmeared cunt of Mrs Courville, who could only remark in reply:

'You sweet, kind, girl, I can only wish you the same pleasure that I have experienced!'

'Tell me, Torrant, candidly if you will, whether you are sincerely attached to your pretty companion?' asked his Lordship, addressing the Captain, on the first opportunity he had of speaking to him privately.

'Well, my Lord,' replied the gallant officer, 'you can see for yourself that she is very nice and fresh; indeed I consider that she has hardly been fucked at all; for although when I got into her – for the first time – I found she had no maidenhead, that may easily have occurred by some other means than a man's prick, for she is at present at a fashionable ladies' finishing school, and I need not tell a gentleman of your Lordship's experience that what with candles, dildoes, and each other's fingers, the young ladies become as open as if they had been married for twenty months.'

'Bless her sweet face and lovely bottom,' exclaimed the peer, 'I should like to buy her from you, Captain Torrant.'

'Oh, dear me, pray don't talk that way, my Lord,' responded Alfred politely, 'I have a certain regard for her of course; but I want to keep her out of my uncle's way (your Lordship knows the rich Mr Bonham of Rutsden Lodge?) and my own cousin Eliza told me she was afraid of his marrying her, which of course would play the devil with my expectations, and Eliza's too; so I thought that if Rosa got a jolly good fucking, it would be pleasant for her and deprive her of the chance of becoming my aunt; though by the way, I should not wonder if the old boy made her his mistress. That would not be so bad; but even then she might have a family! and I would very much rather see her in the position of your mistress than presiding over Rutsden Lodge in any capacity. Miss Bonham requested me to roger her, but if I should carry out the practice to any great extent, that young lady might be addicted to jealousy, so that if your Lordship would take her off my hands and uncle's, and make the dear little thing a good allowance, everybody will be pleased.'

'Well,' replied his Lordship in a reflecting tone, 'I have only one objection to make, she is rather young, and I decidedly require someone with a little experience. You know, Alfred, my boy, that when a man gets to my time of life, he needs certain little refinements in his lasciviousness, such as only a well-trained woman can supply.'

'I understand,' responded the younger gentleman knowingly. 'A little preparatory frigging, or some provocative sucking, an opportune exhibition of plump white posteriors, such as your Lordship seemed to appreciate just now, and no hesitation in submitting the luxurious orifice appertaining thereto to your worship's penetrating prick, while occasionally perhaps a little judicious birching.'

'Ah, I see you understand all about it!' replied the Earl, laughingly interrupting his guest, 'I only wish there was no necessity for my resorting to such stimulants. However, it is a great comfort when one knows where to get them, and if you have no objection, I will consult your little friend as to her capacity and willingness.'

'No objection in life,' returned Alfred, 'I did promise to take her back to Clapham tonight, but if your Lordship makes a satisfactory arrangement with her, she will be quite independent of Mrs Moreen, or my uncle either. Let us withdraw into this alcove and talk to her.'

'Certainly,' said the peer, 'and I'll give her half a pint of champagne with a spoonful of brandy in it, and if that doesn't excite her and make her half tipsy, the devil is in it, and there is always a dildo kept in one of the cupboards.'

Rosa approached Captain Torrant at this moment saying with a half-coquettish air:

'Well sir, I think it is time for me to be getting back to Clapham, you seem so much engaged that I suppose that my company has no longer any attractions for you. I am sure I am very much obliged to you for the attentions you have paid to my humble person, and hope that his Lordship has been gratified, but I suppose that you are no better than the rest of your sex, and having enjoyed my poor little body, such as it is, you don't want me any longer.'

'Indeed Miss Fielding,' replied his Lordship, politely, 'you do discredit to your own attractions, and barely justice to the sensibilities of Captain Torrant and myself. I was just expressing myself in very warmest terms as to yourself and your charms and was consulting my friend here, as to whether you would be willing to leave his uncle's protection for mine; and I must do him justice and say that on his part he seems very unwilling to let you go.'

'Oh, but he must, sooner or later,' remarked Rosa, very briskly, 'I am very glad to contribute to his pleasure, and he fucks me very charmingly and tenderly, and I am sure I try to meet him half way don't I Alfred?' continued the laughing girl, 'but his cock is devoted henceforth to a more legitimate business, and Miss Bonham would half-murder me if she knew how often and what lengths he has pierced into my person. She has a black-haired cunt, hasn't she, Alfred? And I shouldn't wonder if she has a dark fringe around her bottom hole.'

'God bless me!' exclaimed the delighted Earl, 'how knowing we are! How on earth can such a young and inexperienced girl as you are, have picked up such information?'

'From my schoolfellow, Harriet Lovit,' was Rosa's reply. 'She is something like Miss Bonham, though rather younger, and she has black hair and plenty of it. She is a very hot-blooded and lustful girl, and I have seen her exhibit herself, back and front fifty times. Indeed she is very fond of sucking my cunt, and running my finger into her bottom-hole.'

'And I dare say Miss Rosa, if you were to tell the truth she has sucked you many and many a time,' retorted the Earl. 'I suppose young ladies at boarding schools regard spunk good for their complexions? At any rate they seem to get a good deal of it over their cheeks and noses. I wonder how yours would set upon my moustache, it is growing rather grey and wants some reviving fluid.'

At this speech Captain Torrant began to laugh, and
Rosa was beginning to give expression to a blushing
denial, but a tumbler of champagne – slyly laced with
brandy – conquered her scruples; and she consented
to accommodate herself to the Earl's fanciful lusts.
This was performed by her perching herself astride
his face, as indeed, she was not unaccustomed to do,
having put herself in the same position for a somewhat similar purpose with Miss Lovit. In this case,
however, she had rather more duty to perform. His
Lordship was by no means an exhausted man and still
had plenty of semen in his physical nature, but with
every desire to enjoy a perpetual cock-stand, he was
deficient in that qualification except under unusual
provocation.

Thus his walls were covered with licentious pictures, representing fucking, frigging and buggering
under every aspect. His cupboards contained dozens
of exciting books, and he had plenty of dildoes and
birch-rods for the use of his handsome servant girls
and beautiful lady visitors. On the present occasion
when Rosa put her face down upon his private parts,
she found his balls were round and firm, but that his
prick was limp, but by no means despicably sized.
However before inserting his tongue between her
young, delicate, fair-haired cunt lips, he requested
her to take his prick into her mouth. This the good
natured girl did at once, laughing at the same time at
having to perform the operation under the inspection
of Captain Torrant.

As for the gallant officer, there was no mistake
about his prick-stand, his breeches were so near
splitting, that in order to save the stitches he had to
open them and take out Master Priapus. But the
worst of it was that he hardly knew what to do with
it after he had got him out. There he was, cream-
coloured shaft and ruby head, all ready and erect as

you please, and no hole to shove him into. Rosa's mouth and tongue were occupied, she had got the Earl's tool to a beautiful state of stiffness, and was in a fair way of getting a tolerable mouthful of spunk. Her cunt was, as we have said, occupied by his Lordship's mouth and tongue, and his nose all but filled up her little bum hole. Besides as the reader can readily understand from the relative positions of the lascivious pair, it would have been next to impossible for Torrant to have poked that delicate orifice without stifling the noble Earl. After kissing and slapping Rosa's buttocks which were gently undulating with incipient pleasure, and shoving one of his fingers up the vacant hole, he was going to resort with a sigh to the poor expedient of frigging himself, when his noble host who was neither unobservant nor selfish, gave his tongue a moment's holiday, and put it to its more legitimate use, by exclaiming, 'Don't do that, Torrant, I am afraid that all the gayer portion of my fair guests have provided themselves with partners, either in the dance or on the sofa, but there are still half a dozen pretty girls in the servant's hall and kitchen, or there is Lady Forepart. She is sure not to be engaged. To be sure she is five and thirty, and has taken an oath or solemn vow, or something of that kind, not to marry again, but she is a jolly widow enough, and if she is never to be married again that's no reason why she shouldn't be fucked, and I would recommend you to do it, whether she likes it or not. She is in mourning now for quite six months, and if she doesn't want some prick, she should do so – that's all. I shouldn't wonder if she kicks and struggles a good deal, but you don't mind that I suppose!'

'Certainly not,' replied the dragoon, 'I shall rather like it indeed, by way of a change. There is something piquant in rogering a virtuous woman against her will.'

'All right, bricky!' assented the Earl, resuming his occupation of stuffing his tongue up Rosa's cunt and licking her clitoris, for this perseverance was happily rewarded by receiving a small douche of that young lady's liquor all over his moustache and mouth, while Rosa was all but choked by the ejaculation which she simultaneously forced him to make.

When Alfred re-entered the room, he looked around in vain for Lady Forepart. But as women are always amiable to get each other into mischief, or to assist one another in the perpetration of any propriety, the prudent Mrs Harcourt (who did not want any more fucking just at present) and could so afford to be generous, on learning the object of Alfred's search, informed him that the widow had gone into the ladies retiring room to arrange her hair.

'And it is my opinion,' observed the knowing lady, 'that that may possibly mean something else, on the pot-de-chambre likely enough – for she ate a good deal of supper, and prudes must perform the necessities of nature in the way of evacuation just as well as anybody else. The pot is at the far side of the bed, and if you go in quietly and creep underneath, you may very probably find the precise Lady Forepart in the act of doing her little business, and have a good laugh at her mortification.'

Thanking Mrs Harcourt for her information, and chuckling to himself with the glee of a mischievous schoolboy, Captain Torrant proceeded to a large room especially provided for the accommodation of lady guests alone. Indeed from the nature of the orgies at his Lordship's mansion some place of easy access was absolutely necessary, for the retirement of the female guests; and though Lady Forepart had not been treated in such a way as to make it needful for her to make an instant rush to a chamber utensil, still she was availing herself of the accommodations afforded, and was moreover so busily engaged that she did not hear Alfred's entrance, or perceive his soft tread on the carpet. We hope our readers will not accuse us of indelicacy, when we say that he kept himself breathlessly silent, until the splendid woman rose and stooping from him, proceeded to use some soft paper in the necessary way.

Then the prospect of her great white arse, and its fully exposed orifice, slightly open from its recent duty; her round, plump thighs and her well-turned muscular legs, made such an attractive ensemble, that although the lady was clad in the sombre garments of woe our young soldier found her irresistible. Perhaps the very fact of her unblemished character, her habiliments offering such a marked contrast to the gaily dressed company, together with her vow of chastity, all combined to render the fucking or ravishing of such a lady a most desirable act.

At any rate he did no longer hesitate, but striding across the room, almost before the lady had time to finish her operation, he clasped her firmly round the belly with his left arm, while with his right hand he guided his prick to the lips of her somewhat capacious cunt, and lunged into her so furiously as to nearly set her on her head. She screamed out lustily for help, and 'mercy' declaring that 'a brutal lustful man was ramming her to death' and that she would fall on her face.

To all of which Captain Torrant replied by muttered praises of her splendid rump, vowing that he would get into her arse-hole before he had done with her, asking her why she did not lean against the wall or the bed for support. He had even the audacity to ask her whether she liked his cock, or that of her dear departed husband best! and when the insulted and outraged lady raised one of her handsome legs, and endeavoured by shoving it backwards to push him out of her person, he caught hold not only of that but the other leg as well and holding them both up, declared that he was 'particularly fond of a flying fuck' and that although her ladyship was rather heavy for such amusement, yet he would not mind a little exertion for her sake.

Then indeed, without waiting for or requiring an answer from the speechlessly indignant lady, he coaxed up his own lust by enquiring in a mock respectful tone, if she had ever been fucked before marriage, or if Lord Forepart had been lucky enough to have taken her virginity; whether the blood had trickled down her thighs; then cramming one of his fingers up her bum-hole, he kindly asked was that orifice in a state of virginity. And whether she thought it would bleed upon his driving his prick into it!

All these genteel remarks and questions the outraged Lady Forepart let pass in wrathful silence, but when his stalwart weapon began to produce its naturally expected result upon a fine young widow of six months, and she began to push out her rump to meet his shoves, and to wriggle in as lascivious a way as the most licentious woman in the saloon could do, she could no longer restrain her tongue.

'Don't flatter yourself, you brute, that I am exhibiting these natural emotions from any affection for you! Any vigorous woman, deprived as I have latterly been, must do what I am doing now; and it would be all the same if a goat or a donkey or any other suitable sized animal got into my person.'

'All right, my lady,' was the cool reply, 'please yourself. Pray did his Lordship approve of such little games? Now that I come to inspect you more closely, you are tolerably well stretched; pray don't move yet, and I'll see what I can do toward knocking your two holes into one!'

With these words the lustful young soldier made use of some of the mingled juices which were liberally shed in his victim's orifice, to lubricate her lesser hole; the lady protesting that she knew he was going to marry his cousin Miss Bonham, and she would inform that young lady what a lustful tyrant she was about to unite her fate with.

Captain Torrant coolly remarked to that – that Eliza was perfectly acquainted with that peculiarity, and did not wish to have him otherwise, that he had rogered her well both back and front and believed that he had got her with child, that he was going to marry her in a fortnight, and would be very glad to see Lady Forepart at the wedding.

Finally drawing his prick out of her, before the exhausted lady could remonstrate, with a very creditable, and indeed unusual effort of lustful strength, he invaded (apparently her maiden) rectum. This produced a single scream, followed by a storm of sobs, tears, reproaches, from the now thoroughly finished widow; when, after receiving a half a dozen hard slaps on her outraged buttocks, she spent copiously, despite herself. Then she upped and ordered her carriage and took herself off, without saying good night to her host or any of his guests.

Rosa did not go home to Mrs Moreen that night, nor indeed any more. Like a wise girl, she considered that 'a bird in hand was worth two in the bush' and that the offer of a handsome income from his Lordship was worth more than the prospect – rather an uncertain one – of becoming Mrs Bonham.

That gentleman however behaved like a trump (so Mrs Moreen considered at any rate), and consoled himself with keeping a neat little villa at Twickenham, and pretty frequent visits to Mrs Goater's establishment. That amiable lady still flourishes, and keeps around her the same delightful family of young ladies – or some very like them.

Captain Torrant was happily married to his cousin Eliza, and was almost as faithful a husband as could be reasonably expected from one of his natural character, and exposure to such temptations as were to be found in the attractions of the Earl of Longbowles' establishment and Mrs Goater's.

And now as we have accounted for the fate of the principal characters in our short story, we will bid our indulgent readers a cordial farewell.

THE MEMOIRS OF
DOLLY MORTON

Introduction

How I made the acquaintance of Dolly Morton, with a faithful account of the circumstances under which she felt impelled to tell me the story of her life.

In the summer of the year 1866, shortly after the conclusion of the civil war between the North and South, in America, I was in New York, to which city I had gone for the purpose of taking my passage in a Cunard Steamer to Liverpool, on my way back to my home in one of the midland counties of England, after a shooting and fishing trip I had been making in the province of Nova Scotia.

My age at that period was thirty years, I stood six feet in my socks, and I was strong and healthy; my disposition was adventurous; I was fond of women and rather reckless in my pursuit of them; so, during my stay in New York, I went about the city very much at night, seeing many queer sights, and also various strange phases of life in the tenement houses. However, I do not intend to relate my experiences in the slums of New York City.

One afternoon, about five o'clock, I had strolled into Central Park, where I seated myself on a bench under the shade of a tree to smoke a cigar. It was a beautiful day in August, and the sun, sloping to the west, was shining brightly in a cloudless sky. A light breeze was blowing, tempering the heat and making the leaves of the trees rustle with a soothing sound, and I leant lazily back in my seat, looking at the trim, and often pretty nursemaids of various nationalities, in charge of the smartly dressed American children. Then my eyes turned upon a lady who was sitting on the adjoining bench, reading a book.

She was apparently twenty-five years of age, a very pretty little woman with, as far as I could see, a shapely, well-rounded figure. Her hair was a light golden brown, coiled in a big chignon at the back of her head – it was the day of chignons and crinolines. She was neatly gloved, and handsomely but quietly dressed; everything she wore being in good taste, from the little hat on her head to the neat boots on her small, well-shaped feet, which peeped from under the hem of her wide skirt. I stared at her harder than was polite, thinking she was quite the type of a pretty American lady of the upper class. After a moment or two, she became conscious of my fixed gaze, and raising her eyes from her book, she looked steadily at me for a short time; then, apparently satisfied with my appearance, a bright smile came to her face, and she shot a saucy glance at me, at the same time making a motion with her hand inviting me to come and sit beside her. I was rather astonished, as I had not thought from her appearance that she was one of the *demi-monde*; but I was quite willing to have a chat with her, and also to poke her, if her conversation pleased me as much as her looks.

Rising from my seat, I went over to her, and she at once drew aside her voluminous skirts so as to make room for me on the bench beside her. I seated myself, and we began to talk. She spoke grammatically and in an educated manner, and, although she had the American accent, her voice was low and musical – I do not dislike the American accent when I hear it on the lips of a pretty woman – and she certainly was a pretty woman; her eyes were large, clear and blue, her complexion was extremely good, her teeth were white and regular, her nose well shaped, and she had a small mouth with red lips.

She had plenty to say for herself, chatting away merrily, and using quaint expressions that made me laugh. I took quite a fancy to the lively little woman, so I made up my mind to see her home and spend the night with her. She had at once noticed by my accent that I was an Englishman, and she informed me that she had never before spoken to a man of my nationality. After we had chatted for some time, I asked her to dine with me. She seemed pleased at my invitation, and at once accepted it; so we strolled quietly out of the park to a restaurant, where I ordered a good dinner with champagne.

When the meal was over, and I had smoked a cigar, I took my companion, who told me her name was Dolly, to a theatre; and at the end of the performance I engaged a 'hack', as the conveyance is called in New York, and drove the woman to her home, which was in the suburbs, about three miles from the theatre. As it was a bright moonlight night, I was able to see that the house was a pretty little one-storeyed building, with a creeper-covered verandah, standing in a small garden, surrounded by iron railings. The door was opened by a neatly dressed quadroon woman, who ushered us into the drawing-room; then after drawing the curtains and turning up the jets in the gaselier, she went away. The room, which had folding doors at one end, was prettily furnished; there was nothing the least suggestive about it, everything being in good style. The floor was covered with a handsome Oriental carpet, the curtains were velvet; some good engravings were on the walls, and a cabinet contained some choice specimens of old china.

My companion told me to sit down and make myself comfortable, then begging me to excuse her for a moment or two, she passed through the folding doors into the adjoining apartment, which I saw was a bedroom. In a short time she returned, dressed in a white wrapper trimmed with blue ribbons. She had taken off her boots, and put on dainty little French slippers, while her hair was flowing loose over her shoulders nearly down to her waist. She looked so 'fetching', that I at once took her on my knees, and gave her a kiss on the lips, which she returned, at the same time inserting the tip of her tongue in my mouth. Then I put my hand up her clothes, finding that she had nothing on under the wrapper but a fine lace-trimmed chemise and black silk stockings, which were fastened high above the knees with scarlet satin garters, so I was able to feel her whole body with perfect ease.

She was as plump as a partridge; there was not a single angle about her figure. Her skin was as smooth as satin; her bubbies were rather small, but they were as round as apples, quite firm, and tipped with tiny, erect, pink nipples. She had a very good bottom with plump firm cheeks, and the hair on the mons Veneris was silky to the touch.

She gave me a brandy and soda, and we chatted while I smoked a cigar; then we went into the bedroom, where everything was exquisitely clean and sweet. In a short time we were between the sheets; my breast on her bosom, my mouth on her lips, my amatory organ up to the roots in her den of love, my hands grasping the cheeks of her bottom, and I was riding her vigorously, while she was sighing, squeaking, and bucking up under my powerful digs. My member was big, her fissure was small and wonderfully tight, moreover she was a good mount, so I enjoyed the 'flutter' very much, especially as I had not 'had' a woman for a month. But I had knocked all the breath out of the little woman, and when all was over she lay panting in my arms. However, when she had recovered her wind, she said with a little laugh:

'My gracious! you are very big and very strong. I don't think I've ever had such a vigorous embrace in all my life. You seemed to go right through me. But I liked it.'

I laughed, making no remark, but lying quietly resting, still holding her in my arms, and stroking her cool velvety skin until I was ready for action again.

Then making her kneel on all fours outside the bed, I poked her from behind *en levrette*, again making her wince, squeak, and wriggle her bottom. We then got between the sheets again, and I made her turn on her side with her back towards me, while I lay behind her with my belly and thighs pressed against the cool plump cheeks of her bottom, and with my half-stiff tool resting in the cleft of her thighs. In this position we fell asleep.

I slept soundly, not once waking till half-past eight next morning. Sitting up in bed, I looked at my companion, who was still fast asleep, lying on her back with her long hair streaming over the pillow, and her arms stretched above her head. She looked quite young and pretty; and there was a faint pink tint on her round cheeks. I gently pulled the bedclothes down to her feet, and rolled up her night-dress to her chin without waking her; then I took a good look at her naked charms. And they were worth looking at. Her skin was as white as milk and without a blemish; she was really very well-made, and perfectly proportioned. Her little bubbies stood out from her bosom in high relief; her plump, well-rounded thighs were shapely, she had good legs, her ankles were slender, and her belly was without a line or a wrinkle. She evidently had never had a child, and her rose-bud was shaded with fine curly, golden hair. My pintle was as stiff as a poker, so I woke her by gently tickling the edge of her grotto with my forefinger. She looked smilingly up in my face, her big blue eyes twinkling with fun, saying:

'So you have prepared me for the morning sacrifice. Well, I am ready to receive the stroke.'

She then stretched out her legs, and in a few seconds I had given her a strong morning poke, which pleased me more than the ones I had had over night, for while I was working at her, the little woman bucked up more briskly, and wriggled her bottom in the spasm even more lasciviously than on the two other occasions. She really seemed to like the digging I gave her, and I don't think she had pretended to be voluptuously excited merely to please me – women of her profession often simulating passion. Presently we began to chat on various subjects, her conversation showing that she took an intelligent interest in the affairs of the day. Our talk eventually turned to what was at that period a burning topic, the late civil war, and I asked her which side had had her sympathies.

'I am a Northern woman,' she replied, 'so I was always for the union, and am exceedingly glad that the Southerners were beaten, and the slaves set free. Slavery was a horrible thing, and a disgrace to the country.'

'But,' said I, 'from all the accounts one hears, it seems that the negroes in the South were better off before the war as slaves, than they are now as free people.'

'Oh, but they are free now, and that is the great point. No doubt things are bad at present, but they will improve in time.'

'I thought that, as a rule, the slaves were well treated by their owners.'

'So they were in many cases,' she replied, 'but there was no security for them; there was always the chance of their being sold to strange people; and then wives were separated from their husbands, and children from their parents. Besides, there were many owners who treated their slaves badly; working them hard, feeding them scantily, and whipping them cruelly for the least offence. Then again, slaves had no rights of any sort. The girls and women, if light coloured and pretty were not allowed to be virtuous, even if they wished to be. They were obliged to give themselves up to the embraces of their masters, and if a woman dared to object, she was severely whipped.'

'Oh! surely you must be mistaken,' I observed.

'No, I am not. I know what I am talking about, for I lived in a Slave State before the war, and I had special opportunities for finding out all about slavery and the distressing things connected with it.'

'Was it a common thing for women to be whipped?' I asked.

'Yes; I do not suppose there was a single plantation in the whole of the South where the female slaves were not whipped. Of course, on some plantations there was more whipping than on others. And what made the thing more horrid was the fact that the whippings were always inflicted by men, and very often in the most public way.'

'On what part of the body were the slave women whipped; and what instruments of punishment were used?' I enquired.

'Sometimes they were flogged on the back, but most frequently on the bottom; the instruments used were various; there was the hickory switch, the strap and the paddle.'

'What is the paddle?'

'It is a round, flat piece of wood fixed to a long handle, and it was always used on the bottom. It does not draw blood, but each stroke raises a blister on the skin and bruises the flesh. The hickory switch, with any degree of force, will cut the skin and draw blood. There was another terrible instrument of punishment called the cowhide, but it was very seldom used on women.'

'You seem to know all about whipping. Now tell me how it was you came to be living in a Slave State,' said I.

'I was helping to run a station on the "underground railroad"; but I suppose you don't know what an underground station is.'

'No, I do not. What is it?'

' "Underground railroad stations" were houses in which the abolitionists used to conceal the runaway slaves. There were a number of these stations in various parts of the South, and the runaway was forwarded secretly by night from one station to another, until he or she finally got to a free State. It was a dangerous work, as assisting a slave to escape was against the laws of the South, and to do so was considered a very great crime. Any man or woman caught at such a work was sure of getting a long term of imprisonment with hard labour in the State prison. Besides, everyone's hand was against the abolitionist; not only the slave-owners, but also the ordinary white people who did not own a single slave, and it often happened that abolitionists were lynched. They were tarred and feathered, or ridden on a rail, or made to suffer in some other way, by bands of lawless men.'

'Did you ever get into trouble while you were at the underground station?' I asked.

'Yes, I did. I got into bitter trouble, and went through dreadful sufferings. In fact, what happened to me changed the whole course of my life, and was the cause of my being what I am now. Oh! how I hate the Southerners. The cruel wretches!' she exclaimed fiercely, her eyes flashing, her bosom heaving, and her cheeks reddening.

I was surprised at her sudden outburst of anger, and it at once struck me that the little woman had a story. I was curious to hear it, so I said:

'I should very much like to hear what happened to you in the South. Will you tell me?'

After a moment's hesitation, she replied: ·

'I have never told my story to a man yet; but I will let you hear it, as you are an Englishman, and I think you have a sympathetic nature. The story is a very long one, and there is not time to tell it to you now, but if you will come here tonight at seven o'clock and dine quietly with me, I will give you a full account of my life.'

I replied that I should be delighted to dine with her, and that it would give me great pleasure to hear her story.

Just then there was a knock at the door, and the quadroon woman, neatly dressed, and wearing a smart cap on her head, came into the room with tea and buttered toast on a tray, which she placed on a table beside the bed.

My companion sat up, saying to the quadroon:

'Mary, give me my wrapper.'

The woman handed her mistress the garment, which she threw over her shoulders. Then turning to me, she said with a smile:

'Mary was a slave for twenty-five years; and if you like to ask her any questions about her life, she will answer you truthfully. She is not shy. Are you, Mary?'

The quadroon, who was a very buxom, rather good-looking woman, smiled broadly, showing a double row of white teeth between her full, red lips.

'No, Miss Dolly,' she replied, 'I isn't shy.'

I was quite ready to ask Mary to give me some information about herself, so to begin with, I said:

'Well Mary, how old are you, and what State do you come from?'

'I'se thirty years old, Sah, an' I was raised on ole Major Bascombe's plantation, in de state ob Alabama. Dere was one hundred an' fifty field hands on de plantation, an' twelve house-servants in de place. I was one ob de parlourmaids, Sah,' she added, with a sort of pride.

'Was your master a good one?' I next asked the woman.

'Well, Sah, he was a pretty good Massa on de whole; he fed us well, an' he didn't work us too hard; but he was bery strict, an' dere was plenty ob whipping on de plantation, an' in de house too.'

'Were you ever whipped?'

Mary looked at me with an expression of surprise on her face at being asked such a silly question.

'Ob course I was, Sah, many a time,' she replied. 'I got my fust whippin' when I was 'bout seven years old, an' I got my las' one when I was twenty-five; only a week 'fore we was all set free by de President ob de United States.'

'How were you whipped?'

'When I was a little girl I used to get spanked; when I grew big, dey whipped me on de bare back or bottom wid de strap or de hick'ry switch; an' I'se had de paddle on my bottom seberal times,' said Mary as coolly as possible.

'Who used to whip the women?'

'One ob de overseers gener'ly; but sometimes de massa himself used to whip de house-servants. Dere was a room kep' for de purpose, an' when a gal or a woman was whipped, she was tied face downwards on a long bench, den her close was turned up, an' she got her allowance.'

'Were the whippings severe?'

'Oh, dey always hurt us drefful, an' made us squeal out loud an' wriggle; an' sometimes we was whipped till de blood come.'

Here Dolly broke in, saying: 'And when the skin of a woman's back or bottom has been broken by a whipping, the marks never entirely disappear. Mary has plenty of marks upon her body at this moment. Show your bottom to the English gentleman, Mary, and prove the truth of what you have told him.'

The woman, without the least hesitation, turned her back towards me, then she gathered all her clothes up under her arms, exposing the whole lower part of her person, as she was wearing no drawers.

It was a sight!! All women of negro blood have, naturally, big bottoms; and, as Mary was rather stout, her bottom was enormous; the plump hemi-spheres of flesh swelling out, and sweeping in great curves to the massive thighs, and sturdy legs cased in tight, white cotton stockings. Her skin was smooth, and of a light brown tint, and I at once noticed that both the fat cheeks of her bottom, as well as the upper part of her thighs, were marked with long, fine, white lines where the skin had been cut by the lash.

She seemed to like showing her opulent charms, for she was in no hurry to drop her petticoats, but stood looking over her shoulder at me, with a complacent smile on her face, till her mistress said:

'That will do, Mary.'

She then let her clothes fall, and left the room smiling.

'There,' said Dolly, 'you have seen the marks on her bottom, and I can tell you that her back is just as much marked.

'Moreover, she was seduced, or to speak more correctly had to give herself up to her master's eldest son when she was only sixteen. She afterwards passed through the hands of two younger sons; but the fact of her being the plaything of the three young men did not save her bottom from being blistered by the paddle, or striped with the switch whenever she committed an offence of any sort. She has told me that she had sometimes to go to the room of one or another of the young masters while her bottom was still bleeding from a whipping. I have another woman, about thirty-five years of age, in my service as cook; she comes from South Carolina, and her body is even more scarred than Mary's with the marks of the whip.'

Dolly paused for a moment or two while she sipped her tea, then she said:

'Now don't you think it is a good thing that slavery has been abolished in the United States?'

'Yes, indeed I do. I had no idea that female slaves were ever treated in such a way,' I replied.

The details given me by Dolly and the quadroon surprised me very much, and also somewhat moved me; but at the same time I was feeling very randy. The sight of a woman's bottom always has an exciting effect upon me, therefore the full view I had just had of Mary's big posteriors had given me a tremendous cockstand. So taking hold of Dolly, I laid her on her back, pulled down the bedclothes, tucked up her drapery, and poked her again with great gusto. Then, after refreshing myself with a cup of tea and a piece of toast, I got up and had a cold bath in a small dressing-room adjoining the bedchamber. As soon as I had dressed myself, I bade Dolly goodbye, promising to be back again without fail at seven o'clock. Then giving her a kiss and a good present, I left the house and made my way back to the hotel where I was staying. After changing my clothes, I sat down to breakfast with a good appetite, feeling very well satisfied with my night's amusement.

The day passed rather slowly, and at seven sharp I was back at Dolly's house, curious to hear her story, and fully intending to stay with her all night again.

She seemed glad to see me, and was looking very nice in a pretty frock of some soft white material. She gave me a simple, but well-cooked little dinner, with a bottle of excellent Burgundy.

Mary, smartly dressed and beaming with smiles, but perfectly respectful, waited on us, and when the meal was over and we had gone into the drawing-room she brought some really well-made coffee.

Dolly leant back in an easy chair, with her feet, in smart velvet slippers, resting on a stool, and as her skirts were slightly raised, I was able to see her trim ankles cased in pale blue silk stockings.

I lit a cigar and settled myself down in another easy chair opposite her. She then began to tell me her story which turned out to be a very long one: so it was not nearly finished when we went to bed after a little supper at midnight. But as I had got interested in the narrative, I wished to hear the end of it, so I paid Dolly three or four more visits, and she continued her story each time I saw her until at last she had related the whole of her adventures to me, and as I was able to write shorthand, I took down her narrative exactly as she related it, without a break, in her own words.

Chapter One

A young girl's humiliating experiences – Death of my father – How I made Miss Ruth Dean's acquaintance and what came of it – Helping to free the slaves.

My name is Dolly Morton, I am just twenty-six years of age, and I was born in Philadelphia, where my father was a clerk in a bank. I was his only child, and my mother died when I was only two years old, so I have no remembrance of her. My father's salary was a small one, but he gave me as good an education as his means would allow: his intention being that I should gain my living as a schoolteacher. He was a silent, stern, reserved man, who perhaps may have been fond of me in his way: but he never showed any outward sign of affection, and he always kept me under strict discipline. Whenever I committed a fault, he would lay me across his knees, turn up my short petticoats, take down my drawers and spank me soundly with a broad piece of leather. I was a plump, soft, thin-skinned girl who felt pain acutely, and I used to shriek and kick up my heels and beg for mercy; which, however, I never received, for he would calmly go on spanking me until my poor little bottom was as red as fire and I was hoarse with screaming. Then, when the punishment was over, and my trembling fingers had buttoned up my drawers, I would slink away with smarting bottom and streaming eyes, to our old servant who had been my nurse, and she would sympathize with me, and comfort me until the smart of the spanking had passed off.

Our life was rather a lonely one; we had no rela-
tives, my father did not care for society of any sort,
and I had very few girl friends of my own age; but I
was strong and healthy, my disposition was cheerful,
and fortunately I was fond of reading, so although I
often felt very dull, I was not absolutely unhappy
when a child. And so the years rolled on quietly and
uneventfully; my childhood passed, I was eighteen
years old, and had grown to my full height of five feet
four inches; my figure was well rounded, and I was
quite a woman in appearance. I had begun to chafe at
the monotony and repression of my life, and was
sometimes very wilful and disobedient. But I always
suffered on such occasions, as my father still continued to treat me as a child, taking me across his
knees and spanking me whenever I offended him.
Moreover, he informed me that he would spank me,
every time I misbehaved, until I was twenty. This was
very humiliating to a girl of my age, especially as I had
become rather romantic and had begun to think of
sweethearts. But I never dreamed of resisting my
father's authority, so I took my spankings, which I
must confess, were sometimes well deserved, with as
much fortitude as I could muster up. But a change of
my life was soon to come. My father was seized· with
an attack of pneumonia to which he succumbed after
a few days illness.

I was stunned at first by the suddenness of the blow,
but I cannot say that I felt much grief at my loss. My
father had never made a companion of me, and whenever I had tried to interest him in my little affairs, he
had invariably shown himself utterly unsympathetic.

However, I had not much time to think over the
past; my position as it was at that moment had to be
faced, and a most unfortunate one it was. My father
had died in debt, and the creditors were pressing for
payment. I had no money, so the furniture of the
house was sold by auction, and when everything had

been settled, I found myself without a cent, homeless, and quite alone in the world. I lived for a month with my old nurse, who would have kept me with her always, had she been able; but she had her own living to make, so was obliged to go into service again. Then I would have been compelled to seek shelter in the poorhouse had it not been for the kindness of a lady, who hearing of my friendless and forlorn condition, took me into her house.

Her name was Miss Ruth Dean, and she was, at that period, thirty years of age. She belonged to the Quaker sect, or, as she called it: 'The Society of Friends'. She was a virgin, had no lovers, was her own mistress and lived in a large house about two miles from the city. She was well-off, and made good use of her money, spending most of it in charity. Her time was chiefly occupied in philanthropic work of all sorts, and she was always ready to give a helping hand to anyone who needed a start in life.

But before proceeding, I must give you a description of Miss Ruth Dean. She was a tall, slender, delicately-formed woman, with large earnest-looking brown eyes; her hair was also brown; it was long and soft, and she always wore it in plain bands. She had a lovely, clear complexion, but there was no colour in her cheeks, although she was in perfect health, and capable of going through a great amount of fatigue. She was a pretty woman, but there was always a rather prim expression on her face, and she rarely laughed, but was not the least morose. Miss Dean was as good a woman as ever lived, and she was the best friend I ever had in my life. From the first she treated me as a guest, and was most kind to me. I had a bed-sitting-room of my own, prettily furnished, and the servants, all of whom were devoted to their mistress, always treated me with respect. Miss Dean had a number of correspondents in all parts of the States, and now my education proved useful to me, for I was able to help my benefactress in answering her letters, and she, finding that I was sharp and intelligent, appointed me her secretary, giving me a small salary for pocket-money, and also supplying me with clothes. I was very comfortable, and had never been so happy in all my life. There were no cross looks, or sharp scoldings, and above all, no horrid spankings. As time passed, Miss Dean became like an elder sister to me, while I grew very fond of her. She admired my face and fig-ure, and always liked to see me nicely dressed, so she gave me lace-trimmed petticoats, drawers, and che-mises, also several pretty frocks; although she herself was content with the plainest of underlinen and always wore the Quaker costume: a plain bodice with a straightcut skirt of drab, brown or dove-coloured material.

As a matter of course, Miss Dean hated the institu-tion of slavery, and was an ardent member of the abolitionist party. She supplied funds to, and was in constant communication with 'Friends' in the South-ern States who were in charge of 'underground sta-tions', and she frequently received into her house escaped slaves of both sexes whom she kept until they had got employment. She could openly harbour the fugitives as Pennsylvania was a free State.

I need not enter into the details of my life for two years, as nothing eventful happened. I was contented and happy; I had the society of young people of my own age, and I had plenty of innocent amusements. Miss Dean, being a Quakeress, did not patronize places of public amusement of any sort herself, nor would she allow me to go to one, neither did she approve of dancing; but she frequently gave quiet parties, and I was often invited to other houses. I was popular with members of my own sex, and had several male admirers; but as I did not care for any one of them I remained quite heart whole.

At the time of which I am speaking, the friction

between North and South was becoming very great, and there were mutterings of the storm that was soon to break; although few people thought that things would end in a long and bloody civil war.

Towards the close of the year, the North was startled by the execution, or, as we called it: the murder of the great abolitionist John Brown, at Harper's Ferry. Miss Dean was particularly shocked and distressed at the news; she had known John Brown personally, and she considered that he had been quite right in getting up the insurrection which cost him his life. Any act, she averred, was justifiable that had for its object the emancipation of the slaves, and she declared that she would not hesitate to do the same thing herself if she thought it would forward the cause.

As the weeks passed, she became restless, and was not satisfied with merely sending money to the South, but wanted to do something personally to help the slaves, and finally she made up her mind to go south and take charge of an 'underground station'.

She told me one afternoon what she intended doing, and became quite enthusiastic about it.

'Oh!' she exclaimed, 'I am longing to begin the work of rescue. I am sure I could manage a station better than any man. Men are suspected, and constantly watched by the white loafers, but they would not suspect a woman of running a station, so if I live quietly and take all necessary precautions, I am not likely to be found out.'

My sympathies had always been with the slaves, and now Miss Dean's enthusiasm moved me greatly, so I at once made up my mind to go with her, and I told her of my determination.

At first she would not hear of my doing such a thing; she pointed out the risks of the undertaking and remarked that we might possibly be found out, and in that case we should be condemned to a long term of imprisonment.

'Not that I am afraid of imprisonment,' she exclaimed, getting up from her seat and walking up and down the room, her pale cheeks flushing, and her soft eyes sparkling, 'but for you, Dolly, it would be dreadful. You are a young, tender girl, and you could not bear the hard work and coarse fare as I could. Besides, they would cut off all your pretty hair. I have heard that the hair of female prisoners is cut in Southern gaols. No, my dear, I can't let you go with me. For if I did, and anything was to happen to you, I should never forgive myself.'

'I am not afraid of the work,' I said, 'and you have just as pretty hair as I have. If you choose to risk yours, I am ready to risk mine. Do you think, after all you have done for me, that I will let you go alone? I will not be left behind. Where you go, I go, and take my chance with you,' I exclaimed, clasping her hand and pressing it.

I saw that she was much touched by my fidelity to her, but still she tried her utmost to dissuade me from going south with her. But I was firm in my resolve to accompany her, so I met all her arguments, and wound up by saying that 'two heads were better than one,' and that I could be of great assistance to her.

So at last she consented to let me go with her. The point being settled, she kissed me, then sitting down, she wrote to 'Friends' in various parts of the South, asking them to let her know of a place where a new 'underground station' might be advantageously established. We then went to dinner, and when it was over we spent the evening in talking over our plans, and settling what we should do to the best of our ability.

In a few days time, Miss Dean received answers from all her correspondents, and they mentioned several places where an 'underground station' might be set up.

We discussed the advantages of the various sites,

and after a long deliberation, determined to go to a place in Virginia, right in the middle of the Slave States.

The house which had been recommended to be used as a 'station' was situated near the small town of Hampton on the James river, and it was thirty-five miles from Richmond, the capital of the State. Miss Dean at once wrote to a local house-agent, telling him to take the house for her, and have it furnished as soon as possible for the reception of two ladies who wished to spend some time in Virginia.

In a short time she received a letter from the agent, saying that he had taken the house for her, and that it would be furnished and ready for occupation in a fortnight's time. I need hardly tell you that the agent had not the slightest idea that the house was going to be used as an 'underground station'.

Next day, we began leisurely to make preparations for our departure, and Miss Dean decided to take only one servant, a trustworthy, middle-aged, white woman named Martha. She was a Quakeress like her mistress, in whose service she had been for five years. She knew why we were going to Virginia, and was quite willing to accompany us. The other servants were to be left behind in charge of the house in Philadelphia. Miss Dean thought it would be safer not to let anyone in the city know the exact spot to which we were going, or what we intended to do, so she merely let it be known that we were going for a trip to the South.

A fortnight passed, and one fine morning at the beginning of May, we drove quietly to the railway depot and took our tickets for Richmond. On arriving there we stayed at a hotel for a couple of days in order to get some stores we wanted.

Then on the third morning, at half-past eleven o'clock, we left the city in a two-horse buggy driven by a negro coachman, who deposited the three of us with our trunks at the house at six o'clock, after a long, but pleasant drive through a pretty country.

The agent to whom Miss Dean had written was waiting to receive us, with a couple of negro boys to carry in our baggage. He showed us over the house which we found to be in good repair, plainly but comfortably furnished, and everything in perfect readiness; supplies laid in, wood chopped, and the fire lighted in the kitchen.

The house was very secluded, as it was situated at the end of a lane about a quarter of a mile from the main road. It was a wooden structure on one storey, with a veranda back and front; it contained a parlour, kitchen, and four bedrooms; in the rear there was a barn, near which grew two hickory trees; and the whole place was surrounded by a rail fence.

When we had completed the inspection of our new home, the agent bade us goodbye and took his departure, accompanied by the two negro boys. Martha bustled about the kitchen, while Miss Dean and I unpacked our things in our respective bedrooms.

In a short time, tea was ready and we sat down in the parlour to a good meal of ham and eggs, fried chicken, and hot cakes.

The parlour was a good-sized room with rather a low ceiling crossed by heavy beams; there were two bow windows with latticed panes, and on the sills were pots of sweet-smelling flowers. On one side of the room, stood a massive sideboard of polished mahogany, and there was an old-fashioned oval mirror with an ebony frame over the mantelpiece. These two bits of old furniture evidently belonged to the house, and they contrasted strangely with the bright coloured carpet and other modern furniture of the room.

When we had finished our meal Miss Dean wrote to the 'Friends' in charge of the 'underground stations' north and south of us, with which we were to be in communication. The station south of ours was thirty miles distant, and from it we would receive fugitives, whom we would pass on to the station north of us, which was twenty miles away.

Then we had a short chat, but as we were feeling tired after our journey, we soon went to bed.

I got up bright and early next morning, feeling in high spirits, and as soon as I had had my bath and dressed, I peeped into Miss Dean's room; but finding she was fast asleep, I did not disturb her.

Going quietly downstairs, I left the house and went for a morning walk along the tree-bordered road, and down lanes flanked with hedges of bright flowered shrubs of species quite unknown to me. I rambled about in all directions for an hour without meeting a single white person, though I came across several coloured people of both sexes who stared curiously at me, noticing that I was a stranger.

When I got back to the house, I found Miss Dean waiting for me in the parlour, and in a short time Martha brought in breakfast, to which I did full justice, as my walk had given me a good appetite. We soon settled down comfortably, and our new and risky life began, but neither of us had any forebodings of evil. Miss Dean was always cheerful, and I was quite charmed with the novelty of the whole affair. We stored supplies of bacon, flour and coffee in the cellar of the house, and hid a couple of mattresses and blankets under the floor of the barn, in readiness for the fugitives who might arrive at any moment from the station south of ours.

Chapter Two

My new style of life – Redeeming the slave – Our first runaways and how we passed them 'underground'.

The house we lived in was well adapted for our purpose owing to its isolated position. Our nearest neighbour lived three miles away, and the little town of Hampton whence we got our supplies was also three miles distant. The weather was fine but warm; however, it agreed with me, and I was in splendid health and condition. Dressed in a plain linen costume with a broad-brimmed straw hat on my head, I daily roamed about the country, soon making the acquaintance of a number of plantation slaves, who, seeing that I took an interest in them, were always glad to talk to me, and they used to bring me presents of bits of 'possum', and 'coon', two animals that the negroes are very fond of; but neither Miss Dean nor I could touch the meat. I sometimes visited the slaves' quarters on the plantations, and was always heartily welcomed, but I was obliged to pay my visits very secretly; for if the owners of the slaves, or the ordinary white folks in the neighbourhood had discovered that I was visiting the quarters, my motives would at once have been suspected. Though the negroes whose acquaintance we had made never hinted at the subject, I felt pretty sure that they all guessed why we had taken up our abode in their midst.

Three months passed, and during the whole of that period the work at our station had gone on smoothly.

Sometimes in one week we would have two or three fugitives, but often several days would pass without a single runaway arriving. They always came after dark, to the back of the house; and the first thing we did was to give them a good meal, then we put them in the barn for the night. Next day, we fed them well, and as soon as it was dark supplied them with a packet of provisions, and they started off for the next station, walking all night, and hiding in the woods during the day. If, as sometimes happened, the fugitive was a woman who was too tired to go on after only one night's rest, we kept her until she felt able to continue her journey. The runaways were of all sorts: old and young men, old women and girls, and sometimes a woman would arrive with a baby in her arms. Some of the fugitives were in good condition, and decently clothed, others were gaunt and ragged, having come long distances and been many days on the road. Some had even come from the extreme south of Florida. Many were scarred with the marks of the lash, some bore imprints of the branding-iron, and others had open, or half-healed wounds on their bodies. But all the poor creatures who passed through our hands were intensely grateful to us, and we often heard their stories, which were in many cases most pitiful. I need not enter further into details of our management of the station, but I will give you a short account of one of the cases that came under our notice.

One night, Miss Dean and I were sitting as usual in the parlour, chatting and sewing. The lamps had been lit, the curtains had been drawn, and everything was quiet and snug. There had been no arrivals for upwards of a week, and Miss Dean had just said: 'I wonder if anyone will come tonight,' when we heard a low tapping at one of the windows.

I ran to the door and opened it, and as I did so, a girl staggered up to the threshold, then fell fainting at my feet. I called to Miss Dean, who at once came to my assistance with Martha, and we carried the girl into the parlour and laid her on the sofa.

She was a very light-coloured quadroon, with a pretty face and long, wavy, dark brown hair, which was flowing in disorder over her shoulders, as she had nothing on her head. Her age appeared to be about sixteen years, but her figure was fully developed, the rounded contours of her bosom showing plainly under her thin bodice – females of her race soon mature. She was evidently not a field slave, as her hands did not show signs of hard work, while her clothes were a good material, although they were draggled and torn to rags. She was wearing a neat pair of shoes, but they, as well as her stockings, were covered with mud. We soon brought her round, and she opened her great brown eyes which had a haunted look in them, while her face had an expression of pain and weariness. We gave her a bowl of soup, and some bread and meat, which she ate ravenously, telling us that she had nothing for twenty-four hours.

As the girl was so weak and ill, we did not send her to the barn, but as soon as she had finished her supper I took her upstairs to the spare room, telling her to undress to go to bed. She looked bashfully at me, but after a moment's hesitation took off her frock and petticoats – she wore no drawers – and I then noticed that the back part of her chemise was plentifully stained with spots of dried blood. I knew what that meant! Going up to the girl, I raised her chemise and looked at her bottom, finding that the whole surface was covered with livid weals and that the skin was cut in a great many places.

I soon got her to tell me why she had been so severely whipped. It was the old story. She belonged to a planter, a married man with young children, who lived about twenty-five miles away. She was one of his wife's maids. Her master had taken a fancy to her and had ordered her to be in his dressing-room at a certain hour one evening. She was a virgin, and she disobeyed the command. Next day she was sent with a note to one of the overseers, who took her to the shed used as a place of punishment. He then informed her that her master had sent her to be whipped for disobedience. She was then stretched over the whipping-block, her wrists and ankles being held by two male slaves; then the overseer laid bare her bottom and whipped her with a hickory switch, regardless of her screams, until the blood trickled down her thighs. She was then allowed to go, after being told that if she did not obey her master she would find herself on the whipping-block again. She was a plucky girl, and determined not to surrender her maidenhead, so she ran away that night, sore and bleeding as she was, and made her way for twenty-five miles through the woods and by-ways, until she reached our house. She had heard that we were kind to slaves, and she thought we would hide her from her master.

We did hide her, keeping her for a week, then we sent her on to the next station along with a man who happened to arrive just at the right time.

Now I will return to my own story, and that of Miss Dean, for our fates at this period became linked together even more closely than they had been.

Time passed and everything continued to go on quietly. Miss Dean was still full of enthusiasm for the work, but I had got rather sick of it; the stories of cruelty that I was constantly hearing, and the sights I sometimes saw, made my heart ache, moreover I was tired of the loneliness of my life. I wanted some companions with whom I could laugh and chatter freely and frivolously, for although Miss Dean was always sweet and amiable, her conversation was not of a light sort.

Occasionally too, a feeling of fear would come over me. We might be found out. I did not feel so brave as formerly; I dreaded being put in gaol and having my hair cut, and I did not like the idea of the hard labour and the scanty fare. However, so far, I had had no cause for alarm. We had got to be well-known by the people in the neighbourhood, but no one suspected that the two quiet women living by themselves in the lonely house were engaged in unlawful practices. There had never been an instance known of an 'underground station' being run by women. The ordinary white people – and by that expression I mean the white folks who did not own slaves – were always civil to us whenever we had anything to do with them. Many of them were very rough-looking fellows, and there were some lazy loafers, but there was also a number of respectable, hard-working men with wives and families. Strange to say, all these whites, though not one of them owned a negro, were staunch upholders of slavery.

They sold us venison, wild turkeys, and fish, all of which were welcome additions to our usual homely fare.

Chapter Three

I am chased by a bull in the country and saved by an unknown gentleman who, in the sequel, proves a far more savage bull, differing only in the outward shape.

I still continued to amuse myself by wandering about the country; but it was dull work alone and I often wished for someone to talk to, and keep me company during my walks. At last my wishes were gratified.

One afternoon I was strolling along a road, when, on turning a corner, I came suddenly upon a small herd of cows, headed by a savage-looking bull which stopped on seeing me, and began to paw the ground, its head lowered in a threatening way and its eyes gleaming angrily. If I had stood still, the animal might have passed on; but as I was frightened I foolishly turned round and ran away as fast as I could.

The bull, bellowing hoarsely, at once pursued me, and I heard its breathing close behind me as I ran shrieking loudly, expecting every moment to be transfixed by the horns of the creature. Just in the very nick of time however, a gentleman on horseback leaped the hedge, and charging the bull, belaboured it with a heavy whip until the beast turned tail and dashed up the road followed by the cows. The gentleman dismounted and came to me. I was trembling all over and nearly fainting, and would have fallen to the ground had he not put his arm round my waist and held me up. He gave me a draught of wine from a flask which he took out of his pocket, then he made me sit down on the grass at the side of the road while he stood in front of me with the bridle of his horse over his arm, looking down at my face.

'Don't be frightened; the danger is past,' he said. 'It was lucky though that I happened to hear your cries and was able to get to you in time.'

I soon recovered myself, and thanked him warmly, at the same time taking a good look at him. He was a tall, handsome man about thirty-five years of age, with very dark hair and eyes; his face was clean shaven except for a long drooping moustache which hid his mouth, and he was dressed in a well-fitting riding suit. He fastened his horse's bridle to a tree, then sitting down beside me on the grass, began to talk in a lively and amusing way, putting me quite at my ease, so that I soon found myself chatting and laughing with him as freely as if I had known him for a long time. It was delightful to have a merry companion of the male sex to talk to. My spirits rose and I felt quite gay. I think we must have talked for an hour. He told me that his name was Randolph. I had often heard of him, as he was a bachelor, and the owner of one of the largest plantations in the neighbourhood; his place, called 'Woodlands', being about three miles from our house, and I knew some of his slaves. But I did not tell him that. He asked me my name, and when I told him he smiled:

'I have heard of you and also of Miss Dean,' he said. 'In fact I am your landlord, as the house you are living in belongs to me.'

I was rather startled at hearing that, so I merely said:

'Oh, are you?'

'Yes,' he said laughing, 'and somehow I had got it into my head that my tenants were two ugly old Quaker ladies.'

I could not help smiling at the way he had spoken.

'Miss Dean is a Quakeress,' I said, 'but she is not ugly nor old. She is only thirty-two years of age. I am her companion, but I am not a Quakeress.'

'You are a very charming young lady, and I am glad to have made your acquaintance,' he said, looking hard in my face.

I blushed, feeling rather confused by his bold glances; but nevertheless I was pleased with his compliment. I was not accustomed to having compliments paid to me. The few young men I had known in Philadelphia were Quakers, not given to paying compliments.

He went on:

'You two ladies must find it very dull living all alone, especially in the evenings. What do you do with yourselves?'

This was an awkward question.

'We read and sew,' I replied.

'Well, I must give myself the pleasure of calling on you some night. I suppose you are always at home,' he observed.

My heart gave a little jump, and I felt hot and uncomfortable. It would never do to have him calling at the house, so I racked my brains to find something to say that would prevent him paying us a visit.

'I must beg you not to call. Miss Dean would not like it. She is peculiar in her ways, and I have to humour her,' I said, rising to my feet, and thinking I had better get home as soon as possible, so as to avoid being further questioned by him.

He also stood up, saying:

'If that is the case I will not intrude on Miss Dean, but I hope to have the pleasure of seeing you again. Will you meet me here tomorrow at three o'clock?'

I thought there would be no harm in meeting him, besides if I did not he would probably call at the house, and that was a thing to be prevented if possible. So I promised to meet him the following afternoon at the hour he had named. Then, shaking hands with him, I bade him goodbye.

He held my hand longer than was necessary and he also pressed it, at the same time fixing his gleaming black eyes upon mine with a look that made me feel rather uncomfortable again.

'Goodbye then, Miss Morton, till three o'clock tomorrow,' he said.

Then mounting his horse, he touched it with the spur and cantered off, turning round in the saddle to wave his hat to me.

My eyes followed him with admiration, for he was a graceful rider, and his horse was a magnificent animal, moreover I felt grateful to the man, for he had undoubtedly saved me from serious injuries, if not death.

I walked slowly home, thinking over the whole affair, and feeling very light-hearted. A bit of romance had come into my hitherto quiet life, and I was pleased. In future, I should have someone to talk to, and to walk with. I had an idea that Mr Randolph and I would often meet, but I had not the least thought of harm. On reaching the house, I found Miss Dean looking, as usual, sweet and placid, making shirts for ragged fugitives. Kissing me affectionately, she said:

'You are looking very blooming, Dorothy. What has made your cheeks so rosy this evening?'

I laughed, telling her that I had been frightened by a bull, but I did not inform her of the danger I had been in, nor did I mention Mr Randolph. I thought it best to keep silence about him, for Miss Dean was very strict in her ideas, and she would never have allowed me to meet him.

I took off my hat, and we went in to tea, which was also our dinner, and was a plentiful meal, consisting of fried trout, grilled wild turkey, corn bread, buckwheat cakes and honey. The evening was spent in the usual way and we read and sewed till it was time to go to bed.

Next day, at the appointed hour and place, I met Mr Randolph. He was evidently glad to see me, and taking both my hands, he held them, gazing with a look of admiration in my face. A woman always knows when she is admired. After exchanging greetings, he politely offered me his arm, which I took, and we strolled along the road until we came to a secluded dell with mossy banks shaded by trees. In this nook we sat down side by side on the grass, and then he questioned me about myself. I told him I was an orphan, and that I had no relations of any sort. I also informed him how I had become companion to Miss Dean, but of course I did not hint at our reasons for coming to live in Virginia.

His manner to me was perfectly respectful, and I remained chatting with him for upwards of an hour. Then I went home, after promising to meet him again in three days' time.

I did meet him, and from that time we became very friendly, seeing each other two or three times a week. I did not love him in the least, but I liked being in his company, as he was so utterly different from any man I had ever known. He amused me with his stories of adventures – he had travelled all over the world – and interested me by his descriptions of European countries which I was always longing to visit.

I had soon found out that he was cynical, having a very low opinion of women, and from the way he sometimes talked, I had an idea that his disposition was cruel.

However, he seemed to exercise a sort of fascination over me, so I invariably met him whenever he chose to ask me.

So far he had treated me politely, but in a condescending sort of way, and I was quick-witted enough to perceive that he considered me very much his inferior – and so perhaps I was. He was a rich planter, one of the aristocracy of the South, and a member of one of the 'FFV's', as they called themselves, meaning 'First Families of Virginia', while I was only the daughter of a poor clerk of no particular family, earning my living as companion to a Quaker lady.

As time passed, I got to like him a little better, and consequently was more familiar with him, while he became warmer in his manner towards me, but as yet he had not attempted to take the least liberty. He was waiting for a favourable opportunity. He lent me books of poetry, which were a great source of delight to me, and he used often to read aloud to me passages from Byron, Shelley, or Keats.

One afternoon, we were sitting side by side in our favourite nook, and he was reading poetry to me. I do not know who was the author, but I remember that the poem was about love. He had a musical voice, and he read with passionate feeling, every now and then looking into my eyes. I became deeply moved by the sweet but rather warm verse; my cheeks flushed, my heart began to beat rapidly, and my bosom heaved, while a sensuous feeling, such as I had never experienced, took possession of me. I closed my eyes and sat in a soft, waking dream.

He ceased reading, and everything was perfectly still except for the far-off song of a mocking bird. Presently I felt his arm steal round my waist, then he drew me on his lap, and pressed his lips to mine in a long kiss. It was the first time I had ever been kissed by a man, and I felt a thrill pass through me from head to foot, but I did not attempt to get away – the kiss seemed to have mesmerized me. Pressing me to his breast, he covered my face with kisses, calling me all sorts of endearing names and telling me that he loved me. But still I lay quietly in his arms, feeling unable to move.

My quietness emboldened him; so after a moment or two, he put his hand up under my petticoats and felt my bottom through the slit of my drawers. Then my senses returned. The touch of the man's hand on such a part of my body acted like a galvanic shock; my sensuous feeling was instantly changed to a feeling of outraged modesty; I realized my danger, and began to struggle violently in his arms, at the same time calling out to him to let me go. But he paid no attention to what I said, and I was unable to free myself from his powerful grasp.

Laying me down upon my back, he pulled up my clothes, and tearing open my drawers, tried to separate my thighs which I instinctively kept pressed together.

I resisted with all my power, shrieking, and buffeting him in the face with both my hands, but he soon prevented me doing that, by seizing my wrists and holding my arms down at my sides. Then pressing his chest upon my bosom, he crushed me under his weight, and thrusting his knees between my legs, he forced my thighs apart in spite of all my efforts to prevent him; then I felt his stiff member touching my belly in different places as he tried to penetrate me. But he could not; for though I was filled with horror, and burning with shame, I did not lose my head, and I was sure that he could not effect his purpose as long as I kept moving my loins. So I did not exhaust myself by violent struggling, but merely twisted myself about, and every time I felt his 'thing' touch the right spot, I jerked my hips to one side, and by so doing prevented him getting into me.

Again and again, he tried to sheath the weapon, but could not manage to do it. I was strong, healthy, and in good condition, so I fought hard in defence of my virginity, at the same time uttering a succession of loud shrieks.

It was a terrible fight! All my muscles were aching with the strain; every nerve in my body was strung to the utmost tension; the weight of his body was squeezing the breath out of me; my bosom heaved as though it would have burst; my eyes were starting out of my head, and I was filled with a horrible feeling of loathing.

But I continued to resist stubbornly, until at last, fearing I suppose, that my screams would be heard, he ceased his efforts to rape me, and uttering a bitter curse, let me go. Then rising to his feet, he buttoned up his trousers.

I sprang to my feet, panting for breath and trembling all over; tears were streaming down my cheeks, and I was hoarse from screaming. My clothes were torn, and my hair had come down and was flowing in disorder, partly hiding my scarlet face. Overwhelmed with shame, I was about to run away, when he seized me by the arm, and glaring at me with a cruel look in his eyes, hissed out in a savage tone:

'You little fool! Why did you resist me?'

'Let me go you, horrid wretch!' I exclaimed fiercely. 'How dare you look me in the face after what you've done to me? Oh! you beast! But I will have you prosecuted. I will go to the police and have you put in gaol.'

He smiled an evil smile, and darted a baleful glance at me:

'Oh, no, my little girl; you won't go to the police when you have heard what I am going to tell you,' he said, pinching my arm. 'Now you needn't struggle, I've done with you for the present, and I'll let you go in a moment, but you must first listen to what I have to say. I know what Miss Dean and you are doing here. You are keeping an "underground station". I suspected you both from the first, so I watched the house at night on several occasions, and I soon found out the game that was being carried on. For certain reasons, which I dare say you can guess, I did not give information to the police, but you and Miss Dean are in my power, and if I choose now to let the authorities know what you have been doing, you will find yourselves, in a very short time, at hard labour in the State's prison.'

I was startled and frightened, for I saw at once that we were entirely at the man's mercy, but I was so thoroughly upset by the outrage I had suffered, that I could not find a word to say. I could only weep.

Changing his tone, he went on:

'But I don't want to inform against you. I wish to be your friend. I am fond of you, and when you let me kiss you so quietly just now, I thought you were willing to let me go further. I am sorry I treated you so roughly, and I apologize. But I want you. Leave Miss Dean, and come and live with me. You shall have everything a woman can desire; I will settle a thousand dollars a year on you for life, and promise not to lay information against Miss Dean, or to interfere with her in any way.'

As things turned out, it would have been far better for me had I then accepted his offer. But at that moment I was full of rage and shame; moreover, being a perfectly pure girl, I was utterly revolted by the cool way he offered to buy my virtue; and though I dreaded the prison, I said to myself that I would rather go there than yield myself up to this man.

'No! No!' I exclaimed. 'I will not leave Miss Dean. You may tell the police, if you are such a brute. I will go to gaol, but I will not go and live with you. I hate the very sight of you! Oh! go away and leave me, you wretch!'

Again the cruel look came to his face, and he pushed me roughly, saying in a tone of suppressed anger:

'Very well, Miss Dorothy Morton, I will go away

now, but we shall meet again some day, and I think you will be sorry for having refused my offer.'

Then after bowing to me with mock politeness, he turned on his heel and walked rapidly away, leaving me weeping and dishevelled.

Chapter Four

The results of my resistance – The inutility of good-ness – An unwelcome visit, which leads to the humiliation of our persons and the ravishment of my virgin state.

As soon as he was out of sight, I twisted up my hair, and arranged the disorder of my attire as much as was possible; then I hurried home, and fortunately got up to my room without being seen by either Miss Dean or Martha.

Locking the door, I undressed, as my clothes were in a dreadful state; my frock, a white one, was torn at the gathers nearly all the way round, and the back was stained green, the strings of my petticoats were broken, my chemise was torn, and my drawers were hanging in ribbons about my legs. My thighs were covered with black marks made by the pressure of the man's fingers, and I was sore and bruised all over.

After I had put on clean things, I threw myself on the bed, buried my face in the pillow, and cried. But my tears were now angry ones, as the keenness of my shame had somewhat worn off.

I was enraged at my foolishness in having trusted myself alone with Randolph, for whom I had a feeling of distrust ever since he had expressed to me his low opinion of the virtue of women. I also felt degraded in my own estimation, that he should have taken for granted that I was the sort of a girl who would give herself up to a man for the asking. I am sure I had never granted him the least encouragement.

Then I remembered that he had said I should be sorry for not accepting his offer. I had made an enemy of him, so most probably he would give information to the police about us.

It was not pleasant to think of. I felt I ought to let Miss Dean know that we have been found out, but had I done so, I should have been obliged to enter into all the details of my affair with Randolph. And I could not bear to tell her of the outrage I had been subjected to.

Altogether, through my imprudence, we were in a dreadful fix, and there was nothing to be done but wait miserably for the end, which would be the gaol.

Already in my mind I pictured Miss Dean and myself clad in coarse prison garments, and with our hair cropped short, toiling at some hard labour.

Presently, Martha knocked at the door to tell me that tea was ready; so I had to pull myself together and go down to the parlour. I could not eat much, and Miss Dean noticed at once my want of appetite. She also saw that my face was pale and my eyes red, and asked me what was the matter.

I told her I had a bad headache, which was the truth. On hearing that, the kind-hearted woman made me lie on the sofa, while she bathed my forehead with *eau de Cologne*. Then she recommended me to go to bed, so that I might have a long night's rest and sleep off the headache.

But I did not sleep well, as my rest was broken by a succession of horrid dreams, in which I fancied I was struggling in the arms of a man with an enormous member, who always succeeded in overcoming my resistance and taking my maidenhead. In the morning while dressing, I wondered where we should be in twenty-four hours time, for I fully expected that Miss Dean and I would be arrested before the night came.

The day wore slowly away; I was uneasy and restless, and could not settle down to my usual routine of work, but I was constantly peeping out of the window, watching for the arrival of the police.

They did not come. But at nine o'clock, a runaway made his appearance in a starving condition; and in attending to the poor creature's wants, I forgot for the time, my own precarious position.

Several days went by quietly, and I began to think that Randolph after all was not going to be so mean as to inform on us.

But all the same I was very anxious to get out of the state of Virginia, so I said to Miss Dean that I thought we had now done our share of the work, and ought to go back to Philadelphia. Miss Dean however, would not hear of such a thing. She said we were doing good work and that we must go on with it, for some time longer at any rate.

Another fortnight passed, during which period three fugitives arrived, two men and a woman, all of whom we sent on to the next station, without exciting any suspicion as far as I knew, and as nothing had occurred to alarm me, my spirits rose, and I became quite myself again.

I had never seen Randolph since the day he assaulted me, but I often thought of the shameful affair, the recollection of it always sending the blood in a hot flood to my cheeks.

I had hatred for the man and hoped I should never set eyes on him again.

But alas! I was fated to see him before long, under the most painful circumstances. One afternoon, about five o'clock, we were sitting in the veranda at the front of the house. Miss Dean, looking very sweet and pretty in a dove-coloured dress, was as usual usefully employed in making shirts for the runaways, while I was engaged in trimming a hat for myself. Martha was in the kitchen washing up plates and dishes, as we had just finished tea. I was in good spirits, and as I worked I sang to myself in a low voice a plantation song I had learnt from the negroes, called: 'Carry me Back to Ole Virginny'.

It was strange that I should have been singing that particular song, for I was very anxious to get away from 'Ole Virginny', and had I been out of the State I certainly would not have asked anyone to carry me back to it.

Presently the stillness of the evening was broken by the clatter of horses' hoofs, mingled with the sound of loud voices in the distance, and on looking down the lane I saw a number of men, some of them mounted, some on foot, coming towards the house.

Miss Dean and I gazed at them as they came along, and we wondered where they were all going; people very rarely entered our secluded lane.

To our surprise, the party stopped at the house, the men on horseback dismounting and hitching their horses to the fence, then the whole crowd came into the veranda and gathered round us as we sat, in silent astonishment, on our chairs.

I noticed however, that there was a hard stern look on the face of every man, while some of them scowled at us with angry glances. There were fifteen men, all of whom were quite unknown to me, even by sight.

Most of them were bearded, rough-looking fellows, dressed in coarse cotton shirts of various colours, with their trousers tucked into boots reaching to the knees and wearing slouched hats on their heads. But there were some men better dressed, and evidently of a higher class.

My heart began to flutter, and a vague foreboding of evil came over me, for though I had not the least suspicion of what the men's intentions were, I guessed from their looks that they had not come to pay us a friendly visit.

One of the intruders, a man about forty years of age, who was addressed by the others as Jake Stevens, and who appeared to be the leader of the band, stepped forward, and laying his hand on Miss Dean's shoulder, at the same time looking at me, said sternly:

'Stand up you two, I've got sumthin' to say to you.'

We both rose to our feet, and Miss Dean asked in a quiet tone:

'Why have you and your companions invaded my house in this rough manner?'

The man laughed scornfully, saying:

'Well, I should say you orter pretty well guess what's brought us here. You ain't so innocent as you look, by a long chalk.' Then with an oath, he went on: 'It has come to the knowledge of the white folks in these parts, that you are keeping an "underground station" and since you have been here you have got away a great many slaves. Now I jest tell you that we Southerners don't allow no derned Northern abolitionists to run off our slaves. When we ketches abolitionists we makes it hot for them, and now that we've ketched you and your assistant, we are going to bring you before Judge Lynch's court. The boys who have come here with me are the gentlemen of the jury. Isn't that the right talk boys?' he said to the men round him.

'Yes, yes, Jake. That's the talk. You've put it the right way,' shouted several voices.

I sank down horribly frightened on my chair. I had heard dreadful stories of the cruelties perpetrated under the name of 'Lynch'. Miss Dean again spoke calmly:

'If you have found out that we have broken the law of the State, why have you not informed the police? You have no right to take the law into your own hands.'

There was an angry movement among the men, and a hubbub of voices rose.

'We've got the right to do as we please. Lynch Law is good enough for the likes of you. Shut your mouth.

Don't waste any more time talking to her, Jake. Let's get to business,' was shouted.

'All right, boys,' said Stevens, 'we'll go into the garden right away and settle what shall be done with the prisoners. We know they are guilty, so we've only got to sentence them, and then we'll proceed to carry out the sentence of the court.'

Miss Dean and I were left in the veranda, while the men, all trooping out into the garden, gathered in a cluster and began to talk; but they were too far off for us to hear what was being said.

I sat huddled up in my chair, with a dreadful sinking at my heart.

'Oh, Miss Dean,' I wailed, 'what will they do to us?'

'I do not know, dear,' she replied, coming over to me and taking my hand. 'I am not very much concerned about myself, but oh! my poor girl, I am so sorry for you. I should never have allowed you to come here.'

Too miserable to say another word, I sat pale and silent. The men continued talking together, and there seemed to be differences of opinion amongst them, but I could not catch a word that was said. The suspense to me was dreadful, my mouth was parched and I turned alternately hot and cold.

But Miss Dean who still held my hand, occasionally pressing it, was quite calm. At last, the men seemed to have agreed, and they all returned to the veranda.

Then Stevens, assuming a sort of judicial manner, addressed us, saying:

'The sentence of the court upon you two is, that you are each to receive a whipping with a hickory switch on the bare bottom; then you are both to be made to ride a rail for two hours, and further, you are warned to leave the state of Virginny within forty-eight hours. If at the end of that time, you are found in the State, Judge Lynch will have something more to say to you.'

When I heard the shameful and cruel sentence which the lynchers had passed upon us, my blood ran cold and I trembled all over; there was a singing in my ears, and a mist came before my eyes. I rose from my seat, my legs shaking under me so much that I had to hold the back of the chair to support myself.

'Oh, you surely don't mean to whip us!' I exclaimed in piteous accents, stretching out my arms appealingly to the men. 'Oh! don't put us to such awful shame and pain. Have pity on us! Oh! do have pity on us.'

But there was not the least sign of pity on any of the faces surrounding us. All were stern, or frowning, or stolid. And one man called out:

'Sarves you right, you darned little abolitionist. You ought both to be stripped naked, and tarred and feathered after the whipping and then perched on the rail. You would look a queer brace of birds.'

At this coarse joke, there was a burst of laughter from the other men, and I again sank down on my chair, wringing my hands in despair, while the tears streamed down my white cheeks.

Miss Dean, however, faced the men boldly. She had turned very pale, but her eyes were bright and she showed no signs of fear.

Addressing the leader, she said without a tremor in her voice:

'I have often been told that the Southerners were chivalrous in their treatment of women, but I find that I have been misinformed. Chivalrous men do not whip women.'

'I don't know nothing about chivalrous,' said Stevens gruffly, 'but when women acts like men, and sets to running an "underground station" they must take the consekences.'

The men in various terms, garnished with oaths, expressed their approval of what their leader had said.

Miss Dean calmly continued:

'I wish you all to know that I am the only person in this house responsible for what has been done. The young lady is not to blame in any way. She is my paid companion and has acted entirely under my orders. You must let her go free.'

'Oh no! we won't,' exclaimed several voices at once. 'She must have her share of the switch.'

'Let me do the talking,' said Stevens. 'We know very well that you are the boss of this yer show, but the girl has been helpin' you to run it, so she's got to be whipped, but she won't git such a smart touchin' up as you will. Isn't that right, boys?' he asked.

'Yes, yes! That's all right,' some of them answered. 'Let the gal off a bit easier than the woman.'

Just then one of the men called out:

'Whar's the hired woman? She ought to have her bottom switched, and get a ride on the rail as well as the others.'

'Certainly she ought,' said Stevens. 'A couple of you go and bring her here. I guess she's hiding somewhere in the house.'

Two of the men went into the house, and while they were away the others talked and laughed with each other, making ribald remarks that caused me to blush and shiver.

But Miss Dean did not appear to hear what was being said, she stood quite still; her hands loosely clasped in front of her, and with a far-off look in her great soft brown eyes.

In about five minutes' time, the two men returned, and one of them said with an oath:

'We can't find the bitch anywhere in the house though we have looked well. She must have run off into the woods.'

'It's a pity she's got away,' said Stevens, 'but any-how we've got the two leading ladies of the show, and

I guess we'll make them both feel sorry that they ever took a hand in the game.'

'You bet we will, Jake,' shouted the men. 'We'll make them sorry they ever came to Virginny. Let's get to work at once.'

'Very well,' said Stevens. 'Bill, you run to the barn and fetch the ladder you'll find there. Pete and Sam, you go and cut a couple of good, long, springy hick'ry switches and trim them ready for me to use.' Then he added with a laugh: 'I daresay these yere Northern ladies have often eaten hick'ry nuts, but I reckon they never thought they would feel a hick'ry switch on their bare bottoms.'

The men all joined in the laugh, while I shuddered, and my heart swelled with bitterness at our utter helplessness.

The ladder and the switches were brought, then all the men went into the garden.

The ladder was then fixed in a sloping position against the rail of the veranda on the outside, and Stevens took up his position near it, holding one of the switches in his hand; while the other men stood round in a ring, so that they might all have a good look at what was going to be done.

'Bring out the prisoners,' said Stevens.

Some of the men took hold of us by the arms and led us out of the veranda to receive the cruel and indecent punishment.

I was trembling and crying; but Miss Dean was calm and silent. Stevens said to her:

'As you are the boss, you shall be whipped first. Tie her up, boys.'

She was seized by two men, and laid upon the ladder; her arms being stretched to their full extent above her head; her wrists tied with thick cords to the rungs of the ladder, and her ankles also securely fastened in the same way.

She had not made the least resistance nor had she

uttered a word while being tied up, but now she turned her head, and looking over her shoulder at Stevens, said:

'Can you not whip me without removing my clothes?'

'No, certainly, not,' he replied. 'You was sentenced to be whipped on the bare bottom. Turn up her clothes, boys.'

Her skirt, petticoats and chemise were rolled high above her waist, and tucked under her body so that they could not fall down. She had not on the ordinary drawers with a slit behind, such as are usually worn by women, but she was wearing long pantalettes, buttoning up all round, fitting rather closely to her legs, and reaching down to her ankles, round which the little frills at the end of the garment were drawn in with narrow ribbons.

'Why darn me, if she ain't got on white trousers!' ejaculated Stevens in a tone of astonishment. 'I never seed such things on a woman before.'

The other men also seemed surprised, and very much amused at the sight of the trousers, and various remarks were made about them by some of the spectators. I suppose the women of their class in that part of the country never wore drawers of any sort.

'Take down her trousers,' said Stevens.

Again Miss Dean looked round:

'Please leave me my pantalettes. They won't protect me much. Do not expose my nakedness to all these men,' she pleaded earnestly.

But no attention was paid to her entreaty. One of the men roughly put his hands in front of her belly, and after some fumbling, unbuttoned the pantalettes and pulled them down to her ankles, leaving her person naked from the waist to the tops of the black silk stockings she was wearing.

When her last garment had been removed, her pale cheeks blushed scarlet, even the nape of her neck and her ears became red; a shudder shook her body from head to foot, she bent her head down and closed her eyes.

I was being held by two men close to the ladder, so I could not help seeing everything.

Miss Dean, as I have said before, was a tall, slim, slightly-built woman. Her hips were very narrow and her bottom very small, but it was round, well-shaped and fairly plump; her thighs and legs were also well-formed though slender; her skin was of a delicate ivory tint, smooth, and fine in texture.

The men pressed closer to the ladder, and I could see their eyes glisten as they fixed them with lecherous looks on Miss Dean's half-naked body.

And Stevens after gazing for a moment or two at her straight figure, exclaimed with a laugh:

'Je-ru-sa-lem! what a little bottom she's got. It ain't no bigger than a man's. By gosh, boys! perhaps she is a man?'

This was meant for a joke. It amused them and they all laughed, one of the men calling out:

'Well, Jake, you can easily find out whether she's a woman or not.'

'Why so I can, now that you have put it in my head,' drawled Stevens, grinning and affecting to be surprised at the suggestion.

Then he thrust his hand between her thighs.

She flinched convulsively, uttering a startled cry, then looking round at the man with an expression of intense horror on her face, and with her eyes flashing, exclaimed:

'How dare you touch me like that? Take your hand away! Oh, whip me and let me go!'

She writhed and twisted, but the man kept his hand in the cleft of her thighs, saying with a coarse laugh:

'She's a woman sure enough, boys. I've got my hand on her slit.' Then he said to her:

'My hand won't hurt you. But if I and these other

gentlemen were not sorter decent chaps who only intend to carry out the sentence of Judge Lynch, you would soon find something different to a hand between your legs. Now I'll flog you right away, and I guess you'll soon be begging me to stop whipping you.'

He withdrew his hand, and Miss Dean ceased struggling, her head drooped forward; she again closed her eyes, and lay silently awaiting the shameful punishment.

Stevens raised the switch and flicked it about, so as to make it hiss in the air, then he brought it down with considerable force across the upper part of her bottom; the tough hickory spray making a sharp crack as it struck the firm flesh which quivered involuntarily under the stinging stroke.

She winced, drawing her breath through her teeth with a hissing sound, and a long red weal instantly rose on her delicate skin. Swinging the switch high, he went on whipping, laying each stroke below the preceding one, so that her skin was striped in regular lines. Each stroke smacked loudly on her flesh, and raised a fresh, red weal which stretched across both sides of her quivering bottom.

She began to writhe, the clenched her teeth so tightly that I could see the outlines of her jaws through her cheeks, but no sound came from her lips.

The man laid on the strokes with severity, and I wondered how she could bear the pain in silence. I felt inclined to scream, and I shuddered every time I heard the horrid sound made by the switch as it fell on her flesh.

But the brave woman never once screamed, nor did she make an appeal for mercy. Her fortitude amazed me.

At last he stopped whipping, and threw down the switch which had become quite frayed at the end.

Then bending down, he closely examined the marks of his handiwork on the sufferer's bottom.

She had been most severely whipped. I think she must have received forty or fifty strokes.

'There, boys,' said Stevens looking round at the spectators, 'I guess that will do for her. I touched her up pretty smartly, as you can see from the state of her bottom. She won't be able to sit down comfortable for two or three days, and I don't think the marks of the whipping will ever be quite rubbed off her skin.'

He then pulled down her clothes and unfastened her wrists and ankles. She stood up, twisting her loins in pain, with her pantalettes hanging about her feet; her face was now pale and drawn with suffering, her bosom was heaving, her tears were flowing, and she was sobbing.

She seemed oblivious of everything except her pain. But after a few moments she recovered herself a little, and taking her handkerchief from her pocket, wiped the tears from her eyes; then she pulled up her pantalettes, and with some difficulty, as she was trembling very much, buttoned them round her waist, her cheeks again reddening when she noticed the grinning faces and leering looks of the men standing round her.

Two of them took her by the arms and led her into the veranda, where they left her. She laid herself down at full length upon a couch and hid her face in the cushion, weeping.

Chapter Five

I am myself stripped naked and receive a most terrible whipping – The coarse observations of the men – My shame and terror, showing from experience that chastisement by the opposite sex awakens sensations sometimes far from pleasurable.

I have told you all these things precisely as they happened, and I have used the exact words and phrases that were spoken by the band of lynchers who tortured us that day. I daresay you wonder at my remembering all the little details. But such an experience can never be forgotten. All the incidents that occurred during that dreadful period were indelibly printed on my memory, so that I have still a vivid recollection of them.

But to resume. You can imagine my feelings as I listened to the coarse language of the men, language such as I had never heard before, and watched the proceedings, at once so cruel and so utterly revolting to feminine delicacy. I was torn with various emotions. I was horrified at what I had heard and seen. I was filled with pity for Miss Dean, and consumed with impotent rage against the men in whose power we were. I dreaded the coming exposure of my person, and I was awfully afraid of the whipping before me.

I never could bear pain with any fortitude. In fact I must confess that I am morally and physically a great coward.

Stevens picked up the unused switch, and straightened it by drawing it through the fingers of his left hand.

'Now, boys,' he said, 'put the gal on the ladder and tie her up; but let me do the stripping.'

The awful moment had come, and I became quite frantic at the thought of the shame and pain I was about to undergo, and an insane idea that I might escape, came into my head.

The men were holding me loosely, so I easily slipped from their grasp and made a dash for the garden gate.

Several of the men gave chase, and though I exerted myself to the utmost, I was soon caught and dragged to the ladder, shrieking, struggling, and begging them not to whip me.

But my entreaties only evoked laughter. I was lifted up, placed in position with outstretched arms, and securely fastened by the wrists and ankles.

Stevens began to strip me, and seemed to take as long a time over the work as possible, slowly rolling my garments one by one till he came to my drawers; then he paused. I was wearing the usual feminine drawers that are open behind.

'Look, boys,' he observed, 'this gal has got on trousers too, but they are different to the ones the woman wore. These are loose, and are real dandy ones, all pretty frills and lace, and ribbons, and you see there is a big slit at the back. I suppose that's made so as her sweetheart can get at her without taking down her trousers.'

The men all laughed loudly, while I, on hearing the shameful words, shrank as if I had received a blow.

He untied the strings of my drawers and pulled them down to my knees, and then I could feel the breeze fanning my naked bottom and thighs. A sensation of unutterable shame overwhelmed me. To be exposed in such a way before fifteen men!

And such men! oh it was horrible! I knew that

they were all gloating over my nakedness and I seemed actually to feel their lascivious glances on my flesh.

I was hot with shame, yet I shivered as if with cold. But worse was to come. Stevens put his hand on my bottom, stroking it all over and squeezing the flesh with his fingers, making me thrill and quiver with disgust. In fact, my feelings of shame and horror at the moment were far greater than they had been when Randolph assaulted me.

'Ah!' said Stevens, chuckling and continuing to feel me with his rough hand, 'this gal has got something like a bottom. My! ain't it jest plump, and firm, and broad. There's plenty of room here for the switch, and her skin is as soft and smooth as velvet, and you can see how white it is. I've never before had my hand on such a scrumptious bottom. It's worth feeling and no mistake.' I writhed and moaned. He went on: 'I should like you all to have a feel of it, but as leader of this yer party, I can't allow you to touch the gal, for fear some of you might want to do more than feel her; and that would lead to difficulties among us. Now, as to the punishment of the gal, I propose to give her a dozen strokes, but not draw blood. Remember she is only an assistant in the business.'

The men were divided in opinion. Some said that I ought to be whipped just the same as the 'missis'; but the majority was in favour of my receiving only twelve strokes. And so it was settled. Even in my fear and shame, I felt a sensation of relief at hearing that I was not going to be whipped so severely as Miss Dean had been. One of the men called out:

'Mind you lay the dozen right smart, Jake. Make the young bitch wriggle her bottom.'

'You bet I'll lay them on smart, and you'll see how she'll move. I know how to handle a hick'ry switch, and I'll rule a dozen lines across her bottom that'll make it look like the American flag, striped red and white. And when I've done with her I guess she'll be pretty sore behind, but you'll see that I won't draw a drop of blood. Yes, gentlemen, I tell you again that I know how to whip, I was an overseer in Georgia for five years.'

All the time the man was holding forth, I lay shame-stricken at my nakedness, and shivering in awful suspense, the flesh of my bottom creeping, and the scalding tears trickling down my red cheeks. The man raised the switch and flourished it over me; while I held my breath and contracted the muscles of my bottom in dread of the coming stroke.

It fell with a loud swishing noise. Oh! it was awful! The pain was even worse than I had anticipated. It took my breath away for a moment and made me gasp, while I uttered a loud shriek, writhing and twisting my loins in agony.

He went on whipping me very slowly, so that I felt the full sting of each stroke before the next one fell; and every stroke felt as if a red-hot iron was being drawn across my bottom.

I winced and squirmed every time the horrid switch fell sharply on my quivering flesh. I shrieked and screamed, and I swung my hips from side to side, arching my loins at one moment, and then flattening myself down on the ladder, while between my shrieks, I begged and prayed the man to stop whipping me.

I had forgotten all about my nakedness, the only sensation I had at the moment was one of intense pain, and when the twelve strokes had been inflicted I was in a half-fainting state.

I was left lying with upturned petticoats, on the ladder, while the men all gathered round me and looked at me.

As I was a strong healthy girl, the faintness soon passed off, as also did the first intense smart of the whipping, but my whole bottom was sore, and the weals throbbed painfully.

The feeling of shame again came over me as I began to notice the way the men were looking at my naked body, and I tearfully begged them to pull down my clothes.

No one did so however, and Stevens pointing to me said:

'There, boys, look at her bottom. You see how regularly the white skin is striped with long red weals; but there is not a drop of blood. That's what I call a prettily whipped bottom. But the gal ain't got a bit of grit in her. Any slave wench would have taken double the number of strokes without making half the noise. Now the other woman is a plucky one; she took the whippin' well.' He then pulled up my drawers and tied the strings round my waist, saying with a laugh. 'This is the first time I've ever fixed up a woman's trousers, and it's the first time I've ever whipped women who wore pants.'

Pulling down my clothes, he loosed me from the ladder, and led me crying, sore and miserable, back to the veranda where Miss Dean was still lying on her stomach on the couch, with her hands over her face.

The conduct of these wretches towards two women of whom one was young and pretty, and desirable anyway, may appear strange. How was it that their brutal, lustful natures were not inflamed by the intoxicating sight of my dazzling nudity?

The agonizing anticipation of torture did not cause me to prefer the ignominy which was bound to result from the defeat of my virtue, but in the inmost depths of my soul, I hoped nevertheless that the sight of my youthful charms, sharpening the concupiscent instincts of these brutes, might cause them to quarrel among themselves.

Although still innocent, in spite of the lesson the infamous assaults of Randolph had taught me, I knew that the exposure of my frame was capable of awakening the vile desires of these low and bestial men; so I hoped that they might have disputed about the possession of my body, and allowed me to escape under cover of a free fight.

Alas! I knew not then that they were Randolph's own creatures, and generously paid by him to carry out his barbarous orders.

In their hearts, for once, cupidity spoke louder than lewdness.

After Stevens had conducted me to the side of Miss Dean, he went off to the other men, a few of whom I saw were engaged in work of some sort near the fence. But I was so thankful at having got out of their hands and sight that I did not particularly notice what they were doing.

I thought they would soon go away and that all our troubles were over. I had quite forgotten that Stevens had said we would have to ride a rail for two hours after being whipped.

Miss Dean looked mournfully at me, her sweet face very pale and her soft eyes full of tears, but the tears were not for herself; they were for me. She beckoned to me, and when I went to her, she folded me in her arms, pressing me to her bosom:

'Oh! my poor, poor girl,' she murmured in tones full of compassion, 'how I have felt for you! Your shrieks pierced my heart. Oh! the cruel, cruel man to whip you so severely.'

She seemed to have quite forgotten the shame and pain of her own whipping in her pity for me.

'He did not whip me nearly so severely as he did you,' I said. 'He only gave me a dozen strokes and no blood has come. But I could not help screaming. I am not so brave as you are.'

Then we kissed and cried, and sympathized with each other, comparing notes as to our feelings while on the ladder exposed to the eyes of the men.

After a moment or two, I put my hand under my petticoats and touched my smarting bottom, feeling the weals which had been raised on the flesh by the switch. They were exquisitely tender, and I could hardly bear to touch them.

'Oh! dear me!' I wailed, 'How dreadfully sore I am. But you must be much sorer?'

'I certainly am very, very sore,' said Miss Dean, wiping her eyes. 'I can neither sit down nor lie on my back. My bottom is still bleeding I think, and my pantalettes are sticking to my flesh. But oh, oh! the awful exposure, and the shameful touch of the man's hand was worse than the whipping,' she exclaimed, wringing her hands, while the tears again began to trickle down her cheeks.

I pressed her hand in mute sympathy, and she went on:

'Our sufferings are not over yet, Dorothy. Don't you remember the man said we would have to ride the rail for two hours?'

I now did call to mind what Stevens had said about our riding a rail, but I was not much frightened at having to do so. Of course I knew that it would be very uncomfortable, if not painful to have to sit with a sore and smarting bottom on a rail for two hours. That was all I thought about the matter at the moment.

Ah! I little knew what a terrible torture riding a rail would prove to be.

I don't know whether Miss Dean had any notion of what it actually was, but anyway she did not say a word more on the subject, and we stood – both of us being too sore to sit down in comfort – with our arms round each other, weeping silently and waiting miserably for the men to come for us.

We had not long to wait. In a couple of minutes, four of the band came, and taking us by the arms, led us out of the veranda to the fence, beside which the other men were standing some of them holding pieces of rope in their hands.

The fence was about five feet high, and of the

ordinary pattern, made of split rails, the upper edge of each being wedge-shaped and sharp. Stevens, with a cruel smile on his face, said:

'Now you are going to receive the rest of your punishment – a two hour ride on the rail. I guess your bottoms must be very hot jest now, but they'll have plenty of time to cool while you are having your ride, and to prevent you from falling off your horses, we'll tie you on them. Get them ready, boys.'

I thought that we should be merely tied in a sitting posture on the fence with our clothes down. But I was soon undeceived! We were each seized by two men who held our arms, while a third man, in each case, raised our petticoats and pulled our drawers entirely off our legs. Then our garments were held high above our waists so that the whole lower parts of our persons, both behind and before, were exposed to the lustful eyes of the horrid men.

And as they had already seen our bottoms, they all crowded in front of us, gloating over the secret 'spots' of our respective bodies, while we, crimson with a greater shame than ever, struggled and wept, and entreated the wretches to cover our nakedness.

But they only laughed, and two or three of them put their hands on the 'spots' – 'pussies', they called them – the touch of their fingers making us start and shrink with a horrible feeling of disgust.

Stevens, however, stopped them, by saying:

'No, no, boys, you must not touch the prisoners, but you may look at them as much as you like.'

And the men did look, making remarks, speculating as to whether we were virgins or not, pointing out the difference in the shape of our figures, and observing the colour of the hair on our respective 'spots' while we blushed, and cried with shame.

You have seen my 'spot' and know what it is like; there is nothing strange about it. But Miss Dean's 'spot' was somewhat remarkable. I had never seen it before and I could not help looking at it with astonishment. It was covered with a thick forest of glossy, dark brown hair, which extended some distance up her belly and descended between her thighs in curly locks nearly two inches long, the fissure being completely hidden and not a trace of the lips to be seen.

One man, after a prolonged stare, exclaimed:

'By Gosh! I've never seen such a fleece between a woman's legs in my life. Darn me if she wouldn't have to be sheared before a man could get to her.'

The men roared with laughter at the remark, while Miss Dean groaned, and writhed in the bitterness of her shame.

After looking at our naked bodies for fully five minutes, the men went on with their work.

A long piece of rope was passed several times round our bodies, so that our arms and wrists were closely lashed to our sides. We were then lifted bodily up, and to my intense horror, seated astride one of the topmost rails of the fence, facing each other and about six feet apart.

The rail passed between our naked thighs, and our bare bottoms rested on the sharp edge of it. On each side of the fence and close to it, the men had driven stakes into the ground, and to these stakes our ankles were securely tied.

When the men had fixed us in this painful position, they allowed our clothes to fall about our legs. Our nakedness was covered, but our torture had begun.

Stevens looked at us with a grin on his face, saying:

'There now; you are properly mounted on your horses. We've done with you and we're all going away, but at the end of two hours one of us will come back and loose you. And I reckon you'll both be mighty stiff after your ride.'

Then the band of lynchers took their departure,

laughing, and shouting coarse jokes which made us, even in our pain, grow hot with shame. The clatter of the horses' hoofs and the loud laughter of the men gradually died away in the distance; then all was perfectly still.

Chapter Six

On the rack – Moral torture is allied to the physical –
I make the great decision of my life and consent to
become Randolph's mistress – His revolting cynicism.

It was a beautiful, calm, bright evening, the sun was
just setting, so the house, the garden, and our two
unfortunate selves were all bathed in a flood of amber
light.

At first, I had a faint hope that Martha would come
back – now that the men had gone – and release us,
but she never came, and there was not the slightest
chance of any one else coming to the house at that
hour.

There was no escape possible, so we would be
obliged to undergo the whole of our dreadful
punishment.

From the first moment of our being placed astride
the rail we had been suffering pain, and it was increasing every minute. We did not speak to one another, as
our sufferings were too great, so we sat in silence, with
the tears, which we could not wipe off, trickling down
our pale cheeks, while every now and then a shuddering sob, or groan of anguish would break from our
parched lips.

As our legs were rather widely stretched apart, the
rail was in the cleft of our thighs, and the weight of
our bodies forced the sharp edge deeply into the division between the cheeks of our bottoms, and consequently the most delicate part of our persons was hurt
by the pressure of the rail.

Just imagine our position, and think what it meant to individuals of the female sex!

Miss Dean, throughout the whole time we were on the rail, bore her sufferings far more quietly than I did.

The minutes passed slowly, the pain growing more and more excruciating, and in addition, my bottom was still smarting and the weals on it were still throbbing. I felt as if the wedge-shaped rail was slowly splitting me; sharp lancinating pains darted through my loins and up my back, and as my ankles were tightly fastened to the stakes I could not alter my position in the slightest degree.

If my arms had not been bound to my sides, I might have got a little temporary ease by resting my hands on the rail, and thus taking some of the weight off my bottom.

But the men, in their devilish ingenuity, had taken care that we should not have a moment's respite from our tortures. Even if we had fainted, we should not have fallen from the fence. The upper part of our bodies would have dropped either forward or backward, but our legs, tied to the stakes, would have remained straddled over the rail, and its sharp edge would have still remained between the cheeks of our bottoms.

By this time every nerve in my body was thrilling with agony, and a cold dew of perspiration had broken out on my forehead. I groaned and writhed and twisted myself about, but the more I did so, the more the sharp rail was forced against the tender space between the cleft of my thighs.

I began to scream, and I think I cursed.

Miss Dean was crying, and her face showed the anguish she was feeling, but she made no outcry.

A few minutes more of agony slowly passed, then I saw a man enter the lane and come towards the house. He was not one of the lynchers, so my heart bounded with joy. We should be released in a few moments!

I redoubled my cries, begging him to come quickly to our assistance. He did not however hurry himself in the least, but walked on deliberately and when he had got a little nearer I saw that it was Randolph.

A few days previously I had hoped never to set eyes on him again; but now I was intensely delighted to see him.

'Oh! Mr Randolph,' I gasped out in a choking voice, with the tears streaming down my cheeks, 'take me down! Oh! take me down quickly!'

He came close up to the fence and stood looking at us with a smile on his face.

'Oh! dear Mr Randolph, take me down! do be quick and take me down!' I again wailed.

But, to my horror, he did not move.

'Well, Miss Ruth Dean, and Miss Dorothy Morton,' he said mockingly, 'this is what slave-running has brought you to. And it is to me that you owe your present position. I let the white people know of your doings, and you have been rightly and smartly punished. I told you, Dolly, that we should meet again, and we have. I knew the men were to pay you a visit this evening, so I came with them, and although you did not see me, I saw both of you getting your bottoms whipped. And I must say, Dolly, that you squealed just like a pig being killed.'

He paused to laugh, and a sickening feeling of despair came over me. The cruel man, not content with having set the lynchers on us, had come to mock us in our agony.

He continued:

'I am afraid your bottoms, especially yours, Miss Dean, must be very tender after the smart switching, and I am sure you must both be extremely uncomfortable on your present seats. The edges are sharp, and I have no doubt they are pressing sorely on a certain delicate spot between your thighs.'

Miss Dean's face was working with pain, and her eyes were full of tears, but when she heard Randolph's cruel and indecent words, her pale cheeks grew red.

Looking at me, she said in a weak quavering voice:

'Dorothy, do you know this man?'

He answered for me:

'Oh yes, she does. Miss Morton and I were once great friends, but we had a little tiff one day and she told me to go away. Is not that the case, Dolly?'

I hated the man, but at that moment the dreadful pain I was suffering overpowered every other feeling.

'Yes! Yes! that is the case,' I exclaimed fretfully. 'But don't stand talking, take us down at once.'

He smiled, but did not make a movement to release us.

'Oh! Oh!' I shrieked with pain, and enraged at his utter callousness. 'How can you stand there and watch two poor women suffering agony? Oh! why don't you release us? Have you no mercy or pity?'

'I am not a merciful man, and as a rule, I have no pity for abolitionists when they get into trouble for interfering with our slaves,' he replied coolly. 'But I don't mind making an exception in your case, Dolly. I will take you down, if you promise to come and live with me.'

On hearing what he said, Miss Dean again fixed her eyes on me, saying earnestly:

'Oh! Dorothy! don't listen to the man; he is a cruel scoundrel to try and take advantage of your sufferings. But be brave, dear. Don't give way. I am suffering as much, if not more than you are, but I would not accept release on such disgraceful terms as he offers.'

Randolph laughed scornfully.

'I have not the least intention of offering the terms to you, Miss Dean,' he said. 'As far as I am concerned, you may sit on the rail till the two hours are over. The view I had of your naked charms did not tempt me in the slightest degree. You have no figure. You are quite straight up and down. Your bottom is too narrow, your thighs are too small, and your legs are too thin. I like a woman to have a broad bottom, plump thighs, and good legs such as Dorothy has got.'

'Oh! you hateful man,' exclaimed Miss Dean, angrily; as after all she was a woman, and no woman likes to hear her charms, whatever they may be, spoken of in disparaging terms.

'Now then, Dolly, you have heard what I said. Do you intend to come home with me tonight?'

The coarse way he put the question shocked me, so I tried to pluck up a little spirit, and I partly succeeded.

'No, no, I won't go home with you,' I said, but not in a very determined way.

'Very well then, stay where you are. You have an hour and a half more to sit on your perch, and by that time you'll be in a terrible state between the legs, and half dead with pain. Rather a dreadful prospect, isn't it?'

Alas! it was. I moaned and shuddered at the thought of the long period of agony before me, and again I piteously entreated him to take me down.

He made no answer, but coolly lit a cigar and began to smoke. Then leaning his back against the middle of the rail at the ends of which we were straddled, he looked first at one and then at the other, with perfect unconcern, while we writhed, wept, and groaned in anguish, as the sharp edge of the rail pressed harder and harder against the tender flesh between the cheeks of our bottoms.

For a few minutes more I bore the pain which was growing more and more intense: then I gave way utterly. I could no longer endure the anguish. I said to myself:

'What does anything matter, as long as I escape

from this terrible torture. I can't bear it for another hour and a half. I should go raving mad, or die. Oh! take me down! Take me down at once, and I promise to go home with you,' I cried.

No doubt it was weak of me, but I was in a half-fainting state, and as I have before told you, I am physically and morally a coward.

When Miss Dean heard me promise to go with Randolph, she said:

'Don't, oh! don't go with him, Dorothy. Don't wreck your life. Try and bear your sufferings. They will soon be over. If I were you, I would die rather than yield my body to that man.'

'Have you quite made up your mind, Dolly?' said Randolph laying his hand on the knot of the rope binding my arms.

'Yes, yes,' I cried impatiently. 'Oh! do be quick and release me.'

'Oh, Dorothy, my poor girl, I pity you,' said Miss Dean in a sorrowful tone. 'You do not know what is before you.'

Randolph soon untied the ropes that fastened my arms and ankles; then putting his arms round my waist, he lifted me off the rail, carried me into the veranda, and laid me, limp and faint, on the couch. I was stiff and sore, and aching from head to foot, but I was not suffering much pain. Oh! the intense relief it was to find myself no longer astride the sharp rail.

He got me a glass of water which I drank thirstily, as my mouth was parched, and I was quite feverish from the torture I had undergone.

When I had recovered a little, I thought of Miss Dean, and I asked Randolph to release her.

He was however very bitter against her, and at first refused to let her go, but I begged hard for her, and at last he said that he would release her before we went away.

'Now, Dolly,' he said, 'I'll go for the buggy. I left it

just round the corner of the lane. I shan't be gone long, so you lie quietly here till I come back.' Then he added, in a meaning way: 'You had better not attempt to leave the house, for the men are still somewhere in the neighbourhood and if they see you they will put you on the rail again.' So saying, he went away.

But the thought of escape never entered my head. At that moment, I was weak and frightened; all my senses were in a half-torpid state, and I had not fully realized my position. So I lay languidly on the couch, thinking how delightful it was to be free from pain.

Presently, Randolph drove up with the buggy to the garden gate, and after hitching the horse, he came to me:

'Now then, Dolly, come along,' he said. 'Never mind your things. My women can supply you with everything necessary for the night, and I will send for your trunks tomorrow morning. Can you walk to the buggy, or shall I carry you?'

I replied that I could walk, but on attempting to do so, I found myself too shaky and so stiff that I could hardly put one foot before another.

Noticing how feeble I was, he lifted me up in his arms, and carrying me to the buggy, put me in and wrapped a rug round my knees. Then going to Miss Dean, he untied the ropes binding her, but he did not take the trouble to help her down; so the poor thing had to get off the rail without assistance.

She was weak, pale, and suffering, so she had to lean against the fence for support; but her thoughts were still for me.

'Don't go with that man, Dorothy,' she again said in a most earnest way. 'Never mind your promise. It was extracted from you by torture, so you are not bound to keep it. Stay with me.'

I did not want to go with Randolph, and I would have been only too glad to stay with her, but my cowardice prevented me. I was afraid of again falling into the hands of the lynchers. So I only cried, saying feebly:

'Oh! I must go with him, I am in his power.'

'Yes, yes, you are,' he observed, 'and if you were to attempt to break your promise you would very soon find yourself astride the rail again.' Then addressing Miss Dean, he said: 'Remember what the men told you. If you are not out of the State before forty-eight hours are over, you will receive another visit from Judge Lynch.'

He then got into the buggy beside me, and as he did so, I shrank away as far as possible, hating him, and despising myself.

He touched the horse with the whip, and we drove off, leaving Miss Dean standing with drooping head by the fence.

After we had gone a short distance I looked back, and I saw the lonely figure still in the same position. She did not move, and I kept my eyes fixed upon her until the buggy turned the corner of the lane; then I sank back on the seat, and covering my face with my hands, wept bitterly. I had parted with the only friend I had in the world.

Chapter Seven

At Randolph's house – I make Dinah's acquaintance – Her sympathy for me, and her contempt for unsophisticated 'whites'. – My attempts to escape are frustrated.

Randolph did not say a word to me, but just let me cry away, which was the best thing he could have done at the moment.

The buggy, drawn by a fast trotter, rolled rapidly along the road, and as Randolph's plantation was only three miles distant, we soon reached the closed avenue leading to the house. The gates were thrown open by two negroes, and we entered the avenue which was about a quarter of a mile long, shaded throughout its length with tall trees. In a few minutes we arrived at the house, a very large and handsome building, consisting of a central part with a cupola on top, and wings on either side; in front there was a broad terrace sloping down to a lawn, flanked with well-kept beds of beautiful flowers.

Several negroes were on the terrace, waiting to receive their master, and when he pulled up the horse at the door, the men came forward and took charge of the animal.

The wide door of the house was opened; then Randolph, lifting me out of the buggy, carried me through a spacious hall into a handsomely furnished room, and placed me on a couch.

'There, Dolly,' he said, smiling down at me, 'you are safe from the lynchers now.'

He then rang the bell, which was immediately answered by a good-looking quadroon woman, about thirty-five years of age. She was very tall, stout, and broad-shouldered; neatly dressed in a well-fitting print frock, with white apron, collar and cuffs; she had very black, glossy, wavy hair, and on her head she wore a smart cap.

The woman looked hard at me, but there was not the least expression of surprise on her face.

'Dinah,' said her master, 'this lady has met with an accident. Carry her up to the pink room, and attend to her. See that she has everything she wants, and take great care of her. Do you understand?'

'Yes, massa,' she replied.

Turning to me, he said:

'I am going to dinner now, but Dinah will look after you, and I think you had better let her put you to bed. You are quite feverish. You shall not be disturbed tonight,' he added, meaningly.

I understood the significance of the last words, but I made no remark, and a blush dyed my cheeks. I was still dazed and stupid. The rapid succession of painful and startling events had been too much for me.

Dinah came to the sofa, and lifting me in her strong arms, as if I had been a baby, carried me out of the room, up a broad flight of stairs, to a most luxuriously furnished bedroom, and laid me gently on the bed. Then closing the door, she came back to the bedside and looked at me with a kind, motherly expression on her pleasant face.

'I know who yo' is, missy,' she said. 'Yo' is one of de good Northern ladies who keeps the unnergroun' station. All de cullud folks in dese parts has heard ob yo'. But it was none of dem dat set de lynchers on you.' I know de lynchers has been after yo' today, honey. What did dey do to yo'? Did dey ride yo' on a rail? Dey offen does dat to ablishinists. Don't mind tellin' me all about it, little missy. I'se fond of yo' for what yo've done for de runaways.'

The woman's sympathy was most grateful to me, so I told her all that had been done to Miss Dean and myself.

'Oh! you poor young lady! I'se so very sorry for yo',' she exclaimed, in tones full of pity. 'Yo' mus' be drefful sore. But I will bathe yo' an' make yo' as comfortable as I can, an' den yo' mus' go to bed.'

It was rather dark, so she lit the lamps and drew the curtains. She then left the room, returning in a few minutes with a can of hot water.

'Now, honey,' she said tenderly, 'I'll fix yo' up.'

She undressed me to my chemise, then asking me to lie on my face, she rolled up the garment, and after separating my legs a little, examined my body.

'I see dat dose horrid men gave yo' twelve strokes with de switch,' she observed, 'de weals is quite plain on your poor bottom, missy, an' yo' is all bruised an' marked between de thighs where de rail hurt yo'.'

She then sponged my bottom with cold water, and gently rubbed the weals with some soft stuff, saying:

'Dis is 'possum fat, missy, it will take de smart out ob de weals. We always uses 'possum fat to take away de sting of a whipping.' The stuff certainly did seem to make my bottom feel easier. 'What a bootiful figure you've got, and such pretty legs, and such a lubly white skin. I'se never seen such a white one in my life.'

When she had 'fixed' my bottom, she turned me over on to my back, and fomented with warm water the 'spot' and the parts adjacent, uttering all the time expressions of pity for me, and abusing the lynchers whom she called a pack of 'mean white trash'.

It is a curious fact that the slaves in the South used to have a contempt for the white people who did not own a negro. I may also say here that Dinah never knew that it was her master who had set the lynchers on us.

As the parts were very tender and also a good deal

swollen, the fomentation gave me great relief, and when Dinah had finished bathing the sore 'spot', she went to a drawer, which to my surprise, I saw was filled with all sorts of feminine undergarments.

Taking out a lace-trimmed night-dress she brought it to me, then removing my chemise, put the night-gown on me, and made me get into bed.

She then went away, but soon returned with a tray, on which were dishes and plates, and also a small bottle of champagne.

She placed a little table by the bedside, and spreading a cloth, laid out the good things she had brought, saying:

'Now honey, here is a nice wee dinner. Yo' must try and eat a bit, and drink some of dis wine. It will do yo' good.'

As I had been a teetotaller all my life I did not want the wine, so I asked Dinah to get me a cup of tea.

She soon did so, then propped myself up in the bed, taking care to press as little as possible on my bottom, and as I was feeling very faint, I began to eat, and was able to make a very fair meal, forgetting, for the moment, the past, and not thinking of the future. While I was having my supper, Dinah talked to me freely, but always with perfect respect. The fact of my having been indecently whipped by a band of men had not lowered me the least in her estimation. To her, I was still a white lady from the North, while she was only a slave.

She informed me with an air of pride, that she was the housekeeper, and had twenty female servants under her. Then she gave me some particulars about herself. She had been born on the plantation, and had never been more than twenty miles from it in all her life. She had once had a husband, but was now a widow without a child. She further informed me, in a most matter-of-course way, that she had often been whipped.

When she had cleared away the dinner things, she brushed my hair – it was the first time I had ever had such a thing done for me since I had become a woman – then she put a bell on the table beside the bed, and, after turning down the lamp, she bade me good-night, and left the room.

When I woke next morning, the hands of the handsome Dresden china clock on the mantelpiece pointed to half-past eight. Sitting up in the bed, I looked about me with the puzzled feeling one always experiences on first waking in a strange place.

Then my brain cleared, and I vividly remembered all the dreadful incidents of the previous day. The horrible exposure of my most secret parts before a number of rough men, the ignominious and painful whipping, and the agonizing ride on the rail! I shuddered. Next I thought of Randolph, and of the promise I had given him. He might come to me at any moment! I felt my cheeks flush, and in a sudden, unthinking impulse, I jumped out of bed, and ran to the door to lock it. But there was no key. Then it struck me that locking the door – even if I had been able to do so – would not save me. I was in the man's power, and would have to submit to him sooner or later. So I crept back to bed again, lying trembling, and wondering whether he would do the horrid deed some time during the day, or wait till the night.

However, as it turned out, I did not meet my fate that day or night.

At nine o'clock, Dinah came in with a cup of tea for me, bringing with her a letter from Randolph, saying that he had been unexpectedly called to Richmond on urgent business which would probably detain him four or five days. He also said that he had made arrangements for my trunks to be brought to Woodlands; and he had given orders to all the servants that they were to look upon me as their mistress, and he finished the note by telling me that Dinah knew where everything was, and that she would take good care of me. Feeling very thankful for my temporary respite, I drank the tea and lay down again.

Presently, a smart young quadroon chambermaid brought in a large tin bath which she filled with water; then after laying out towels and all the other articles necessary for my toilet, she left the room. I had my bath, and while drying myself, looked at my bottom in the pier-glass, finding that the weals had gone down considerably, but they still showed in long red stripes on my skin, and were still tender to the touch. I was also still very sore between the legs, where the rail had bruised the flesh. In fact, it was a week before all the marks and bruises on my body had entirely disappeared. The tears rose to my eyes, and my heart swelled with rage and bitterness as I gazed at the traces of the shameful punishment that had been inflicted on me.

Dinah came back, helped me to dress, and also arranged my hair. Then she showed me down to a snug, well-furnished room, where I sat down – my bottom was rather tender – to breakfast, waited on by two pretty quadroon girls, who gazed at me curiously with their big, soft, black eyes, but treated me with the utmost deference.

Just as I had finished breakfast, Dinah came to inform me that my trunks had arrived; she told me also she had heard that Miss Dean and Martha were going to start that evening for Richmond on their way North.

Oh! how I wished I was going with them. Then the idea of escape flashed across my mind, and I determined to try and get away from Woodlands. If I could get to Miss Dean, she would be delighted to see me, and to know I returned to her as pure as when I left her. She would take me back with her to Philadelphia. Filled with new hope, I went up to my room, finding that Dinah had unpacked all my things and put them away in the drawers.

I was glad to be able to change my clothes, so I dressed myself in clean garments from head to foot; and then putting on my hat I went downstairs to the hall, finding Dinah standing near the open door. I told her I was going out for a walk.

'Oh! missy,' she said, 'I know what yo' is thinkin' of. Yo' wants to get away to Miss Dean. But oh, honey, yo' can't. De massa has gib strict orders to de men at de gate not to let yo' out, an' all de place is watched. Yo' can't get away nohow.'

My hopes of escape were dashed to the ground. I felt utterly miserable, and throwing myself on a seat I wept bitterly; while Dinah hovered about me, looking sympathetic, but saying nothing.

I saw at once that if I could not reach Miss Dean before she started, all chance for me was gone, for even if I managed to get away from Woodlands, I had no money, nor had I any place to go to; moreover, I had been warned by the lynchers to leave Virginia in forty-eight hours. If they caught me wandering about – which they would be sure to do – they would either whip me or ride me on a rail again, perhaps both.

The prospect was too awful to contemplate, so with a heavy heart I gave up all thought of leaving Woodlands. I would have to remain and submit to my fate when the time came.

After a few minutes I grew calmer, then Dinah, with the intention of diverting my thoughts, asked me if I would come and see the house.

I answered in the affirmative, and she showed me all over the place from the attics to the kitchen.

It was a very large mansion, beautifully furnished throughout: it had long corridors, and two flights of stairs, one at the front of the house and one at the back, and there were twenty bedrooms, each one decorated in a different style. There were several sitting-rooms and boudoirs, a spacious dining-room and an immense drawing-room; there was also a billiard table, and a large library, well filled with books of all sorts.

I had never before been in such a grand house, nor had I seen such splendid furniture – the pictures though, in some of the rooms, made me blush.

There were twenty female servants, slaves of course, living in the house. All were dressed alike in well-fitting pink print frocks, with white aprons, caps, collars and cuffs. They all wore neat well-polished shoes and white cotton stockings, and everyone of them looked trim and clean. In fact they were obliged to be always tidy and properly dressed, any slovenliness being punished. The cooks and kitchen servants were black, or mulatto women, but all the parlourmaids and housemaids were young quadroons, or octoroons, from eighteen to twenty-five years of age.

All of them were pretty, while two or three of the octoroons were really quite handsome and so light in colour that they might easily have passed as white girls anywhere except in the South. People there can at once detect the least trace of black blood in a man or woman.

Some of them had full, voluptuous-looking figures, and as none wore stays, the rounded contours of their bosoms were plainly outlined under their thin bodices. There were several children of both sexes about the place, but no male servants lived in the house.

When Dinah had shown me everything that was to be seen in the establishment, she left me, and I went out in the grounds. They were extensive and beautifully kept. There were flower gardens, fruit and kitchen gardens, shrubberies, and hot-houses, the whole place being surrounded by high iron railings, the only means of exit being the gate at the entrance to the avenue.

I wandered about listlessly, but I noticed that the men who were at work about the grounds kept a watch on my movements. I walked down to the gate, and just to see if I was really a prisoner I tried to open it, but two men instantly came out of the lodge, and one of them said civilly:

'Yo' can't go out missy. De gate is locked, by de massa's order.'

I then returned to the house, and went up to my grand bedroom, all pink and white and gold, with two large windows looking on to the gardens at the back. It was partly furnished as a sitting-room, with a comfortable sofa and easy chairs, a round table, and a large, well-fitted writing cabinet.

Drawing an easy chair to one of the windows, I sat down and had a long think. I thought what a cruel man Randolph was to have betrayed us to the lynchers and then to have taken advantage of my agony to extract the promise from me.

Oh! why had I not sufficient fortitude to bear the pain? If I had refused to accept release on the shameful terms he had offered me, I should in a few hours have been on my way to Richmond with Miss Dean.

I thought of her, and contrasted her position with mine. She was all right, except for the whipping, and in a couple of days she would be safe at home in Philadelphia, still in possession of her virgin treasure, while I would be at Woodlands, a prisoner in the hands of a man who had shown himself to be utterly unscrupulous.

And what was to become of me afterwards?

'Oh, dear! oh, dear!' I said to myself. 'How I wish I had never persuaded Miss Dean to let me come to Virginia with her!'

The morning passed, and at one o'clock Dinah came to tell me that lunch was ready. I went downstairs and managed to eat something, then I betook myself to the library where I remained for the rest of the afternoon trying to divert my thoughts by reading a novel.

At seven o'clock, I sat down to a dainty, well-cooked little dinner – a better dinner than I had ever seen, as Miss Dean always lived very plainly. The two quadroon parlourmaids, whose names were Lucy and Kate, waited on me, while Dinah, as 'Butler', overlooked them.

Dinah had the key of everything, and was entirely trusted by her master. She offered me champagne, claret, and bottled ale, but I refused them all. However I made a fair meal, as I was a healthy girl, and my appetite asserted itself in spite of the depressing nature of the position I was in at that moment. When dinner was over, I went into one of the smaller sitting-rooms, where the lamps had been lighted, the curtains drawn, and everything made snug for me. But the evening seemed very long, and I felt very lonely. I should have liked Dinah's company even, as her quaint talk would have amused me a little, but I did not think it would be quite correct for me to send for her, while she, I suppose, did not think it right to intrude upon me, so I did not see her until I went up to my room, when she came to brush my hair and help me to undress.

Chapter Eight

News arrives that the 'massa' is returning – My virginity to be sacrificed – Fears and dread – I am given a scented bath – Tortured in the tyrant's bed – The pain and horror of the 'wedding-night' – The 'lust of his eyes' – The terror of his tearing, iron-made tool.

Four days passed in the quiet way narrated in the preceding chapter. On the fifth morning of my captivity, when Dinah came in with my usual cup of tea, she informed me that she had received a letter from her master – she could read, but not write – telling her he would be home at seven o'clock to dinner, and that she was to take care it was a good one.

I sat up in bed, looking blankly at Dinah, and feeling a sinking sensation at my heart, for though I had known the fatal moment would come, I was startled at hearing that it was so close at hand.

I got up, had my bath, and dressed myself mechanically, then went downstairs; but I could not eat any breakfast, though I thirstily drank two cups of coffee. All day long, I was restless and uncomfortable, roaming about the great house with a sort of feeling that I was in a dream, and would soon wake. Sometimes I would sit down on a chair, with my mind quite blank, then, in another moment, the thought of what was going to be done to me would strike my brain with a sudden shock that sent the blood to my cheeks.

I dreaded the ordeal before me, morally as well as physically. Even a newly-wedded bride on the day of her marriage feels a little shame and fear at the thought of what her husband will do to her at night.

The afternoon wore slowly away, and at five o'clock I was sitting listlessly in my room, when Dinah came in, followed by one of the chambermaids carrying the bath. Placing it in the middle of the room she filled it with warm water, then she went away, but Dinah remained.

As I had taken my bath in the morning, I could not understand why the girl had again filled it, and with hot water too. I was not in the habit of bathing in hot water.

'I don't want a bath, Dinah,' I said.

'No, missy, I knows yo' don't, yo' is bootiful clean. But I'se had orders in de letter from de massa, to give yo' a scented bath. I must obey his orders whatever dey is, or he will whip me. Now den, honey, yo'll let me give you de bath.'

I flushed with a strong feeling of indignation. I also felt deeply humiliated. The victim was to be bathed and perfumed before the sacrifice!

However, Dinah could not help it, she had to obey orders, so I told her that she might bathe me.

She was evidently relieved, and at once began to prepare the 'scented bath'.

First, she poured some fluid from a phial into the water; she next threw in a quantity of white powder which had a delicate perfume of roses; then she stirred the water till the powder was completely dissolved. I found out afterwards that the fluid and the powder were Turkish preparations used by the ladies of the harem to impart a softness and gloss to their skins.

When everything was ready, she undressed me, then making me stand up in the bath, she sponged me all over with the warm perfumed water, at the same time praising the symmetry and plumpness of my figure and the whiteness of my skin.

When she had finished bathing me, she dried me

with soft warm towels, then rubbed me with her hands from head to foot, and with her fingers gently kneaded my titties and arms, also my bottom, thighs, and legs, until my flesh seemed to become firmer, and my skin smoother and more velvety than usual.

She then began to dress me, putting on my nicest things, and I had some pretty undergarments. She first put on me a lace-trimmed chemise with blue ribbons on the shoulders, then my finest drawers with deep lace frilling and bows of pink ribbon at the knees. Next she drew on my legs a pair of white silk stockings, fastening them above my knees with dark blue satin garters with silver buckles – these garters were produced from her pocket; I did not possess such fine ones.

Then she cased my feet in my neatest shoes, put on my nicest petticoats, and laced me tightly in my stays, and finally helped me on with my prettiest white frock. Then she brushed my hair, and arranged it most elaborately. She was delighted with my appearance and after turning me round two or three times, exclaimed:

'Oh, missy! yo' is a bootiful young lady for true. De massa will be pleased when he sees yo'.'

Dinah knew that she had bathed, perfumed, and dressed me for the sacrifice, but she did not understand what a dreadful thing it would be to me. She was not a virtuous woman herself, and her ideas, like those of most slave women, were very loose on the subject of feminine virtue.

Besides, I think she considered I was rather a lucky young lady to have attracted the notice of 'de massa', who in her eyes was a very exalted personage indeed. Now that I was dressed, she suggested that I had better go down to the drawing-room so as to be in readiness to receive the master on his return.

Accordingly I went down to the great room, which had been brilliantly lighted, and seated myself on a sofa.

I had become dully resigned to my fate, but my heart

was heavy as I waited in the gorgeous apartment for the man who was going to rob me of my virginity.

If I had had the slightest liking for him, I should not have felt the thing so much. But I did not like him. I hated him. Presently I heard the sound of wheels on the terrace, and then I heard the hall door being opened and shut. He had arrived! My heart began to flutter, though not with the pleasurable anticipation of a young girl waiting for her lover.

But he did not make his appearance, so I supposed he had gone straight to his own room to change his travelling garments. Such was the case. In a short time he came into the drawing-room, dressed in evening clothes.

I rose from my seat, and he came to me, took both my hands in his, and kissed me hotly on the lips, making me shrink and tremble. Then, holding me at arms length, he looked at me from head to foot in a critical way, as if he were appraising my charms, while I stood with flaming cheeks and downcast eyes.

'You are looking very charming, Dolly,' he said. 'The frock you are wearing becomes you, but in future you must always put on a low-necked dress for dinner.'

He already considered me his property!

'I have not got one,' I murmured, without looking up.

'Well, you shall soon have more than one,' he observed, laughing and patting me on the cheek. 'Now tell me, have you been comfortable during my absence; has Dinah taken good care of you, and have the servants been attentive?'

I did not answer the first part of his question, for though my body had been comfortable after it had recovered from the first severe effects of the punishment, my mind had been extremely uncomfortable the whole time. I replied:

'Dinah has taken very good care of me, and the

servants have been attentive.'

'So much the better for them. If they had not, I would have made all their bottoms smart, from Dinah downwards,' he observed, coolly.

His words jarred upon me. I thought he need not have said anything about the women's bottoms.

He asked two or three other questions, which I answered, and then one of the parlourmaids announced dinner, so we went into the big dining-room.

The table had been beautifully decorated with flowers and fruit; the glass, linen, and other appointments were of the finest description, and the great sideboard of old, polished mahogany glittered with massive silver plate which had been in Randolph's family for generations. It was the first time I had seen the precious metal. The dinner was of many courses, with all sorts of dishes that I had never heard of, and it was accompanied by wines whose names were also new to me.

Randolph talked away gaily, eating heartily, and drinking a bottle of champagne; but I, being nervous and depressed, hardly ate anything. I could only answer in monosyllables, and I blushed whenever I happened to catch his eye. I was constantly thinking of the dreadful thing he was going to do to me that night.

In order I suppose to cheer me up, he filled my glass with champagne and insisted on my drinking it, but the wine only went to my head and made me giddy without exhilarating me in the least. So when he saw the effect the liquor had on me, he did not give me any more.

When dinner was over and he had smoked a cigar, we went back to the drawing-room. Seating himself comfortably in an easy chair, he continued to talk, not taking any notice of my silence, or making any remark about my downcast looks.

He was in high spirits, induced I suppose, by the thought that he would soon be in possession of my virgin body.

He told me he had heard that Miss Dean had got safely home to Philadelphia, and he added with a laugh:

'I don't think the prim Quakeress will ever again take to running an "underground station". She got a real smart whipping and she will always carry the marks of it on her bottom. But you won't be marked in the least, Dolly, as your skin was not cut.'

I shuddered, and my bottom seemed to tingle as I thought of the whipping.

At ten o'clock he rose from his seat and said jocularly:

'Now, Dolly, as this is our wedding night, we'll go to bed early. Come upstairs.'

I blushed furiously and began to cry. After all, I could not resign myself quietly to my unhappy fate. I thought I had become resigned, but now that the moment had arrived, all my feelings of modesty rose in revolt against the sacrifice of my maidenhead. I made a despairing appeal to him for mercy:

'Oh! Mr Randolph,' I exclaimed, 'will you not spare me?'

His countenance grew dark, he frowned, and a hard look came into his eyes.

'Don't be a fool, Dolly,' he answered harshly, 'you gave me your promise, and I thought the whole affair was settled. Come along.'

'Oh, do not hold me to my promise!' I wailed. 'You know that when I made it I was half-mad with pain. Oh! do let me go away from your house.'

'Now listen to me,' he said, in cold, incisive tones. 'I am not going to stand any nonsense. You are completely in my power, and I don't intend to spare you, as you call it. If you do not come upstairs and submit quietly, I'll have you carried up by four of the women, and I will make them hold you down upon the bed, so that I shall be able to do what I like to you at my ease. Now, will you come quietly, or must you be carried up and held?'

My appeal for mercy had failed, and I was thoroughly frightened by his threats. To be held down by four women while the deed was being done would only add to my shame, the very idea of such a thing made me thrill with horror. Resistance would be useless. So there was nothing left for me but to submit.

'I will go quietly,' I sobbed out in a low voice, with the tears trickling down my cheeks. Oh! how wretched I felt as I said those words.

'That's right,' he said.

Then taking me by the hand he led me up to my own room.

The shaded lamps had all been lit, so the apartment was filled with a bright soft light, and I at once noticed that a large bath towel had been spread over the silken coverlet of the bed, and a nightshirt of his had been placed on one of the pillows.

He closed the door, then turning to me, said:

'I am glad you have come to your senses. I hate struggling with a woman, but I would have had my way in the end. Now continue to be sensible, and let me do whatever I like to you, without making any more remonstrances. First of all, I am going to undress you with my own hands. I like undressing a pretty girl.'

He did the work in a way that showed it was by no means the first time he had stripped a woman.

Making me stand in front of the pier-glass, he unfastened my dress, and taking it off, threw it on a chair, then he deftly unlaced my stays and removed them, thus exposing the upper part of my bosom which I endeavoured to hide by crossing my arms over it.

Next he loosed the strings of my petticoats, letting

them fall to the floor and making me step out of them, then kneeling down, he took off my shoes, after which he slipped his hands up my legs, unbuckled my garters, and pulled off my stockings. Then putting both his hands under my chemise, he untied my drawers and drew them off my legs. As his hands strayed over my body and limbs while he was thus slowly stripping me, I shivered, but offered no resistance. It would have been of no avail. He had determined to do the deed in his own way, so there would have been no use in my resisting. Nothing now remained but my chemise, and that he soon pulled off over my head, leaving me standing nude before him, and I saw my whole figure reflected in the pier-glass. I could not help uttering a little cry of shame, and I instinctively covered the 'spot' with both my hands, while my face, neck, and the upper part of my bosom became scarlet. I shut my eyes, but the tears forced their way between my closed eyelids and trickled down my cheeks.

Of course it was very horrid to be obliged to stand naked before a man, and I had a strong sense of shame, but I did not feel so horribly ashamed as at the time when my person was exposed to the lascivious eyes of the lynchers, and my ears shocked by their obscene remarks.

He turned me round and round, looking at me on every side, and holding my hands so that I could not screen any part of my body, but he did not feel me. When he had sufficiently gratified the lust of his eyes, he lifted me up in his arms, carried me to the bed, and laid me down upon it on my back. Covering the 'spot' with one hand, and with the other hiding my scarlet face, I lay trembling, while he quietly undressed himself and put on his nightshirt.

I hoped he would extinguish the lights, but he did not. Getting up on the bed beside me, he removed my hand from my face, then clasping my naked body in his arms, he kissed my lips, eyes, and cheeks, saying:

'Now my dear little girl, I've got you at last!'

It was the first time he had made use of a tender word to me that night. While stripping me, he had not spoken a word but had treated me as if I had been merely a lay figure. After kissing me, he proceeded to gratify his sense of feeling. Laying both his hands on my bosom, he played with my titties, squeezing them, tickling them, and moulding the flesh with his fingers, then bending his head, he took one of my nipples in his mouth and nibbled it with his teeth.

Uttering a startled cry, I shrank away from him, plucking my nipple out of his mouth.

'Keep still, whatever I do,' he said sharply.

Then taking my other nipple between his lips, he sucked it, and rolled his tongue over it as if it had been a bit of candy.

I forced myself to lie still, and after a moment or two he let go my nipple. He next stroked my belly and ran his hands several times over each of my thighs; then separating my legs a little, he touched the 'spot', twining his fingers in the hair and pulling it rather hard, then he inserted the tip of his forefinger between the lips, making me squirm, and quiver from head to foot – but not with pleasure – and extracting from me a stifled shriek.

'Oh! oh! don't do that!' I exclaimed. 'Oh! do take your hand away!'

'Don't be silly,' he said. 'You'll feel something else there in a minute or two.'

With a strong effort I controlled myself and lay quiet again. Turning me over onto my face, he looked at my bottom, saying: 'The marks of the whipping are not quite gone; there are still a few faint pink lines on your skin.'

Then he played with my bottom in all sorts of ways, stroking it, pinching it all over, gently spanking it, and squeezing the flesh with both his hands; finishing up by separating the cheeks and rubbing his hand up and down the division from the upper part to the cleft of my thighs.

The whole of these proceedings had been intensely repugnant to me, making me feel quite sick; moreover they were totally unexpected. When he laid me down on the bed, I thought he would at once have embraced me. I had not the slightest idea that I should first have to go through so much preliminary handling.

I afterwards discovered that Randolph was a man who always liked to spin out his pleasure as long as possible.

He now turned me onto my side and again took me in his arms, kissing my face, throat, and bosom, and inhaling the sweet odour emanating from my flesh. He was evidently pleased with the charms of his victim.

'You are a pretty little woman,' he said. 'Your figure is very good, and you are plump without being fat. Your skin is beautifully white and smooth, your flesh is firm, and you are as fresh as a rose, and as fragrant as one. I am fond of the delicate perfume of roses on a woman when I have her naked in my arms, and that is why I told Dinah to give you the bath with the Turkish powder in it.'

After toying with me a moment or two longer, he laid me on my back, saying:

'Now, Dolly, I am going to do the job. To use plain words, I am going to poke you. You will feel a little pain, but you must bear it. Every woman suffers more or less, the first time she is poked by a man; but afterwards she feels no pain at all, but only pleasure when in the arms of her lover.'

The fatal moment had come!

Closing my eyes, and covering my face with my hands, I waited for the stroke, feeling greatly frightened, very much ashamed, and intensely sorrowful.

Taking hold of my knees, he stretched my legs widely apart, then getting between them, he laid himself down upon me with his breast on my bosom, at the same time removing my hands from my face and pressing his mouth on my lips. Then with his fingers he opened the way, and immediately after, I felt the tip of his member inserted between the lips of my 'spot'. I shuddered and uttered a low cry. My martyrdom had commenced!

Clasping his arms round me with his hands under my bottom, and holding me tightly, he began to move his loins up and down, and I felt the column beginning to penetrate me.

As I was utterly ignorant of the size of the erect male organ, and as I was in a state of great fright, the weapon seemed to me to be of enormous dimensions – it really was not very big – and I thought it could not possibly be got into the sheath.

He worked away steadily, gradually forcing the implement deeper. I felt as if a wedge was being driven into me, and that I was being split. I winced under his thrusts.

The weapon, however, was driven deeper and deeper, until its further progress was checked by something inside the sheath.

My ravisher – for such in reality he was – had reached the membrane that barred the passage: my maidenhead! Increasing the vigour of his strokes, he battered at the opposing membrane. I writhed, and I squealed, but at the same time I instinctively arched my loins to aid his in his efforts to break through the barrier.

He paused for a moment to take breath, then gripping me tighter he again began the assault vigorously.

He quickened his strokes, the membrane began to yield, then suddenly it gave way and his member went right into me up to the roots, and at the same instant I felt a sharp pain which made me utter a shrill cry.

He went on working, while I, quite involuntarily, moved my bottom up and down, keeping time with his thrusts, though I had not the faintest sensation of pleasure.

His movements became quicker and quicker, I writhed with pain but still kept heaving up my bottom to meet him. He gave me two or three more furious pushes, then the gush of fluid came, and at the same moment a curious spasm seized me, and I could not help wriggling my bottom, and squirming from side to side as I felt the stuff spurting in hot jets up to my very vitals.

However, the warm thick fluid, as it flowed over the lacerated edges of the ruptured membrane, seemed slightly to assuage the pain, and when all was over, I lay in his arms panting, my naked bosom heaving, my face wet with tears, and my whole body jerking spasmodically. There was a buzzing in my ears, a mist before my eyes, and I thought I was going to faint.

After a moment or two he got off me, and giving me a kiss, said:

'There, Dolly, it's all over now. It won't hurt you so much next time.'

When I had recovered myself a little, I became aware that I was wet between the legs, and that something was trickling down my thighs. So sitting up on the bed, I looked at the 'spot', and saw that blood was oozing from it, I also noticed that the towel under me was stained with the proof of my virginity. I was dreadfully frightened, as I had no idea that there would be an effusion of blood, and my terrified imagination made me think that I had actually been split open.

'Oh! Oh! I am bleeding. What shall I do!' I exclaimed, wringing my hands and beginning to cry again.

He took me in his arms, and petted and soothed me, saying:

'That's nothing, Dolly. You needn't be alarmed.

Every woman bleeds a little the first time she is poked.'

Then getting off the bed, he brought a basin of water and a sponge, and making me again lie on my back with outstretched legs, sponged the 'spot' and my thighs until he had removed all outward traces of his bloody deed. He then told me to put on my night-gown and get between the sheets.

I did so, glad to be able at last to cover my nakedness.

After he had washed himself, he put out all the lamps, except a small one, then he got into bed beside me, but did not touch me. He seemed to be tired, and after giving me a kiss, he turned over onto his side with his back towards me, and in a short time I knew by his quiet breathing that he had gone to sleep. I heaved a sigh of relief, heartily glad that all was over – for a time at any rate. The 'spot' was sore, and the parts felt stretched; I had a curious sensation as if his stiff member was still sticking in me, and I kept as far away from him as I could in the broad bed.

At first I could not go to sleep. I was far too miser-able, and I lay crying bitterly for the loss of my virginity.

'Oh what an unfortunate girl I am! What shall I do? What shall I do?' I kept on saying to myself des-pairingly.

After a time, however, my tears ceased to flow, though I continued to sob, then a dull apathetic feel-ing came over me, I grew drowsy, and at last I sobbed myself to sleep.

Strange to say, I slept soundly, and when I woke it was broad daylight. Sitting up in bed, I looked at my ravisher who was still sleeping calmly and I wondered how he could rest so quietly after having ruined a poor defenceless girl.

I had a headache, and also a heartache, and on looking at myself in the glass on the toilet table near the bed, I saw that my face was pale, and that there were some dark patches under my eyes. I felt very wretched and forlorn, but my brain was quite clear, so I was able to review my unhappy position with a certain amount of calmness.

And it was an unhappy position without doubt. I was a ruined girl. I had no money, and I had lost my only friend, for I felt that I could never, under any circumstances, go back to Miss Dean. What then was to become of me?

I thought over everything and at last came to the conclusion that I should have to remain at Woodlands, for a time at any rate; after all, it was the only thing I could do, so I determined to try and make the best of my position as it was at the moment and to trust to chance for the future.

As I have already told you, I disliked Randolph, but as I was going to stay at Woodlands, I made up my mind to conceal my true feelings, and let him think that I was quite willing to live with him. It would be to my interest to do so.

Presently he woke, and after yawning and stretching himself, he kissed me, saying with a smile:

'Well, Dolly, how do you feel this morning? A little sore between the legs, I suppose.'

I blushed, but acting up to my resolution to make the best of things, I forced myself to smile answering lightly:

'Yes, I am rather tender, but I suppose the soreness will soon pass off.'

He kissed me again, saying:

'I'm glad to see you are taking the affair sensibly, not whining or complaining. The thing's done and can't be undone. I'll make you very comfortable at Woodlands, and it will be your own fault if you are not happy. I am an easy man to get on with, when I have my own way,' he added with a laugh.

He then played with my titties, and felt my bottom

till he was ready, then placing me in position, he rolled my nightdress up to my chin and got into me for the second time. As there was now no obstacle in the way, a very few movements of his loins were sufficient to drive the weapon up to the hilt in the sheath, and then he poked me with full force.

I suffered a good deal while the great thing was being worked up and down in the sore, raw folds of my 'spot', the pain making me grind my teeth and utter little cries, but again I was forced by nature to heave my bottom up and down to his strokes, and again when the spasm seized me, I wriggled and squirmed till I had received every drop of his offering.

I did not by any means like my second poke, but it had not been so intensely repugnant to me as the first.

Randolph sat up and looked at me as I lay on my back, breathing hard, with flushed cheeks, and moist eyes.

'It did not hurt you so very much that time, did it Dolly?' he observed.

'No'o, not-so-very-much,' I replied in a shaky voice, and feeling rather inclined to cry, for the 'spot' was smarting dreadfully.

'Oh, you'll soon get used to it, and then you'll like it,' he remarked, laughing at my woebegone face.

I thought to myself that I might get used to it, but I did not think I should ever get to like it.

Just then there was a knock at the door, and Susan, one of the chambermaids came in with tea and toast. She came to the bedside and placed the tray on a little table, her eyes resting for a moment on us as we lay side by side.

The girl's face was perfectly expressionless, but I felt ashamed that she should see me in bed with her master; my cheeks grew hot, and I did not know which way to look.

She got my bath ready and tidied the room, picking up my clothes which were all scattered about the floor, where Randolph had thrown them when he stripped me overnight.

Then she left the room, and we drank our tea, which was most refreshing to me, as I was faint and thirsty.

Randolph then got up, and taking his garments, went away to his own apartments leaving me alone to dress.

While having my bath, I examined the 'spot' finding that the inner lips were red and swollen, so I bathed them well with cold water. After completing my toilet I went downstairs, and going out to the garden, betook myself to a secluded spot where I sat down on a long cane chair under a magnolia tree.

It was a beautiful morning, the sun, though not high, was shining brightly in a cloudless sky of pale blue, the birds were twittering, a soft breeze was blowing, drops of dew were still sparkling on the gossamer festooning the bushes, and the air was filled with the sweet scent of flowers.

I felt very languid, so putting my feet upon the chair, I leant back, inhaling the fresh morning air and feeling a great sensation of relief at being alone.

After the trying time I had gone through, the calm and quiet of everything had a soothing effect upon me, and my heart seemed to grow a little less heavy.

In about half an hour's time I returned to the house, and went into the breakfast room. Randolph soon made his appearance and we sat down to the morning meal.

My appetite was not so good as usual, I felt ill at ease in the presence of the man who had taken my maidenhead, and whenever I caught his eye I could not help blushing. He, however, was quite at his ease, chatting away gaily throughout the meal; when it was over, he ordered his horse to be brought, and then went off to the plantation to make a round of inspection after his absence.

Shortly after he had gone, Dinah came into the room, and handing me a basket of keys, asked me respectfully to give her my orders for the day. I noticed that she no longer called me 'missy', but addressed me as 'missis'.

As I did not want to be bothered with the house-keeping of such a large establishment, I told Dinah to keep the keys, and to carry on the management as before.

She appeared glad to hear that she was not going to be deprived of her authority, and taking the basket of keys went away smiling. Randolph did not come back to lunch, so I had it by myself in the big dining-room, waited on by Lucy and Kate.

When I had finished, I went to the library where I spent the afternoon, reclining on a couch, reading.

I did not feel inclined to take walking exercise that day. Randolph came home later, so I did not see him till we met at dinner at seven o'clock. My appetite was returning, so I managed to partake of some of the tasty dishes, and I also drank a glass of champagne, which I liked, as it exhilarated me slightly without affecting my head.

The evening passed, and we went away upstairs to my room at eleven o'clock.

Randolph allowed me to undress myself, and while I was doing so he sat on a chair watching me. We were soon in bed, and a few moments afterwards I found myself groaning and wincing, as the dart was being forced for the third time into my still tender flesh.

And before I got up in the morning, I had twice again wriggled my bottom and squirmed in Randolph's arms.

Chapter Nine

*I learn some cunning tricks of the 'ars amandi';
loving, without loving – Randolph's amorousness –
I become a 'past-mistress' in the joyful craft of arse-
wriggling, but find withal no mental joy therein.*

Some time passed. I had settled down to my life at
Woodlands, adapting myself to my surroundings at
the time, and endeavouring not to think of the future.

A dressmaker from Richmond had paid several visits to the house, and I was well supplied with pretty
frocks of all sorts, for morning and evening wear, as
well as a quantity of fine, richly-laced undergarments,
silk stockings of all colours, and numerous pairs of
shoes. I had also a riding costume with breeches and
boots, a horse was always at my disposal, and I was
learning to ride. Randolph had also given me a lot of
jewellery, he always made me dress for dinner in a
low-necked frock, and one of the octoroons, a girl
named Rosa, had been specially appointed to act as
my maid.

Randolph was a clever man, and well read, but he
was a thorough libertine who considered women
merely toys to be used for the gratification of his
sensual desires.

Before my arrival at Woodlands, all the pretty
quadroon and octoroon slave girls had been his con-
cubines. Not that he had been in the habit of sleeping
with any one of them, but whenever he wanted a girl,
he would give her orders to be in his room at a certain
hour of the day, or night, as the case might be, and

then after he had amused himself with her for an hour or two, he would send her away.

But though he used the girls as playthings whenever he felt inclined, he had not the slightest soft feeling towards them. They were his slaves, nothing more; and whenever a girl misbehaved or offended him in any way, he would either send her to one of the overseers to be whipped, or he would inflict the punishment with his own hands.

He did not love me in the least, but he admired me, often telling me that I was a pretty girl and that I had a good figure: he was fond of seeing me naked, and posing me in various positions before the large pierglass in my room, in order that he might be able to see both the back and front of my body at the same time. He soon made me acquainted with the meaning of all the naughty words in the vocabulary of 'Love' – words that I had never heard before – and in course of time he taught me practically, all the different positions in which it is possible for a man carnally to possess and enjoy a woman, either by day, or night; in bed, or out of bed.

I was invariably submissive to all his whims; he was a masterful man, and his strong will dominated my weak one; moreover I was always rather afraid of him. In my innocence I had thought that there was only one way of administering the stroke, and, at first, I was greatly astonished at the number and variety of the positions in which he rogered me. He would 'have' me lying on my back, or on my side; also standing, kneeling, sitting, or on all fours. He would 'do it' to me from behind, while I leant over the side of the bed, or the back of a chair, or the edge of a table, and he would sometimes lie on his back and make me straddle over him on my knees with my back turned towards his face, so that he could see my bottom; then I had to fix the weapon in the sheath, and do all the work by raising myself up and down on my knees.

Sometimes he rode me when I was stark naked, or when I was half dressed, or in my chemise, stockings and shoes, or perhaps with nothing on but my drawers, and frequently after dinner he would 'have' me in full evening dress with tightly-laced stays.

On these occasions he would sit on a chair while I would stand in front of him with my back turned; and putting his hands up my clothes, he would feel me until he was properly excited. He would then unbutton his trousers, letting out his member in full erection, with the red tip uncovered ready for action. I had then to pull open the slit of my drawers myself, hold my petticoats above my waist; and lower myself down upon the dart until it was into me as far as it could go, and my bottom rested on his thighs.

In that position he would possess me. He used to say that a woman should never be 'had' twice in succession the same way, and he told me that if a man always poked a woman in the same position, he would get tired of her sooner than if he varied the embraces.

After my shame had worn off, and I had got used to being stroked in this way, I discovered that there was a strain of voluptuousness in my disposition, and although I never liked Randolph, I was not averse to his embraces, so I always let him do what he liked to me by day or night, without murmuring; and he often told me: 'I was a very good mount.' Randolph was a man who always called 'a spade a spade'.

I don't think that after my arrival in the house he had much to do with the slave girls; anyhow he always slept with me, and it was rarely that a night passed without his poking me once at least.

I should have been better pleased had he let me more alone at night, for I was a sound sleeper, and I hated being woke up to be pulled about in all sorts of ways, and then poked in some uncomfortable position. I had gradually got accustomed to him, and called him by his first name, George, and though he was often very ill-tempered, and sometimes spoke extremely harshly to me, he never laid his hand upon me in anger during the whole time I lived with him.

Randolph was one of the richest planters in Virginia, and his family was one of the oldest, but I soon found out that he was not, so to speak, in 'society'. His character as a libertine was well-known throughout the State, consequently no ladies ever came to the house. But he often gave dinner parties, at which I always took my place at the table opposite him.

On these occasions, all the young women in the house, chambermaids as well as parlourmaids, were very smartly dressed in well-fitting black frocks, with white caps and aprons, and it often happened that three, four or even more of the gentlemen, who had come from a distance, would remain in the house all night.

These parties wound up regularly with high card play, during which a good deal of liquor was drunk, and the house became a regular 'Liberty Hall', as Randolph allowed his guests to do whatever they liked. I always went to bed as soon as the gambling began.

If a guest took a fancy to any particular girl he had seen about the place, all he had to do was to inform Randolph, who would at once send for the damsel. The gentleman would then take her up to a bedroom and poke her, returning afterwards to the card-room. And every guest who stayed in the house for the night could take a woman to bed with him if he felt inclined to do so. However, I was never treated but with respect by the men – to my face at any rate – for Randolph having chosen to put me at the head of his table, always insisted on his friends behaving as if I had really been the lady of the house, and as he was known to be a dead shot with a pistol, and always ready to use it, not one of the gentlemen who visited Woodlands ever attempted to take a liberty with me, nor did one ever speak to me in an improper manner.

Chapter Ten

The slaves get to know me – Voluptuous effects of flagellation – My maid, Rosa, is whipped for impertinence – Description of her bottom and legs – Randolph's opinions on the right of raping coloured women – Randolph puts me on the sofa and does the 'usual thing'.

The weeks slipped away. My health continued good, my spirits had revived and I was not unhappy. I had plenty of books to read, I rode nearly every day, sometimes alone, sometimes with Randolph, and he also often took me for a long drive in the buggy.

We occasionally spent a few days in Richmond, staying at the best hotel, and going every night to the theatre, or some other place of amusement. Before that time, I had never been in a theatre, so I enjoyed the performances immensely, and wished very much that I could go on the stage. I told Randolph so one day, but he only laughed, telling me that I was 'a little goose', and that I had not enough 'go' in me to make an actress.

At Woodlands I often amused myself by roaming about the plantation, which was a very extensive one, with upwards of two hundred field hands, male and female, all of whom were engaged in cultivating the cotton. Randolph fed his slaves well and did not overwork them, but otherwise he was a hard master; and his four overseers had orders never to pass over a fault, or allow the least shirking of work, consequently the strap, switch, and paddle were constantly being used on the plantation, both to men and women.

The slaves' quarters were divided into three blocks of 'cabins' – as they were called – one block was for the married couples, another for the single men, and the third for the unmarried women and girls. But as soon as work was over for the day, all the slaves of both sexes met together round a fire, where they spent most of the night, dancing, singing, and playing the banjo, and as a matter of course there was a great deal of poking. However, no notice was taken of what they did with themselves at night, so long as they were present next morning, when the roll was called by the overseers, before the gangs were marched off to work.

The slaves soon got to know me well, and as I took an interest in them, and was often able to do them little kindnesses, they all became fond of me. I liked the poor good-natured creatures who were always lighthearted, except when they happened to be smarting from a whipping.

Although I had often seen the marks of the lash on the bodies of the runaways who had passed through our station, I had hitherto never seen a slave whipped. Dinah, in her capacity as housekeeper, maintained strict discipline, so she often brought one of the women or girls before Randolph for neglecting her work or some other offence, and he sometimes himself gave the offender a whipping on her bottom with the switch. I had occasionally heard the squeaks of a culprit, but I had always avoided being present at the punishment.

Whipping a girl seemed to have an exciting effect on Randolph, for, after switching one, he used invariably to come to me, wherever I happened to be, and poke me with great vigour.

I thought it strange at the time, but I have since found out that men's passions are inflamed by whipping the bottom of a female till she cries and writhes with pain, and if they can't do it themselves, they like seeing it done. This is a curious, but undoubted fact, and it shows what cruel creatures you men are.

I have already mentioned that an octoroon girl named Rosa had been appointed to act as my maid. This girl had formerly been Randolph's favourite, but since my arrival at Woodlands he had had nothing to do with her.

When Rosa found that she was entirely neglected, and obliged to serve as my maid, she had been filled with resentment. In fact the girl was bitterly jealous; she had shown her vexation from the first, by constant sullenness, and at times she was very impertinent to me. But I had borne with her ill-temper, and had always been kind to her, trying to make her like me, as I pitied her and all the other slave girls. However, nothing that I could do had any effect in softening the girl; she continued to be sulky and disrespectful, though I had managed to make all the other women and girls fond of me.

I knew that if I reported her to Randolph he would have her punished, but as I did not wish to get her into trouble I did not say a word. Rosa was twenty years of age, a tall, handsome girl, and as she was an octoroon, she was not darker than an ordinary brunette; her complexion being a clear olive, with a tinge of pink showing on her cheeks. She had a well-rounded figure, with a full bust and broad hips; her feet were small, and her hands were smooth, as she had never done any hard work. She had a profusion of long wavy, dark brown hair; her eyes were also brown, large, and soft; she had white, regular teeth, and full, red, moist lips. Her voice was low and musical, but she was perfectly uneducated, not being able to either read or write, and she spoke in the usual slave fashion.

One morning, when she was assisting me to dress

she appeared to be in a worse temper than usual, and while brushing my hair, she pulled it so roughly that I several times had to tell her to be more careful. I spoke gently, but my remonstrances only seemed to irritate her. Tossing her head, and giving my hair a nasty pull, she said in a most saucy way:

'I oughtened to be brushing yo' hair at all. Becos, you is white, yo' tinks yo' is a very fine lady; but yo' is not a bit better dan me. Yo' isn't married to de massa, yet yo' sleeps wid him ebery night.'

I flushed with anger, and rising from my seat, ordered the girl to leave the room. She did so, laughing.

The tears came into my eyes, my heart swelled, and I felt a deep sense of degradation. It was hard that owing to a series of misfortunes, I should have come to be spoken to in such a coarse way by a slave girl. But, alas! what she had said was the truth. I really was no better than her.

After a moment or two, I put up my hair, finished dressing, and went down to breakfast. I had not intended to say anything to Randolph, but he noticed that I was put out, and asked me what was the matter.

'Oh, nothing much,' I replied, 'Rosa has been a little impertinent to me.'

Not being satisfied with my answer, he insisted on knowing what the girl had said to me.

So I told him what had occurred, adding that she had always been more or less impertinent to me, and I suggested that if he spoke to her, she would probably be more respectful in future.

'I will speak to her presently,' he said. Then he went on quietly with his breakfast.

I thought no more about the affair, and when the meal was over we left the room, and went into an adjoining apartment, where I amused myself reading the newspaper, while Randolph smoked his cigar. When he had finished, he rang the bell, which was answered by one of the parlourmaids, named Jane.

'Go and tell Dinah and Rosa I want them here, and come back yourself,' he said to the girl.

She went away, returning in about five minutes accompanied by the two other women. Randolph rose from his seat with a stern expression on his face, and turning to Rosa, who was looking rather frightened, said angrily:

'You young hussy! I have been hearing about your conduct. How dare you speak to your mistress in the way you have done? Did you think I would let you insult a white lady? You are getting too saucy, but I will take the sauce out of you. I am going to whip you.'

Rosa turned as pale as her olive complexion would allow, a frightened expression came into her eyes, and she burst into tears.

'Oh! massa!' she exclaimed. 'Don't whip me! Oh! please don't whip me! I'se very sorry I was sassy to de missis. Oh! do let me off an' I will be a good gal and never be sassy again.' Then turning to me, she said imploringly: 'Oh! missis, forgib me, an' ask de massa not to whip me dis time.'

I did not wish the girl to be whipped, so I asked Randolph to let her go away, saying that I was sure she was sorry for what she had said, and I did not think she would offend again.

But her master was very angry with her, and would not consent to let her off, although I begged him hard to do so.

Turning to Dinah, he said curtly:

'Take her up.'

I had no idea what was meant by the words, but Dinah knew what to do. She had often 'taken up' naughty slave girls on her broad, strong back. Going up to Rosa, she seized her by the wrists, and turning round, drew the girl's arms over her shoulders; then bending well forward, she raised the culprit's feet off the floor, so that her body was brought into a curved position.

Not wishing to see the punishment inflicted, I walked towards the door, but Randolph peremptorily ordered me to remain in the room.

'Turn up her clothes, Jane, and mind you hold them well out of the way,' he said.

Jane went to the right side of the delinquent, and rolling up her skirt, petticoats, and chemise, held them high above her waist.

The girl's underlinen was perfectly clean, but she wore no drawers – none of the slave women possessed drawers.

She had a fine, big, well-shaped bottom, and owing to the curved position in which she was being held, the large, plump, round cheeks swelled out in high relief at a most convenient angle for receiving the switch. Her olive-tinted skin was perfectly smooth, her thighs were large and well-rounded, her legs were shapely and her ankles were trim. She was wearing tightly fitting white stockings, gartered with bows of blue ribbon and she had on neat shoes. Randolph went to a cabinet from which he took out a hickory switch – he kept a switch in nearly every room – then placing himself at the left side of the culprit, said:

'Now, I'll teach you to respect your mistress. I have not whipped you for some time, but I'm going to make your bottom smart now.'

Rosa had not struggled or uttered a word while she was being 'taken up' and prepared for the switch, but now she turned her head, looking at Randolph, with a dog-like expression of appeal in her great, brown eyes, and said beseechingly, while the tears ran down her cheeks:

'Oh massa, don't whip poor Rosa hard.'

He began to flog her, laying on the strokes smartly, and as calmly as if he were merely beating a dog. The girl winced, drawing in the cheeks of her bottom with a jerk each time the switch fell; weals rose on her skin, her plump flesh quivered, and she kicked up her feet, squealing shrilly and exclaiming in gasps:

'Oh, massa! – Oh, massa! – Don't, oh! whip – me – so – hard! Oh! massa! Oh! – good massa please – don't whip – me – so – hard! Oh! Oh! Stop massa! Oh! please – please – stop. My bottom – is – so – sore! – Oh! Oh!'

The switch continued to stripe her writhing bottom, extracting loud cries from her, making her struggle and plunge violently, but Dinah, slightly separating her legs and bending well forward, easily held the shrieking girl in position. Randolph whipped away steadily; Jane held up the girl's petticoats and Dinah gripped her wrists tightly, while Rosa, squealing and twisting herself about, drew up her legs one after the other, then kicked them out in all directions, and in her contortions opened her thighs so that I could see the curly dark brown hair shading the 'spot' and every now and then I caught a glimpse of the pink orifice.

Then throwing down the switch Randolph said:
'Let her go.'

Jane let the sufferer's petticoats fall, and Dinah released her wrists. She then stood on her feet, twisting her hips and wailing with pain, while she wiped the fast-flowing tears from her eyes with her apron.

'There, Rosa,' said Randolph, 'I have let you off rather easily this time, but don't let me ever again hear that you have been saucy to your mistress. Now you can all go back to your work.'

Rosa, still wailing, slunk out of the room with her hand pressed to her smarting bottom; the other two women followed, and Randolph and I were left alone.

He put away the switch, then turning to me, said:
'I don't think she'll give you any more trouble, but if she does let me know.'

'Oh, George!' I said. 'How could you bring

yourself to whip the girl so severely? She is a pretty creature and I know you have often "had" her.'

He laughed.

'Yes. I have often "had" her and will "have" her again if ever I feel inclined to do so, and I will also whip her whenever she requires punishment. You are a Northern girl, so you don't understand how we Southerners look upon our slave women. When they take our fancy we amuse ourselves with them, but we feel no compunction in whipping them whenever they misbehave. Their bodies belong to us, so we can use them in any way we please. Personally I have no more regard for my slaves than for my dogs and horses.'

Though I had got to know Randolph pretty well by that time, I felt rather shocked by his unfeeling sentiments; however, I made no remark. He was standing in front of me, and I noticed that there was a protuberance in a certain part of his trousers. I guessed what was coming!

He went:

'You know, Dolly, that whipping a girl always excites me, so I am going to "have" you.'

Then laying me on the couch, he pulled up my petticoats, took down my drawers, and entered me with more than usual vigour. Whipping Rosa's bottom had certainly acted on him as a powerful aphrodisiac.

When all was over, and I had fastened up my drawers, we went to our respective rooms, and made ourselves tidy. Then he ordered the buggy, and we went for a long drive in the country, lunching at a farm house, and not returning home until it was time to dress for dinner.

When I got to my room I found Rosa there, as usual, waiting to assist me in making my toilet. She was looking very subdued, and her manner was humble and submissive. She had received a severe whipping, and her bottom must have been very sore. I felt for her, knowing as I did, how dreadfully the switch could sting.

'I am sorry for you Rosa,' I said. 'Did the whipping hurt you very much?'

'Oh! yes, missis,' she answered, giving a little shudder at the remembrance, 'it did hurt me most drefful. De massa never gib me such a hard whippin' before. Dinah has rubbed my bottom wid possum fat, an' dat has taken de sting out of de weals some, but I'se very sore, an' I can't sit down easy.'

She helped me to dress, seeming very anxious to please me in every way, and always speaking most respectfully. From that day she was a changed girl, so far as regarded her behaviour to me, and I never had occasion to find fault with her during the rest of my stay at Woodlands.

Chapter Eleven

A Rabelaisian banquet of nude damsels – A shocking orgie – Ten naked waitresses and their bashfulness – Hot viands and bottom-spanking escapades – Original racing in the corridors, and the inevitable sequel.

Three months passed, during which period I went through some varied experiences, and saw some curious sights, but if I were to relate everything that occurred, my story would be too long.

However, I will describe one or two of the incidents, just to give you an idea of the sort of man Randolph was.

I have already mentioned the dinner-parties he frequently gave to his male friends, and I have told you that these gatherings were always of a very free and easy sort.

At one of these dinners the proceedings were of a more licentious character than usual. Randolph had invited ten guests, which was the usual number – the parties, including our two selves, never exceeding twelve.

He was very particular on these occasions that all the girls should be nicely dressed, so Dinah used to parade them for my inspection just before the guests arrived. I merely had to see that the girls should be nicely attired outwardly, but Dinah before bringing them to me, had to see that each girl was clean in person, and that she had on fresh underlinen.

On the day of which I am speaking, after my own toilet had been made, I went down to the hall and inspected the girls, finding them all looking clean and smart.

Then I went into the drawing-room where Randolph was lounging on a chair turning over the leaves of a large illustrated book of Rabelais, which he was very fond of reading.

I told him I had seen the girls, and that they were all looking very nice in their black frocks. To my astonishment, he burst out laughing, and said:

'Oh, they won't wear frocks this evening. I have got such a splendid idea from a picture in this old book. I wonder it never struck me before.'

'What is it?' I asked.

'I have just been reading the chapter which tells how Pantagruel and his companions were entertained at a banquet by the Papimanes, and were waited on by a bevy of nude damsels. The dinner tonight shall be a reproduction of the scene described. There are ten men coming, and each man shall be waited on by a naked girl. It will be great fun, and also quite a novel entertainment for my guests.'

Although I was accustomed to his vagaries, this new freak horrified me. I should have to sit at the table with ten men, while the same number of women displayed their naked bodies.

The idea was most repugnant and I blushed, a thing I had not done for many a day.

'Oh George!' I exclaimed, 'don't do such a thing. It is too shameful.'

'Yes, I will,' he said, laughing heartily. 'Why Dolly, you are actually blushing! I thought you had got over all your squeamishness by this time.'

'Oh, but this is a particularly horrid idea,' I observed. 'And if you are determined to carry it out, don't make me come to table. Just fancy what a dreadful position it would be for me to have to sit among a lot of men, surrounded by naked women. I should not know which way to turn my eyes!'

He again laughed, but there was in his pupils a stern gleam which I had got to know, meaning that he had determined to have his way.

'It does not matter which way you look,' he said. 'You are looking very pretty and that's sufficient. You will have to take your place at table as usual, and you must appear to be quite unconscious that the women are naked. None of my guests will insult you by word or glance.'

I still remonstrated, but he sternly told me to shut up, or it would be the worse for me. I held my tongue, for I was afraid of him, knowing him to be a man who would stick at nothing, and it struck me that if I made any more objections he might take it into his head to whip *me*.

Sending for Dinah, he told her what he intended to do, and gave her orders to have ten of the young women stripped naked in readiness. He named the ones he wanted, selecting those who had the best figures. Seven of them were quadroons, the other three were octoroons, one of them being Rosa. Dinah received the order, and also some further instructions he gave her, with a perfectly unmoved countenance.

'All right, sah,' she said. 'De gals shall be ready.'

She then left the room.

It was nearly seven o'clock, and the guests began to arrive. Some came on horseback, others in buggies, and in a short time the whole party had assembled. All the gentlemen were more or less known to me, and everyone on entering the room shook hands with me in a most polite manner. They were of all ages, the youngest being about twenty-five years of age, while the oldest was upwards of fifty. Most of them were bachelors, but I knew that some of them were married men.

Presently Dinah, looking very smart in her black frock and white cap, made her appearance with a tray of cocktails, and while the guests were imbibing them, Randolph said with a smile on his face:

'I suppose, gentlemen, that most of you have read Rabelais. Those who have perused the book will remember the description of the banquet given to Pantagruel in the island of Papimany. I intend our dinner tonight to be, as nearly as possible, a counterpart of that celebrated banquet. I think I can give you as good fare and as good wine as Homenas gave Pantagruel and his companions. I also think that the "she-butlers" will please you. They may not be so fair-skinned as were the damsels of Papimany, but in all other respects you will find that the "waitresses" will answer the description of the ones mentioned in the book. They are "tight lasses", good-conditioned; comely, waggish, and fit for business.'

The men who had perused Rabelais and knew what was coming, laughed and clapped their hands, but the men who had not read the book looked puzzled. However, knowing Randolph's little ways, they guessed that something funny was going to happen. In a short time, dinner was announced, and then the oldest of the guests, a gentleman named Harrington, who I knew had grown-up daughters, offered me his arm and led me into the brilliantly lighted diningroom. The other men followed, and we took our places at the table, which was beautifully decorated with flowers, and glittering with plate and glass.

Randolph took his place at one end of the table; I faced him at the other end, and five of the guests sat on each side.

When everyone was comfortably settled, Randolph touched a small handbell beside him, and then the door at the far end of the room was opened. Dinah came in, followed by the ten naked young women with their long black, or dark brown hair flowing loose on their shoulders; each girl, without hesitation, taking up her position behind one of the guests. Dinah had told each waitress where she was to go. They all, without exception, showed signs of bashfulness, for although every one of them had passed through the hands of gentlemen on various occasions, singly in a bedroom, they had never been exposed stark naked before the eyes of a number of people. Some of the girls blushed, the colour showing plainly on their olive cheeks; others cast down their eyes and fidgeted as they stood, while all of them placed their hands over the 'spot' between their legs.

I felt horribly uncomfortable, hot thrills passed over me, and my cheeks grew scarlet. The men smiled, casting amused glances at one another, then they looked with gleaming eyes at the naked girls. Some were slim, and some plump; some tall, some of medium size, and some short; but all of them were pretty and had shapely figures, with firm, round titties and good bottoms, while the brilliant light, shining on their naked bodies, made their smooth, olive-tinted, and in some cases, nearly white skins, glisten. The hair covering the 'spots' was, in all cases, black or dark brown, and one of the quadroons, a plump little girl, nineteen years of age, named Fanny, who had been whipped a couple of days before, still bore on her bottom the pink stripes left by the switch. Rosa was the prettiest of all the girls; she had also the best figure, and she was the lightest in colour; consequently she attracted the most admiration. The dinner was soon in full progress; the girls, directed by Dinah, bustled about bringing in the dishes, changing the plates, and filling the glasses with champagne. Some of them, not being accustomed to waiting at table, were rather awkward, but whenever a girl made a mistake she received from Randolph the next time she came within reach of his arm, a sounding slap on the bottom which made her jump and squeal, and clap her hand to the place.

But no one took the least notice of these little occurrences, the gentlemen continuing to talk and laugh as unconcernedly as if they were quite accustomed to being waited on by naked women, and also to seeing them smacked whenever they made a mistake. But it was a most trying time for me. I sat with my eyes fixed on my plate, and with a very red face, making a pretence of eating, and hardly listening to the conversation of Mr Harrington, the old gentleman who had taken me into dinner, and who was sitting on my right. He chattered away to me, but I noticed that he kept leering lecherously at Rosa's full bosom and broad bottom, as she tripped gracefully here and there. She had evidently taken his fancy more than any of the other girls, and I felt sure that later on, my pretty maid would be poked by the old satyr. The dinner was a long one, but at last it was over, and the gentlemen settled down to smoke their cigars and sip their coffee, while the conversation turned upon slaves, and the price of cotton.

No improper remarks of any sort were made by the men, but their eyes were frequently turned with lustful looks on the naked girls standing in various attitudes about the room.

When the cigars had been smoked, we all went into the drawing-room, the girls being told to follow. I tried to slip away, but Randolph ordered me to remain. He told his guests to sit down on a row of chairs at the end of the room, and when they had done so, he posed the naked girls in groups in various positions with their arms round each other, some standing, some kneeling, and some lying on their sides at full length, so that their figures could be seen both back and front. These *poses plastiques* greatly pleased the spectators, and they gloated over each lascivious tableau, applauding vigorously; while the girls, utterly astonished at what they were being made to do, gazed timidly at the men with their big, ox-like eyes. At last, Randolph exhausted his ingenuity in inventing fresh tableaux, and I thought he would at least let the girls put on their clothes. But he did not. He had not yet done with their naked bodies.

'Now gentlemen,' he said, 'if you will go into the corridor I will let you see young mares' races. Some of them are rather fat, but I dare say I shall be able to make them show their best paces.'

The men, laughing boisterously, trooped out of the room and stationed themselves at intervals on each side of the long, broad corridor. The races were to be run in heats, the course being from one end of the corridor to the other and back, twice over. Before starting the girls, Randolph got a long heavy whip, and cracking it in the air, warned them that they had better run as fast as they could. Then as soon as the first lot was off, he took up his position at one side of the corridor half-way down, and as the runners dashed past him in the several heats, he flicked the bottom of any girl who appeared not to be exerting herself, the touch of the whip extracting a shrill cry from the victim, and making her increase her speed, while a red mark instantly showed on her skin where the end of the lash had fallen.

The men grew excited, they laughed, cheered and betted on the girls as they raced up and down the corridor, their long hair flowing loose behind them, their titties undulating and their bottoms swaying.

The final heat was won by a tall, slender octoroon girl, twenty-one years of age, named Jenny.

After the runners had a rest, there was what Randolph called a 'jockey race'. The five strongest girls had to take on their backs the other five girls, who held on by putting their arms round the necks, and their legs round the loins, of their respective 'mounts'.

This time the course was once up and down the corridor, and heavy bets were laid by the men on the women they fancied.

The signal to start was given, and the race began, the gentlemen whooping and shouting as they watched the extraordinary sight. Five naked women staggering along the corridor as fast as they could, each woman carrying on her back another naked female!

The muscles of the thighs and bottoms of the carriers quivered under the strain, while the legs of the riders, being stretched apart by the position in which they clung to their steeds, the cheeks of their bottoms were slightly separated, so that the spectators could see the hair in the cleft of the thighs. And nearly every one of the bottoms was marked either with the prints of Randolph's fingers, or with the red dot made by the flick of the whip. Two of the girls had both finger-marks and whip-marks, and when all was over only three girls out of the ten had spotless posteriors.

The men's eyes gleamed, their faces were flushed, and I could see that they were all in a state of great sensual excitement. After a close struggle, the race was won by a sturdy young quadroon woman, twenty-five years of age, named Eliza, who had carried the youngest of all the girls, a slightly-built, shapely octoroon named Helen, who was only eighteen years old.

Then we went back to the drawing-room, the girls being allowed to sit down, and Randolph told Dinah to give each of them a glass of wine and water. They were all very thirsty, some of them had tears in their eyes, and one or two were rubbing their bottoms, while the girls who had been carriers were panting for breath; their bosoms heaving tumultuously, and their naked bodies moist with perspiration. As soon as they had recovered their breath, the ten were made to stand in a row with their hands by their sides. Then Randolph said:

'Now, gentlemen, will you each choose a girl, either

for a short time, or for the whole night? You can please yourselves.'

The men laughing and joking, began to make their selections, and in cases where two or three wanted the same girl, the matter was settled by tossing up a coin.

Rosa was the favourite, five of the men, including Mr Harrington, wanting to have her, but finally the old gentleman, as the senior member of the party, was allowed to take her. The selections being made, each man, followed submissively by the naked girl he had chosen, left the apartment and went upstairs to a bedroom.

Randolph and I were left alone.

He had been very much pleased with his evening's amusement.

'Oh Dolly,' he said laughing, 'what fun it has been! I've never had such a game before. I'll do it again some day or other and when I do, every woman in the house shall strip for the races.'

I did not feel at all mirthfully inclined. I had been wretched and uncomfortable throughout the whole proceedings, moreover the sight of so many bare bottoms, naked bosoms, and uncovered 'spots', had given me a feeling of disgust. A woman is not excited by seeing the nakedness of other women. At any rate I never am.

'I think it was all very horrid and shameful,' I observed.

'I don't care what you think,' he replied. 'It pleased me, and amused my guests, and that's all I care about. But it has been very exciting work, I am feeling very randy, and my tool is aching from its prolonged erection, so I must take the stiffness out of it at once. I will "have" you sitting down, so as not to crumple your pretty frock.'

So saying, he seated himself on a chair and let loose his member, which stood straight up with its red tip uncovered.

'Come along now, Dolly, you know what to do,' he said impatiently.

I did know what to do. Turning my back to him, I raised my petticoats above my waist, and pulled open the slit of my drawers as widely as possible, exposing the whole of my bottom; then straddling over his thighs, with a leg on each side of him, I lowered myself down upon his upstanding member, which he guided between my thighs into its place, and the weight of my body forced the weapon up to the hilt in the sheath.

He clasped me round the waist under my clothes, while I, raising myself up and down on my toes, did all the work until the spasm seized me, and I felt the hot torrent inundating my inside. Then I lay back panting against his breast. As soon as I had received all he had to give me at the moment, I got off his lap, pulled my drawers into their place, and shook my petticoats straight, as some of the men might be coming back at any moment. As it was, we got done only just in time, for we had hardly sat down before one of the gentlemen made his appearance, and he was followed at intervals by others, until at last all had re-assembled except three, who had elected to stay all night with their girls. The other lasses, after being poked, had been allowed to go away to their own part of the house. Dinah brought in a tray of liquors and the men refreshed themselves. Then they all sat down to play cards, and I slipped out of the room and went to bed, glad to get away from the men, although not one of them had said an improper word to me during the evening.

It was very late, or to speak more correctly, it was early in the morning, when Randolph came to bed. I was fast asleep, but he soon woke me up by pinching my bottom, and then in a moment or two he was working away at me. As I was very tired and sleepy, I did not respond to his movements in the least, so when he had finished, he said crossly:

'Damn it, Dolly, you lay just like a log of wood. You did not even move your bottom at the finish. What's the matter with you?'

I said that there was nothing the matter with me only that I was sleepy. He growled out something uncomplimentary, then turning his back to me, went to sleep, and I speedily did the same.

Chapter Twelve

Mr Harrington's copulative capabilities – Randolph goes to Charleston on shipping business – I am left in charge with instructions to whip and spare not – I witness more whipping scenes – How the overseers lashed delinquent women – How differently women bear punishment – Description of the bottom in the Quadroon and Mulatto female.

We got up late next morning, and after he had gone to his dressing-room, Rosa came to help me as usual. While she was brushing my hair, I asked her how she had got on with Mr Harrington during the hour she had spent with him the previous night.

She looked at me with a comical expression on her pretty face.

'Oh, missis,' she replied, giggling, 'I tell yo' all 'bout it. De ole gentleman was no good at all. He couldn't do nuffin to me. He try, an' he try, an' he try. He feel me all over, he play with me with his finger, an' dat did make me squirm, an' he make me rub him, but it was all no use, his ting would not get stiff enough to go into de place. Den he lay me on my face, an' say I got very fine bottom, an' he asked me if de massa often whip it. I tole him dat de massa sometimes whip it. He laugh, den he gave me a little spankin', an' afterwards he gib me two dollars, an' say dat I was a pretty wench, an' dat he would buy me if de massa would sell me.' I smiled, and Rosa went on: 'But, oh, missis, ask de massa not to sell me to de genterman. I'se fond ob yo' now, an' I don't want to leave de ole plantation. I was born on it.'

I told her that I was sure her master would not sell such a pretty girl as she was to anyone. She seemed pleased at what I said, and went away with a smile on her face.

I went down to the breakfast-room, where I found Randolph, and in a short time the three gentlemen who had stayed in the house all night came into the room.

They greeted me politely, without the least sign of embarrassment, but I felt rather uncomfortable when I met their eyes. The cook had sent up an excellent breakfast, to which we all did justice. The three girls who waited looked fresh and clean, for though they had taken part in the races, and had been poked, they were not the three who had been kept at work all night.

When breakfast was over, and cigars had been smoked, the buggies were brought round to the terrace; the gentlemen bade me goodbye, and smilingly thanked their host for the pleasant night's entertainment he had given them. Then they drove away to their respective homes; Randolph went off to look round the plantation, while I betook myself to the library and amused myself with a novel.

A few days after the 'races', Randolph found that he would have to go to Charleston on some business connected with the shipping of his cotton. So Dinah was told to pack her master's portmanteau with things for an absence of ten days. On the morning he left Woodlands, he spoke to me about the slaves, telling me that I was on no account to interfere with the overseers in their management of the field-hands, but he gave me full authority over all the women and children in the house. And he said that if any of them misbehaved, I could, with Dinah's assistance, whip the offender myself, or send her to the overseers to receive the whipping. In the latter case, I was to send a note to the man specifying the instrument of punishment that was to be used, whether strap, switch, or paddle, and also stating the number of strokes the culprit was to receive.

I told him I would look after the women, but I said to myself that I would neither whip them with my own hands, nor send one to be whipped, under any circumstances. The idea of grown-up women being whipped was intensely repugnant to me, and is still, but I think that children of both sexes require an occasional spanking. Randolph went away, and I was glad to be temporarily my own mistress. It was pleasant to be able to come and go as I pleased, and not to be at the beck and call of a master; for such Randolph was to all intents and purposes, and as I have before told you, I was always more or less afraid of him.

The days passed quietly. Dinah was most attentive to me, and I had no trouble with any of the women. I read a good deal, and nearly every afternoon I took a long canter in the country on the quiet old horse Randolph had given me. I had learnt to ride pretty well, but I was always rather nervous when I was on horseback. I also often walked about the plantation, watching the field-hands at work under the supervision of the overseers, each of whom carried a whip. It was the cotton-picking season, the picking being done entirely by women. Every one had to pick a certain quantity each day, and at the hour when work ceased, each picker carried her basket of cotton to the weighing-shed, where one of the overseers was in waiting to check the day's work.

Each woman's basket was weighed to find out if it contained the right quantity, and if it did not turn the scale, the woman who brought the basket was whipped there and then, receiving twelve strokes. No excuse was ever taken, and the punishment was always inflicted with the strap, which gave great pain, but did not cut or injure the skin. I once heard an overseer say that he could whip a slave wench's bottom with the strap for half-an-hour without drawing a drop of blood, and her skin at the end of the time would be as smooth as a peeled onion. There were seventy female field-hands employed in the cotton-picking, and nearly every evening one or two, and sometimes three or four of the women, would be punished for not bringing in proper weight. I will give you a description of what I once saw, and you must remember that it was almost a daily occurrence, not only on Randolph's plantation, but on most, if not all, of the other plantations in the South.

I have often heard people – not Southerners – defend slavery and say that it was a fine institution, but those people had never seen what slavery really was. To this day the thought of slavery makes me indignant. But to proceed.

One evening, I was returning from a stroll, and happened to be passing near the weighing-shed, just at the hour when work ceased for the day, and the women were bringing their baskets of cotton to be weighed. I stopped to watch the scene, and, as there was a hedge between the shed and the path where I was standing, no one saw me, though I could see through the leafy screen. I knew the rules of the plantation, and as I looked at the women, I hoped for their own sakes that they had all picked their proper weight of cotton. They were of all ages, from eighteen up to forty. Some were married, but most of them were single, and of various shades, the majority being black, but there were many mulattoes and also several quadroons. All of them were strong, healthy-looking women, dressed in cotton gowns of divers colours; their heads, as a rule, being covered with brightly-coloured handkerchiefs, but some of the younger and lighter-skinned women wore linen sun-bonnets or wide-brimmed straw hats, while every one had on shoes and stockings. They came along the path carrying their baskets on their heads, chatting and laughing as if they had not a care in the world, but I noticed that a few of them were looking rather grave, and I thought to myself that they had probably been idling, and were not quite sure that they had picked the full weight. The overseer, with a notebook in his hand, and attended by four field-hands, stood in front of the shed, near a large pair of scales. The women came up one by one, each handing her basket to be weighed by the men. If the weight was correct, the overseer ticked off the woman's name in his book, and she went away to her cabin, free to do what she liked till next morning, but if a woman's basket proved to be of short weight, the overseer put a mark against her name and told her to remain. The weighing was quickly done, so in a short time all the women had gone, except six poor things whose baskets had been found to be light. They knew what they were going to get, and stood in a row, all of them looking doleful, while three of them were also whimpering.

If I had possessed any authority on the plantation, I would have saved the women from the lash, but I had none. If I had showed myself to the overseer at that moment and asked him to let the culprits off the regulated punishment, he would have laughed at me. I knew all the delinquents; three of them being black women, two mulattoes, and one was a quadroon.

The overseer did not make a single remark to them, nor did they attempt to excuse themselves – they knew that no excuse would have saved them. Turning to the woman whose name was first on the list, he said sharply: 'Lie down.' The woman, without hesitation, extended herself upon the ground. Two of the men then knelt down and held her arms stretched out at full length, while the other two men, also kneeling, grasped her legs by the ankles. She was a big, very stout coal-black woman, forty years of age, married; and having two strapping daughters, both of whom were pickers in the same gang as herself. The two girls, who were both over twenty years of age, and quite black, had brought in their proper weight, and had walked away a little distance from the shed, but when they saw their mother had been kept back, they stopped, and standing side by side, looked on in silence while she was being whipped. I dare say it was not the first time they had seen such a sight. Members of families, of both sexes, were often whipped in each other's presence on Southern plantations. The overseer turned up the woman's scanty garments, which consisted only of a skirt, a stuff petticoat, and a coarse chemise, laying bare her great posteriors. Her bottom was enormous, and so fat that it was dimpled all over. Her thighs were colossal, and her legs immense; her black skin however, was quite smooth, and it shone like polished ebony. It was the first time I had ever seen a black woman's bottom fully exposed, and the sight of it rather astonished me.

The overseer took out of his pocket a strap about two feet and a half long, three inches broad, and an eighth of an inch thick, and then standing over the prostrated woman, he gave her twelve sharp strokes, the leather making a loud crack, like the report of a pistol, each time it fell on the culprit's great big bottom.

The tears rolled down her cheeks, and her fat buttocks quivered involuntarily, but otherwise she did not move a muscle, nor did she utter the least sound during the whipping, and when it was over, she got up and went to her daughters, who put their arms round her, and then the three walked away. I noticed that the broad stripes made by the strap showed a livid colour on her black skin.

The next on the list was the quadroon: a slim, rather pretty girl, not more than eighteen. She was in a great fright, tears running down her cheek, and she did not place herself in position when ordered.

'Put her down,' said the overseer.

She was seized by the men, and in a moment more was lying flat on the ground, with her petticoats up to her shoulders. Her bottom was small, with pear-shaped cheeks, and at the upper part of her thighs there was a small space through which peeped the crisp black hair shading the 'spot'.

She received her dozen, and although the overseer did not whip her as hard as he had the black woman, the girl twisted her loins, and squealed loudly from the first stroke to the last, and when all was over, her olive-skinned little bottom had become a dusky red colour. When she rose to her feet, she danced about for a moment with the smarting pain, and then she walked stiffly away, wailing loudly, with both hands pressed to her bottom.

The third culprit was a sturdy mulatto woman, thirty-five years of age. She submissively laid herself down when ordered to do so, and the overseer soon stripped her. She had a big, round, plump bottom; its skin was smooth, and of a yellowish tint, not at all pretty. The strap cracked on her yellow bum, striping it with twelve red bands, and making her wince, wriggle, and cry aloud, but she never once screamed.

The other delinquents, two black women aged respectively twenty-seven and thirty, and a mulatto girl aged twenty, were then disposed of by the overseer in the same way. The black women bore their punishment with a certain amount of fortitude, but the mulatto girl writhed and squealed, making almost as much outcry as the quadroon.

I will here state that from what I saw of whipping during my residence in the South, I came to the conclusion that the light-coloured slave-women had finer skins than the darker women, consequently the former felt more pain while being whipped than the latter. Moreover, the whipping of females by men, besides being cruel and most indecent, was also in my opinion, extremely unfair as a punishment. For instance: if an octoroon woman and a full-blooded black woman, both of the same age and physique, were to undergo exactly the same punishment, the octoroon would suffer far more than the black.

When the overseer had finished whipping the last culprit, and she had gone whimpering away, he told his assistants to go to their quarters, then rolling up the strap, he put it in his pocket, and strolled leisurely away in the direction of the overseer's house. The four men lived together, and I have no doubt they had carnal intercourse with all the best looking field-girls. But the man had been perfectly unmoved throughout the whole affair, not appearing to be the least excited at seeing the naked bottoms of the women writhing and twisting with seemingly lascivious movements under his strokes, and he had whipped the poor creatures with as little compunction as if they had been dogs. However, as it was his almost daily work, he was quite accustomed to it, and I don't suppose that the cruelty of the thing ever struck him. Slavery had a demoralizing effect upon most of the white people in the South; and they hardly looked upon slaves as human beings. But I am again digressing.

Chapter Thirteen

Randolph is detained – Dinah wants a woman whipped – Her opinion on the disciplinary power of chastisement – Dinah's delight.

By this time everyone had disappeared, and I was left alone in the fast-gathering dusk. My ears still seemed to be ringing with the sharp cracking sound of the strap striking the flesh of the women, and I kept fancying I heard the cries of pain. I felt pity for them, but my feelings of commiseration were not so keen as they had been a few months previously. I had grown accustomed to seeing women whipped, although I had never before seen six turned up one after the other. Moreover, since my own shameful whipping and the events that had followed, my nature had become hardened.

I walked back to the house without meeting anyone, and went up to my room, where I found Rosa waiting for me. I changed my dress and bathed my face, and after having my hair brushed, I went down to dinner, which I ate with my usual good appetite, although now and then I could not help thinking of the scenes I had witnessed. After dinner, I amused myself with a book until bedtime. Next morning, I received a letter from Randolph, telling me that business matters would oblige him to go on to New Orleans, and he did not know exactly how long he might be detained. The news did not trouble me. I did not care for him, so I did not miss him, and I liked to be sure of having the days to myself without being poked. A nice quiet embrace in bed at night was all very well, but I disliked being poked by day with all my clothes on, and that was what Randolph often did to me. He was a man of strong sensual passions, and the least thing inflamed them: a paragraph in a newspaper, a picture in a book, or a passage in one; an unexpected glimpse of my ankles, or some other trifle would set him off, and then in a twinkling, I would find myself turned up in some ridiculous position.

After breakfast, I went to the library to answer his letter, and just as I had finished writing, Dinah, looking annoyed, came into the room, with a long story of how Emma, one of the mulatto kitchen-girls, had lately been neglecting her work. Said Dinah:

'I scold her, an' I scold her, but she don't mind me one little bit, an' dis very mawnin' de ornery wench was sassy to me, who am de housekeeper of Woodlands,' added Dinah, her ample bosom swelling with wrath. She continued: 'Now missis, yo' jus' send for her, I'll take de gal "up", an' den yo' gib her a good whippin' wid de switch.'

'No, Dinah, I cannot do that,' said I.

'Well den, missis, send her to de oberseer.'

'No, I won't do that either.'

Dinah looked very much surprised. She could not understand why I would neither whip the girl nor send her to the overseer.

'Oh, but, missis,' she said, 'if dis yer gal isn't whipped for her sassiness to me, all de odder wenches will get sassy to me, an' I shan't be able to keep dem in order.'

I could hardly keep my countenance on hearing the contemptuous way Dinah spoke about the other girls. Although she was a slave herself, and liable at any moment to be whipped if she committed an offence, she had a great idea of her own importance as housekeeper of Woodlands. I said:

'Wait until Mr Randolph comes home, then report

Emma to him, and he will very likely punish her.'

Dinah was not satisfied with my suggestion, so she remarked that if I did not like to whip the girl with the switch, or to send her to the overseer, I might at least give her a spanking with a slipper.

But as I would not consent to do even that, she went away fuming and muttering something about my being too easy with 'sassy wenches'.

A week passed before Dinah and I resumed our usual good relations. Then, one night after dinner I asked her several questions about Woodlands, and as she was always ready to chatter to me on the least encouragement, I heard some very curious stories about the doings of slave-women and girls. She also gave me many particulars, that I had not heard before, about herself and the Randolph family. Dinah was very fond of hearing herself speak, and she used a great many more words than were necessary, so I will only give you a summary of what she told me.

She was exactly the same age as Randolph, both having been born on the same day, thirty-five years back. Her mother had been Randolph's nurse, and the two children had been brought up together, and had played with each other in their young days. But when George grew to boyhood, he became the young master, and she had to submit to all his caprices. He was the only child, and his parents spoilt him, allowing him to do what he liked. He was very precocious, and when he was sixteen years of age he had begun to feel her, and whenever she offended him, he would throw her down upon the floor, turn up her petticoats, and spank her.

When they were eighteen years of age, he took her maidenhead, and he continued to possess her whenever he felt inclined, for three years. Then he went to travel in Europe. He was away for a couple of years, and after his return he occasionally had further carnal relations with her.

When she was twenty-five years of age, she had got married to a quadroon man a few years older than herself, and from that time Randolph never touched her. But, as she pithily expressed it:

'Massa George had plenty ob odder gals in de house.'

When Randolph was thirty, his father and mother died within a short time of each other, and he became master of Woodlands. When that event occurred, Dinah was a widow, and was head parlourmaid, but after a time, Randolph made her housekeeper, and gave her a certain amount of authority over the other slave women, though he had never hesitated to whip her if she happened to displease him. It was, however, nearly two years since she had received a whipping.

Dinah, when once started, would have gone on chattering all night about Woodlands and its people, but as I was beginning to feel very sleepy, I sent her away and went to bed.

Chapter Fourteen

I learn something of Randolph's previous copulating proclivities – I go for a ride and am rogered in my tight-fitting riding-dress – Spanked and again rogered – I respond to his lunges and give the Southern Bluebeard satisfaction.

Next morning, I received a letter from Randolph, informing me that he would be home in three days' time, and telling me to have a good dinner ready for him at the usual hour, with gumbo soup, stewed terrapin, and roasted canvas-back ducks. He was very fond of those three things, two of which: gumbo soup and stewed terrapin, can only be got in perfection in the Southern States.

Sending for Dinah, I told her that her master was coming back, and gave her orders about the dinner, also telling her to warn the cook and kitchen-women to be careful. Randolph, being a great *gourmet*, was most particular about the cooking of everything, and if a cook, through carelessness, spoilt a dish, her bottom was generally made to smart.

After lunch on the day he was to return, I interviewed Dinah, who told me that she had got the terrapin and the canvas-back ducks, and that the cooks were preparing a very good dinner.

It was only two o'clock, and as I did not expect Randolph to be home until six o'clock, I thought I would go out for a ride. There would be plenty of time for me to have a long trot and afterwards to dress before he arrived. I knew he would scold me if he did not find me dressed for dinner, and waiting in the drawing-room to receive him. So after ordering my horse to be brought round to the terrace, I went up to my room, and assisted by Rosa, dressed in full riding costume, with a short chemise reaching to my knees, and a dark blue habit. On my head, I wore a soft felt hat of tan colour, and I had tan gauntlets on my hands. Rosa was always amused when helping me to dress in riding costume, and on this occasion, while buttoning my breeches round my broad hips, she laughed, saying:

'Oh, missis, how funny yo' does look in dem tight trousies. Dey does show de shape ob yo' figure, an' no mistake.'

However, when I was completely attired, the girl gazed admiringly at me, remarking that I looked 'real lubly'. And I think I may say without conceit, that I did look well in riding costume. I went downstairs, and out on the terrace, where one of the negro grooms was walking my horse up and down. He was getting old, but he was a very handsome creature, a thoroughbred, dark bay with black points; and he knew me well, as I used to visit him every day, giving him bits of bread, lumps of sugar, and slices of carrot, of which he was very fond. The groom put me up on the saddle, and then I trotted off alone. I never took a man with me.

It was a bright, cool day, the old horse was fresh, but perfectly under my control, and as he ambled with an easy action along the smooth, level road, the breeze fanned my cheeks, bringing an increased colour to them; my eyes began to sparkle and I felt in very good spirits. I rode seven miles to a farmhouse, where I dismounted and had a glass of milk, while the old horse had a bucket of meal and water. Then after a short rest, I again mounted, and rode slowly back to Woodlands, arriving there at five o'clock.

The groom was waiting for me on the terrace, and

as he helped me down from the saddle he told me that 'de massa' had been back about an hour. Hurrying into the house, I went straight to the drawing-room, where I found Randolph lying on the sofa.

'Oh, George!' I exclaimed, 'I am sorry I was not in when you returned, but I did not think you would be home until six o'clock.'

I expected he would be very cross with me for not having been waiting for him; but to my great relief, he was in a good humour.

'Never mind, Dolly,' he said, 'it doesn't matter.'

Then getting off the sofa, he lifted me up in his arms and kissed me on the forehead in a gentle affectionate way. He seldom kissed me, and when he did his kisses were coarse and sensual. I was surprised at his soft manner and tender kiss, and I thought to myself that if he would only treat me more as a woman and less as a subject for the gratification of his passions, I might get to like him a little.

But his soft mood did not last many moments. I saw the sensual look I knew so well come into his eyes as they roved over the curves of my bosom and the outlines of my hips, which were clearly defined by my tightly-fitting habit.

After a moment, he said:

'You are looking very fresh and rosy, and your habit does show off your figure to perfection. In fact you look so nice that I am going to "have" you this minute just as you stand.'

'Oh!' I exclaimed, rather taken aback, 'that will be very uncomfortable. I've got on breeches and boots. Come to my room and let me take them off.'

'No, I won't go to your room,' he said laughing, 'I intend to keep you here, and poke you just as you are. I've "had" women in all sorts of dress and undress, but I've never "had" one in full riding costume. It will be a decided novelty, therefore my pleasure will be increased. I've not touched a woman since I left you. Now take off your hat and gloves, but don't remove anything else.'

When I had first seen him that afternoon, I was not disinclined for a poke, after three weeks abstinence, and if he had taken me quietly upstairs to my room, let me undress, and then poked me properly on the bed, I should have been pleased. But now I was annoyed by the coarse way he had spoken, and I disliked having to submit to his embraces while dressed as I was.

However, I knew it would be useless to remonstrate, so taking off my hat and gloves I waited for his next move. He took off his coat and waistcoat, and then made me lean over the back of a low, broad armchair with my hands resting on the seat. I was not surprised, as he had often placed me over a chair before. He next rolled up the skirt of my habit to my shoulders, and as my body was curved by the position in which I was leaning, my bottom was well stuck out and my breeches tightly stretched. After a little fumbling under my corset, he unbuttoned the breeches, and with some difficulty pulled them down to the tops of my boots, then carefully tucking up my chemise, leaving me bare to the attack. He was always fond of looking at me, and feeling my bottom, so he stroked it, saying:

'Why, Dolly, your bottom seems to be plumper, prettier, and whiter than ever, but I am going to redden it a little with a spanking.'

When I heard him say that, I was frightened. He had never offered to do such a thing to me before. Raising my head, and looking over my shoulder, I said in a pleading tone:

'Oh, don't spank me, I can't bear pain.'

But I did not attempt to move from the position he had placed me in. Somehow or other, I never could resist his will.

'I won't hurt you,' he said, 'I'll only make you feel

a pleasant tingling sensation.'

He then began to spank me; not with much force, but yet sufficiently hard to cause my skin to tingle more than I liked, and he applied the slaps to one side of my bottom only, leaving the other side quite untouched.

When he had spanked the whole surface from the upper part down to the thigh, he stopped, saying with a laugh:

'There, Dolly; one cheek is as pink as a rose, and the other is as white as a lily. The contrast between the two is charming. It is a pity you cannot see your bottom at this moment.'

Then going to work again, he spanked the white cheek till it also turned a rosy pink colour, but I can't say that I only felt a pleasant tingling sensation; in point of fact my bottom decidedly smarted. But strange to say, the slight spanking had excited a voluptuous feeling in me, and I was anxious to receive the stroke. He unbuttoned his trousers, and then making me separate my legs slightly, he clasped his arms round my body, as stooping a little, he thrust his 'thing' into the 'spot' between the cleft of the thighs. Holding me in a close embrace with his belly pressed against my bottom, he began to lunge at me strongly, giving me the full length of his member, while I, pressing my thighs together, clipped the weapon tightly in the sheath, at the same time moving my loins briskly backwards and forwards to meet his powerful thrusts. He worked away in fine style, and I gave him every assistance, so in a few seconds the supreme crisis arrived. He discharged copiously, while I squirmed and twisted myself about, wriggling my bottom in the voluptuous spasm until all was over. Then my knees gave way under me and I should have fallen had he not held me up. He put me on my feet.

'That was a good one, Dolly, wasn't it? And you did your part very well,' he remarked.

I smiled, and pulling up my breeches, buttoned them round my waist; while he fastened the front of his trousers and put on his coat and waistcoat. I do not know whether during his absence he had touched a woman or not, but anyhow the poke he gave me that day was the most vigorous one I had ever received from him.

I had liked it, but I would rather have had it properly done to me on a bed. Since that time, I have learnt by experience that all men are fanciful; they like change, and are fond of 'making love' to women in all sorts of ways. But women do not care to be 'had' in fancy positions with their clothes on; they prefer to be embraced in the old-fashioned way, lying on their backs in or on a comfortable bed, with nothing on but a chemise or a nightdress.

We went to our respective rooms and dressed for dinner, meeting each other at table at seven o'clock. It was an excellent dinner; the cooks had done their best, and the gumbo soup, stewed terrapin, roast canvas-back ducks, and all the other things, were cooked to perfection, and as we were both hungry, we did full justice to the various dishes, also to the champagne, and other wines.

Chapter Fifteen

'Spoon fashion' – The irony of woman's destiny – I am futtered in the place where, when a virgin, I defended my honour – The calm is broken – Dinah receives an awful spanking – Her majestic bottom.

After dinner, when we were in the drawing-room, he told me that he had great trouble with his business matters, owing to the unsettled state of affairs between North and South. Randolph, like all Southerners at that period, hated the Northerners, speaking of them most contemptuously, and calling them 'damned Yankees'. He also said that he did not think they would dare to push matters to extremes with the South.

Being a Yankee myself, I did not like to hear Yankees spoken of with contempt, and I felt convinced in my own mind that they would be quite able to hold their own with the Southerners. However, I did not argue the point: I had long given up trying to argue with Randolph, for whenever I attempted to hold an opinion different to his, he always told me that I did not know what I was talking about, and to 'shut up'.

The evening passed, and at eleven o'clock we went to bed; but before going to sleep, he made me lie on my side, while he also on his side, lay behind me, with his arms round me, and his bare belly pressed close against my naked bottom, so that his stiff member passed between my thighs into its place. Then, grasping one of my titties in each of his hands, he poked me. This was rather a favourite position of his, when we were in bed, and he used to call it 'spoon fashion'. Next morning after breakfast, he went out to make an inspection of the plantation, to see how things had been carried on during his absence. He found everything in fair order, so he came back in a good humour to lunch, and when it was over ordered the two-horse buggy, and we went for a drive. It was a bright, hot afternoon, so he drove through the shadiest lanes, and we happened to pass the little dell where he made the assault on me.

He pulled up the horses, and pointing with his whip to the spot, said, with a laugh:

'Do you remember this place, Dolly?'

I did remember it well! and I thought of the long and desperate struggle I had made to keep my maidenhead, which I had to surrender to him after all.

'Oh, I remember the place very well,' I replied. 'Do you think I could possibly forget it?'

He again laughed, saying:

'How you did kick, and scream, and fight; you quite astonished me. I would not have believed that a little woman like you could have made such a strong resistance. It was an exciting struggle, and the thought of it has given me an erection, so I intend to have a roll on the grass with you.'

I said nothing, but I thought a great deal. I was going to be rogered by him on the very spot where I had once successfully resisted his assault. It was surely the very irony of fate.

He got out of the buggy, and hitched the horses to a tree; then lifting me down, he carried me to the little hollow, and laid me on the grass. Then after some amorous dalliance, he placed me in position, turned up my petticoats, and poked me strongly, making me bounce under him.

'Ah, Dolly,' he remarked when all was over, 'if you had let me get on the top of you that day, you would not have had your bottom whipped by the lynchers, nor would you have ridden the rail.'

I made no answer, but arranged my somewhat disordered attire; then we got into the buggy again, and continued our interrupted drive, not returning home until it was time to dress for dinner.

The days passed, and everything went on smoothly in the establishment. The women gave very little trouble; their conduct being so good that not a single one of them had had her petticoats turned up since Randolph's return. I mean turned up for a whipping, as I have no doubt that most of them, if not all, had their petticoats turned up for a poke in the evenings. Plenty of lovemaking went on, as a certain number of the women and girls, in turns, were allowed to be out every night till half-past ten o'clock. Anyone who was late in returning to the house was brought by Dinah next morning before Randolph, who either whipped the offender himself, or sent her to the overseer. She was also further punished by not being allowed out of the house at night for a month. So it was very seldom that a woman stayed out beyond the hour fixed for her return.

But the calm that had lasted for so many days was one afternoon ruffled by a breeze. I think something had gone wrong on the plantation; I don't know what it was, but anyhow Randolph, who had been out for a couple of hours, came back to the house in a vile temper. He blew me up because I happened to be wearing a pair of easy slippers without heels, asking me what the devil I meant by going about slipshod, 'like an untidy slave wench!' When he had quieted down a little, he informed me that he had a business appointment with a gentleman – one of the neighbouring planters – and that they were to meet each other in an hour and a half's time at a certain crossroad, a few miles from Woodlands. He was then going to ring the bell, to give orders for his horse to be saddled, when Dinah happened to come into the room to ask me a question about dinner.

I answered her question, and as she was leaving the room, Randolph told her to order his horse to be brought round at once. He then went up to dress, returning in about half an hour's time, in riding costume. The groom, however, had not made his appearance with the horse, so Randolph kept walking up and down the room, fuming with impatience, constantly glancing at his watch, and every now and then looking out of the window, wondering why the horse had not been brought, saying that he would most likely miss his appointment, and vowing that if he did, he would have the groom cowhided by the overseer.

At last he rang the bell furiously, telling the parlourmaid who answered it to send Dinah up, and when the girl had left the room, he turned to me, saying:

'I think that confounded woman must have forgotten to send word to the stables.'

Presently Dinah, looking calm and placid, came into the room.

'Did you order my horse?' shouted Randolph, in an angry voice.

A frightened expression at once appeared on the woman's face.

'No sah, I didn't. I quite forgot dat yo' tole me to order de hoss,' she answered, in a faint voice, glancing deprecatingly at her angry master.

He flew into a violent passion – he was a most violent man – the veins of his forehead swelling, and his eyes gleaming with rage.

'Oh, you forgot, did you!' he exclaimed. 'I'll teach you to forget my orders.'

Rushing at Dinah, who stood cowering, he seized her, and sitting down on the end of the sofa, threw the great big woman across his knees, just as if she had been a little girl.

I could see by her astonished face that she was utterly

taken aback, but she did not struggle. Ejaculating once: 'Oh massa!' she lay quietly over Randolph's thighs, with her hands resting on the floor at one side of him, and her feet on the other.

With one sweep of his arm he threw her petticoats up over her head, completely hiding her face, and laying her bare from her waist to her garters.

Dinah, being a tall, strapping woman, had large posteriors; her bottom was really a splendid one: broad, deep, and very plump, and as she was lying in a much curved position, the great half moons were raised high on Randolph's lap. She had large, round, muscular thighs, and the plump calves of her big legs seemed ready to burst through her tight, white cotton stockings. Her dusky olive skin was smooth and wholesome-looking, and all her drapery was clean. Holding her firmly in position, with his left arm over her naked loins, and with his right leg over the back of the lower part of her thighs, he began to spank the woman, raising his hand as high as he could in the air, and laying on the strokes with his full force. Each time his hand fell on her big bottom, a loud 'smack' echoed through the room, and the red prints of his fingers and thumb instantly showed on her skin. Dinah winced under the stinging slaps, her plump flesh twitching and quivering, but she did not utter a sound, nor did she attempt to put her hands behind her. He went on spanking her ruthlessly, and after a moment, she shook her head clear of her petticoats, and looked round at her master with a pleading expression in her great, brown, ox-like eyes. Her cap had fallen off, her hair had come loose, her lips were quivering, tears were rolling down her cheeks, and she writhed and twisted her loins in pain, but still she was silent.

He continued to rain down the shower of slaps, the red marks of his fingers spreading all over her bottom till not a part of it was left unmarked. Dinah's fortitude at last gave way, she began to utter little shrieks, and to kick her legs about, while she jerked her hips from side to side, and putting her hands over her bottom, tried in vain to shield it from the tremendous spanking, at the same time gasping out entreaties to her master to stop.

At last he did so, and pushed the woman off his knees onto the floor, where she lay with her petticoats still up to her waist, so that her great red bottom remained exposed. After a moment or two, she got on her feet, wiping the tears from her hot, flushed face with her apron, and then she twisted up her hair, picked up her cap, put it on her head, but not very straight, she shook her petticoats into their places, and stood sobbing before her master.

'There, you careless hussy,' he said, 'I think you'll remember my orders in future. Go away.'

Dinah, holding her apron to her eyes, walked rather stiffly out of the room. Randolph rubbed the palm of his hand, saying:

'Damn the thing, I have made my hand quite sore on the woman's bottom; her flesh is very firm, and I felt as if I were spanking a board. I ought to have used the switch and saved my fingers. But,' he added, 'if my palm is so sore, what must her bottom be? I fancy she won't forget that spanking in a hurry.'

'I think it was a shame of you to spank Dinah at all,' I observed.

The laughing expression instantly left his face, and he glared furiously at me, saying in a loud angry tone:

'You had better keep what you think to yourself. It is no business of yours what I do to my slaves. Why, damn it,' he exclaimed with increased anger, 'no one has ever dared to make such a remark to me before. I have a great mind to take you across my knees and give you a smart spanking, too.'

My blood ran cold, and a lump came into my throat. He was quite capable of doing what he said.

'Oh, I beg your pardon. I am very sorry I spoke,' I said earnestly.

'So you ought to be. I thought you knew by this time that I will stand no interference,' he said, scowling at me.

He then left the room, much to my relief, and shortly afterwards I saw him canter down the avenue. I was very sorry for poor Dinah; she had always been most attentive to me, and I liked her very much. I wondered how Randolph had the heart to expose and whip so severely the woman who had been his foster-sister; had lived all her life in the house with him, and had also been the toy of his passions. Feeling rather upset by the scene I had witnessed, and also by my narrow escape from a spanking, I went up to my room, and ringing for Rosa, told her to take down my hair and give it a good brushing, a thing which always has a soothing effect upon me. The news that Dinah had been spanked had already got about the house; she was not liked by her fellow slaves, because, as housekeeper, she kept them in order, reporting any woman or girl who misbehaved, or neglected her work.

Rosa brushed away at my hair for a few moments in silence, but I could see that she was bursting to say something, and at last she said:

'All de women is glad dat Dinah got a good spankin' from de massa. She tinks too much of herself. An' she always tells on a gal if she don't do exactly right, an' gets her a whippin'.'

'Dinah only does her duty,' I remarked. 'If the women and girls always behaved as well as they have been doing lately, Dinah would not have to tell of them.'

Rosa tossed her head, but made no further remarks, and when she had brushed my hair well, and re-arranged it, I sent her away, telling her to send Dinah up to me. I was rather curious to see how she was after her terrible spanking. In a short time she came into the room looking as smart and tidy as ever. Her hair was neatly arranged under a clean cap, and she had put on a clean apron, collar, and cuffs; her face wore its usual placid look, but her eyelids were red and rather swollen.

'I am sorry for you, Dinah,' I said. 'Your master spanked you so very severely.'

She seemed to be a little surprised at my expressing sympathy, but she was very grateful for it and she thanked me. Then she said:

'I'se had plenty ob spankins' an' whippins' in my life, but I never thought dat I'd come to be spanked again like a little gal. Why, missis, I ain't had such a ting done to me since I was thirteen years ole. But, oh my! dis one was a spankin'! It hurt most drefful. De massa laid on powerful heavy, an' his hand is bery hard. I'se been paddled twice, but I tink de Massa's hand hurt me today, near as much as de paddle did. My bottom is bery sore an' bruised, an' it'll be black an' blue all ober tomorrow.'

Dinah had spoken without emotion. She evidently did not think it strange that a woman of her age should have been whipped in such an ignominious way, and did not appear to bear her master the least malice. She was his slave; her body belonged to him, therefore he could do what he liked with it. Such was the degrading effect of slavery on the minds of the human chattels.

I sent her away and dressed for dinner, putting on a new frock which I had lately received from the dressmaker in Richmond. Then I went down to the diningroom, where I found Randolph, and as the dinner was ready, we sat down to table. He had missed his appointment he said, which was an important one, consequently he was very cross and snappish; but after he had eaten a good dinner, drunk a bottle of champagne, and smoked a cigar, he got into better humour.

When we went into the drawing-room, he seated

himself in an easy chair, saying to me waggishly:

'Come here, Dolly, and let me see if you have taken off those beastly slippers you were wearing this afternoon.'

I went to him, and held my skirts above my knees, while he looked at my feet and legs. I had on a pretty pair of high-heeled boots and pale blue silk stockings, fastened with silver-buckled pink satin garters.

'Ah, this is something I like,' he observed; running his hand up and down my legs and ankles.

Then he put his hand higher up under my drapery, and opening the slit of my drawers felt my bottom.

'You are looking very pretty tonight, Dolly, and that new frock becomes you,' he said, drawing me closer to him while his eyes began to sparkle.

I knew what he was going to do! Taking me up in his arms, he carried me to the sofa and laid me down upon it, then he turned up my garments one by one, looking at my fine white petticoats deeply flounced with lace, my prettily-trimmed drawers, and my filmy chemise; as he always made me wear the daintiest undergarments in the evening.

When everything had been turned up, and my drawers had been taken down, he stretched my legs widely apart, and gazed for a moment or two at the 'spot', then inserting his finger he tickled the sensitive little 'point' till it distilled a few drops of moisture, while I squirmed and kicked up my legs. He seemed to be very much excited, kissing me hotly on the lips, eyes, and cheeks several times, then throwing himself upon me he pressed his lips upon mine, and thrust his tongue into my mouth, as putting his hands under me and grasping the cheeks of my bottom, he fixed his weapon deeply in the sheath, and 'sworded' me vigorously.

When all was over and we had made ourselves tidy, he rang the bell, and ordered the parlourmaid to bring a bottle of champagne, and when the girl had brought the wine, we soon disposed of it, as our exciting combat had made us both thirsty. Randolph was pleased with himself and he was also pleased with me, so he was in very good humour. We had a long conversation on various subjects, and as he did not snub me when I differed with him, I passed a more pleasant evening than usual. At half-past eleven o'clock we went to bed.

Chapter Sixteen

After four months – The 'spirit of unrest' – My sym-
pathies are with the North – An escaped Negress
taken and flogged – A most awful flagellation –
'Paddling' described – A blistered bottom.

I will now pass over a period of four months.
During that time, events had been marching rapidly,
and stirring things had happened. The slave States
had seceded from the Union. Jeff Davis had been
elected President of the Southern Confederacy. Fort
Sumter had been taken, and the war had begun. All
those events are matters of history, so I need not enter
into details of them, but I will confine myself to
relating the things that were connected with Woodlands, and with my own fortunes.

The work on the plantation was carried on as
usual, notwithstanding the very unsettled state of
affairs, but there was a spirit of unrest among all the
field-hands, and they were inclined to be insubordinate, so Randolph and his four overseers always went
about armed with revolvers, and whippings were of
more frequent occurrence than ever. The overseers in
all cases inflicted the punishments, the male slaves
being tied to the whipping-post and cowhided, while
the females were stretched upon a bench, and either
switched or paddled. By these severe means, discipline had so far been thoroughly maintained. Even
the women in the house, with a few exceptions,
became very troublesome, but here again Randolph
would stand no nonsense. He became stricter with

them than before, and whenever a woman or a girl had misbehaved in the least, Dinah, and another stalwart woman named Milly, were sent for, and the offender was taken up and prepared for punishment. Then in a few seconds, she would be squealing, writhing, kicking up her heels, and promising amendment, while Randolph, wielding the switch with vigorous arm, striped her bottom with red weals. This treatment reduced to order all the women who were inclined to be unruly, and they soon returned to their ordinary behaviour.

For some time past, business in the State had been almost at a standstill, therefore Randolph could not dispose of his cotton, which had accumulated in the sheds, which were full to overflowing. He was a rich man, but most of his income was derived from the sale of his cotton, and now that there was no market for it, while at the same time the great expenses in keeping up the plantation were going on, he became very much pressed for ready money. However, he thought it would only be a temporary inconvenience, as he was quite convinced in his own mind that the South would eventually prove victorious in the war.

My sympathies, of course, were with the Northerners, and I wished them speedy success, but I dared not express my sentiments. I really don't know what Randolph would have done to me if I had said what I thought. He rarely left the plantation, and he never gave any dinner parties, as all his friends had either left the State, or joined the Confederate Army. He would have done so himself, only that he was too old to go as a private soldier, and he was unable to get a commission as an officer, owing to his having no knowledge of military affairs; but he had been elected a member of Congress for the Southern Confederacy. As he would not leave Woodlands, he was obliged to fall back upon my society, and he seemed glad to have it; he also seemed to appreciate it. His manner became a little more tender; he did not speak to me so coarsely as he had often been in the habit of doing, and he treated me with less indecency. But with his slaves, both outdoor and indoor, he was more strict than ever. Since the breaking out of the war, several of the field-hands had run away, and had managed to get clear off, although the 'underground stations' had been closed. Randolph had offered two hundred dollars reward for the capture of each runaway, but strange to say, not one of them had been brought back. These losses had vexed him very much, the runaways having been some of his strongest and finest young men and women, each of whom was worth from fifteen hundred to two thousand dollars. So far none of the house-women had run away, but at last one of them did. One morning, when Randolph and I were at breakfast, Dinah came in and told her master that one of the women named Sophy, who had been out the previous night, had not returned to the house, and it had been found out that she had taken away some of her clothes. Sophy was one of the kitchen-maids, a fine, big, healthy young mulatto woman, twenty-six years of age, and worth about eighteen hundred dollars. There was no doubt that she had run away, so Randolph at once wrote out copies of advertisements, describing the woman, and offering the large reward of four hundred dollars to anyone bringing her back to Woodlands, or lodging her in a gaol. He sent the advertisement to all the local newspapers, and also ordered bills to be printed and posted up in various places. Several days passed, the advertisements appeared in the papers, and the bills were stuck up all about the neighbourhood; but nothing was heard of the runaway. However, as all the white loafers were eager to secure the large reward, Randolph had hopes that the woman would be caught sooner or later. And so she was.

About five o'clock one evening, a couple of rough-looking white men drove up to the house in a ramshackle wagon, bringing with them the runaway, whom they had found concealed in the slave quarter of a plantation, twenty miles from Woodlands. The woman, whose wrists were tied together with a piece of rope, had evidently not suffered any privations during the time she had been absent. Her frock was clean, and she was in good condition bodily, but her face was looking very doleful, as she knew there was a severe whipping before her.

The men who had hunted her down received the four hundred dollars, and drove off in their wagon, while Sophy was taken away to the servants' quarters, and after she had been given something to eat, was locked up in a small bedroom by herself for the night.

Randolph was much pleased at having got the woman back, consequently he was in a very good humour all through the evening, so when we were in the drawing-room after dinner, I ventured to ask him what he intended to do to Sophy.

'Never you mind, Dolly,' he replied smiling. 'It's no business of yours. I've not quite made up my mind what I shall do to her, but anyhow, I intend to make the hussy smart tomorrow, and if you like, you can see the punishment.'

I asked no more questions, and he told me to come and sit on his knee. I did so. Then as a matter of course, the usual toyings took place, and in a very short time I found myself impaled as I sat on his lap. Afterwards, we talked about the war and I had to carefully conceal my real opinions. In due course we went to bed. Next morning at breakfast, he told me he had determined to make an example of Sophy, therefore he intended to whip her with the paddle, in the hall, before all the other women in the house.

I was sorry for Sophy – I was always sorry when a woman was whipped – but I dared not say a word, in fact, if I had said anything, it would only have irritated Randolph, and made him harder on the woman; moreover, it would have brought his wrath upon me. When he had finished his breakfast, and smoked a cigar, he left the room to make preparations for the punishment. In about twenty minutes he came back and said:

'Everything is ready now. You can come out to the hall if you would like to see a paddling.'

I had seen many women switched; some whipped with the strap, and several spanked, but I had never seen one paddled, and I was rather curious to see how the punishment was inflicted. I followed Randolph to the hall. I was sorry for the woman, as I have before said, but my curiosity overcame my pity. I had grown somewhat callous.

In the middle of the long wide hall, there was a machine I had never seen before, though I had heard of it. It was the whipping bench, a long, low, curved wooden structure about two feet broad, supported on four legs, each of which was furnished with buckled straps.

On the floor beside the bench was the paddle, a round flat piece of wood an eighth of an inch thick, and eight inches in diameter, fixed to a handle two feet and half long. It was very much dreaded by all the female slaves, as it caused great pain, bruising the flesh and blistering the skin, so that after a paddling the sufferer's bottom remained sore and tender longer than after a switching or a strapping.

All the women and grown-up girls in the house were present, and they were twenty-one in number, ten of them in a row at one side of the bench and ten of them at the other; Dinah stood by herself. Randolph ordered her and Milly – a strong black woman whom I have mentioned before – to go for the culprit. They went, returning in a couple of minutes with Sophy, who the moment she caught sight of the preparations for her paddling, burst into tears and hung back, so that the two women had to drag her up to the bench. Sophy was not a bad-looking woman, for a mulatto, and on ordinary occasions her yellow-tinted complexion was clear, but at that moment, fear had turned her face a sort of dull grey colour.

'Oh, massa! massa!' she cried, stretching out her arms appealingly, with the tears running down her cheeks, 'don't paddle me. Whip me wid de switch or de strap, but don't, oh don't paddle me!'

'Put her on the bench,' said Randolph.

The woman, in an agony of fear, threw herself upon the floor. Dinah and Milly lifted her up, and then she began to struggle and kick, but in spite of her resistance, the two big, strong women soon had her stretched at full length on the bench, with her wrists and ankles securely fastened with the straps. Dinah then stripped her, and as her head and feet were lower than the middle of her body, which was raised by the curve of the bench, the part of her person to be operated upon was thrown well up.

She would have had a good figure, only that her bottom was out of all proportion. It was too big, but nevertheless it was fairly well-shaped, with well-rounded cheeks meeting each other closely; her thighs were large, and she had a sturdy pair of legs; her skin was smooth and of a clear yellow tint.

Randolph took up the paddle, and standing at the culprit's left side, said:

'Now, you bitch, I'll make your fat bottom smart. You've cost me four hundred dollars, and I intend to take the value out of your yellow hide.'

He raised the paddle high in the air over the trembling, crying woman, who in dread of the coming stroke, drew in the cheeks of her bottom until the division between them looked like a fine line.

Down came the paddle with great force, and with a

resounding 'smack' on the upper part of the right
cheek of her bottom; she gave a convulsive start, and
gasped for breath, then she uttered a long shrill
squeal, and at the same instant a great red blister-like
patch, the exact size and shape of the blade of the
paddle, sprang up on her yellow skin.

The second stroke fell on the left cheek, and again
the loud sounding 'smack' was followed by a shriek,
and another round patch showed red on her skin. He
went on paddling her with great severity, laying the
strokes alternately on the right and on the left side of
her bottom, and striking a fresh place each time.

Finally, Randolph threw down the paddle, telling
Dinah to release the woman, and as soon as she was
unstrapped, she rolled off the bench, and lay crying
loudly. While she was being paddled, the other
women had looked on in silence, the majority of them
showing no signs of emotion, but some of the
younger girls had tears in their eyes. They had all,
with few exceptions, seen each other at various times
receive a whipping, and everyone of them, without
exception, had been whipped herself more or less
frequently.

Randolph told Dinah and Milly to take Sophy
away and attend to her. They lifted the sufferer up
and, clasping their arms round her, led her wailing
out of the hall, to bathe her blistered bottom with
cold water. He then ordered a couple of the women to
take the bench and the paddle back to the shed where
they were kept; the other women and girls he sent to
their work, and I was left alone with him in the
hall. Being well aware that whipping a woman always
excited him, I felt pretty sure that I was going to be
poked. I was not wrong. Putting his arm round my
waist, he led me into the drawing-room, and made me
lean over the high end of the sofa. Then he turned up
my petticoats, let down my drawers, and gave me a
strong poke from behind. He then went out, and I

was off to my room to make myself tidy, as I was in rather a dishevelled state after his vigorous onslaught. When I had removed all traces of what had occurred, I rang for Rosa, and sent her to see how Sophy was getting on. When she came back she said:

'Dinah is bathin' Sophy's bottom with cold water. It looks drefful sore an' it's swelled up twice its size. I'se never seen such a bottom as dat woman's got. She won't be able to do no work for three or four days. I'se never had de paddle, an' I hopes I never shall. It's far wuss dan de switch.'

I sent Rosa away, and went into the garden, where I sat until Randolph came back to lunch. In the afternoon we went for a long ride together.

Chapter Seventeen

Defeat of the Federals – Randolph goes to Richmond – I am left in charge – Endeavours to stop the whipping of women – An eventful afternoon – The soldiers arrive – I meet Captain Franklin.

The weeks passed, and in their course, the tide of war flowed nearer to us at Woodlands. The Federal troops had entered Virginia, and many skirmishes had taken place with various results. Then came the battle of Bull's Run, in which as you know, the Federals were utterly defeated. When the news of the Confederate victory arrived at Woodlands, Randolph was jubilant, and he said to me that the damned Yankees would soon be driven out of Virginia. He gave the field-hands a couple of days' holiday, with an extra supply of food and liquor; the house-women also had a treat and were allowed to invite their sweethearts to a dance in the servants' quarters.

I was very sorry to hear of the defeat of the Federal troops, but I did not think that they would be driven out of Virginia.

A short time after the battle of Bull's Run, Randolph was summoned to Richmond to attend the first meeting of the Congress of the Confederate States. As he expected to be away a considerable time, he gave me full instructions as to what he wished me to do with regard to affairs on the plantation during his absence; and told me I was to write twice a week, informing him exactly how things were going on. He went away a couple of days later, and I was for the second time left alone, but on this occasion I had full charge of everything at Woodlands. He had latterly been treating me with a little more consideration, and though I had not the least love for him, I missed his company a little at first. But I soon settled down contentedly to my solitary life and did what I could to keep up the usual routine of work on the plantation, my efforts being well assisted by the overseers, who had been told to take any orders I might give them. They were trustworthy men, and though rather rough creatures, were always civil to me. I determined that as long as I was mistress on the plantation, there should be as little whipping as possible, at least as far as the women were concerned. So I gave orders that no woman or girl was to be whipped in any way without my sanction. The overseers were very much surprised at my order, but I believe they obeyed it, and at any rate as far as I knew, no woman or girl was whipped during the time I was in charge of the estate. The days passed quietly and uneventfully on the plantation, but outside of it, everything was in a most disturbed state.

Fighting was always going on somewhere, the Federal troops were concentrating in force, and were pressing on Richmond: many of the neighbouring plantations had been occupied by parties of the Union soldiers, and I was daily expecting them to make their appearance at Woodlands. I wrote twice a week to Randolph, giving him particulars of everything that happened, and he wrote to me once a week, his letters always being business ones without a word of love.

At last 'the boys in blue' did come. One afternoon about four o'clock, I happened to be looking out of one of the drawing-room windows, when I saw a party of soldiers led by an officer, and accompanied by an army waggon, coming up the avenue towards the house.

In a few minutes they halted on the terrace, piled

their arms, and unpacked the waggon, which contained blankets and other things belonging to the soldiers. My heart began to beat with excitement, and I sat down on the sofa to await the *dénouement* of the affair. In a minute or two, Dinah ushered in the officer, who saluting me politely, said:

'Madam, I have been ordered to occupy this plantation, but I assure you that you shall not be interfered with in any way. I will put my men in the slaves' quarters, but I must ask you to give me a room in the house.'

I rose to my feet, smiling. It did my heart good to see the dear old blue uniform again.

'I am very glad to see you, and your men, sir,' I said. 'I am a Northern woman, and all my sympathies are with you. Take a seat, and I will have a room prepared for you at once.'

He took a chair, looking very much surprised. Then I rang the bell for Dinah, and gave her the requisite orders. The officer was about twenty-seven years of age, a tall, handsome, fair man, with a bronzed face, clear grey eyes, and a long silky blond moustache. His uniform was a little worn, but it fitted him to perfection, and he was evidently a well-bred gentleman. We entered into conversation, and as there was already a bond of sympathy between us, we were soon chatting and laughing as if we had been old friends. He told me he was a captain in the United States Army, that his name was Franklin, and how he came from Pennsylvania – my own State. This fact made me feel even more friendly towards him, and I informed him that I also was a Pennsylvanian. Then we laughed and shook hands. I could see that it puzzled him how it happened that a Northern woman, and one who openly expressed her sympathy with the Union soldiers, should be apparently the mistress of a Southern plantation. But he was too well-bred to ask questions, and I did not volunteer any explanations. I could not tell my own shame. After talking for some time, he rose from his seat, saying that he must go and see to the quartering of his men. I told him that dinner would be ready at seven o'clock, then he bowed and left the room.

I sent for Dinah, and asked her if she had seen that everything had been got ready for the officer. She replied that she had seen to everything, and had had his valise taken up to the room. I then told her that now the United States troops had come, she and all the other slaves would soon be set free.

'Oh, missis! is dat a fac'?' she exclaimed, showing her white teeth in a broad smile.

'Yes,' I replied.

'Den I'll look after de ossifer myself. He is a fine-looking young gentleman,' she said, bustling away.

I went to my room, dressed for dinner, putting on one of my prettiest frocks, and then I went down to the drawing-room to wait for Captain Franklin. Presently he came in, and after making me a bow, thanked me for the comfortable chamber I had allotted him. I think he was rather surprised to find me in full evening toilette with bare arms and shoulders. He had changed his rather warworn uniform, for an undress jacket and braided pantaloons, and he looked smart, soldierly, and very handsome. Dinner was announced and we went into the dining-room. The meal was a good one, and I had ordered Dinah to get out some champagne, as well as claret and sherry. As Captain Franklin had been campaigning in a very rough way for six months, he thoroughly appreciated the dainty well-cooked dishes and the good wine, and said with a smile, that he was a most fortunate man in having been detailed to occupy Woodlands, instead of having to live in a damp muddy tent, and fare on tough ration beef and hard biscuit. I laughed, saying that I was glad to hear he liked his quarters. Then we talked about all sorts of things, and I thoroughly enjoyed the conversation, finding that I had plenty to say, and was quite able to hold my own in an argument when not snubbed. He was polite and agreeable, treating my opinions with consideration, and never contradicting me. When we went into the drawing-room, he bade me good night, saying that he had to visit his men and mount a guard. He then went away, and I felt quite lonely. His coming to the house had excited me, and I found that I could not settle down quietly to anything that evening, so I went upstairs to my room and got Rosa to brush my hair for half an hour, and then I went to bed.

Some days passed, and I soon found that the presence of the soldiers had caused nearly all the work on the plantation to come to a standstill. The field-hands did pretty much as they pleased, although as yet they were slaves, the proclamation of their freedom not being made until some time afterwards. I had written to Randolph, making him fully acquainted with the state of affairs, and had received a letter in which he said that he would not come back to Wood-lands just then. It would be no use, and would only annoy him to see his old home overrun by a lot of damned Yankees. He did not think he would be able to stand it quietly, and there would probably be trouble, which most likely would end in shooting. He also said that he was thinking of taking a house in Richmond, and if he did, he would at once send for me. He wanted me badly, as there was not a decent-looking woman to be had in the place. He wound up by saying that when I came away, I could leave everything in charge of the overseers; if there was anything left to take charge of.

The letter was typical of the man. It was utterly selfish; there was not a word of tenderness in it, and he had not even thought it necessary to be silent about his doings with other women. However, his unfaithfulness did not trouble me in the least, and I only smiled when I read that part of his letter. During the time that had passed, I had seen very little of the soldiers, as they kept well out of the way, but I was pretty well sure they were having a good time with the women and girls belonging to the plantation. I knew that Rosa had secured the sergeant for her beau, as I had seen her one afternoon in a summer-house with him in a rather suspicious attitude. But I did not care how many sweethearts the girl had, or what they did to her, as long as she was at my service whenever I wanted her. And she always was.

Captain Franklin had never obtruded his presence on me, but we met at meals, and he always used to spend an hour with me in the drawing-room after dinner. It was a most pleasant time to me, as he was always agreeable and amusing; moreover, we had many ideas in common, and our natures were sympathetic. I saw that he admired me, and before long I felt pretty sure, from the way he looked at me, and by various other little signs, that he had more than a mere liking for me, although I had but little doubt that he guessed the relations existing between me and the owner of Woodlands. But whether he had or not, he always treated me with respect, and I could not help contrasting his courteous, gentlemanly manner, with the coarse, and often brutal way, in which Randolph had nearly always treated me.

Chapter Eighteen

My first love – Captain Franklin's reserve – I employ the courtesan's art of seduction – Low-necked dress and violet perfume – Unwinding a skein of wool – I faint in Franklin's arms and what happened – The violence of his attack – Our mutual passion – The end of the romance.

From the day Captain Franklin came to the house, I liked him, and as I got to know him better, my feelings had gradually grown warmer, until at last I fell in love with him. It was the first time in my life that I had felt the passion. It took full possession of me, and I was always thinking of Franklin when he was not with me. Then I began to want to feel his kisses on my lips, and I longed to lie in his arms. I had not disliked being poked by Randolph, for whom I had not the slightest affection, therefore I thought how delightful it would be to be embraced by the man I loved. Randolph had never cared for me; he had not scrupled to tell me he was unfaithful to me, and above all he had possessed himself of me originally by most cruel means, therefore I did not consider that I was in the least way bound to be faithful to him.

He certainly had given me plenty of fine clothes, and a quantity of jewellery, but then – as he would probably have said himself – he had taken the value out of my body. Anyhow, I thought he had most fully. I became quite lovesick on account of Franklin, or to put it more truly, though in coarser language, I wanted to be well poked by him. But although he had plenty of opportunities, he never made love to me, even in the mildest manner, and yet I felt sure that he did love me. I could not make out whether his reserve was caused by shyness, or by a sense of honour that would not allow him to make advances to a defenceless woman who was quite in his power. Three or four more days passed without his showing more warmth, and as my 'lovesickness' was increasing, and as there was only one cure for it, I determined to make the first advance. Randolph had instructed me well in all the little artifices by which a woman may allure a man. I would try the effect of one or two of them on my cold lover. I remembered that Randolph had told me that if a man happened to be fond of perfume, the odour of it on a woman increased his sensual desire for her. Franklin liked the perfume of violets; so that night when I was dressing for dinner, I sprinkled my chemise and hair with the delicate but strong essence. I then put on my finest petticoats, and a pair of very dainty drawers, with deep frills of lace, drawn in at the knees with bows of pale blue satin ribbon. I then encased my legs in pink openwork silk stockings, and put on my feet a pretty pair of bronze leather high-heeled shoes, with silver buckles. I next made Rosa lace me tightly in my corset, and finally I put on a very low-necked frock. When I was fully dressed, I gazed at myself in the pier-glass, feeling perfectly satisfied with my appearance. My dress fitted me to perfection, my cheeks were tinged with a faint pink colour, my eyes were bright, and my bare shoulders and arms looked very white and plump. I went down to the drawing-room, where I found Franklin, whom I had not seen all day, as he had been away on some military duty since early in the morning. We shook hands, and I let my hand linger in his, but he did not press it, although I saw he noticed my more than usually elaborate toilette.

The dinner passed over quickly, and we were both

in good spirits, chatting and laughing merrily. When we went into the drawing-room I began to exercise my arts. Seating myself on a footstool, just under the lamp, I asked him to hold a tangled skein of wool for me while I wound it. To do this, he would have to stand close to my knees and look down at my hands as I wound the wool. He took up his position in the very way I wanted, and while I moved my arms to and fro winding the wool, I at the same time, in an apparently unconscious manner, swayed my body so that he could if he chose, see the upper part of my bosom and the division between my titties. At first, he kept his eyes steadily fixed on my hands, but after a few moments his gaze was turned upon my half-naked bosom, and I saw his eyes begin to sparkle as he looked into the depths of my corset. I smiled inwardly, saying to myself that I had at last made him show some sign of feeling. Affecting a serene unconsciousness, I continued to show my titties and to wind the wool till it was all done. Then putting my hand to my forehead and closing my eyes, I complained of a sudden faintness, saying that I would lie down on the sofa for a few minutes.

He appeared to be very much concerned, and he asked me anxiously, if he could get me anything. I shook my head, then rising feebly to my feet, I stood swaying about as if I was on the point of fainting, and he, thinking I was going to fall, put his arm round my waist to hold me up. The moment he did so, I collapsed limply in his arms with my head against his breast, and my eyes closed. I ought to have turned pale, but I was not able to do that – however, it never struck him that it was strange I should have kept my colour all through my 'fainting fit'.

With an ejaculation of pity, he tenderly raised me in his arms, carried me to the sofa, and laid me down upon it. I pretended to be quite insensible, but I kept my eyes half-open, and I had managed to slyly raise my skirts nearly up to my knees, so that my feet and legs were exposed. He began to chafe my hands, but I saw that his eyes were fixed on my legs, and I noticed that his face had become a little flushed. Opening my eyes, I said smiling:

'Oh, I am all right now. It was only a slight attack of giddiness and it has quite passed off.'

As I spoke I stretched myself, so as to show more of my legs, and bring into view the frills of my drawers. Still holding one of my hands, he sat down close beside me, looking in my face most tenderly and affectionately.

Taking my handkerchief from my pocket, I passed it over my forehead, and then I let my hand drop, as if by accident, on the upper part of his thighs. I felt him start, and I saw a soft light shining in his eyes, which were again fixed upon my legs. I pressed his thighs with my fingers. Then all his reserve disappeared; he bent down and kissing me on the lips, said in a tone of passion:

'Oh, my darling girl I love you! and have loved you, from the first day I came here.'

His kiss was a fervent one, but tender. It was a kiss of love; the first I had ever received; and it made me thrill with a delicious sensation from head to foot.

Throwing my arms round his neck, I exclaimed:

'And I love you too. Give me another nice kiss.'

Again he kissed me on the mouth, then pressing his lips upon my bosom just above the edge of my dress, he inhaled the violet perfume, saying: 'How sweet you are dearest! Violet is my favourite scent.'

I again closed my eyes, and settled myself well down upon the sofa, feeling pretty sure that I would soon have my desire gratified. It was! Now that the ice had been broken, Franklin was no 'laggard in love'. He felt my legs, praising their shape, admiring my pretty shoes and stockings, and also the dainty lace frills of my drawers. But he soon put his hands up my petticoats, and untying the strings of my drawers, pulled them down, then his hands roved all over my bottom, and he did not neglect the 'spot' between my thighs. However, he did not waste much time in dalliance. In a moment or two, he prepared himself, then raising my petticoats, he stretched out my legs, and opening the way with his fingers, inserted the tip of his member in the 'spot' which was ready to receive it. Clasping me in his arms, and pressing his lips upon my mouth, he gently but firmly forced the dart deeply into my body, with a few strong movements of his loins, and then he began to poke me in the most powerful way. He was eight years younger than Randolph, larger made, and much more vigorous.

The force of the attack almost took my breath away, while the size of the weapon stretched the sheath to its utmost extent, but I only felt a sensation of intense pleasure at being at last embraced by the man I loved. All my voluptuous feelings were excited to a high pitch by the friction of his large member in the folds of the sensitive 'spot', so I was not backwards in the amorous combat. Pressing him to my bosom, and throwing my legs round his loins, I met each of his strong down-thrusts with a brisk upward heave of my bottom. He increased the length of his strokes, his member seemed to go deeper into me, and as the end approached his movements became quicker and quicker, while I bounded under him, arching my loins, and sighing and groaning in an ecstasy of voluptuous pain. At last, with a final tremendous dig, he 'spent', while I wriggled my bottom convulsively, and squirmed till I had received every drop of my lover's offering. Then heaving a deep sigh of gratified desire, I lay quietly in his arms, while he kissed and petted me. It had been a most delightful embrace. I had never before so thoroughly enjoyed being poked. I think that a man always enjoys poking a woman whether he loves her or not;

but I am sure that a woman never really enjoys a man's embrace unless she loves him.

After a moment or two of kissing and soft words, he withdrew his still half-stiff member from the clinging lips which were loath to let it go, and then he pulled down my clothes, and buttoned up his trousers. I got off the sofa, and after arranging my disordered attire, I sat in an easy chair, and looked with a smile at my stalwart lover. He smiled lovingly back, and coming to me lifted me out of the chair; but sitting down in it himself, he took me on his knees, and putting his arms around my waist, held me, while I nestled close up to him with my head on his breast.

After a little love talk, I told him why I had originally come to Virginia, afterwards relating what had been done to me, and how I had been forced by torture to come to Woodlands. He was moved by my story, and when I had finished it, he kissed me and sympathized with me. Then he said:

'I am not a rich man, so I cannot offer you a house and luxuries such as you have here. But I love you, and when the war is over, I will gladly take you to live with me, if you will come.'

'Oh, I shall be only too delighted to go to you,' I replied earnestly. 'But are you sure you really love me?'

'I do really love you,' he answered, kissing me affectionately on the forehead.

It delighted me to hear him say those words, and I made him repeat them. Nestling closer up to him, I returned his kisses with interest, and as my desire was not yet satisfied, I unbuttoned his trousers and let out the thing I wanted. He laughed, and after a little play with my bottom, was ready for action. He then again laid me on the sofa, and gave me another delicious poke, followed by a long chat, sitting side by side on the sofa. When it was bedtime, he wanted to come to my room and sleep with me, but I would not let him, as I did not want the women to know anything about my doings. So after a long and loving kiss we parted for the night. I must say though that I should have very much liked to have cuddled up to him all night 'spoon fashion'.

Next morning we met in the dining-room, both of us bright and cheerful, and after kissing each other affectionately we sat down to breakfast with good appetites. When the meal was over, I took my sweetheart to my favourite little arbour which was an ideal place for lovemaking, and in a short time I was sighing in his arms. Then there passed several days of quiet happiness. Franklin was constantly with me; we wandered about the garden together, or sat in the arbours with our arms round each other's waists like the fondest of lovers. And we *were* lovers. I think he really did love me, and I know I did love him. He rogered me every day, some time or other, and I seemed to get fonder and fonder of his embraces. They were done so vigorously and yet so decently. He always had me in the one position – lying on my back – and he never exposed my person more than was absolutely necessary. I think a man copulates with the woman he loves differently to the way he pokes the woman he merely lusts for. We used to talk and make plans as to what we would do in the future, when the war was over, and we were back in Pennsylvania. It was all very nice, and we both hoped that the fighting would soon cease, so that we might live together.

In the meantime I would have to remain at Woodlands. But our lovemaking was suddenly put an end to by Franklin receiving orders to withdraw his detachment, and return to the headquarters of his regiment. I was deeply grieved at his having to go, and he was equally grieved at having to leave me, but as we had both known that the order was bound to come sooner or later, we made the best of it, and cheered each other up.

Next morning when we had finished breakfast, he laid me on the sofa and gave me a farewell 'visit'. Then after bidding me goodbye, and promising to write to me, he kissed me tenderly and left the house. I stood at the window, with tears in my eyes, watching my lover at the head of his men marching down the avenue, and when they reached the bend leading to the gate, Franklin turned round, and waved his sword to me in a parting salute.

And so ended my little romance. It had not lasted long, and I have never had another in my life so far.

I may as well here tell you that I never saw my soldier lover again, as he was killed a year afterwards at the battle of Cedar Mountain. At that time, I was living in New York, but I mourned for him sincerely, as I had never ceased to love him, and I still keep the letters he wrote to me, and also a lock of his hair that he gave me the day he parted.

Chapter Nineteen

The country is occupied by the Federals – The slaves demoralized – Randolph instructs me to join him at Richmond – 'Bushwhackers' and their depredations.

But to resume. A fortnight passed, and a very wretched time it was to me in every way. I missed my lover; the slaves on the plantation were very insubordinate; and I was troubled at the idea of having again to live with Randolph.

I had written to tell him that the soldiers had left Woodlands, and asking him when he intended to return. He answered saying that he had not made up his mind what to do, whether to come back or to send for me, but he would let me know in due course. Meanwhile I was to see that the affairs on the plantation were carried on as usual. I was so vexed at his letter that I sat down and cried. It was very easy for him, amusing himself in Richmond to tell me to see to his affairs, but things had got into such an utterly disorganized state, that it was quite impossible for me to keep order. I was only a girl, not twenty-two years of age. All work on the plantation had come to an end, as the whole country for miles round was occupied by the Federal troops, and the slaves, knowing that their freedom was at hand, would hardly do anything, while the overseers, under the circumstances, no longer dared to enforce the discipline by their usual methods. Many of the field-hands had run away and no attempt to capture them could be made, while others had openly joined the negro regiments which were being raised by the

United States authorities. The majority of the house-women too, had become utterly demoralized, and several of them had gone off, but others, among whom were Dinah and Rosa, had remained faithful. After a few more days, I wrote again to Randolph, telling him that things were getting worse and worse, and saying that I was afraid to remain any longer by myself at Woodlands. This time, I received a letter saying that as things at the moment were in such a bad state in Virginia, it was no use his trying to keep the plantation going any longer. I was, however, to tell the overseers that he would continue to pay them their salaries if they would remain on the estate and do the best they could for him. He had taken a furnished house, and I was to go to him as soon as possible. The house at Woodlands was to be shut up, and left in charge of Dinah and the other women who had remained.

I was glad to get at last some definitive instructions; for the strain on me had been almost more than I could bear, and I had got into a low nervous state.

Sending for the faithful Dinah, I told her that I was going to join her master in Richmond, and that I intended to start in three days' time. I also informed her that she was to take charge of the house, and I gave her instructions about shutting up. Then I wrote to Randolph, telling him when to expect me.

Next day, I saw the overseers, and gave them their employer's message. The men said they would remain on the plantation and do the best they could to prevent things going to ruin, but they added that there was no chance of getting the slaves to do much work as long as the Federal troops were in the neighbourhood. I spent the following day in packing my trunks, and settling affairs, as far as I could, with Dinah and the other women. They were all sorry that I was about to leave them, though delighted at the idea of being left alone in the house to do as they pleased without fear of a whipping.

The only way for me to get to Richmond – which was thirty-two miles distant – was by driving, and I intended to start at four o'clock in the afternoon, so as to arrive at my destination about eight o'clock. I chose four o'clock as the hour of starting in order that I might escape the heat of the day. All the horses were still in the stables, and some of the grooms had remained; one of them being an old and faithful negro coachman, named Jim, who had taught me to ride, and in whom I had perfect confidence. I sent for him and told him that I wanted him to drive me to Richmond next day, and that he was to have the pair-horse buggy ready at four o'clock.

'Very well, missis,' he said. 'I'll put yo' through all right if I kin. But don't yo' take no money or joolery along with yo'; 'cos de road nowdays is 'fested wid dem low down cusses ob bushwhackers; an' if we was ter come across any ob dem, dey would most sholy rob yo' .'

It had never struck me that there would be any danger in the drive to Richmond, but now that Jim had mentioned the bushwhackers, I remembered that I had lately heard several stories of the lawless doings of these men. 'Bushwhackers', I must tell you, were low white loafers, who, while pretending to act as guerrillas against the Federal troops, were in reality highwaymen, who robbed and sometimes murdered defenceless people, whether they were Northerners or Southerners. Bands of these ruffians infested the Southern States during the war.

I sent Jim away, but I thought I would follow his advice; so going upstairs, I opened my trunks, and taking out all my jewellery, locked the articles up in a safe that was built in the wall of Randolph's bedroom.

The rest of the day wore slowly away; I was restless and nervous; I could not eat my dinner, and I went to bed early.

Chapter Twenty

Farewell to the plantation – On the road – Stopped by the bushwhackers – Robbed, kidnapped, and the awful consequences.

I had a good night's rest and got up next morning feeling well and also much calmer in my mind. After breakfast, I made a few final arrangements, and at four o'clock the buggy, with a fine pair of horses, was driven round to the terrace by Jim. The two trunks I intended taking with me were brought down, and put into the vehicle. I shook hands with Dinah and Rosa, my two favourites, bidding them goodbye and telling them to take care of everything in the house as well as they could. Then climbing up into my seat, I waved a general farewell to all the other women who had come out to the terrace to see me off; and they shouted in shrill chorus: 'Goodbye, missis!'

Then Jim touched the horses with the whip, and we started on our journey. It was a beautiful afternoon, but very hot, though there was a faint breeze stirring; however, as I was lightly clad, I did not feel the heat oppressive. We were soon out of the avenue, and as the comfortable buggy rolled smoothly and quickly along the road, the rapid motion caused the warm, scented air to lightly kiss my cheeks; my spirits rose, and I had a feeling of exhilaration such as had long been a stranger to me. I was not looking forward to seeing Randolph, but I felt glad because I was at last free from the load of care that had been weighing me down during the past few weeks at Woodlands. The road we were travelling was a good one, and, before the war, there had always been a great deal of traffic on it, but now it was almost deserted, so we did not meet a single vehicle until we had gone several miles, and there were very few pedestrians. To pass the time, I talked to Jim and was rather amused by his quaint but shrewd remarks on things in general. When I told him that most likely all the slaves in the South would soon be set free, he remarked in his own jargon, that no doubt it would be very nice to be free, but that, after all, freedom would not fill his belly, and that he would not be able to make a living if Mr Randolph did not keep him. Old Jim had been born at Woodlands, and had never been out of Virginia.

As there was no necessity for hurry; I told him not to press the horses, so we trotted along at an easy pace, and by six o'clock had completed half our journey. We then reached the top of a very steep hill, and entered a long stretch of road running through a thick wood. Jim had just pulled up the horses to give them a short rest, when four rough-looking men suddenly appeared from the bushes, and covered us with their revolvers.

'Drop the reins and hold up your hands!' shouted one of the men.

Exclaiming in a low tone: 'By gosh, missis, de bushwhackers has got us!' Jim held up his hands, while I dreadfully frightened, uttered a shriek, and cowering down, averted my eyes from the threatening muzzles of the pistols. Two of the men lowered their weapons, and came to the side of the buggy, while the other two kept their revolvers levelled at us. Then one of the bushwhackers, a burly, black-bearded ruffian, said with an oath:

'Get out of the buggy, the pair of you; but don't attempt to run away, or you'll both git holes bored in you.'

We got out, and stood on the road, side by side. Jim

was quite unmoved, and though I had been alarmed at first, I was beginning to feel less frightened. I thought the men would merely take everything they wanted, and then let us go on. Seeing that we had no idea of attempting to escape, the bushwhackers returned their pistols to their belts, and began their work of pillage. The traces of the horses were cut; then one of the men mounted one of the animals and, leading the other, rode off at a brisk trot down the road. It had never struck me that they would take the horses, and I wondered how I was to get to Richmond. The three men who remained threw my trunks on the road, and breaking them open, tossed out all my dresses and linen, searching for articles of more value to them than a woman's clothing. But finding nothing, they broke into loud curses and kicked my things all over the road. The black-bearded man, who appeared to be the leader, then told me to hand over my purse.

I did so, but as there was only five dollars in it, he gave vent to his feelings of disappointment in a fresh volley of oaths that made me shiver. The men then going a short distance away, talked with each other in low tones, occasionally bursting out laughing, while I stood in suspense, wondering what was going to happen next. After a minute or two, the leader came back to us and addressing Jim, said:

'See here now, old darkie, I know whar you come from, so jest you start off and go straight back to Woodlands, and don't as much as look back or it'll be the worse for you. Now git!'

Jim gazed at me for a moment, with a dog-like expression of faithfulness in his eyes and a resolute look on his rugged black face, then turning to the man, said firmly:

'No, sah, I'll not leave my missis.'

The man drew his revolver, and pointing it at Jim, said savagely:

'You damned fool! We'll take care of your mistress, and if you don't start right away, I'll put a bullet through your woolly head.'

Jim never flinched, but stood quite still, looking steadily at the man. I am a coward, but at that moment I felt brave. I could not allow Jim to sacrifice his life uselessly. It struck me that the men meant to keep me prisoner to extract money for my ransom, so I said:

'It will be no use your remaining with me, Jim. So you had better go back to the house.'

'Oh, missis,' he said, 'I don't like to leave yo', but if yo' tink it ain't no good my stayin' I'll go, an' praps I may be able to do sumthin' for yo' .'

He then walked slowly away, turning round every now and then to look back at me. I watched the faithful old negro, who I know would have sacrificed his life for me, till he had passed out of my sight down the slope of the hill, then I burst into tears, feeling utterly forlorn. Two of the men picked up some of my things, and made them in a bundle, while the leader said to me, in a quiet tone:

'Now come along with us, and we'll put you up for the night in our shanty, and tomorrow I daresay you'll be able to get a lift on to Richmond, if you want to go there.'

Then taking me by the arm, he led me through the bushes at the side of the road onto a path. The other two men followed, and we walked through the gloomy wood for about a mile, until at last we came to a small shanty. They took me in, and as it was quite dark, one of the men lighted a rude lamp, which enabled me to see the place in which I was to pass the night. It was a squalid-looking place: the floor was the earth, the walls were of squared logs, and the ceiling was made of shingles. The furniture consisted of an unpainted wooden table, three or four benches and stools, a couple of tin buckets holding water, and three rough-looking beds covered with deerskin. On the open hearth a fire of logs was smouldering, and there were a few cooking utensils scattered about.

Chapter Twenty-One

In Bill Jackson's gang – The supper in the shanty – I am violated by the three ruffians – 'Spread-eagled' and stark-naked – Observations on the difference in the members of the ruthless scoundrels.

I had been a little relieved at hearing that I was to be allowed to go in the morning, but I did not like the prospect of spending the night in the dirty shanty with the three men. One of them threw some fresh logs on the fire, and when it had burnt up, he fried some bacon, which he put on the table in the frying-pan along with a piece of corn bread, a bottle of whiskey, and some tin plates and pannikins. The men, each one drawing his sheath knife, sat down to the rough supper, and they offered me some, but I could not eat a morsel, though I drank some water. Then sitting down wearily on a stool at the far end of the room, I watched my captors as they devoured their food. All three were coarse-looking fellows; the black-bearded man, who was called by his companions Bill Jackson, was about forty-years of age; the other two men, who addressed each other as Frank and Tom, were respectively about thirty and thirty-five years old. While the meal was in progress, they did not talk to each other, nor did they speak to me, but every now and then, one of them would glance at me with a smile on his face. And yet, strange to say, it did not strike me that my person was in danger. When they had finished eating, they smoked corn-cob pipes, chatting a little, and passing round the bottle of whiskey till it was finished, but they were all perfectly sober.

Then the man Jackson rose from his seat, and coming over to me, said with a coarse laugh:

'We've been greatly disappointed at not havin' found anything in your trunks wuth a dollar to us. Now we ain't men who works for nothin', so we're bound to git sumthin' out of you.'

'Oh,' I exclaimed eagerly, 'I shall be glad to give you anything you want. If one of you will come to Richmond with me tomorrow, my husband, Mr Randolph, will pay you the money.'

I called him my 'husband', thinking to impress the men. But they burst out laughing, and Jackson said:

'We know better than that. Randolph is not your husband an' I guess he would not pay much for you; but whether he would, or not, nary one of us 'ull go to Richmond to see. There is rather a prejudice agin us in the city, and if we was to go there we would never get away again. So as it is impossible for us to make any money out of you, we intend to make you pay us in another way. We are going to fuck you.'

To adequately describe the horrible events of that night I shall have to use the words the ruffians used. Aghast and utterly horrified, I sprung to my feet, and bursting into tears, exclaimed in a choking voice:

'Oh, don't do such a thing to a defenceless woman! I will send you any money you like if you will not touch me. Oh! Let me go!'

They laughed. Then my terror changed to anger, and I threatened them with the consequences that would follow if they dared to outrage me. But they only laughed more. Then I tried to wheedle them and coax them into letting me go, but without effect, and then again I begged and prayed them to spare me. But all my tears, threats, coaxings and entreaties were useless – in fact, my abject fear and intense misery seemed highly to amuse the wretches – and Jackson said:

'Now see here, young woman; you may jest as well shut up. We are going to fuck you. Will you take the fucking quietly or will you not?'

'No! No! No!' I cried. 'I will not let you do it to me! You shan't do it to me! Oh, you miserable cowards! Don't dare to touch me! Oh, you beasts! You wretches!'

The more I raved in my rage and fear, the more they laughed.

'Well,' said Jackson, 'if you won't take it quietly, you'll have to take it fighting. Now lads, let's strip the little bitch and "spread-eagle" her.'

The three then seized me, and I fought, kicked, scratched, and tried to bite, at the same time uttering loud shrieks, but, in spite of my frantic struggles, the men easily carried me to one of the beds and laid me on it. Then, holding me down, they began to strip me, turning me over and over, wrenching off the buttons, breaking the strings of my garments and pulling them off roughly, until I was stark naked, except for my shoes and stockings, while I resisted with all my strength, screaming, crying and begging them not to 'do it' to me.

Laying me on my back, they stretched out my arms and legs as widely as possible, fastening my wrists and ankles with ropes to the side of the bed. I was thus 'spread-eagled', and entirely at their mercy. Standing beside the bed, they looked down upon me, their eyes gleaming with lust as they scanned every part of my naked body, while at the same time they made admiring remarks on my shape, the whiteness of my skin, and the golden colour of the hair shading the 'spot'. From words they proceeded to deeds. They began to feel me, and I had three pairs of hands on my body at the same time. While one was squeezing my titties, and pinching the nipples, another was pulling the hair on the 'spot', and tickling the lips with his finger, while the third was feeling my thighs and bottom.

Then they would change about, so that at last everyone had felt my shrinking body from head to foot. They touched me roughly, their hands were coarse and hard. When the wretches had felt me to their hearts' content, a difficulty arose. Each man wanted to be the first to 'have' me and so they came to high words, but no one would give way. At last one of them suggested that they should settle the matter by cutting a pack of cards, the man who cut the highest being allowed to poke me first, and the next highest to follow. This was agreed to. Then a dirty pack of cards was produced, and cut by the men in turn. The youngest man cut a knave, the man Jackson came next with a ten, and the third man cut a seven. You can imagine what I felt while my body was being disposed of in such a way. It had been intensely revolting to me to be pawed all over by three men simultaneously, but it would be still more revolting to be poked by three coarse ruffians, in succession. The thought was maddening, and I lay writhing in my bonds, my bosom heaving, my heart swelling, and the scalding tears running down my scarlet cheeks.

The man who was to 'have' me first, unbuttoned his trousers, letting out his member, which stood stiffly erect, and I could not help looking at it with a sort of fascination, noticing that it was long but not very thick. Saying:

'Here goes for the fust fuck,' he threw himself upon me like a tiger seizing its prey, and clasping my naked body in his arms, tried to get the weapon into the sheath.

But at first he could not succeed, for although my extremities were tightly secured; I could move my loins, and so I twisted about as much as was possible, thus for some time preventing his entering me.

The other men meanwhile stood looking on, laughing and jeering at their companion's vain efforts, and telling him that he didn't know how to get into a woman. The struggle lasted for some time, but at last I became exhausted and lay still for a moment. Then before I could recover my breath and renew the fight, the man got his long 'thing' into me, up to the roots, and began to poke me furiously, at the same time pressing his lips to mine with loathsome kisses.

Filled with disgust, I lay shuddering under him while he worked away at me, but as he was highly excited, the end soon arrived, and though I could not help receiving his copious discharge, and though nature forced me to 'come', I had no feeling but one of loathing, so I never moved at the supreme spasm.

He got off me, saying in a tone of vexation:

'She is a damned bad poke! I thought my prick was long enough to have stirred her up, but the bitch had no more life in her than a log of wood.'

The brutes laughed. The man Jackson then made ready for the assault, displaying to my horrified eyes a tremendous weapon, which he shook up and down, saying with a horrid laugh:

'I'll bet this yer little thing will make her squeak if it does nothing else.' He added: 'This'll be the first time, to my knowledge, that I've ever "had" a buttered bun.'

He then got on the bed between my widely-stretched legs, but he did not at once attack me like his predecessor. Turning to the other two men, who were looking on grinning, he said:

'I always take my time over a job of this sort, and I like to play with a woman before fucking her.'

Then he played with me, feeling my titties with both his hands, and also sucking the nipples one after the other. He then passed his hands over every part of my body, stroking my thighs, pinching my bottom, and pulling the hair on the 'spot', and finally he thrust his finger deeply in, hurting me dreadfully, and making me utter a shriek, while my body quivered all over, and I entreated him not to torture me in such a way.

Removing his finger, he inserted his member – I made no useless resistance this time – and with some difficulty forced the great thing into its place. Then gripping me firmly, with his hands under my bottom, he began to poke me slowly with long thrusts, each time drawing the dart out till only the tip was left between the lips, then driving it in again with great force, each tremendous dig shaking me all over and making me wince, and as the parts were stretched to the utmost by the great size of the column as it was worked up and down in me. He spun the affair out as long as he possibly could, while I lay groaning under the terrible battering, and trying to hold myself back, but again nature obliged me to 'come' before he did. Oh! it was horrible! At last he quickened his movements, then in a few seconds he 'spent' and the jets of fluid spurted up me, while I heaved a sigh of relief when I felt his great 'thing' shrink in size inside the folds of my 'spot', but I never moved my bottom. My disgust was increasing.

He withdrew, saying:

'Well, she certainly ain't much as a poke, but she's got a nice little c . . t, and my big p . . . k made her squeak, as I said it would.' Then turning to the third man, he said laughing: 'But you'll be able to get into her easy enough, Tom, as her tight slit is well greased by this time.'

The man laughed, saying, 'Yes, her c . . t is well buttered.'

He then prepared himself, and I saw that he was the smallest of the three, though the instrument he displayed was in full erection. He lost no time in preliminaries, but at once laid himself down on me and with his two forefingers separated me without the least difficulty, and began to poke me quietly, but with plenty of vigour, so that in a few seconds I was for the third time deluged with hot sperm, and for the third time I received the discharge without stirring, but with a sickening sensation of disgust. He then got off me without making any remark, and I thought the horrible ordeal was over, and that they would release me. But to my horror, they did not, though I begged them piteously to let me go.

'We've not done with you, my girl,' said Jackson.

Leaving me tied up on the bed, weeping and shivering with shame and despair, the men filled their pipes, and sitting down on stools, chatted coolly with each other about me and the way I had behaved while being poked, and while they talked they gazed at my naked palpitating body. When they had smoked their pipes they came to the bedside again. Faint and sick, I wailed pitifully, beseeching them to have mercy on me, and not to touch me again, saying that it would kill me. I might have spared my breath. They only laughed and Jackson observed that a woman could take twenty men without being a bit the worse. Again I begged and prayed them abjectly to let me go, but nothing moved the brutes. They had neither pity nor compassion.

However, I need not enter further into the details of my martyrdom; it will suffice to say that they all three poked me again one after the other, and when the last man had withdrawn his member from my quivering body, the receptacle was filled to overflowing by the six copious discharges it had received, so that the hair was covered with the stuff, and it was also trickling in thick drops down my thighs.

They unfastened my wrists and ankles which had red marks round them where the ropes had chafed the skin, and then Jackson threw a blanket over my naked body, telling me that I might go to sleep if I could, as they had got as much out of me as they wanted. Drawing the blanket over my head, I huddled myself up, crying miserably. The men took no further notice of me, but sat smoking and talking in low tones for about half an hour; then leaving the lamp burning, they threw themselves in their clothes upon the other beds, and in a short time I knew by their snoring that they were fast asleep.

My mouth was dreadfully parched, and the 'spot' was throbbing painfully. I wanted a drink; so slipping quietly off the bed, I got a tin cup, and going to the bucket of water, quenched my thirst. I then bathed the red and swollen lips of the 'spot', and washed off my body all outward traces of the horrible pollution. I dressed myself in my tumbled garments, and lay down again on the bed, hoping to forget for a time in sleep the horrors through which I had passed. But though I was physically and mentally worn out, sleep would not come to me. I shall never forget the misery of the long night I spent in the shanty, tossing and turning on the dirty bed. I was feverish at one moment, and chilly the next, but all the time I felt sick with disgust, haunted moreover by a dreadful fear that the wretches might not let me go in the morning. I would have run away to the woods and tried to find my way back to the road, but the door was locked and the small window was closed by a heavy shutter. But if I had managed to get out of the shanty, I should have lost myself in the thick wood and been starved to death.

Chapter Twenty-Two

Daybreak and breakfast – Renewed fears and forced kisses on the mouth – I am liberated – The friendly carrier – Arrival at Richmond and meeting with Randolph.

I don't think I ever lost consciousness during the weary hours, and I thought the morning would never come, but at last I saw the welcome daylight showing through the chinks in the shutter. Presently the men woke, and getting off the beds, stood yawning and stretching themselves for a moment or two; then looking at me, they laughed, making remarks about my pale cheeks and red eyes, while I lay in dire suspense, fearing that one or another of the ruffians would take it into his head to poke me again. But to my intense relief no one touched me. The window was opened, and the fire was lighted, some bacon was fried and a pot of coffee made; then the men sat down to breakfast, ordering me to sit at the other side of the table and join them in their meal.

With downcast eyes and flaming cheeks, I seated myself opposite the three brutes who had outraged me so shamefully, and as I was very faint, I tried to eat a bit of bread, but it stuck in my throat. I managed however to drink a pannikin of the milkless coffee, which, bad as it was, refreshed me a little.

When the rough meal was over, and the men had lighted their pipes, I raised my eyes, and addressing Jackson, reminded him of his promise to let me go.

'Oh, do please let me go,' I pleaded earnestly,

bursting into tears, and stretching my hands towards him, appealingly. 'Surely you won't be so cruel as to keep me.'

He looked at me for a short time, and my heart seemed to stand still. At last he said:

'You are a pretty girl, and though you are a bad poke, you are better than nothing. We'd like to keep you for further fucking, but you'd be in our way, so we'll let you go. I'll put you through the woods to the road, and then you can either go back to Woodlands, or on to Richmond; both are the same distance away, about sixteen miles. You can come along at once if you like.'

A dreadful weight was lifted from my heart, and I rose from my seat eagerly.

'Oh, I am quite ready to start.'

He laughed.

'All right,' he said, 'but you must first shake hands with us, bid us goodbye and give us each a nice kiss on the lips.'

So I had to kiss each of the ruffians in turn, bidding him goodbye, and as I did so, each man put his hands up my clothes and felt the 'spot'. Jackson then left the shanty, and I followed him; he evidently wished to confuse me as to the exact position of the place, so he led me by devious paths through the woods for at least a couple of miles before bringing me out onto the road. Then, after pointing to the direction in which Richmond lay, and telling me that I could not miss my way, he disappeared in the bushes.

There was not a person in sight, and I sat down on a log at the side of the road, uncertain what to do, whether to go back to Woodlands, or on to Richmond. But I did not quite see how I was to get to either place, as I could not possibly have walked the distance. Under ordinary circumstances, I was a good walker, and would have thought very little of a walk of sixteen miles, but at that moment I was weak and faint, sore and stiff; every movement of my legs causing me pain. Not knowing what to do, I began to cry in sheer helplessness, thinking what a dreadfully unfortunate woman I was in every way. But a bit of luck came to me. I had been sitting by the roadside for about ten minutes, when I saw in the distance, a farm-waggon coming along the road in my direction, and when it had got close to me, I perceived it was being driven by a respectable-looking middle-aged man. Rising from my seat on the log, I tearfully asked him if he would kindly give me a lift towards Richmond.

He pulled up his horse at once, said he would, and then giving me his hand, helped me into the waggon and made me as comfortable as he could, looking rather curiously at me, but asking no questions. I gave him a short account of how I had been stopped on my journey and robbed by bushwhackers, but I was silent as to the other things that had been done to me.

He was full of sympathy for me, and anger against the bushwhackers in general, who he said ought all to be lynched. Then he added:

'I reckoned thar was suthin' wrong when I see a lady like you a settin' by the roadside cryin'. Dern this war! There's no law or order now in the whole state of Virginny. I wish I was out of it and back in Connecticut, whar I come from.'

I was glad to hear that he was a Northerner, the fact seemed to give me greater confidence in the man. I had got to be frightened and suspicious of all Southerners. I told him that I also came from the North, and heartily wished I was back there. On hearing that he insisted on shaking hands; then he informed me that he was going all the way to Richmond, and expected to get there in about three hours – it was then ten o'clock. The waggon was heavily laden, so we jogged along the road slowly, and almost in silence. He was a taciturn man, while I, as you may suppose, was not inclined to talk at that moment. In fact, it was as much as I could do to prevent myself crying.

When at length we reached the outskirts of the city, the man said most kindly that if I would give him my address, he would drive me to it.

I thanked him gratefully, telling him where to go, and in about half an hour we reached the house which Randolph had taken furnished. It was a comfortable-looking, three-storied, detached building standing in a garden, and situated in one of the best parts of Richmond.

The kind man got out of the waggon and helped me down; then I asked him to come into the house and see 'my husband', who would like to thank him, and also reward him for the service he had rendered me. But the good fellow said he wanted no reward, and that he was glad he had been able to help a Northern lady in distress. Then he bade me goodbye, and drove off.

I knocked at the door, which was opened by a good-looking, smartly-dressed, white servant-girl, and I asked her if Mr Randolph was at home. She looked curiously at me for a moment, then asked civilly if I was the lady Mr Randolph had expected to arrive the previous night? I said that I was, and she at once asked me to come in, and then ushered me into a handsomely furnished dining-room, where I found Randolph seated at lunch.

He did not rise from his chair, but sat staring at me in surprise, noticing my pale face, red eyes, and generally draggled appearance, then he said in an aggrieved tone:

'Why, Dolly, what an object you are! Where on earth have you been? What has happened to you? I expected you at eight o'clock last night. Where is Jim and the buggy?'

I had not expected to be received with much show of affection, but his cold manner annoyed me very much. I was in need of sympathy and kindness at that moment.

'Oh, don't bother me with questions,' I said sharply. 'I have had hardly anything to eat for twenty-four hours, and I am faint with hunger, so I mean to have something to eat and drink before I tell you what has happened.'

He looked quite surprised at my unwonted display of spirit, but drew a chair to the table for me, poured me out a glass of wine and helped me to a cutlet. I really was famishing, so I made a good meal, drank a couple of glasses of wine and had a cup of black coffee; then feeling much better, I sat down in a comfortable easy chair and told him something of what had occurred. How Jim and I had been stopped the previous night by bushwhackers who had taken the horses, broken open my trunks and robbed me of everything I had in my possession. But I could not bring myself to tell him that I had been outraged by the three men. He listened attentively to all I told him and when I had finished, he asked:

'Where did you pass the night, and how did you get here this morning?'

I had expected the questions and was ready with the answers.

'I stayed in the woods all night' – so I had, in the shanty – 'and this morning I met a man going by with a waggon and he brought me on to the city.'

I do not know whether Randolph thought I was keeping back something or not, but anyway he did not ask me a single awkward question. He was very much vexed at the loss of his two valuable horses, but he was rather amused at my description of the way the bushwhackers had kicked my clothes about in disgust.

'Damn the thing,' he said. 'I would not have sold those horses for less than eight hundred dollars, but we can easily replace your finery, Dolly. It was lucky you left your jewellery behind you. I will go to the police and give information, but I am pretty sure nothing can be done, as the whole country is in such a disturbed state. When you want to go to your room, ring the bell, and Clara, the girl who let you in, will attend to you.'

He then went away, and I remained reclining in the easy chair for a short time. Then I rang the bell, and when Clara came, I told her I wished to go to my room.

She showed me upstairs to a long, airy, prettily furnished bedroom, with a bathroom adjoining, and as soon as she had gone away, I stripped myself, and had a most refreshing bath, scrubbing myself all over with scented soap, till at last I felt that my body was thoroughly cleansed from all outward impurities. When I had dressed myself, the girl came back, and brushed my hair, and although she was quite aware that I was not Randolph's wife, her manner was respectful.

I put a few questions to her, and as she was by no means reticent, I soon found out that Randolph had been in the habit of poking her whenever he felt inclined. However, the knowledge of that fact neither surprised nor annoyed me. It was just what I had expected to hear, from the moment I had seen the girl's pretty face and neat figure.

After she had finished brushing my hair, and had left the room, I lay down upon the bed and fell into a profound sleep.

When I woke, I saw by the clock on the mantelpiece that it was seven. I had slept for four hours, and I felt quite fresh; the colour had come back to my cheeks, my eyes had lost their heavy look, and the ill-treated 'spot' was feeling fairly easy. I was just about to get up and go downstairs, when Randolph entered the room, and coming to the bedside looked down upon me.

'Well, Dolly,' he said, 'I suppose you've had a good sleep? You're looking all right again, so I intend to have a poke, to give me an appetite for dinner. It will be as good as a cocktail for me, and I will make you "cock up your tail", ' he added laughing.

I loathed the very idea of being poked again, and I heartily wished there was not such a thing as a male organ in the world. Six times in less than twenty-four hours had the horrid weapons pierced my poor little 'spot' and now it was going to be transfixed for the seventh time. However, I knew that if I made any objection, it would only make him angry and excite his suspicions, so I did not say a word.

He proceeded to 'cock up my tail', by laying me in a curved position over the side of the bed with my feet on the floor, then turning up my petticoats, and letting down my drawers, he took a long look at my bottom, then he stroked it, and spanked it harder than was pleasant, saying coolly:

'Well, Dolly, I must say that I have not seen a prettier bottom than yours, or spanked a plumper one, since I came to Richmond.'

He then began to ram at me from behind, with evident pleasure to himself, but with pain to me, for though outwardly the 'spot' was apparently all right, the inner lips were excoriated; consequently I suffered a good deal and had to clench my teeth to keep myself from crying out. But to prevent him suspecting anything was wrong, I worked my bottom backwards to meet his thrusts, as if I had been really enjoying the embrace, and when he 'spent', I wriggled myself briskly. But I was exceedingly glad when all was over and he had withdrawn his member from the sore 'spot'. However, he was pleased with me, and giving me a kiss, complimented me on the way I had done my share of the work. After the necessary ablutions, we went down to dinner, which was a good one, and also well cooked, the waiting being done by a neatly dressed, but rather elderly, white parlourmaid. All the servants in the establishment were white women, whom Randolph had taken over along with the house, the owner of which had gone to Europe with his wife and family at the outbreak of the war.

During the progress of dinner, Randolph and I talked about the state of affairs at Woodlands, and he asked me a number of questions, all of which I was able to answer fully and truthfully. Strange to say, he did not ask me a single question about the Federal officer, Captain Franklin. When dinner was over and we were in the drawing-room, we conversed about the war, and he said that most of the planters in the Southern States would be ruined if the Federals eventually proved victorious in the struggle. He further said that though he himself would be hard hit by the abolition of slavery, he had fortunately a large sum of money invested in foreign securities, so that whatever happened he would still be comparatively a rich man.

At eleven o'clock he told me to come to bed, adding that he wanted to have a good naked roll with me. I was glad to go to bed, but I did not look forward with pleasure to more lovemaking; however, I followed him meekly upstairs to the bedroom. After locking the door, he lit all the candles, so that the chamber was brilliantly illuminated. Then he made me take off all my clothes, doing the same himself, and when we were both stark naked, he put his arm round my waist, and waltzed round the room with me till I was quite out of breath, while all the time, his bare breast was pressed against my naked palpitating bosom, his stiff member rubbing against my belly, and he occasionally stimulated my flagging steps by applying a smart slap to my bottom. When he was tired of 'dancing', he lifted me onto the bed, and then holding me in his arms, twining his legs round mine, he rolled over and over, clasping me in a tight embrace, finally finishing up by laying me on my back and sabring me lustily.

Then he allowed me to put on my chemise – I had

no nightdress – and get between the sheets, where he soon followed me.

I thought he was done with me, but I was very much mistaken. He was in great form, so I got very little sleep, as he kept playing with me, at short intervals, all night, besides poking me thrice in a different position each time. It was late next morning when we got up, and it was noon before we had finished breakfast. He then left the house on some business or other, while I sent for my dressmaker and ordered a fresh stock of frocks, hats and bonnets. I then went out shopping and bought a full supply of dainty undergarments, silk stockings and shoes. Randolph always liked me to be prettily dressed, and he never objected to pay the bills for the clothes that adorned me, but he did not give me much money to spend; in fact he was rather stingy. In a few days, I was completely fitted out again, and was able to go out with him, by day or night, wherever he wished me to accompany him.

Chapter Twenty-Three

The battle of Fair Oaks – Departure for New York – No more sights of beaten slaves – Randolph's fresh 'amours' – He starts for Europe – My last spanking – The only reminiscence of 'tenderness' – I begin housekeeping.

A few weeks passed; Randolph paid a visit to Woodlands, and found that everything on the plantation was in a most neglected state, but the house had been kept in order by Dinah and the other women. When he came back, he brought me my jewellery.

A week after his return, the battle of Fair Oaks was fought, the Federal troops drew closer to Richmond, and everything in the city became more dull and wretched than ever. On my former visits I had liked the place well enough, as it had been brisk and lively, and there was always something to be seen, but now there were no amusements of any sort. The shadow of the war was over everything and everybody. It was a dreary place to live in. I was very tired of it, and I would much rather have been at Woodlands.

Randolph, also, had got very tired of Richmond, and of the everlasting fighting that was going on all round, which never seemed to be decisive in any way, although hundreds of lives on both sides were sacrificed.

At last, he made up his mind to leave the South altogether, and go to New York, taking me with him. So he told me to pack up, and be ready to start in a week's time. I was delighted at receiving such an order, and I soon had everything in perfect readiness. The day of our departure arrived; we left Richmond, and in due course reached New York. And as it turned out, we left the city just in the nick of time, for a few days after our departure, the place was regularly infested by the United States troops, and after that event happened it became a difficult matter for persons, even if they were non-combatants, to pass through the Federal lines.

We put up at one of the best hotels in New York, and for a time I was as happy as a woman in my precarious position could be. I was away from the dreadful fighting; I could come and go as I liked without any fear of being whipped by lynchers, or outraged by bushwhackers. I had plenty of pretty clothes of all sorts, and also a considerable amount of jewellery. Randolph frequently took me to places of amusement, and I saw that I was always admired. He was fairly kind to me, and he gave me more money to spend than he had ever given me before. Moreover, I was delighted to have got away from the horrid slave States, and I was glad to know that I should never again see a poor slave woman writhing in agony, and shrieking for mercy while her naked bottom was being wealed by the switch, striped by the strap, or blistered by the paddle, wielded by a man. I had determined, whatever happened, never to go back to the South.

The weeks slipped by. Randolph had made a number of friends, both male and female, so I saw very little of him by day, and he very frequently stayed away from me all night.

I knew he went with other women – in fact he made no secret of his amours – but the knowledge of them did not trouble me in the least. I took a poke from him whenever he chose to give me one, but I never tried to get him to embrace me. I had a number of admirers myself, and could have had plenty of poking had I wished, but I was always faithful to Randolph, not from any feeling of honour towards him, but simply because I did not care for strange men.

At that time there was no necessity for me to allow myself to be poked if I did not wish to be. Captain Franklin was the only man who ever 'had' me, with my own consent, during the whole time I lived with Randolph.

As the days passed, I saw less and less of him, and even when he was with me he never touched me in any way, while his manner towards me became very cold, although he never was actually rude to me at that period. I guessed what it all meant. He got tired of me, and I had a presentiment that he would soon turn me adrift. However, I had always known that our relations would come to an end, sooner or later, and that then I should have to do what many a woman has had to do when finding herself deserted by the man by whom she has been ruined. It was not long before Randolph gave me the news I had been expecting. One morning, after an absence of three days, he came to me and said he had something to tell me. My heart gave a jump. I knew what he was about to say, but I made no remark. He said:

'I am going to Europe with a party of friends, so I cannot take you with me. In fact, Dolly, the time has come for us to part altogether. But although I am leaving you, it is not through any fault of yours. You have always been a good-natured girl, and done whatever I asked you. Therefore I wish to do the best I can for you. I intend to buy you a little house, and furnish it well for you. I will also give you a sum of money to start with. You are only twenty-two years of age; you have a pretty face and a very good figure. You also have lots of good clothes and a quantity of jewellery. You will soon make friends, and I am quite sure you will manage to get on very well here in New York.'

It was a hard way of putting the matter before me and the tears rose to my eyes, but nevertheless I felt a certain amount of gratitude to him for what he intended doing for me. He had ruined me, but he might have cast me off with nothing at all. I thanked him, and he gave me a short kiss saying that he would take me out next day to look for a house. He then went away, leaving me to think over my future prospects. They did not seem to be very bright to me at that moment, but they might have been worse, so I made up my mind to face my position as bravely as I could. I did not see Randolph any more that day, or night, but next day, after lunch, he came for me and we looked at several houses in various parts of the city, but did not find one that was suitable. I need not, however, lengthen out my story by telling you of our house-hunting: it will suffice to say that eventually he bought this house, furnished it throughout, and engaged a couple of white female servants. I afterwards sent them away, and got two coloured women, who I have at this moment in my service. I find them much easier to get on with, and also far more faithful than white servants.

When everything was in order, he brought me here one afternoon, handed me over the title deeds of the house, and gave me a thousand dollars. We then sat down and had a chat, while he drank a glass of wine and smoked a cigar. When he had finished, he rose from his seat, saying with a laugh:

'You know, Dolly, that I am fond of whipping a woman's bottom. Now I don't suppose I shall ever have a chance of doing such a thing in Europe, so you must let me give you a farewell spanking, a real smart one.'

I did not like the idea at all, and a cold shiver ran down my back, as I knew he would hurt me dreadfully, but I had not the strength of mind to refuse his farewell request, so in a rather faint voice, I said:

'I will let you spank me, but do not be too hard upon me. You know that I cannot bear pain.'

Taking a handkerchief from his pocket, he tied my wrists together, a proceeding that alarmed me.

'Oh, don't tie me!' I exclaimed.

He laughed, saying:

'I am going to whip you as if you were a naughty slave girl, so your hands must be tied to prevent you putting them over your bottom during the spanking.'

Thoroughly frightened, I made some feeble remonstrances, but he seized me, and sitting down on a chair, placed me in the orthodox position across his knees; then he turned up my petticoats and took down my drawers.

'Now,' he said, stroking my bottom, 'don't make too much noise, or the servants will hear you.'

Then holding me firmly down, he began to spank me very severely. Oh, how hard his hand was, and how it did sting!

I burst into tears, wriggling and squirming about on his thighs, and as I did so, I could distinctly feel his stiff member pressing against my belly. Clenching my teeth and holding my breath, I kept down, for a short time, the cries that rose to my lips, but at last the stinging became so intense that I began to squeal shrilly, kicking my legs about, and begging him to stop.

But he went on spanking me till my bottom burned and throbbed in a most agonizing way, and I screamed out as loudly as I could.

Then he stopped, and laying me in a stooping position over the end of the sofa, poked me while I was still crying and smarting with the pain of the spanking.

When all was over, he untied my wrists and laid me on the sofa, while he stood beside it, looking down at me, with a smile on his face, as I lay with the tears trickling down my cheeks, all my clothes rumpled, and my drawers hanging about my ankles. My face was red, but I am sure that my poor bottom must have been much redder, judging from the way it was throbbing and tingling. It was black and blue the next day. Bending down, he gave me a kiss, saying laughingly:

'There, Dolly, that is the last spanking, and the last poke you will ever get from me!'

'It was very cruel of you to have spanked me so severely,' I said tearfully. 'I cannot understand why you should have taken pleasure in giving me such pain.'

He was not a bit sorry for having whipped me with such wanton severity, but said:

'Oh, you will soon find that many other men besides me are fond of spanking a woman till she squeals.'

I have since found out that such is the case; many men are very fond of taking a woman across their knees. I have often been asked to allow myself to be spanked, but I have never consented. Randolph is the only man who has ever taken me on his knees, for a spanking. He went on laughing at his own poor joke:

'You know, Dolly, that when a man sets up a new establishment, he generally gives a housewarming. Well, I have given you a bottom-warming instead. I have always admired your bottom, and I shall always have a pleasing recollection of it as it appeared today. It looked very pretty while the plump white cheeks were blushing at the touch of my hand.'

He then again kissed me on my tear-bedabbled face, bade me goodbye and calmly left the house, leaving me lying on the sofa, sore, angry, and indignant. Fortunately, the servants had not heard the shrieks I had uttered while being spanked. I lay quietly until the intense smarting pain of my bottom had somewhat subsided; then I fastened up my drawers, and going into the bedroom, bathed my flushed face, thinking to myself what an utterly heartless man Randolph was. There certainly had never been any sentiment in the relations between us, but I thought he might have parted with me in a more tender way. However, I had no tender feeling for him after the way he had treated me, and so the only 'tenderness' there was about our parting was the 'tenderness' of my sorely spanked bottom.

Chapter Twenty-Four

*The last of my tyrant – I make other friends –
How my present life began – Hate of the Southerners
justified.*

He sailed for Europe next day, and I have never
seen him or heard from him since, but I know that he
remained abroad until the war was over, and then he
returned to Woodlands, where I believe he is now.

As soon as I had got fairly settled in my new home, I
put five hundred dollars in the bank, and went on
keeping house with the remainder of the money.

At first, I did nothing but amuse myself, and I
thoroughly enjoyed being mistress of a house of my
own, doing just what I liked, without anyone to
bother me. But after a time, as money was constantly
going out and none was coming in, and as I had determined not to touch the five hundred dollars in the
bank except in case of absolute necessity, I saw that I
should have to replenish my purse. And there was
only one way for me to do it.

I did not like having to adopt the life, for notwithstanding all I had gone through, I was still a modest
woman to a certain extent. But I made the plunge, and
as I had a pretty face, a well-shaped figure, good
clothes and handsome jewellery, I attracted admiration and soon made a number of friends. I hated the
life at first, and I dislike it still, but have got accustomed to it – like other women in the same position.
Nearly four years have passed since that time, and I
have done well in the 'profession'. I have many good

friends, some of whom are rich and liberal. I have saved money and am still saving, and I have had a couple of offers of marriage.

Perhaps I will get married some day, if I get an offer from a man whom I could love, for although I am what I am, I will never marry a man unless I love him.

About a year ago, I paid a visit of a couple of days to Philadelphia and while there, I heard that Miss Dean was still unmarried, and was as charitable as ever. It had never got to be known that she had been shamefully whipped during her stay in the South. I need hardly tell you that I did not call upon her, though I should have liked to have seen and spoken to the sweet woman again.

My story is finished, and now you know why I said I hated Southerners. Don't you think I have good reason to hate them? They were the cause of all my misfortunes. If they had not whipped me and ridden me on a rail, I should not have been outraged by three ruffians, nor been compelled to adopt my present life.

Conclusion

I remained in New York for three weeks after Dolly had related her story to me, and I frequently paid her a visit, not only because she was a pretty little woman and a splendid poke, but because I had got to like her, and I also pitied her very much. She certainly had been hardly dealt with by men while she was in the South.

On the day I bade her goodbye, I gave her my address, and told her that I should like to hear from her if ever she felt inclined to write to me.

I think she was a little sorry to part with me; for there were tears in her eyes, and her voice shook, when she wished me goodbye.

Next day, I sailed from New York in the *Scotia*, and after a rather rough passage arrived in Liverpool, from which place I went straight home and settled down to my usual life.

Six months afterwards, I received a letter from Dolly, telling me that she was going to be married to a man in a good way of business, a few years older than herself, who loved her, and whom she really loved.

I was glad to hear the news. She was a good-tempered, amiable young woman, who although weak in many respects, would, I was convinced, make a good and faithful wife to the man she loved.

I wrote her a letter of congratulation, and sent her a wedding present, which she acknowledged in a nicely-worded letter. Our correspondence was never renewed, but I hope she is a happy wife.

The poor little woman, who had suffered so much from no fault of her own, deserved to have some luck after all her troubles.

LAURA MIDDLETON

Laura and I were old friends. She was about two years older than I, a very handsome, fine-looking girl but, as I had then fancied, upon rather a larger scale than quite suited my taste. We had always been on very good terms as children, but she had a sort of haughty, imperious air which, joined to the difference in our ages, had operated in a manner that would have prevented me from thinking of taking any liberties with her; and she was about the last person in the world I should have been disposed to imagine addicted to the amusements in which Emily had participated with her.

When I again met her on arriving at the Middleton's country seat, I found that a considerable change had taken place in her person, but probably this was merely the natural result that the preceding two years, during which I had not seen her, had worked upon a girl at her time of life, by fully developing the proportions and fining down the parts of the figure which at an earlier period might have appeared too prominent. I too had grown considerably during this period, more so in proportion than she had, and now her height by no means appeared to me to be too great; and altogether, I could not help acknowledging to myself that I had rarely seen a handsomer or finer-looking woman. She still retained somewhat of her haughty air, though softened down, and I could hardly fancy, when looking at her, that Emily's account of her behaviour in the hours when she gave herself up to enjoyment could be true. I soon, however, became aware of circumstances that tended to corroborate that tale, and which put me in the way of making advances to her, which I hastened to do.

When it came to be time to dress for dinner, Lady Middleton said to me that she had presumed on our relationship to put me into the family wing of the house, as the arrival of some unexpected visitors had made her change the destination of the room she had previously intended for me. She said no doubt I would find the one set apart for me quite comfortable, for the only objection to it, and which prevented her from being able to put a stranger into it, was that it opened into another room which would have to be occupied by her son Frank, who was expected home from school in a short time. This last room, in consequence of some alterations made in building an addition to the house, had no separate entrance, but opened into the two rooms on each side, and as the one on the other side was occupied by his sister and aunt, Frank would have to enter through mine. She said I must keep him in order and make him behave himself, and if I had any trouble with him to let her know. I had not seen my young namesake for about two years, but I recollected him as a fine, high-spirited, very handsome boy always getting into some scrape or other and always getting out of them somehow in such a fearless, good-humoured manner that it was impossible for anyone to be angry with him. So I said I should be delighted to renew my acquaintance with my young friend, and that I had not the least doubt but that we should get on very pleasantly.

On going to my room to dress for dinner, I found a servant-girl engaged in making some of the arrangements which the change of apartments had necessitated. On my entrance she was going to leave the room, but seeing that she was a very nice-looking young girl, I said she need not run away in such a hurry, that surely she was not afraid of me. She gave me an arch look as if taking the measure of my capacities, and replied with a smile that she did not think she need be afraid of such a nice-looking young gentleman. This I thought was a fair challenge, and it induced me to take a better look at her. I found she was a very well-made country girl of about nineteen, with some very promising points about her. I therefore kept her in conversation for a short time, while I went on with my washing operation. Finding she was in no hurry to leave me, I went up to her as she was engaged in putting the bed in order and snatched a few kisses. I then commenced playing with her bubbies and taking some further liberties with her. As my proceedings met with very little resistance, beyond a few exclamations of 'Oh for shame, I did not expect such conduct from you,' I proceeded with my researches and without much difficulty I succeeded in raising her petticoats and getting possession of her stronghold. On insinuating my finger within it, I found it to be tighter and even more inviting than I had anticipated.

She soon became excited with my caresses and the titillation which my finger kept up without her fortress, and I succeeded in laying her upon the bed and throwing up her clothes so as to disclose it fairly to my view. I found a fine, fresh white belly and a pair of plump, handsome thighs with a very pretty little opening tolerably well shaded with light brown hair. Altogether it was a very desirable prospect, and I thought that failing anything better I might manage to find a good deal of enjoyment in her charms. Slipping off my trousers, therefore, I jumped up beside her on the bed, and throwing my arms round her, I got upon her and attempted to introduce myself into the fortress. But here I found greater resistance than I had anticipated from her previous conduct.

I had observed, however, the effect my caresses had produced on her senses. I thought the best plan would be to endeavour to excite them still more. So, insinuating the finger of one hand again into the critical spot, and with the other drawing my shirt over my head so as to leave myself entirely naked, I raised myself on my knees beside her, exhibiting my standard fully erected, flaming fiercely before her eyes. While continuing to excite her by the movements of my finger, I said I was sure she would not be cruel enough to refuse me, but would take pity upon the little suppliant that was begging so hard for admittance. Taking hold of her hand I placed it upon the stiff object and made her grasp it as it throbbed and beat with the excitement under which I was labouring. Her eyes were fixed upon the lovely object thus exposed to her gaze, and I could easily see from the flushing of her face and the sparkling of her eyes what a powerful impression I had made upon her.

All she said was, 'Oh, but if John should know of it.'

I immediately replied, 'But why should John know anything about it? You don't suppose I am such a mean wretch as to tell anybody of what we may do, and if you only keep your own secrets no one need ever know anything about it.

'But perhaps,' I continued, 'you think this little gentleman,' and I shoved the furious member backwards and forwards two or three times in her hand as she still continued to grasp it, 'is not so big as John's and won't give you so much pleasure, but only let me try and I shall do all I can to pleasure you.'

'Oh no, it is not that,' said she hastily, squeezing the little object convulsively in her grasp, and as I bent down to kiss her, she whispered, 'I can't resist you any longer, but you must bolt the door, and if anybody comes I can get away through Miss Laura's room. She won't tell anything; I can easily make her keep quiet.'

This speech not a little astonished me, for from what I knew of Laura I thought she was the last person in the world to make a confidante of her waiting-maid. But I was aware that this was not the moment to expect any explanation, so I jumped out of bed, bolted the door, and speedily returned to the charge, when I found that the opposing party had given up all idea of defence and was quite ready to meet my advances. Stretching herself out in the most favourable position, she allowed me again to mount upon her and, taking hold of the instrument of love, she herself guided it to the proper quarter.

To my surprise, however, the entrance was much more difficult than I had expected and I soon found that I had overrated Master John's capacities and that the fortress, though not a maiden one, had not previously been entered by so large a besieging force. With some little exertion on my part, aided by every means in her power, though she winced a good deal at the pain I put her to, I at length succeeded in effecting my object and penetrated to a depth which from her exclamation of delight when she found me fairly imbedded within her, and from certain other symptoms, I felt certain had never been reached previously. Once fairly established within my new quarter we mutually exerted our utmost endeavours to gratify each other as well as ourselves, and the result of our efforts soon led, much to the satisfaction of both parties, in the temporary subjugation of both the contending forces. Gratified by finding that the issue had been much more satisfactory than I had expected, and not having had an opportunity for some time previously of indulging myself so agreeably, I, much to her surprise and joy, retained possession of the stronghold with my forces so slightly weakened by their late defeat as to give immediate promise of a renewed attack.

Telling her to be still for a few minutes and that we should shortly enjoy ourselves again, I began to question her regarding the matters in which I felt interested. I thought it better at first not to allude to Laura, so I commenced by enquiring about John, and I soon found that the one subject led to the other. It appeared that John was the under-groom whose duty it was to attend upon Miss Laura when she rode out. John had courted Betsy for some time previously and had been admitted to all the privileges of a husband on condition that he should marry her as soon as he could obtain a situation which would enable him to support her.

Betsy, it seems, was rather jealous, and John, to tease her, had pretended that he was on terms of intimacy with his young Mistress, a statement for which there was not the slightest foundation. Betsy's suspicions, however, being once roused, were not easily set at rest, and this led her to pay more attention than previously to her young Mistress's proceedings. She had sometimes wondered what induced Laura to go out by herself almost every morning before breakfast, and now fancying that it might be for the purpose of meeting John, she resolved to watch her and ascertain if her suspicions were correct. She accordingly followed her, and found that she invariably made her way to a smaller summer house at a little distance from the house. Here John never made his appearance, but curious to know what Laura was about, Betsy continued her spying until she one day ascertained that, instead of amusing herself with John's article, Miss Laura resorted to the place for the purpose of consoling herself with a very insufficient substitute for what Betsy had suspected to be the offending member.

As Laura slept in the same room with her aunt she had no opportunity of thus indulging herself.

I drew all this gradually from her, leading her on by

degrees, and trying to make it appear that I had no particular interest in the subject. Her story, however, had such an effect upon a certain part of my body, which was still imbedded within her, that she could not help feeling as she proceeded with her tale the impression it made upon me. Indeed when she came to relate the discovery she had made, I was obliged to stop her and proceed to a repetition of our enjoyment in order to allay the fire which had been so fiercely lighted up within me. When I had brought the second engagement to a still more satisfactory conclusion than the first, I found it was time for me to get on with my dressing so as not to be too late for dinner, and Betsy volunteered her services to assist as valet. The lewd little monkey, however, was too intent upon examining the course from which she had derived so much pleasure to do anything except fondle and caress it, and seeing the pleasure it evidently gave her, I allowed her to do as she liked. While she amused herself with tickling and squeezing the accessories, handling the principal object, kissing it, inserting it in her mouth and sucking it, and doing everything in her power to restore it to the imposing attitude which had pleased her so much, I endeavoured with as much apparent unconcern as I could assume to ascertain every particular as to Laura.

Betsy however was too quick not to discover what I was after, and said to me, 'Come, come, I see quite well how it is with you – you would like this pretty little gentleman I am playing with to take the place of its substitute between Miss Laura's thighs. Oh! you need not try to deceive me – I felt how it swelled up within me whenever I mentioned her name, and how firm and stiff it grew when I told you what I had seen. Well, it would be almost a pity not to let you take compassion upon her; it is very hard she should be reduced to such a miserable contrivance when she might have such a delicious charmer as this to amuse herself with. But I am afraid you would have some difficulty in getting it in, more than you had with me, why her little plaything is not much bigger than my finger; even John's, though it is not near so big as this, is better than it. But as for this wicked fellow I can hardly grasp it in my hand, and I don't see how you will ever be able to make it enter into such a little chink as she has. However, I dare say you will be able to manage it somehow. Come, I shall make a bargain with you: if you will take John as your groom, so as to let us be married before my belly gets big, as I am afraid it will do after this naughty fellow has been into it, I shall do all I can to enable you to enjoy Miss Laura, and I have no doubt we shall soon find means to accomplish it. What do you say?'

I replied that I was afraid such an arrangement would hardly answer. In the first place, I could not turn away my present servant, and secondly, I was afraid that if John were in my service he might perhaps be apt to be jealous of his master.

She laughed and said that would never do. She, however, soon came to an agreement that I should exert myself to find a better situation for John, and I promised her that if I succeeded with Laura, she should make her a present of fifty pounds as a wedding gift on condition that she acted in all respects as I desired and exerted herself to promote my object and conceal our proceedings from everyone. She stipulated that she was sometimes to have the enjoyment of the charming article which she still continued to fondle, and this I willingly promised, but I warned her that she must be very careful that her Mistress should not suspect our intercourse in the least, as I was quite sure from what I knew of her proud disposition it would ruin all my hopes, as she would never consent to be the rival of her waiting-maid. I easily satisfied her that even for her own sake the utmost caution was absolutely necessary, and having now obtained all the information she could give me and the dinner bell ringing, I hastened to the drawing room.

If I had perceived an alteration in Laura's appearance, she had evidently been no less struck with the change that had taken place in my person, and she expressed her surprise at my having grown so much. I fancied I could perceive that there was some curiosity to ascertain what was the extent of the change which had taken place in a certain quarter, and I caught her eyes more than once glancing in a direction where she must have perceived symptoms of a growth at least corresponding to that of the other parts of my body. I was induced to think that she was by no means displeased with the discovery from her manner towards me, which instead of being as formerly haughty and condescending was now frank and friendly. On entering the drawing room I found that Sir Hugh had not yet made his appearance, and that it would still be a few minutes before we went to dinner. I was conscious that the fingering which Betsy had kept up during the whole time I was dressing had again raised a flame in me which I had not had time to quench, and I turned into the music room to take advantage of the few minutes to calm myself down, that I might not make an exhibition before the rest of the party. Laura had observed me, and thinking that the movement arose from shyness at meeting a party of comparative strangers, she came to me and entered into conversation. The charms of her person, more especially after all that had just passed with Betsy regarding her, again raised the flame to an even greater height than before, and the effect was plainly visible through a pair of thin trousers. I soon saw by her heightened colour that the consequences were not unobserved by her. I was afraid at first that she might be annoyed by so open a demonstration of the effects of her charms, but to my great delight she showed no symptom of being offended, but continued to converse with me, and, I thought, rather enjoyed the confusion which the rampantness of the offending member at first occasioned me. Finding this to be the case, I soon recovered my self-possession, and being desirous to make as great an impression on her senses as possible, I placed myself so that I could not be observed by any of the party in the drawing room, and instead of attempting to conceal it, I allowed the protuberance in front to become even more prominent, indeed so much so, as to enable her to form a pretty accurate idea of its size and shape. She took no notice of this, but I knew it could not escape her observation. When a general move was made to the dining room, she took my arm and said that, as I was a stranger, I must allow her to take charge of me, until I became a little better acquainted with the company. I willingly assented, and for the rest of the evening I attached myself to her. Without attempting to take any liberties with her, I omitted no opportunity of letting her see the full effect of her beauty and charms upon my senses.

The next morning I was up early and on the lookout. From Betsy's description I had not been able exactly to understand how I could manage to surprise Laura during her amusement, and I determined to watch and follow her and be guided by circumstances. Sometime before the breakfast hour I saw her leave the house by a side door and proceed through a part of the park which was a good deal shaded with trees. I took advantage of the shelter thus afforded me to trace her steps, unperceived, until I came in sight of the summer house, but to my dismay, I found that it was impossible to follow her any further without being discovered. The building was circular, consisting of woodwork to the height of about four feet and above that glass all round. It was situated in the centre of a flower plot of considerable extent in which the bushes were kept down and not allowed to attain any size.

It was therefore admirably adapted for the purpose

to which it had been applied, as no one approaching it could well see what passed within, while the party in the interior could command an uninterrupted view all round and discover any intruder at some distance. I was quite aware that it was most important to avoid giving her any alarm or making her suspect I had any idea of her proceedings, and I resolved not to attempt to approach her that morning. So, selecting a tree which was situated in such a manner as to command a complete view of the summer house, I swung myself up into it and soon gained a position from which, with the assistance of a small telescope I had taken with me, I could obtain a good view of her proceedings. I very soon discovered that Betsy's story was perfectly correct. She had apparently no time to spare, for, taking out the little instrument from its place of concealment, she seated herself on a couch from which she could command a view of the approach from the house. Then, extending her thighs, she drew up her petticoats and, inserting the counterfeit article in the appropriate place, began her career of mock pleasure.

I watched all her proceedings with the greatest enjoyment, and such was the effect produced upon me that I could not help following her example. I drew forth my excited member and, as she thrust the little bijou in and out of the delicious cavity in which I so longed to replace it with a better substitute, I responded to every movement of her hand by an up-and-down friction upon the ivory pillar, with such effect that, when she sunk back upon the couch after having procured for herself as much pleasure as such a makeshift could afford, I felt the corresponding efforts produce a similar effect upon my own excited reality, which, throbbing and beating furiously, sent forth a delicious shower of liquid bliss.

I allowed her to get up and return to the house without her perceiving me, and when we met at breakfast she was not even aware I had been out. The day passed very pleasantly. She was evidently flattered with the devotion I showed her and seemed noways indisposed to try to what length her encouragement might carry me, probably thinking that she could at any time check my advances should they become too forward.

In the course of the day I again visited the summer house and ascertained that I had no chance of surprising her there without making some alteration in it, which it would take a little time to effect, but which I resolved to have made if I found I could not succeed otherwise. In the meantime, I resolved to try the effect of a bold stroke.

Getting up early the next morning I proceeded directly to the summer house and waited there till she made her appearance. Having made certain that she was alone, I stretched myself on the couch as nearly as possible in the attitude she had assumed the previous morning. I then unbuttoned my trousers and drew them down below my knees and at the same time turned up my shirt above my waist thus exhibiting the whole forepart of my person entirely naked. Then grasping my stiffly erected weapon in my hand, I exhibited myself performing the same operation which I had witnessed her engaged in the previous morning. She came in without the least suspicion and, on entering the place, had at once a full view of my nearly naked figure extended at full length on the couch and engaged in performing an operation the nature of which she could not possibly misunderstand.

She seemed struck with astonishment – so much that she remained motionless for more than a minute, during which I watched her with intense curiosity. Her face and neck, so far as visible, flushed till they were almost of a purple hue, and her eyes were fixed upon the stiffly erected column up and down which my hand was gently moving. I was in great hopes that the sight had produced the effect I desired. But no. Suddenly recovering herself, she exclaimed, 'For shame, Sir,' and turning away hastily left the place before I had time to rise and interrupt her. I would fain have followed her and tried to induce her to return, but I would not allow my passions to carry me so far as to do what might injure her irreparably in the event of anyone being about the grounds and seeing me in the condition in which I then was.

Before I could replace my dress so as to be able to venture out, she had gone so far that she had reached the house ere I could make up to her.

When we met at breakfast she took no notice of what had passed; nor could I discover any difference in her manner to me, beyond her heightened colour, when we exchanged the morning greeting as if we had not met before. But she carefully avoided any opportunity of our being left alone, though I could sometimes detect her eyes glancing towards me when she thought she was not observed, and more particularly in the direction of the part of which she had obtained a first glance that morning.

Having gone so far with her, I was determined to try at least whether I could not get a little farther. So in the evening when a dance was got up I asked her to waltz with me in such an open manner that she could not easily make any excuse for not doing so. As soon as I got an opportunity of saying a few words unheard, I whispered to her, 'Come, come, Laura, this is too bad of you to be offended at me for doing the very same thing I saw you doing in the same place yesterday morning.'

In an instant her face turned perfectly scarlet and then as pale as death, and I am certain she would have fallen to the ground had I not supported her. In a few seconds she recovered herself a little and in a suppressed but earnest tone she whispered, 'Hush, hush for God's sake.'

I led her out of the room into the conservatory and pressed her to sit down on a bench. She objected to this, saying, 'Not here; not here,' pointing at the same time to the door at the opposite side leading into a rosary which was not overlooked from the drawing room. I there placed her on a seat and sat down beside her and waited for a few minutes, till her emotion should subside.

Finding that she was still quite overcome and remained silent, trembling, and evidently greatly agitated by the discovery that her secret was known to me, I said to her, 'Laura, dearest, you need not be in the least alarmed, your secret is quite safe with me, and nothing shall ever induce me to say a word to anyone regarding it, nor need you fear, my own darling, that I shall take advantage of it to make you do anything you don't like.'

She made no reply but at the same time she offered no resistance to the caresses I ventured to bestow upon her, and I even fancied that the warm kiss I imprinted on her lips was faintly returned. I went on to say, 'I cannot tell you what bliss it would give me if you would only allow this little charmer to take his proper place, instead of the wretched substitute I so much envied yesterday. I am quite sure it would give you as much pleasure as it would me.' And at the same time, while I supported her with one arm round her waist, I placed her hand upon the object to which I drew her attention, and which, throbbing fiercely, lay extended along my thigh. Emboldened by her allowing her hand to remain upon it, I unbuttoned a few buttons and removed my shirt, when out it started stiff and erect as a piece of ivory. When I again placed her hand upon it, I felt it grasped with convulsive eagerness. Excited beyond measure by this, I slipped my hand under her dress, bringing it up along her thighs until it reached the object of my adoration, and gently insinuated a finger within its moist lips.

The touch of my finger, however, within such a sensitive spot seemed to rouse her at once, for she started up, saying, 'Not now, Frank, not now, dearest. You must let me go. I must have time to think over this. I know you won't refuse me when I tell you I cannot remain with you at present. There, that is a good boy, go back to the drawing room, and I shall follow you immediately.' At the same time she gave a fond pressure on the sensitive plant she still held in her grasp, imprinted a warm kiss on my lips, and then tore herself from my arms.

I felt that the place was not such as to enable me to attempt to carry the matter farther at present, and delaying for a minute or two in the conservatory that I might calm down my excitement a little, I slipped quietly back to the drawing room. To cover the agitation I still felt, I again joined in the waltz with the first partner I could find. In a few minutes Laura returned to the room, nor could anyone have possibly discovered from her manner that she had so recently undergone such violent emotion. I could hardly believe it possible that the seemingly proud and haughty girl was the same panting, trembling creature who had so recently been in my arms.

I soon, however, found reason to regret I had not chosen a more fitting reason for my denouement, in which case I might perhaps have turned it to greater profit than I appeared likely to do. With the morning, she had recovered all her coolness and self-possession, and had evidently determined on the course she was to pursue. She did not leave her room till breakfast time, and afterwards evaded all my stratagems to obtain a private interview with her.

After luncheon the horses were brought to the door, and a large party started out for a ride. When we had gone a short distance, she contrived to let the others get ahead of us, so as to leave us alone together, for I had got her to dispense with Master John's attendance when I accompanied her. She then turned up a quiet lane which led to a common where there was little chance of our meeting anyone, and where the many bushes, scattered in large clumps over it, were high enough to conceal us from observation.

Then, without any hesitation, she entered at once on the subject which engrossed all my thoughts. She said she could not imagine how I could possibly have discovered her secret, but that as it was clear I had done so, it was no use for her now to attempt to deny it, and that she was quite sure I would not make any use of it that could be injurious to her.

'But don't suppose,' said she, 'that I am offended at the manner you took of showing me you had found out my propensity. It was a very good idea, and I shall be delighted to become better acquainted with my new friend,' at the same time placing her hand upon him. 'He is a very handsome little fellow, but I must tell you frankly that though I shall be happy to contribute as far as I safely can to afford him amusement, you must not expect that I can allow him to do what might get me into most serious difficulties. Perhaps after a time even this may be managed, but at present it is out of the question, so he must be contented for the present with the pleasures I can safely afford him.'

As she spoke, she continued to unbutton my trousers and remove my shirt, until she had fairly uncovered her new acquaintance, which started out under the pressure of her soft fingers showing his head proudly erect. She loaded it with caresses, at the same time expressing in the warmest terms her admiration of its size and beauty. I saw at once from her manner that she had made her mind up on the subject and that there was no chance of complete success on that occasion at least. So I resolved to make the best of the opportunity and humour her inclination, and do all in my power to gratify her in her own way, trusting that on some more propitious occasion I might obtain my wishes in their fullest extent.

Ascertaining, therefore, that there was no one in sight and that we were in such a position as to be able to command a view all round of some considerable distance so that no one could approach us without being observed, I said that all I desired was to contribute to her happiness, and that I only wanted to know in what manner that could be best done, and that I was quite ready to use every exertion in my power to effect it; that if she had any curiosity about her new acquaintance, I was quite prepared to do anything I could to gratify her. She said she was curious about it, and would be delighted to have a better view of it and see what it could do.

I immediately unbuttoned my braces and let down my trousers and tucked up my shirt under my waistcoat, then, bringing my leg over the horse so as to sit on one side in her own fashion, exposed everything to her view. She seemed perfectly enchanted as she took hold of and played with the ivory column and uncovered its ruby head and explored the secrets of the pendant receptacles of the liquid of life. She seemed to be fully aware of the effect of her soft hand moving up and down upon the object of her worship, and she watched with eagerness the consequences her operation produced. I did not attempt to conceal my emotions from her in the least, and gave myself up to the voluptuous sensations which her proceedings could not fail to occasion, till they attained such a height that a full overflow of the precious liquid, spouting from the overexcited tube, fairly attested the effect produced upon me. She gazed upon the charming sight with evident delight, and dwelt upon every excited motion I made, endeavouring by every means in her power to heighten and increase my enjoyment.

When I had in some measure recovered from the pleasure-trance, I threw my arms around her and thanked her for all the pleasure she had afforded me and said it was not fair that I should enjoy all the delight, and I trusted she would allow me to repeat upon her the lesson she had thus practised on me. She said at once that she would not get off the horse, but that if it would afford me any pleasure she was quite willing that I should do anything I liked with her in that position. I saw it was no use to attempt more, so I resolved to make the most of my situation.

Dismounting from my horse, I removed her leg from the horn of the saddle, and raising up her clothes discovered her most exquisite thighs and the enchanting object between them almost completely hidden under a cluster of dark-auburn curly hair. After kissing and caressing it for some minutes, parting the moist lips, and tickling the surrounding moss, I tried to introduce my finger. The tightness of the aperture and the difficulty I had in getting it in beyond an inch or two soon satisfied me that either the pain or the fear of doing mischief had prevented her from using the substitute to such an extent as to deprive the first living entrant of the glory and pleasure of a victory over her virgin charms, and this discovery increased tenfold the desire I felt to be the conqueror in such a splendid field of battle. I did the best I could in the situation in which I was placed, and partly with my finger and partly with my tongue I succeeded in creating such a degree of titillation upon her sensitive clitoris and the adjacent parts that, sided as it was by the excitement of the scene that had previously been enacted, it produced such an effect upon her as she had never previously experienced. When her convulsive motions ceased, and the stream flowed over my fingers down her thighs, she bent down her head and fondly kissed me, acknowledging that I had contrived to afford her more pleasure than she had believed it possible she could enjoy.

I seized the opportunity to point out to her the

effect which her wanton hand had upon my champion,
for she had now bent down to grasp it and play with it
again and it still held up its proud head as erect as
ever. I endeavoured to persuade her that what she had
experienced was nothing in comparison with the bliss
he could bestow upon her. But she remained firm, and
would not allow me to give her a practical illustration of my theory, though she was so delighted with
her little friend that she continued to caress and
fondle him whenever she could, almost all the way till
we reached home.

Two or three scenes of this nature followed in the
course of the few following days, and still I could not
contrive to get further with her. I therefore resolved to
try the effect of a stratagem that had occurred to me.
Though she had resisted all my entreaties to meet me
at the summer house, I had told her the day after our
explanation that I would not act so cruelly to her as
she did to me, and that I was desirous to contribute to
her amusement in any manner she liked best, and,
therefore, as she seemed determined that her visits to
the summer house should be solitary ones, I would
put some books and pictures in the hiding-place which
I was sure would divert her and add to her enjoyment
whenever she would take a fancy to repair thither. I
kept a watch upon her, but never could catch her
there, though I soon became aware from the change in
position of the books that she occasionally visited the
place when she knew I was away and could not surprise her.

I selected a day on which a party was made up to
visit some objects of curiosity in the neighbourhood,
and when she had announced her intention to stay at
home, having already been often at the place, and to
allow another lady of the party to ride her horse. In
the morning I arranged with my groom that he should
file off the heads of the nails of one of my horse's
shoes, so that the shoe should come off easily, and I

appointed him to meet me a short distance from the house on the road we were to take.

After I had proceeded with the party for a few miles, I pretended to think that my horse was going lame, and dismounting, I exhibited one foot with the shoe nearly off. As the horse was a valuable one, the excuse was readily accepted that I could not proceed farther, but must walk him back quietly. As soon, however, as the party had got out of sight, by the aid of a hammer and a few nails I had taken in my pocket, I fastened the shoe, and started back at full speed. Meeting my groom at the place I had appointed, I told him to get the horse properly shod and then take him to a small inn in a retired place a few miles off, so as not to have my return known at the hall. I then hastened to make my way across the fields to the summer house, having a strong hope that Laura would take advantage of the opportunity for visiting it, as my absence would render it safe for her to do so and would at the same time preclude the chance of her being able to have any gratification in my company and reduce her to her solitary amusement.

On making a more minute inspection of the summer house, I had discovered a circumstance which was not apparent at first sight and which had inspired me with the idea of my present operation. The ceiling was formed of small branches, split and nailed together in the form of panels. One of these, I discovered, was moveable and gave access to a small apartment above, part of which was floored over and occasionally used by the gardener to dry seeds. To this apartment the only access was by means of a ladder. The ceiling however was low enough to admit of my catching hold of the sides of the opening when standing on a stool, and thus swinging myself up into the interior. I had contrived, by means of oiling the hinges well and attaching a weight with a pulley, to make the entrance open easily and without the least noise, and I had also made some small apertures in the roof from which I could keep a lookout.

I immediately took possession of my hiding place and closed the entrance, resolved to take the chance of Laura's coming if I had to wait there the whole day, for I knew the precaution I had taken would prevent anything being known of my being in the neighbourhood until the return of the party, who had made the necessary arrangements for taking refreshments with them, and were not to be back till the evening.

I waited with patience all the forenoon, comforted with the idea that in all probability Laura would find herself at leisure after luncheon, at which time some of the elder part of the company who had not joined the expedition usually drove out.

It happened as I had anticipated and very soon after the ordinary luncheon hour I was rejoiced to see Laura approaching. I was very certain, from the manner in which she looked about her as she drew near, what her object was, and I made my arrangements before she arrived so as to be able to keep perfectly still till the proper time came. After taking a walk round the place apparently to make certain that no one was in the neighbourhood, she came in, and taking out one of the books, sat down to peruse it. Convinced that my only chance of success was to catch her in the critical moment when she would be too much overwhelmed by her voluptuous sensations to offer any resistance, and afraid that any precipitate movement on my part might enable her to retain that self-command of which she possessed so large a share, I waited quietly for the effect of the seductive entertainment I had provided for her. Now was it long before it began to produce the expected result. Her colour heightened, she moved backwards and forwards upon the couch apparently unconsciously, and at last her fingers stole under her petticoats and reached the part which was the principal scene of her excitement and which I could see from the motions of her arm she was attempting to allay. In a few minutes she appeared to be unable longer to withstand the temptation which the opportunity offered, and rising up, she went to the hiding-place and took from it some lascivious pictures and the little object with which she intended to solace herself.

After heightening her desires by an attentive examination of the seductive plates, she raised her dress and stretched herself on the couch, much in the same attitude in which I had previously seen her, and after a little toying with her finger she separated the ruby lips and introduced the mock representation of that part of me which I was so eager to enable her to judge how much more pleasure the reality would afford her. Even then I had the patience to wait until she had made use of it for some little time and until I could discern from sundry sighs that the pleasure it was giving her was approaching a climax. Then gently raising the trap door and catching hold of the sides, I quietly let myself drop into the apartment below. A slight rustling noise I made attracted her attention, and looking up from her book, she beheld my almost naked body with the most prominent object of it standing fiercely erect, for I had let down my trousers and turned up my shirt so as to afford her a complete view of my person.

At this sight, so suddenly and unexpectedly presented to her, without her at first being able to discover who it was that thus presented himself in such a guise, she was so struck with surprise and astonishment that she was in the utmost consternation and completely lost her presence of mind, remaining motionless even after I had fully appeared before her and approached her so that she must have recognized me. Aware that, if I was to profit by the opportunity, I must not lose a moment in explanation, I at once got between her thighs which were stretched out widely extended, and withdrawing the wretched mock article from its darling retreat, I threw myself upon her and instantly without the least hesitation replaced it with reality. I was quite aware I should find some difficulty in getting admission, but most fortunately her situation was so extremely favourable that I was enabled so far to effect my object as to get the head of my weapon fairly inserted within the delicious lips of her charmer before she had recovered from her surprise sufficiently to offer any opposition. Then, indeed, she attempted to rise up, exclaiming, 'Oh! Frank, Frank, this will never do.' By this time, however, I had got my arms fairly round her waist and held her locked in a close embrace, and while I endeavoured to stifle her remonstrances with burning kisses on her fair lips, I exerted my utmost efforts to improve my position. My thrusts and heaves, driven with the greatest vigour my burning passion could inspire me with, evidently hurt her severely, but this I had expected and was fully prepared for, as I was aware from my previous inspections of the charming spot that it never had been stretched to such an extent as to enable me to attain free admission, and consequently I was not disposed to relax in my efforts on that account, trusting that the overwhelming pleasure that would ensue would fully make up for all suffering, and that I should obtain full possession, as soon as she should be enabled to join in my transports.

Her very struggles, caused partly by pain and partly by apprehension, as she endeavoured to rise up, only aided me in effecting my purpose, and after a short contest, I had the satisfaction and delight of feeling the resistance which her virgin obstacles had offered to my progress entirely give way, and my victorious champion had penetrated her inmost secret recesses in such an effectual manner as to produce the most delicious conjunction of the most sensitive parts of our bodies that can possibly be conceived. The effect upon her, however, was not so immediately delightful as it was upon me. The pain occasioned by the last few thrusts by which I had completed the achievement had been so severe as to make her abandon her resistance, and when it suddenly ceased, on my weapon obtaining complete entrance, she sank back on the couch as if exhausted. I followed her example and sank down upon her, pressing her more closely in my arms, and being now relieved from the necessity of using force, I regulated the movements of my victorious champion so as to try to avoid as far as possible giving her any further pain, and endeavoured to replace it with more delightful sensations. But with the removal of the pain her apprehensions revived, and she again entreated me to let her rise. Her request, however, now came too late – even had I been disposed to comply with it, which I certainly was not, the excited state into which she had worked herself previous to my appearing on the scene had produced such an effect upon her frame that very few up-and-down movements of my pleasure-giver within the now thoroughly opened up premises were quite sufficient to remove all traces of the pain and to produce the consummation he was labouring to effect and was so eager to join in. Before she had time to repeat her request and even before I was quite prepared to respond to the tide of joy, her head again sank back and she exclaimed, 'Oh! Oh! Delicious, oh! Dearest, oh! I can bear it no longer.' Her ecstatic movements, while in the act of enjoyment, were all that was required to make me join in her delight, and pouring forth a torrent of bliss I sank motionless on her breast enjoying a happiness that may be conceived but cannot possibly be described.

When I had recovered a little from my transports, still retaining my place, I thought it was time to endeavour to appease her indignation which I feared might have been aroused at the trap I had evidently laid for her. But I soon found I had no occasion to be alarmed on this subject. She had no hesitation in admitting that, though she had so long resisted my entrance, it had only been from the fear of the consequences and she had all along been as anxious as I was for the crowning pleasure from the first moment when she had viewed the potent charms of my pleasure-giver, and she had been as much disappointed and annoyed at the unsatisfactory manner in which our intercourse had hitherto been conducted; and she even went on to say that whatever the consequences might be to her she was rejoiced I had had the courage to make her break through the restraint she had imposed on herself.

Accordingly, when I asked her whether her new acquaintance had not justified, by the result he had produced, all that I had predicted as the consequences of his being admitted into his present delicious quarter, she frankly confessed that though she at first had suffered dreadfully from the tearing open of her interior, the final close had much more than gratified all her expectation and had fully made up for all she had endured. And she added that she never would have forgiven me, if I had yielded to her entreaties and left the performance unfinished.

'But now,' said she, 'that this little darling has done his duty so well, do get up and take a look about, in case anyone should stray in this direction. I don't want to part with you so soon, but it would never do for anyone to come in and catch us in this situation.'

'No, no, dearest,' I replied, 'you only half enjoyed yourself the last time, and I am afraid if I were to withdraw this little gentleman I might have to give you more pain in replacing him, and as I want you thoroughly to enter into all the blissful sensations of this occasion, you must let him remain where he is.'

'What,' said she, 'do you mean to say he can do it

again? Oh! That would be delicious! But I am so frightened for anyone coming.'

'Well, dearest, just keep your arms round me, and I shall raise you up till we can take a look about us.' And clasping her round the waist so as to keep us still firmly united by the pleasantest of all links, I raised her up to a position from which we could command a view all round us, and thus satisfy ourselves that all was safe.

Then gently laying her down, I again commenced operations; at first thrusting my weapon cautiously and gradually in and out of the charming orifice so as to avoid the risk of hurting her. But I soon found there was no danger of this. The elements of pleasure were so fiercely aroused within her that my exertions occasioned very different sensations from those which had accompanied my first entrance into her delicious quarters, and in a few minutes her efforts to promote our mutual bliss vied with, if they did not exceed, my own. For the first time in her life she thoroughly enjoyed the most exquisite of all sensations a woman can be blessed with, that of having her most sensitive region fully gorged with the masterpiece which first works her up to the most amorous frenzy and then subdues her by making her die away with itself in melting bliss. There was not a moment from the time when I half withdrew and again inserted the delicious morsel, the possession of which she so much enjoyed, till the overwhelming bliss of mutual emission took away our senses, that she did not evince both by her gestures and her words the most excessive and frantic delight, and I need hardly say that my enjoyment equalled hers.

When our second course was finished, I withdrew my still unexhausted weapon, which notwithstanding its double victory still held up its head bravely, but I was somewhat horrified at the mingled tide which now poured out its crimson stream down her thighs.

She was in great distress less it might betray her, but I managed to prevent any of it getting upon her dress and persuaded her to accompany me to a small fountain a little way off where, dipping my handkerchief in the water, I first removed all marks of the conflict, and then continued to bathe the swollen and tender lips which still bore traces of the fierce nature of the combat. Finding the cooling sensation was grateful to her, I continued the application until the sight of her charms, thus freely exposed, made the author of the mischief so wild at the contemplation of the effects of his own deeds that I was obliged to show the state he was in, and tell her that it would require another defeat before he could be quieted. She hesitated a little from the fear of the pain accompanying his re-entrance in the present tender state of her interior. But seeing that he also bore bloody marks of the fray, she insisted on reciprocating the good offices I had bestowed upon her, and taking the handkerchief, she proceeded to remove them by tenderly bathing the little gentleman.

Pretty well aware what would be the consequence of this proceeding, I allowed her to take her own way. And as even the application of the cold water failed to quench his ardour, she at length admitted that there was nothing for it but to renew the combat and we accordingly returned to the summer house.

Notwithstanding all my care, the pain I occasioned her while getting fairly established within her was very severe; but she persevered in her efforts to introduce him to his old quarters until she had effectually accomplished it to our mutual satisfaction. As soon as I had fairly reached the bottom, I desisted from the attack, and allowed her to remain quiet till all her suffering had entirely subsided and she was again in a condition to be able to enjoy the perfect pleasure.

The first hot eagerness of novelty being now over, we both felt disposed on this occasion to prolong our enjoyment as much as possible and we accordingly proceeded with the operation more leisurely, watching the effects to our mutual efforts to produce the greatest enjoyment, and telling each other when to quicken or retard our movements, so as to keep the delicious sensations at their highest pitch, and at the same time delay the final crisis as long as possible. Sometimes it was I who would urge the fierce intruder backwards and forwards in his career of pleasure; and sometimes, making me remain still, it was she who, with up-and-down heaves of her delicious buttocks, would make the lips and sides of her charming, tight-fitting sheath move over my entranced weapon, creating within it the most voluptuous sensations it is possible to conceive. But at length we could restrain ourselves no longer, and then again commenced a furious struggle of mutual heaves and thrusts intermingled with burning kisses and fond caresses, which soon resulted in drawing from us a pleasing stream of such enchanting ecstasy that Laura declared it was even more delicious than the previous one, which she had believed could not have been surpassed.

By this time she began to be afraid that her absence might be noticed and insisted that it was time for her to return to the hall. Before she left me I easily persuaded her to resume her morning visits to the summer house, and to allow me to meet her there. I satisfied her that there was no risk in this, as in the event of anyone coming to the place by chance, I could easily take refuge in my hiding-place so that no suspicion could arise if she were found there alone.

For several mornings we continued to indulge ourselves with a repetition of our amorous pranks and every meeting only added to the zest with which we gave ourselves up to every mode of enjoyment we could devise.

The sole drawback to our pleasures was the impossibility in such an exposed situation of enjoying the sight and the touch at once of the whole of each other's charms, and I anxiously watched for any opportunity when we might be able to accomplish this. One forenoon Lady Middleton had accompanied the rest of the party on a visit to some friends in the neighbourhood from which they were not to return till night, leaving at home only Sir Hugh, Miss Middleton, Laura, and myself. I had made some excuse for not accompanying the party, but my real reason was the wish to have an opportunity of meeting Laura, as she had been unable to keep her appointment with me that morning, though I little expected that I was to be thereby enabled to arrange for the full accomplishment of our most anxious wishes.

I was sitting with the two ladies when a servant brought in a note for Miss Middleton saying that the messenger waited for an answer. She read it and said to Laura, 'This is very provoking, it is a note from Mr Percival asking me to come over and meet the Savilles at dinner. I should like so much to go, as all our party are away today, and I shall not have another opportunity of meeting my old friends; but I am afraid there is no conveyance to take me. If the pony were able to go, I should drive over in the pony-chaise, but I fear he is not sufficiently recovered from his accident.'

Laura's eyes and mine met, and all the advantage of getting her aunt away for the night flashed upon us. I gave her a look to urge her aunt to go. She reflected for a minute, and then said she did not think the pony was fit for work yet, but that her aunt might send for a carriage from the town, which was some miles distant, and that she would arrange with her mother to come for her the next morning.

To this, however, Miss Middleton objected, saying that before a messenger could go on foot and bring the carriage it would be too late, even if he succeeded in getting it, which was doubtful.

I now thought I might venture to interfere, and

addressing Miss Middleton I said, 'I did not think you would have treated me with so much ceremony. You know there are two horses of mine standing idle in the stable which are quite at your service; if you wish to send a messenger into town, my servant shall go directly, but I think the best plan will be for you to allow me to drive you over in my dogcart, and as you may not like coming home in the dark, I shall come back for you tomorrow at any hour you may fix.' She appeared to hesitate, but Laura had little difficulty in persuading her to accept my offer. She accordingly went to prepare, while I ordered the dogcart to be got ready. Before setting out I arranged with Laura that as it might appear strange were I to insist on returning to dinner when she was alone at home with her father, I should, if invited, remain at the Percivals till evening. She agreed to go to bed at her usual hour and to leave the door connecting her room and mine unlocked and to tie a white ribbon to the door-handle, if all was safe for me to come to her. I started with Miss Middleton, and as I had expected was urged to remain till next day. I at once agreed to stay for dinner, but refused all their pressing to remain all night on the plea that I had made no preparations for so doing. I remained till pretty late and then started for the Hall, promising to return the next forenoon for Miss Middleton.

By the time I arrived everyone had gone to bed, and I hastened to follow their example.

My first impulse was to examine Laura's door, and I was rejoiced to find the agreed-on signal. I hastily stripped off my clothes, and opening the door softly, found her still awake, awaiting my arrival. Throwing down the bedclothes I was about to jump into her arms, when it occurred to me that the operations we contemplated might perhaps leave some traces behind, which might lead to suspicion if discovered in her bed. I therefore said to her that it would be safer for her to repair with me to mine. Ascertaining that her door was locked so as to prevent all intrusion, I took her round the waist and led her to my room.

As soon as we reached the bedside I threw off my shirt and said, 'Now, dearest, since we have at last obtained the long desired opportunity we must endeavour to avail ourselves of it to the best of our abilities. I shall try to contribute as much as I can to your happiness and I am sure you will not hesitate to do anything in your power to add to mine. Now, the first thing to be done is to get rid of all these obstacles to my fully seeing and enjoying all your charms.'

She made no objection to my removing the envious veil which covered her person. Indeed I think she was quite as anxious as I was to enjoy the delight which the contemplation of each other's beauties was sure to produce upon us. However, at last we were both too eager to enjoy the *summum bonum* of earthly felicity to give up much time to the preliminaries.

After a cursory inspection of each other's persons, I stretched her at full length upon the bed and getting upon her I made her herself insert my stiffly distended champion into her delicious pleasure-sheath, and enabled her for the first time to enjoy the delicious sensation occasioned by the complete contact in every quarter of our naked bodies. Making her clasp her arms around me, and twist her thighs and legs about my hips, I drove my rammer into her as far as it would go and then commenced a more voluptuous encounter than any we had yet sustained. Fired by the sight she had enjoyed of my naked person and animated by the delicious sensations which our close contact was sure to occasion, she responded at once to all my movements and there ensued a fierce combat between us, each of us striving by every artifice and exertion in our power to prove the victor, and while conquering, to add to the enjoyment of the vanquished. She proved the conqueror by forcing me to be the first to yield up my tribute; but not wishing to be outdone in the capacity of conferring pleasure, I continued my vigorous heaves and thrusts in the delicious receptacle in which I was engulfed, while I felt the warm life-drops bursting from me in a torrent of bliss, until I was sensible that she also had yielded to the potent spell and shared my enjoyment by mingling her contribution with the tide which flowed from me. Then with a warm kiss we ceased our efforts and lay for a while locked in each other's arms, still joined together by the tender tie that bound us in a perfect heaven of luxurious delight.

If we could have reckoned upon a similar enjoyment every night, we would both have remained thus closely embracing for the whole night without desiring greater pleasure.

But the slight view of her splendid charms I had already enjoyed had only heightened my desire for a more minute inspection of them, and I could not afford to lose the opportunity thus fortunately presented to me. Getting up, therefore, and lighting some additional candles I had prepared for the purpose, I stretched her out all naked as she was on the bed and commenced a thorough examination of all those beauties which I had so eagerly longed to inspect, and which as yet I had only been able partially and cursorily to investigate. No part of her escaped my ardent gaze and eager touch. She willingly yielded to my wishes, nay, she even seemed gratified by my eagerness, and placed herself in every position in which she fancied I should be able to detect a new beauty. Every portion of her body, both before and behind, was in succession the object of my adoration and was covered with the most passionate and thrilling kisses and caresses. The effect of this may easily be imagined, and it was not long before the imposing majesty of my overjoyed pleasure-giver showed to her, and equally convinced me, of the necessity we were under of cooling our ardour by a repetition of the same delightful process which we had already undergone.

After this was happily concluded, she insisted on having in her turn the same privilege I had enjoyed, and she made me undergo the same minute investigation to which she had been subjected. Her curiosity was excessive; every object underwent the most searching examination and of course all those parts in which there was a difference between us were more particularly and vigorously explored and discussed. It was impossible for me to remain insensible to her lascivious caresses which again roused the fire within me. My staff of love started up proud and erect as if eager to exhibit its full proportions to her ardent gaze. Upon me the effect was most delicious. To find myself lying there stark naked before a lovely girl and undergoing the delightful touches with which she covered every part of my person as she explored my most secret charms, and at the same time to gaze on all her splendid beauties which were as freely exposed before me, was bliss indeed which roused me to the highest pitch of excitement, and again I repaid her in the most delicious manner for all the pleasing sensations her charming researches had excited in me. After this we lay for some time in each other's arms luxuriating in the blissful feelings caused by our complete conjunction, till morning beginning to appear, I suggested that she should endeavour to obtain a little repose to prevent the fatigues of the night exhibiting their traces upon her too obviously the next day. Not yet satisfied, however, she laid her hand on the weapon of love, as if to ascertain whether it was yet capable of again conferring upon her the bliss she desired. Quite understanding and appreciating her object, I soon satisfied her in the most practical manner that his powers were by no means wholly exhausted, and having achieved another victory over our raging desires, we at length fell asleep locked in each other's arms.

When I awoke, the sun was shining brightly into the room. During her sleep Laura had somewhat changed her position, and instead of fronting me, had turned upon her left side, presenting her splendid posteriors to me, between which my champion was nestling himself. Judging by his imposing appearance, his powers did not seem in any way impaired by the exertions of the previous night. Turning down the bed-clothes, I for some time quietly revelled in the sight of her charms, and then getting excited beyond endurance, though unwilling to disturb her peaceful slumber, I thought I might perhaps be able without awakening her to take up a more satisfactory position than the one I enjoyed. So gently raising her right leg and creeping as close behind her as I could, I placed my right leg between her thighs in such a manner that my champion shoved himself between her legs, stretching up almost to her navel. In this position I lay for some little time till some half-muttered words and certain movements of her body made me suspect that Laura in her sleep was acting over again the scenes of the previous night. Convinced that she would have no more objection than myself to the illusion being converted into the reality, I gently separated the lips of the seat of pleasure and inserted the tip of the appropriate organ. His sweet touch in such a sensitive spot at once broke her slumber. She opened her eyes, and glancing downward got a full view of my stiffly distended weapon with its ruby head quite uncovered just entering within the charming precincts of her lovely retreat, and she said smiling that it was just what she had been dreaming of. She was then going to turn herself round towards me, but I told her to remain as she was and that I thought we should be able to accomplish our wishes in that position. I pointed out to her that although we could not so well enjoy the pleasure of kissing each other, we could at least better watch and observe each other's operations while my weapon was perforating her, as the reflection of our figures in a large mirror, which I had purposely placed so as to produce the best effect, would add greatly to our enjoyment. Looking towards it, she blushed deeply at beholding exposed to her full view her own lovely face, exquisite swelling breasts, snow-white belly and ivory thighs, with the upper part of the mount of pleasure beautifully shaded with its appropriate fringe and the lips swollen and distended with the shaft of love, while my leg, holding her thighs apart, exposed to view between them the pleasure-yielding receptacles of its liquid treasures, and at every heave I gave exhibited at full length the staff of my weapon as I alternately penetrated and then partly withdrew it from its delicious sheath. This exquisite sight delighted us so much that we determined to prolong it as much as possible, and regulating each other's movements so as to keep up the enjoyment to the uttermost and at the same time hold back the crisis, we lay in the most ecstatic bliss for upwards of an hour, enjoying the thrilling delight which this perfect combination of the most exquisite sensations of touch and sight can confer. At length, in spite of our endeavours, we could no longer restrain the tide of passion, a few furious heaves of my maddened and thrusting pleasure-giver completed our bliss, and the genial shower sprinkled the field of pleasure and calmed our overexcited senses.

One other soul-stirring enjoyment was all we had time to accomplish before the approach of the hour at which Laura was usually called warned us that we must separate, and with the most poignant regret that we might not have another opportunity of again enjoying ourselves in such a delightful manner, we parted.

In the forenoon I drove out for Miss Middleton. As her friends wished her to remain, I of course endeavoured to persuade her to do so and offered to come back for her on any day she might fix, but she insisted on returning home that day. I had, however, the satisfaction of finding that she had made an arrangement with the friends whom she had gone to meet to pay them a visit for some weeks as soon as they returned to their own abode, which they were to do in about a week.

One circumstance, however, occurred the same day which rather counterbalanced the pleasure with which I received this intelligence. Young Master Frank on leaving school had gone to pay a visit to a school-fellow, but a letter had arrived from him that morning to say that he would be home the next day. Now his arrival and consequent occupation of the room between Laura's and mine threatened to prevent the constant agreeable intercourse which I had expected to be able to keep up with her during her aunt's absence.

I felt very much annoyed at the idea, and urged her, if possible, to get some arrangement made by which he might occupy some other apartment. She said, however, that she was afraid to make any such proposal to her mother for fear of exciting suspicions as to her object, or of occasioning my removal to another room, which would be equally destructive for our projects.

On the whole she took the matter so quietly and coolly that I was rather astonished, considering the enjoyment she evidently had in our intercourse. A little annoyed at this, I made up my mind that if my young friend retained any portion of the youthful beauty I remembered him to possess, I would endeavour if possible to make up in his arms for the enjoyment he would deprive me of by keeping me out of his sister's.

His first appearance at once decided me to follow out the idea that had occurred to me. At sixteen, some years younger than his sister and just of that delightful age when the passions of manhood have begun to exert their influence on the senses but before they have taken away the attractive and charming bloom and graces of youth, he was, if possible, more captivating than his sister. Indeed, when upon one occasion I dressed him up as a girl, it was almost impossible to distinguish between them and he might easily have passed for her even among her intimate acquaintances. We became good friends at once. When the ladies left the table after dinner, I made a sign to him to come over beside me, and he was very soon communicating to me all his secrets. I easily led him to talk of his school-fellows and their amusements, and when the party rose to join the ladies he was in the midst of the details of the history of one of the elder boys to whom a married lady had taken a fancy at a house where he had been visiting, and who had conferred a favour on him of which it was very evident my young friend was somewhat envious. When we went to the drawing room, he wanted to continue the history, but I said to him that it would be better not to do so there, but that as he slept in the next room to mine, he might come to me after we had retired for the night, when we would have a better opportunity for discussing the subject. He said he would, but that I was not to expect him till everyone had gone to bed, in case his mother or sister should come into his room. Although a little surprised at this allusion to the latter, I was quite satisfied from what he said that all was right, as, unless he somewhat comprehended my object, he would not have thought it necessary to make any mystery or take any precaution on the subject.

I went to bed, and taking a book, remained awake reading until I heard my door open, and my young friend entered with only his nightshirt on. When he came to the bedside I at once threw down the bedclothes and made room for him beside me. He jumped in instantly, and clasping him in my arms I pressed him to my bosom. He warmly returned my embrace, and the idea I had formed as to his appreciating my intentions was immediately confirmed by my finding something hard and stiff pressing against my belly, and I soon managed to ascertain that his instrument was in a state of fierce erection. After a few kisses and caresses, I led to the subject of his young friend and the lady, asking how old he was, and then laying my hand upon his organ of pleasure, asked him whether his friend's plaything was bigger than this. He said at once it was, and then taking hold of mine, which as may be supposed was standing stiff enough, he added that it was not so big as mine. Continuing to caress his little charmer, I said I was afraid it was a very naughty little gentleman, and asked whether he had ever had a lady to teach him how to behave himself properly. He said, 'Oh! no! I have not been so fortunate, but I do wish I could get someone to do it with me. I can think of nothing else night or day, and I shall go wild unless I can manage it before long.'

The manner in which my caresses affected him showed plainly how excitable he was. He pressed me to him, and as I grasped his instrument he twisted himself backwards and forwards endeavouring to make my hand serve as a substitute for what he so eagerly desired, while he begged of me to tell him whether I could not put him in the way of obtaining fulfillment of his wishes. I at once promised that if he would get permission to pay me a visit at the Hall, I would arrange that he should have as much of it as he liked, if he would only allow me to witness and partic-ipate with him in his pleasures. In his delight and gratitude he at once said that he would do anything I liked, that I had only to tell what I wanted and he would be as eager as I could be to do whatever was in his power that would contribute to my enjoyment.

During this conversation I had been playing with

his pretty little instrument as he had been with mine, and I had occasionally introdueed it between my thighs squeezing them together so as to compress it between them and meeting and returning the thrusts which he could not help giving on finding his little charmer so agreeably tickled by my soft flesh. This drew from him exclamations of delight.

'Why, my dear boy,' said I, 'if this gives you pleasure, as I imagine it does, I think I could manage to make you do it in a manner that will be more agreeable still.' Turning round to him I presented to him my posteriors, and retaining hold of his instrument I inserted it between my hips, and squeezing and pressing it in the same manner as formerly, I enabled him to enjoy the pleasing friction over a larger portion of the surface of his now inflamed weapon. This seemed to gratify him extremely, and he repeatedly thanked me for the nice way in which he said I made him do it, and protested that he had never enjoyed it so much before. I told him I thought I could make it even pleasanter still. I had still retained my fingers round the root of his sensitive plant, and I now drew it back a little, and raising the point, directed it to the orifice between the cheeks of my posteriors. Opening the lips so as to permit the head to penetrate a short way, I made the cheeks of my bottom close round the head of the intruder so as to produce a most delicious compression upon it, which drew from him the exclamation, 'Oh! This is splendid!'

I then asked him whether he had ever put it in here before. He seemed a little surprised at the question, and said, 'No,' and then putting down his hand and ascertaining the little charmer's head was actually within the lips of the orifice, he immediately asked, 'Will it go in?'

'Just try, my dear boy,' was my answer.

He did not wait for any pressing, but immediately pressed forwards, and as I favoured the insertion as much as I could, a very few thrusts sufficed to lodge the charming intruder fairly within me, evidently as much to his delight as it was to mine. As soon as it was driven completely home, and his thighs and belly came in close contact with my buttocks, he ceased his movements and lay still for some minutes apparently in the greatest ecstasy. The complete constriction which was thus established on every part of his stiff-standing instrument – so tightly fitting and pressing upon it and yet so deliciously tender and soft – was so different from anything he had ever previously felt, when his own or a school-fellow's hand had procured from him an emission, it seemed quite to overpower him.

After fully enjoying himself for a little time, he withdrew the inflamed morsel which I felt burning hot within me, bringing it out nearly to its full extent and then replacing it.

He then said, 'Tell me, my dear fellow, may I do this, it is so delicious, but I am afraid of hurting you.'

'Hurting me?' I replied. 'You need not be very afraid of that. Does that feel as if you were hurting me,' taking his hand and placing it upon my inflamed member of which in his excitement he had lost his hold, and which throbbing and burning stood up fiercely erected along my belly, excited to the utmost by the charming pressure which his member exerted upon its sensitive root. 'No, no, the little charmer is not quite big enough yet to do any harm, he is just the size to give me as much pleasure as he will give you. So don't be afraid to do anything you like, and I shall do my best to help you!'

Encouraged by this, he commenced operations which I seconded and with all my might. At first he pushed backwards and forwards, gently and regularly, and I had no difficulty in keeping time with him, but after a little he became so excited and thrust followed thrust with such velocity and so irregularly that

I found it quite impossible to keep in unison with him, and could only aid his frantic efforts by the compression of the muscles upon his raging champion, which I exerted whenever he gave me an opportunity by making a more prolonged thrust than usual within me. In the meantime his panting sobs and sighs bore testimony to the excess of his enjoyment and the near approach of the voluptuous crisis, which was speedily announced by an exclamation, 'Oh, goodness, oh!' I felt my delightful invader pressed into me with all his force, as if he wished his whole body could follow. I endeavoured to add to his delight by a few movements on my part, for he was now so overcome with pleasure as to be almost incapable of motion, and contracting the mouth of the orifice as much as I could, I pressed upon his swollen and throbbing column and strove to prolong his pleasure by delaying as long as possible the passage of the precious liquid through it, which was now bursting from him in furious jets. I succeeded in this so well that he has often told me since that in all the amorous encounters he has subsequently been engaged in, and they are not a few, he has never enjoyed such delicious sensations as he did on this occasion when he first felt the ravishing delight of his pleasure-giving member being completely engulfed within, and compressed by, the magical circle of living flesh.

After he had lain quiet for a little while, I felt his somewhat attenuated weapon slip out of me. He then turned himself round, presenting his buttocks to me and, still keeping his hold on my member which he had maintained during all his raptures, he gently drew me round also, nothing unwilling, and presenting his captive at the entrance to its destined prison, he opened the lips of his orifice as much as he could, and tried to get him in.

I was amused and delighted with his eagerness about it, but fearful of hurting him, I did not attempt to force my way in, until he asked me why I did not assist him in getting it farther in. I said simply because I was afraid that, as he had not tried it before, I might hurt him the first time, but that if he would allow me to try, I would endeavour to do it with as little suffering to him as possible. He at once told me to do anything I liked, that he could not expect me to allow him to enjoy himself within me again unless he reciprocated the pleasure and that he would willingly suffer any amount of pain to be permitted again to taste the delight he had already felt. I was in no way averse to take him at his word and accordingly set to work. As he gave me every facility, I was enabled with the aid of a little cold cream to make my way in with less difficulty than I had expected. My first penetration no doubt hurt him a little, but he bore it manfully and urged me to proceed till, to my infinite delight, I was fairly lodged within him up to the hilt. The avenue was as tight and delightful as possible, but it was of that charming elasticity which yielded sufficiently to admit the invader, and at the same time pressed upon him with that degree of force which occasioned the most consummate voluptuous gratifications. As soon as I was fairly in, all annoyance seemed fairly at an end and, judging from the rise of his thermometer which I held in my hand, there succeeded an increase of the pleasure heat which I had hardly anticipated. The result was that eagerly availing himself of the lessons I had given him, he set to work so deliciously and exerted himself so much to promote my pleasure that in spite of my efforts to prolong the enjoyment, he drew down from me in a very few minutes the first flow that had saturated his virgin premises.

After some little fondling of each other he again wished to repeat the operation. I told him I was afraid of his exerting himself too much, and proposed that we should put it off till morning, but he would not be satisfied with this, and urged me to comply by appealing to an argument the strength and beauty of which I could not withstand. Again this fascinating charmer was plunged into my interior with the same lascivious results and again I was rewarded for my compliance by the full enjoyment of his delicious charms, and after we had each thus attained again to the height of felicity we fell asleep locked in a close embrace.

I awoke early in the morning before he did, and I delighted myself with a view of all his naked charms while he still slumbered. I was unwilling to awaken him even to satisfy my own raging desires inflamed by the sight of such beauty, for I saw that his lovely champion was already raising his head proudly aloft, as fiercely as if he had not undergone any fatigue on the previous night, and I was convinced that if he once awoke, nothing would prevent him from at once commencing and continuing the delightful game till it was time to appear at breakfast.

I therefore resolved to keep quiet as long as possible, and creeping gently as close to him as I could, I placed my throbbing weapon in the hollow between his buttocks, and in that delicious position remained quiet until he awoke. When he did open his eyes, he turned his head round, and finding how he was situated and that I had been awake for some time, he scolded me for wasting so much valuable time, and while he took hold of and insinuated my pleasure-giver into the appropriate niche with which it was in such close contact, he vowed that he was much disposed to punish me by not allowing him to enter.

The joys of the previous evening were repeated. He in his turn penetrated into my interior, and revelled in the same lascivious enjoyment. After we had each thus allayed our fires a little by a copious discharge, we proceeded to a minute examination of our respective persons, while I was highly delighted with the unrestrained exhibition of such charms as have seldom fallen under my notice.

I found that he was not less struck and pleased with what I in return placed at his disposal. Anything of the kind he had previously seen had been of boys of his own age, and this merely by stealth when he had no opportunity of making minute observations. My somewhat more mature proportions, occasioned by the difference of a few years in our ages, were therefore fully appreciated and drew from him the warmest encomiums and the most luxurious caresses.

While Frank and I were thus agreeably occupied in a minute investigation of each other's charms, I reverted to what had fallen from him the previous evening, and asked if he really meant to say that his sister was in the habit of visiting him after he had gone to bed.

'Not now,' he replied, 'I only wish she did, and I would soon repay her the lessons she used to give me. Do you know it was she who first taught me how to do anything in this way?'

I expressed my surprise and curiosity to know what had occurred between them, and he at once proceeded to enlighten me, saying that from the kindness I had shown him he was sure he need have no reserve with me.

'It was,' he said, 'just last holidays when I had returned from school, that our first amusement began. We then slept in the same rooms we now occupy, and as some of my younger brothers were in the room where you are, I used often to lock the door at night to prevent them from coming in and tormenting me. Laura used generally to come to bed before her aunt. She somehow ascertained that I shut myself up in my room and probably imagined that I was better informed on certain subjects than I really was.

'One evening on which there were some old people

at dinner who were likely to occupy our aunt's attention and keep her up late, Laura said to me that she was tired of the party in the drawing room, but that she was not inclined to sleep, and that if I left the door open between our rooms she would come and sit with me for a while. I sat up for some time, expecting to hear her come to her room, but at length I grew tired of waiting, undressed, and went to bed. I suspected she must have crept softly to her own room and waited there without my being aware of it till this took place, for I had hardly got into bed and put out the candle when I heard her come in. She came to the bedside and enquired in a low voice if I was awake. On my answering her, she said we had better not talk loud in case of disturbing the young people in the next room. She sat down by the bedside and leaned over me, putting an arm round my neck and kissing me warmly. Then, putting her hand under the bedclothes, she began to caress my naked bosom. This seemed a little strange to me, but very pleasant. And it was still more agreeable when, putting my arm round her neck, I found that she also was undressed and had nothing but her nightshift and a dressing gown which was quite open at the front. This she accounted for by saying she must be ready to slip into bed if she heard her aunt coming.

'The touch of her naked breasts, with their full, round form, quite delighted me, and it was while playing with them that the first voluptuous sensations were awakened within me. I had previously been sometimes surprised, especially on awakening in the morning, to find a certain little gentleman quite hard and stiff, and had been at a loss to ascertain what was the cause. And I was now still more surprised that as I played with her soft yielding globes, the same effect occurred, but although the sensation was most agreeable, I was too ignorant regarding such matters to be able to connect the cause with the effect. Laura continued to kiss and play with me for some time, and at last I became aware that while with one hand she caressed me, the other was employed in some movement about her own person, the object of which I did not understand and did not think of investigating. The effect, however, seemed to be pleasant to her, for her kisses and caresses increased in ardour till at last with a heavy sigh they ceased at once; and she remained for a few minutes perfectly still. Then after another kiss she said she was afraid her aunt might come and find her away. So making me promise to say nothing of her visit she left me.

'Our interview had been so agreeable to me that I pressed her to renew it on the succeeding night, which she willingly agreed to do, and somewhat of the same procedure occurred on that and several subsequent occasions. I gradually began to discover that as her caresses increased and as her hand came to wander lower down on my person the effect which was produced upon a certain part came to increase in force and to be accompanied with more pleasant sensations. This aroused a suspicion in my mind that there must be some connection between them. So one night, when my little plaything was particularly stiff, and she was very much excited, I took her hand which had never before strayed below my navel and, certainly by no means unwillingly on her part, drew it down and placed it on the throbbing object that had raised my curiosity. She made not the least objection to my making her grasp it, and after handling it for a little, she asked me what was the meaning of it and what I wanted her to do with it. I said I did not know, but that I suspected she knew better than I did, as it was only when she played with me that it became in its present state. She laughed and asked me if it gave me any pleasure for her to play with it. I told her it did, and begged of her to continue to fondle it. She complied very willingly, and then began to question me how long it was since it had commenced to get into this state and whether I had ever played with it myself, or done anything to procure myself pleasure with it. I told her that it was only of late that it had often been in the way of getting stiff, and explained how much it had been affected by her caresses. She then said she thought she might perhaps be able to procure for me still greater pleasure with it, but that it would take a little time to do so, and as she could not remain long enough that night she would come back and try what she could do on the first favourable opportunity.

'The next evening she complained of a headache and retired to bed earlier than usual. As soon as she came into my room, she lighted my candle, stripped down the bed-clothes, made me take off my night-shirt, and at once began to amuse herself with my little plaything. It swelled out and increased in size under her playful fondling to an extent that surprised me. After she had satisfied her curiosity respecting it and its appendages by a strict examination of every part, she took it in her hand and began to rub it up and down. She then put out the candle, so that I did not see what was probably the case – while endeavouring to procure me pleasure, she was at the same time operating upon herself for the same agreeable purpose. I certainly very much enjoyed her performance upon my sensitive article, but still I felt as if something was wanting, and I was greatly disappointed when as usual she sunk almost fainting on my bosom and ceased her efforts.

'After a little she recovered herself and said she was afraid I was still too young to be able to enjoy the full pleasure of what she had been doing, but that she would try again the following night. Still two or three nights passed without anything occurring to heighten my enjoyment.

'By this time I had begun to express some curiosity with regard to her person and to wish to be allowed to extend my researches over it as freely as her hands roved over mine. With some little difficulty I prevailed on her to remove her dressing gown and nightshift and stretch herself naked on the bed beside me. I had been aware from what I had seen of some girls that there was a considerable difference in our formation, but I was astonished at first on finding her centre-part so thickly shaded with hair. I, quite delighted with its beauty, was soon tempted to get my fingers between the moist ruby lips of the charming little slit which I discovered within the curly forest, and to begin to explore its recess. The sensitive little organ I found within so closely resembling, though on a smaller scale, my own organ of pleasure, did not escape my observation, as wakened up by my lascivious touches it darted its little head out from its hiding-place. It was not long before I discovered that this invasion of her inmost recesses occasioned Laura the greatest delight. She seemed at first to hesitate a little, but summing up courage she took hold of my hand and, inserting my fingers within the warmly moist cavity, made me move it up and down within her. At the same time she grasped my weapon and rubbed it backwards and forwards more rapidly and more forcibly than she had ever done before. I felt greatly excited and continued the titillating movements of my fingers within her with the greatest zest, until I saw her stretch her legs out and sink backwards on the bed sobbing violently, while with quick hurried movements of her buttocks she responded to every thrust I made in her inflamed interior. These violent emotions only lasted a few seconds, and then I felt something wet apparently issue from her, trickle over my fingers and down her thighs. She still retained her grasp of my machine, which I felt throbbing and burning more fiercely than ever and giving me more pleasure than I had ever previously experienced, though in her crisis of delight she had ceased to operate upon it. I now begged for her not to stop, but to continue her employment which afforded me so much delight. Suspecting what was indeed the case, that the sight of her charms and of the enjoyment she had undergone had stirred me up to an unwonted pitch of desire which might perhaps be attended with a happy result, she good-naturedly resumed her efforts, and every succeeding movement of her hand upon the throbbing and inflamed member evidently added intensely to the flame that consumed me. She persevered until she had produced the desired result, and I saw a drop or two of white liquid burst from the inflamed point, while at the same time a most delicious sensation pushed through the part affected and from thence seemed to thrill through my whole frame, as overcome with the exquisite delight I fell back upon the bed, she kissing me tenderly and congratulating me on having at length attained the powers of a man; then she left me to my repose.

'After this we omitted no opportunity that was afforded us of amusing ourselves together in the same way. My ignorance on the subject, however, prevented me from thinking of carrying our enjoyment farther, and though doubtless she knew better, she allowed me to return to school without enlightening me any farther. She made me promise two things, first that I was not to indulge myself in any repetition of our pastimes until we met again, and secondly not to say anything to my school-fellows regarding such subjects. I cannot say that I kept my promise on either point. I tried as well as I could to do so with regard to the first, but I could not help occasionally breaking through. But my curiosity was too much excited by our late proceedings not to endeavour to ascertain how some of my elder companions felt regarding such subjects. On sounding them cautiously I discovered that some of them were better informed on such affairs than I was, and from their revelations I became aware of the amount of pleasure I had lost through my want of knowledge to avail myself of it. Since then I have endeavoured to prevail on her to afford me an opportunity of repeating our amusements, but she always puts me off, laughing and saying that I am grown too old for her to allow me to play these tricks now, so that I never have been able to show her what a change had taken place in the size of her old acquaintance or to prove to her how much pleasure I am sure it could now give her.'

This detail produced such an exciting effect upon both of our organs of pleasure that we were obliged again to quench our raging fires in each other's interiors. In the course of the mutual operation I questioned him as to whether, if he had an opportunity, he would like to repeat his former amusements with Laura and even carry them further. He said at once it would be most delightful to do so, and nothing would give him greater pleasure. Then referring to her close neighbourhood to us and to her aunt's approaching departure, he said that there would be such a capital opportunity for our all enjoying ourselves together, if she could only be persuaded to agree to it, that he was determined to try whether he could not persuade her to renew their meetings, and he even showed me a key to the door leading into her room which he had got made on purpose to enable him to have access to her.

His story had somewhat enlightened me as to Laura's ideas, and I could now understand to some degree her not feeling so much annoyed as I had been at Frank's arrival. I strongly suspected that rather than be deprived of her favourite amusement, she would not object to his again being a participator in it. I thought it better, however, not to say anything to him at present regarding my intimacy with her until I had ascertained what her intentions really were. After mutually agreeing that we were both to endeavour to prevail on her to join in our sports, and that if one succeeded he was to do all he could for the benefit of the other, we went down to breakfast.

I had an opportunity sooner than I expected of coming to an explanation with Laura. She had told me that she could not meet me that morning at the summer house, but in the course of the forenoon she found she could get away for an hour, and she gave me the usual signal for me to repair there. When, as she was accustomed to do, she opened my trousers and uncovered her little darling and proceeded to give him his usual caress before introducing him into his nest, her quick eye at once discovered that he was not in his ordinary trim to satisfy her desires. With a flushed cheek, she looked me full in the face, and asked what was the reason for this and what I had been about to occasion such a state of things.

I was very well pleased to have such a good opportunity of coming to the point, and I at once answered that, having been deprived of the pleasure of seeing her in the morning and despairing of being able to accomplish a meeting with her that day, I had been reduced to the necessity of seeking consolation in the embraces of one whose charms put me so much in mind of her that I had almost believed it was her in reality and had been tempted to exceed the limits I had intended to have placed upon myself.

She enquired with some heat and astonishment what I meant. But she blushed scarlet when I replied that Frank and I had been rehearsing some of her lessons. She was at first rather annoyed at what I told her; but when I explained to her that I had not made Frank aware of what had passed between us until I was sure of her approbation and that his reason for confiding in me was the hope of my being of use in enabling him to obtain the bliss he so much coveted – of again regaling himself in her charms – she was quite appeased.

I had little difficulty in discerning that she was

highly delighted with the glowing description I gave of his youthful charms and especially of the size and prowess of her old acquaintance. I dwelt on this and on the necessity there was of taking him into our confidence, and even making him a partner in our amusements, unless we were to give them up entirely, for there could be no doubt if we went on that he would soon discover the footing we were on. Although I could not get her to say that she would consent to this, I was tolerably well satisfied she would make no great opposition. I therefore ceased to urge the point, telling her that she must leave it to me to arrange matters with Frank, if I found it was necessary, and that I would take care not to commit her more than was absolutely requisite.

We had continued to caress each other during this conversation and her charms producing their usual effect upon me I was soon able to point out to her the flourishing condition of her favourite.

I exerted myself notwithstanding my previous night's work to show her that it had not quite exhausted me; and at length she left me quite reconciled by the result of three vigorous encounters.

When Frank came to me that night he was somewhat surprised at the state of my rather enervated champion, which he with great glee contrasted with the vigorous condition of his own. But he was still more surprised when I frankly confessed that I could not attempt to cope with him on that occasion, and explained the cause from which the deficiency arose. He was greatly delighted to learn the footing on which I stood with Laura, and at once concluded that she would not be able to resist the temptation of adding to her enjoyment by making him participate in it. I quite agreed with him, but at the same time I told him the objection she had made and that it would probably be necessary to devise some plan by which at least the appearance of her not voluntarily complying with his desires might be kept up.

After some deliberation on this subject, occasionally interrupted by a renewal of our previous evening's amusements, in which, however, I generally allowed my young friend to take the more active share, we arranged our plan which was carried into effect in this manner.

Laura was now afraid to venture to the summer house every morning, so we had few opportunities of meeting. But ascertaining that her mother and her aunt were going two days afterwards to pay a visit at a distance, which would occupy them the whole forenoon, I arranged with her that if she were left alone, she should come to my room where I would be waiting for her. I then arranged with Frank that at breakfast he should say he was going to take a ride to call upon a companion in the neighbourhood, but that instead of doing so he should conceal himself in a closet in my room and upon my giving a certain signal he should make a noise which would lead to his discovery without it appearing that I knew he was there.

Everything happened as I anticipated. As soon as the carriage drove off with her mother, Laura came to my room, where I was awaiting her. Saying that it seemed an age since I had had the opportunity of fully enjoying the sight and touch of all her charms, I at once stripped myself quite naked and proceeded to perform the same operation upon her. As she enjoyed this as much as I did, she made no objection whatever, and even assisted in getting rid of her clothes as fast as possible. I placed her in several different postures, in order to allow the delighted boy to enjoy the voluptuous sensations I was sure her charms would produce upon him, and then proceeded to the final enjoyment. When this had been completed to our mutual satisfaction, I again displayed all her attractions, and when by kisses and caresses and lascivious touches I had again roused her desires for a repetition of the encounter, I made the agreed-on signal to Frank. He immediately responded by pushing down some article of furniture. Laura started up, exclaiming, 'Good heavens, what is that? Can anyone be there?'

I jumped out of the bed and seized a pistol which was lying on the dressing table and opened the door saying I would take good care to silence any intruder so that he should never be able to tell upon us. On opening the door and disclosing Frank, I exclaimed, 'So it is you, Master Peeping Tom. Well, it is lucky it is only you, for anyone else would have had a good chance of having a bullet through his head. But I shall deal somewhat differently with you. Don't suppose, however, you are to get off unpunished for thus stealing in upon us. I see there is a good rod here, and you shall have a sound flogging for your impertinence and curiosity. So strip instantly and remember the longer you are about it the more severe your punishment will be.'

Frank appeared nothing loth to submit to the proposed infliction and with my assistance was soon as naked as we were.

All this time I watched Laura closely to observe how she was affected by our proceedings. At first she had been dreadfully alarmed, but on finding it was only Frank she was quite aware she was perfectly safe. As I proceeded to strip him, and disclosed his exquisite figure and symmetrical proportions, she evidently became much interested, and when at last I drew his shirt over his head and revealed the full contour of his body with his delicious charmer standing fully erect and exhibiting its rosy head completely developed, I could see a flash of pleasure and delight steal over her lovely features and impart still greater animation to her sparkling eyes. Convinced that I might now proceed to any extremities I said, 'Now, Laura, you must assist me to punish this young rogue properly.'

I then gave her the rod, and sitting down on the side of the bed, I placed him across my knees and turned up his beautiful posteriors to her. She instantly entered into the sport and gave him two or three cuts with the birch which, though not very severe, were quite sufficient to give him an excuse for tossing his legs about and exhibiting all his charms in the most voluptuous manner possible, in which I gave him every assistance in my power. After this playful enjoyment had been continued for some time, I said to Laura that she was too gentle with him and did not punish him half so severely as he deserved, and proposed that she should change places with me and let me take the rod. She laughingly assented and asked me in what position she was to hold him for me. I told her the best plan would be to do as they flogged the boys at school, and I would show her how it was done. Making her lean forward upon the bed, I placed him behind her, and putting his arms over her shoulders, I made her catch hold of his hands, telling her to hold them fast. She did as I directed, while I applied a few lashes to his plump, handsome posteriors which, as I expected, made him cling closely to Laura, bringing his instrument into direct contact with her buttocks, against which it beat furiously, as if eager to effect an entrance somewhere.

I said, 'Ah, I see you have got a very unruly little gentleman there, I must try if we can't hold him fast also.' And at the same time I inserted it between her thighs and again inflicted a few blows.

The near approach of his furious weapon to the seat of pleasure caused him to make fierce efforts to endeavour to penetrate it, and I could no longer resist the imploring glances he cast upon me, expressive of his urgent desire that I should enable him to complete his enjoyment. So making Laura rest her belly on the bed and stretch her legs as far asunder as possible so as to afford him a fair entrance from behind, I loosened her hold of his arms so far as to enable him to stoop down sufficiently low, and then taking hold of his flaming weapon I guided it into the heaven which I felt was burning with desire and eager to receive it. Laura at once accommodated herself to all his proceedings and finding that her hold of his hands rather obstructed his progress, she loosened it, and they were soon transferred to her splendid swelling globes, and then, as he became more and more excited in the hot struggle, were firmly clasped round her waist so as to bring their bodies into the closest possible contact. Animated by the delicious scene before my eyes the fiery impatience of my excited organ of pleasure could no longer be restrained. I threw myself on the lovely young man and almost at the first thrust was plunged up to the hilt in the delicious buttocks which he thus so temptingly exposed to my eager assault.

Once engulfed I had nothing to do but to keep my place and leave to the energetic struggles of the other two combatants the task of bringing the warfare to a successful termination.

After a hard fight, during which the utmost endeavours of both parties seemed to be to try which should be vanquished soonest, it terminated in a drawn battle.

And as I contributed at the same time my share of the spoil, poor Frank's beautiful little balls of delight were quite inundated both before and behind with the stream which flowed from himself and me and which mingled with the first tribute his manly prowess had drawn down from woman and poured in torrents along his thighs. The dear boy was so overcome with the delight that I thought at first he must have fainted, but I soon discovered it was only the swoon of pleasure. Raising him up in my arms, as soon as I could disengage my unruly member from the pleasant quarters it still clung to, I laid him on the bed by the side of Laura who was not in much better condition and stood equally in need of my assistance.

It is wonderful, however, how soon one recovers from such exhaustion, and in a few minutes they were both as lively as ever and were actively engaged in the mutual contemplation of each other's exquisite charms. This pleasant proceeding was enlivened by an animated discussion regarding the alteration and improvement which each of them discovered the other's beauties had undergone since they had last been submitted to their mutual inspection, and it cannot be doubted that Laura was greatly delighted to witness the change in size of the pretty little champion to which she had given the first lesson. All this, of course, produced the usual effect upon us, and Frank seeing that I was quite ready to renew the combat proposed to resign Laura to me. I fancied, however, that they would like repetition of their previous engagement, and he was evidently perfectly able to renew it, for, indeed, the wanton boy had been so wound up by the preliminary scene that his former encounter had produced hardly any relaxing effect upon his lovely weapon. I therefore drew him upon the not unwilling Laura, and again guiding the fiery courser into the lists of pleasure, had the satisfaction of seeing them once more commence the amorous encounter, which proceeded to the ordinary happy result, evidently to the great delight of both parties.

Frank, revelling in the blissful conjunction of every part of their naked bodies, clasped Laura round the neck and imprinted burning kisses upon her lovely lips, while his rampant steed plunged violently backwards and forwards in the abyss of pleasure and his charming buttocks bounded and quivered with the excess of wanton delight. Greatly interested in watching the delightful encounter, I endeavoured to promote their enjoyment by tickling and playing with them in the most sensitive places, till their excitement reached its height and they both sunk down in the swoon of pleasure.

Laura had no sooner recovered a little from the effects of this engagement, than Frank insisted on seeing me perform the same pleasant operation in which he had just been engaged. Nothing loth, I immediately humoured his fancy, getting upon Laura, who was still lying on her back in the bed. The lascivious and not yet exhausted boy had no sooner got us fairly placed and my weapon inserted in Laura's sheath and set to work, than I felt him separate our legs so as to enable him to kneel down between them behind us. Having established his position satisfactorily, he instantly plunged his still rampant champion into my rear, producing in me the most rapturous sensations, which soon caused me in conjunction with Laura to die away in bliss before he was ready to join our sacrifice.

Finding that he was determined to complete his third pleasing operation, I proposed that he should change his position and take up my place in Laura's palace of pleasure and allow me again to stimulate him in the rear, and assist him to attain his object. He highly approved of this proposal, and immediately took up his position in Laura's arms, while, getting behind him and inserting my weapon in his delicious sheath, I proceeded to render him the same agreeable service he had just done me. This speedily had the desired effect, and a delicious emission from all the three parties brought our undertaking to a most successful and satisfactory conclusion.

By this time, Laura for once had had enough to satisfy her, and we separated, sadly grudging the loss of the two days which were still to pass before the departure of her aunt would admit to a renewal of our joys in security. We faithfully proposed on our part that we should be abstinent in the meantime with the view of being the better able to enjoy ourselves thoroughly when the happy time for our all again meeting together should arrive. Upon the whole, with the assistance of an occasional solace from her in the summer house, when an opportunity afforded, we kept our promise tolerably well, though as Frank would insist on coming to my bed, and we could neither of us refrain from indulging in a sight of each other's charms, it was sometimes a hard struggle to restrain our desires.

At length Miss Middleton's departure enabled us to give free course to all our wanton inclinations, and night after night my room was the scene of a repetition of the most exquisite and voluptuous enjoyments it is possible to conceive. When our exhausted frames could no longer furnish us with the means of indulging in the performance of our soul-stirring rites, we were never tired of gazing on and caressing the delicious forms which were constantly exhibited without reserve for the delectation and amusement of one another, for we all seemed to feel that our own delight was heightened by aiding to promote the happiness of the others. We had no secrets from Laura; in fact, she had witnessed with delight the pleasures which Frank and I mutually conferred upon each other. On one occasion when she was disqualified from joining in our amusements, she watched Frank and me stripping and enjoying by ourselves the pleasures she was unable to participate in.

The evident delight they afforded us affected her so greatly that she declared she must try the effect of the same operation upon herself. Accordingly, the next night she insisted upon us both operating on her at the same time. Frank offered to me the choice of routes. But as I was aware that he had often contemplated with great pleasure the idea of opening up the new way, which he thought would be peculiarly well suited to his yet somewhat undeveloped proportions, I at once gave him the precedence. I told him that, as I had already had one victory over a maiden citadel, it was only fair that he should enjoy the next and that it was better he should do so, as in all probability he would obtain it with less suffering to the conquered fair one than if my larger battering ram were at first introduced. Laura quite approved of this arrangement. Having all stripped quite naked, I laid myself down in the bed at full length and then drew her upon me, making her place herself so as to bring her cavity just over the stiff pole which was standing up ready to enter it. She herself inserted and adjusted it in the most satisfactory manner. When she was quite impaled upon me and firmly fastened by the wedge being fairly driven home in her, Frank got between her legs on his knees, and with lance in hand, proceeded to insert it in her hinder cavity. Being, however, his first attempt at storming a maiden fortress, he was not very expert at it, and the coveted way proving very narrow and confined, it was not without some difficulty he effected his object. The obstacles, however, only increased the ardour of his desires, and, with the assistance of a little cold cream, they were at length happily surmounted, and his weapon forced its way into the interior of the citadel. During this time I endeavoured to keep as quiet as possible, and as Frank's efforts occasioned her some pain, Laura also remained nearly motionless, only exerting herself a little occasionally to humour his movements and assist him in effecting an entrance. As soon, however, as I found from his exclamation of delight that his weapon had overcome all resistance and was as fully embedded in the lascivious, fleshy sheath as mine was, I began at first gently and quietly, and then more rapidly and vigorously, to join in the combat, heaving my buttocks up and down and urging the lusty pole backwards and forwards in its delicious quarters, only pausing now and then to receive and return the burning kisses which Laura, now rendered quite frantic with the double enjoyment stimulating her both before and behind, showered upon me. I soon found that any further efforts on my part were quite unnecessary. Maddened by the novel excitement, Laura heaved and thrust alternately, displacing and replacing the sturdy instruments above and below, and declaring she really knew not which of them afforded her the greatest delight. I, therefore, confined myself to favouring her movements so as to give them the greatest possible effect, till at last with her eyes flashing fire and her whole body panting and heaving with the excess of her emotion, she almost shouted out, 'Oh, heavens, this is too much!' Her grasp round me slackened, and she sunk entranced on my bosom, while Frank and I responded to her call, and a few frantic heaves on both our parts served to cause our rivers of delight to flow into her where, mingling with her own flood, they somewhat served to calm our over-excited senses.

It was some time before Laura came to herself, but when she did she was delighted to find that we still retained our respective positions within her. On my enquiring whether they felt disposed for a renewal of the combat in a similar manner, they both declared with the most impassioned caresses that nothing would give them greater delight.

Telling Frank that as the entrance to both fortresses was now well lubricated, we might venture to carry on the warfare more boldly without the risk of doing any damage, I desired him to keep time with me and thrust his weapon as far in and out as he could at each heave, first alternately with me and then on a given signal both together.

At the same time I advised Laura to remain quiet and try what would be the effect of our efforts. The result far surpassed her expectations. When, after heaving alternately for some little time, I gave Frank the signal and we made a simultaneous thrust together, burying both our weapons as far as they would go within the soft yielding flesh, she exclaimed,

'Oh, this is exquisite, it could not possibly be more heavenly.' We continued this mode of action for some time, alternately changing from one variety to another, while she responded merely by twisting and wriggling her buttocks, and in turn compressing and squeezing the darling object before or behind, which for the moment affected her senses the more powerfully. Gradually, however, she became too much animated to adhere to any settled plan, and she could not refrain from meeting and returning our lusty efforts to promote her enjoyment. This only animated us to fresh exertions in which we were so successful that we were soon rewarded by as overpowering an overflow of bliss as before.

As soon as it was over, she insisted on laying us both out at full length on the bed quite naked, bring our organs of pleasure so close together that she could caress them at the same time, and placing herself upon us so that her mouth came in contact with them. In this position she remained for a long time – kissing, caressing, and sucking the instruments of delight and thanking us in the warmest manner for the excessive joy we had given her until her luscious caresses, exciting us almost to madness, forced us again to allay the irritation produced on our burning weapons by again bringing them into her delightful sheaths.

In such exquisite amusements a few weeks passed rapidly away without any interruption to our joys, when we were startled by learning from Laura that there was a derangement of the usual symptoms which she feared indicated pregnancy. This greatly alarmed us, for trusting to our youth we had had no fear on this subject. I lost no time in consulting an eminent London surgeon, but his reply was that the symptoms were usual in cases of pregnancy, but that they were not infallible signs of it, as they sometimes occurred from other causes. It was, however, obvious that some arrangement must be made to provide for the occurrence of the possible event. I, of course, told Laura that if it should turn out as she feared, we must make up our minds to run off together and getting up a story of her having been previously privately married, keep out of the way until the noise of the affair blew over. This plan, however, did not meet her approbation. She said that whatever might really have been the case, everyone would at once say from the difference in our ages that she must have seduced me and that she would never be able to show her face again in society, and that moreover she could not think of inflicting such a penalty on me as to saddle me for life with a wife older than myself, when she had been as much to blame in the matter as I had.

After a great deal of consideration I ventured to hint whether her best plan would not be to accept Sir Charles Tracy, marry him at once, and get the ceremony over without delay, so that if a child did come, there might be at least the lapse of six months to admit of the possibility of his being the father.

I must here explain that Sir Charles had been an almost constant resident at the Hall ever since my arrival, and was evidently looked upon by the family as a suitor. He was a young man of about twenty-seven, of large fortune, tall, handsome, and well made, not particularly clever, but almost the best-tempered and most good-natured person I ever met. His object in remaining so long was quite obvious. Although she would never admit it, I had all along fancied that Laura liked him; but since I had become so intimate with her, she certainly had shown more coldness towards him than she did on my first arrival.

At first, Laura said this plan would never do. But, as we could devise nothing else, on my pressing her a little on the subject she admitted that before I came she had made up her mind to accept him if he proposed, but that she was afraid to do so now for two reasons: first, she feared he might discover on his first attack that someone had had access before him to the sanctuary of love and secondly, from the dread that in the event of a child coming before the usual time he might denounce her and turn her adrift.

I considered a little, and then asked her whether if these difficulties could be got over she would still be disposed to marry him.

She said it was no use thinking of it, but that if it were not for the objections she had mentioned, she certainly would, as she thought she could live happily with him.

I then told her that as to the first objection she might set her mind perfectly at ease, for from what I had already seen of Sir Charles, his instrument I knew was so much larger than anything that had found its way into her and he would find so much difficulty in getting it in for the first time that he would never suspect any intruder had been before him, and that if, as she easily might, she insisted in the operation being performed in the dark, I could supply her with a contrivance by which a little red liquid might be applied so as to produce the natural appearance of an effusion of blood. Then as to the second objection, I told her I thought there would be little fear of his making any complaint at least in public on the subject, if she had the power to hold out to him that she could bring forward a matter which it would be equally unpleasant for him to have disclosed.

She said that in such a case the matter might perhaps be arranged, but she could not imagine how she was to obtain such a hold over him.

I told her I thought she might leave that to me. I then explained to her that Sir Charles had taken a fancy to me on my arrival, and had shown me every kindness and attention, evidently wishing to be on an intimate footing with me.

The poor fellow no doubt was in an awkward predicament. Inflamed by the constant sight of the charms of Laura, of whom he was greatly enamoured, he was afraid to console himself in the arms of any of the women in the neighbourhood for fear his infidelity might come to her knowledge, and unable wholly to restrain his desire to give vent in some manner to his pent-up passions, he had made some overtures to me of which I clearly understood the meaning, though with Laura, Betsy, and Frank on my hands, I had quite enough to do in that way, and consequently I had pretended not to understand his intentions. I now suggested to Laura that by complying with his wishes I might get him to come to my room where she and Frank would have an opportunity of seeing us enjoy each other, so that if at any future period he should accuse her of infidelity prior to her marriage, she might retort upon him.

Laura was quite satisfied that, if this could be accomplished, she would be perfectly safe; as with his good temper she said she had little doubt, even in case of the worst we dreaded occurring, she would be able to persuade him that it would be for the interests of both that he should keep quiet, seeing she had such a hold over him. She now admitted that she really was fond of him, though her curiosity and my boldness had lately enabled me to gain the advantage over him, and I easily drew from her that she did not like him the less for the report I had made of his evident ability to perform satisfactorily in the battles of Venus. I therefore told her that, though I was afraid that the performance of the instrument that would probably afford the greatest pleasure to her might prove to be martyrdom to me, I was prepared to undergo it for her sake, and we signed and sealed the agreements in our usual happy way.

As I have always found that where a thing is once determined on it is better to lose no time in carrying it into execution, I set to work immediately. I dressed for dinner that day sooner than usual, and about half an hour before the ordinary dinner hour, I made my way to Sir Charles' room, taking with me an amorous work he had lent me and making a pretext of wishing to borrow another. When he found who it was that knocked at the door he asked me to come in, saying that he wanted to see me as he had that day received a packet from town with some things he had ordered down for me. He then told his servant to lay out some things for him, and that he would not be required further. As soon as the servant had left the room, he took from a drawer a large parcel, and selecting a packet of drawings, told me to sit down and amuse myself with them while he finished dressing.

This was coming to the point even sooner than I had anticipated, but as it was just the opening I wanted, I sat down and began to examine the drawings which consisted of a most beautifully executed series of voluptuous designs. When he had dressed himself, all except his coat and waistcoat (and he was a very few minutes about it), he came and leaned over me, looking at the drawings and making observations upon them. After we had gone over them, he said there were some more which he liked still better and he hoped I would be equally well pleased with them. He went to the drawer for them, while I rose up to lay aside those we had been looking at. He selected two packets, and then coming back to the easy chair in which I had been sitting, he sat down, and wished to draw me on his knee.

This, however, I did not allow, but I sat down on the arm of the chair allowing him to put his arm around my waist. He exhibited some more illustrations of luscious scenes, many of which were new to me, and I did not attempt to conceal the effect which was produced upon me, while I told him, which was the case, that I had never seen anything of the kind more beautifully designed and executed. I could see that he was watching the impression made not only on my face but also on another part of my person, which had now become somewhat prominent. He seemed satisfied with this, and then opened the other packet, which was a series of drawings executed by a first-rate artist in the most admirable style delineating the seduction of a beautiful boy of about sixteen by another handsome youth a few years older. Every scene in the progress was illustrated by an appropriate and admirably drawn portrait of the two characters, commencing with taking him on his knee and impressing the first amorous kiss; the laying of his hand upon the organ of pleasure; the maiden bashfulness of first feeling the naked weapon grasped by a strange hand; the first starting out of the beautiful object on the trousers being unloosened; the full development of all its beauties on their being removed; the drawing his bridle over the fiery little head of the charger; the playing with the beautiful little appendices; the opening the thighs to get a glimpse of the seat of pleasure behind; the turning him round to obtain a full view of the exquisite hindquarters; the first exposure to his gaze of the second actor in the scene of pleasure; the making him caress and play with it; the complete exposure of all their naked charms as their shirts are drawn over their heads; the close embrace as they strain each other in their arms; the turning him round to present the altar for the sacrifice; the entrance; the combat; the ecstasy; the offering the recompensing pleasure; the introducing the virgin weapon for the first time; the ardour of the first enjoyment; the first tribute and the mutual embrace of thanks as they kissed and caressed each other's organs of pleasure after the work happily was accomplished. All these were depicted with a beauty and a truth to nature that forcibly reminded me of my own sweet experience of similar enjoyment on my first initiation in the secrets of pleasure. As I gazed with admiration upon them, he could not help observing how much I was interested, and was no doubt encouraged to think, as I intended he should be, that there would be little objection on my part of his proceeding to enact a similar scene. His hand gradually slipped down over my stiffly distended weapon. I made a little faint resistance, but gradually allowed him, without much difficulty, to handle and feel it, to unloosen my trousers and make it appear on the stage. He had no sooner got possession of it, than he loaded it with kisses and caresses, declaring that he had never seen anything to surpass it in beauty. He had not much more difficulty in loosening my braces and completely removing my trousers so as to give him a full opportunity of seeing and handling my naked person.

I affected to be so much engrossed with the pictures as not to observe that he had not only done this, but had also drawn down his own trousers and raised up his shirt displaying his magnificent weapon, until taking my hand he tried to make me grasp – for my fingers could not meet round it – by far the most splendid and largest champion I had ever met with, one which, indeed, I have never seen surpassed. He seemed much amused by my surprised exclamation. 'Oh, goodness, what a monster,' and, laughing, asked if I had never seen one so large before. But on my expressing my wonder that he should ever get it into a woman at all he seemed to be a little apprehensive that I might be too much frightened to allow it to enter where he wished it should go, and he tried to persuade me that after all there was not so very great a difference between it and mine.

In truth I had begun to be somewhat terrified on the subject and to wish at least to delay the operation, if it must be undergone, until it could be effected in a place where the object desired could be secured. I knew that in a few minutes the dinner bell would ring, and I therefore determined to temporize as long as possible and escape on the present occasion by holding out hopes of his attaining his object on a more favourable opportunity.

But I found that it was easier to make the resolution than to keep it. His evident passion for me and the means he adopted to excite me to an ardour equal to his own – keeping up a titillatory friction over the most sensitive points of my body – soon produced their effect, and in spite of my resolution, I could not make any effort to oppose him. Having drawn me on his knees, he raised me up, and opening my buttocks and holding apart the lips of the orifice, he presented the enormous head of his charger and tried to gain admittance. He seemed to be aware that there must be considerable difficulty, and he not only anointed the parts with cold cream, but he also refrained from attempting to force it in by any violent exertion on his part, apparently wishing that the junction should be brought about in a manner that would run less risk of occasioning me pain by my pressing gently down upon it myself. This he urgently begged me to do, and I could not withhold feeling sensible of this attention to my feelings on his part. I thought it would be hardly fair of me not to show that I was so by at least endeavouring, as far as I could, to aid in accomplishing his wishes. I therefore pressed down upon the impaling stroke with as much force as I could venture to exert, and with great difficulty and some pain did get the head fairly within the entrance. Having attained this, I desisted from my efforts for a moment and was pleased to find that the pain ceased entirely. As for him, he was perfectly enchanted and loaded me with kisses and caresses. Just then the bell announced that dinner would be on the table in five minutes. Although I had previously been anxiously expecting this announcement, I must confess I felt sorry when it did come, for I had now got so interested and excited in our proceedings that I would willingly have contributed by every means in my power, even at any sacrifice of pain, to bring the enterprise to a successful termination. But there seemed no help for it, and I turned my head round to him and said that I was afraid we must go downstairs. He caught me round the neck, pressed my lips passionately to his, and entreated me to have patience with him for a few moments; he said he would not attempt to do anything that would give me more pain, but that he was then enjoying the most transcendent pleasure from the kind assistance I had already afforded him in getting his instrument so far imbedded in the abode of bliss, and if I would only allow him to remain where he was for a few seconds longer, he would be overwhelmed with the excess of his joy and would never cease to be grateful to me for having thus contributed to it. I could not resist his appeal, seeing clearly from his excited and flashing eyes that the tempest was nearly at its height, and on the eve of bursting forth with all the fury of a torrent.

He did not attempt to force his way further in, but supporting me with his arms he wriggled and twisted his buttocks making his weapon move about within me in the most surprising and delicious manner. Wishing to gratify and assist him as far as I could, I put one hand behind and grasping as well as I could the lower part of the splendid pillar, I rubbed and squeezed it, endeavouring to increase the excitement and promote his object; then passing the other hand between my thighs, I tickled and played with the massy round globes I found just beneath my own and which instead of hanging down, pendant as at first, were now closely drawn up in their wondrous purse. He kissed me again fervently and was in the act of thanking me for my kindness in thus increasing his pleasure, when he suddenly stopped short with a passionate exclamation of a single 'Oh!' My hand, which grasped his splendid weapon, was sensible of the instant rush of the fiery liquid through it, and the next moment, I felt the warm gush driven into my entrails as if it had been forced up by a pump. I continued the motion of my hand gently upon his instrument until the fit of pleasure was entirely over. Then, with some difficulty disengaging myself from the link that bound us together, I wiped the ruby head of the still rampant champion, and stooping down, first kissed it and then his lips as he still lay reclining in the chair and then proceeded to arrange my dress. He soon recovered himself and earnestly begged that I would come to his room that night that he might have an opportunity of thanking me and of endeavouring to repay, as far as he possibly could, the delicious treat I had afforded him. This, however, I would not promise to do, saying I was too much afraid of being seen when I could have no excuse for being in his room, but I allowed him to understand that I would try to devise some plan for another meeting.

I contrived to give Laura a hint before dinner that all was right and that she would get the details at night. She was so delighted with this that the distance and hauteur with which she had lately treated Sir Charles were greatly removed, and he on his part, animated by the scene which had just taken place and his victory, as he thought, over my virgin charms, was more lively and bolder than usual. So that by the end of the evening they were on a better and more familiar footing than they had ever been before. When the ladies retired to bed, Sir Charles again urged me to go to his room. I still refused, but at last I suggested that perhaps he might come to me early the next morning, as this would be less liable to suspicion, for if anyone saw him we might go out immediately together, when it would be supposed he had only come for the purpose of calling on me, while if he was not observed, he might remain for a time with me. Of course, that night I explained to Laura and Frank all that had passed, and we contrived to make two apertures in the partition wall of the closet between Frank's room and mine, from which they would have an uninterrupted view of the scene of operations.

The next morning I heard Sir Charles open my door, but I lay quiet as if still asleep. I was conscious that he fastened the door and then came round to the side of the bed where I was lying. He removed the bed-clothes, raised up my nightshirt, and remained for some minutes contemplating me. Of course, the principal object of his worship was my virile member which, as was usual at that period of my life, always held up its head proudly erect when I awoke in the morning. I heard him undress himself and get into bed, and then kneeling down by my side, after kissing and caressing my organ of pleasure, he took the point of it into his mouth and commenced sucking it and moving it backwards and forwards between his lips. I opened my eyes, as if just awakened, and beheld him kneeling beside me perfectly naked with his tremendous member standing stiff and erect. He immediately made me take off my shirt, and employed himself for a time in examining me all over and caressing all my charms. During this time I also made a more minute inspection of my acquaintance of the preceding evening, and I was even more than ever astonished at its proportions, and at how I had managed ever to get it within my narrow aperture as far as it had been.

After some little time had elapsed in these preliminaries, he said that it was his turn now to contribute to my enjoyment, and taking hold of my weapon, he was going to turn himself away from where Laura and Frank were placed. As they had both been greatly interested by the account I had given them of Sir Charles' tremendous weapon, I wished that they should have an opportunity of seeing as much as possible of its proceedings. So I got him to change his position and to place himself where they were and where they could have the gratification of observing every motion he made in the approaching encounter. He immediately placed himself as I wished, and I then, at his request, took up my position behind him, and he proceeded to introduce my weapon into the sheath of pleasure. But if I had been surprised at the largeness of one of his proportions, I was no less so at the smallness of the other, as in fact I had almost as much difficulty in getting into him as he had had with me. At length, with his assistance, I succeeded and gradually penetrated within the delightful cavity, till I was completely imbedded within it. Of course, the opposition I met with and the extreme tightness of the place, when it was once fairly overcome, only increased the pleasurable sensations I experienced after I had fairly accomplished my entrance. When he found I was completely buried within him and was beginning to proceed with the work of pleasure, he took my hand and placed it on his majestic champion, saying that if I would be good enough to operate upon it at the same time it would not only give him exquisite pleasure by being combined with the performance going on behind, but would also, by depriving it of a little of its vehement fury, make our after-proceedings more easy and agreeable to me, when, as he hoped I would allow him to do, he should again try to introduce it into the delicious aperture that had given him so much delight the previous day. I immediately acquiesced, and grasping as much of the pillar as I could manage to do with one hand, I commenced a series of movements upon it, gently rubbing it up and down and titillating the shaft as much as possible, which drew from him the warmest encomiums. In this manner, combining the movements of my hand in front with those of my excited weapon in the rear, I managed to pour my tribute into him at the same time that he sent a shower of love's balsam spouting beyond the bed far into the room.

This scene acted so powerfully on Laura that unable to restrain herself, as Frank afterwards told me, she seized hold of his hand, conveyed it to her pleasure-spot, and made him cool her raging fever in a similar manner where she stood.

Sir Charles then asked if I would allow him to endeavour to accomplish the undertaking which it had given him so much delight partially to accomplish the preceding day. I could not well make any objection, after having availed myself of his complaisance, to his now proceeding to carry out his wishes to their entire fulfilment. I therefore disposed myself so as to endeavour to stand the attacks in as favourable a position as I could, and at the same time afforded my friends as good a view of the proceedings as was possible.

I placed all the pillows and cushions I could find on a heap in the centre of the bed and lay down with my belly resting on them so as to raise up my posteriors and present them to him in an attitude that would be propitious to his purpose. He thanked me, and told me to let him know if I found that he hurt me too much and he would at once stop, as he would be sorry to enjoy even such a gratification if it were to be at the expense of occasioning me any suffering. He had provided some ointment with which he lubricated the whole of his weapon, and then with his finger inserted some of it in my aperture. He then applied the point of the dart to the mark, and endeavoured to insert it. For some time it baffled his endeavours, the head slipping upwards and downwards, away from the entrance, whenever he attempted to thrust which he did very gently and carefully. I saw he was too much afraid of hurting me to be able to succeed, and getting excited myself by this time, put my hand between my thighs and taking hold of his splendid weapon I kept its head at the mouth of the aperture, and desired him to thrust a little more boldly. At the same time, trying to push back and stretch the aperture as much as possible, I met his advancing thrusts with all the firmness I could muster. This brought about the junction I desired, and again to his great delight the head of his weapon got lodged between the extended lips of the aperture. The pain, however, of this proceeding was so great that I was obliged to ask him to pause till it should abate a little, which it very soon did. Then summoning up courage, I told him to thrust again gently. This he hastened to do in the most delicate manner possible. The first few thrusts, till the upper part of the pillar got fairly inserted within the cheeks, were even worse than before. But as soon as this was accomplished, and the hollow part at the junction of the pillar with the head passed the Rubicon, all feeling of uneasiness vanished and was succeeded by the most delicious sensations, as inch by inch he gradually fought his way into my interior, the intense pleasure increasing at every thrust he gave, until the whole of the monster was fairly established within me, and I could feel the hair on his thighs and belly in close contact with my buttocks, and his delightful soft bullets beat against mine at every motion he made. As soon as he was fully lodged to the utmost extent within the citadel, he stopped and inquired how I felt and expressed the greatest satisfaction at finding my sufferings had now been converted into pleasure. After enjoying the voluptuous sensations of the elastic constriction the nerves of the sheath in which it was plunged exerted upon his throbbing weapon for some minutes, during which his hands roved over my body in nervous agitation, he resumed his delightful exercise, and thrust after thrust of his delicious weapon was driven into me with the most intense enjoyment to both parties. At length, his lusty efforts were rewarded with success, and, from the warm gush within me, I felt that a torrent of bliss must have issued from him, while his nervous frame shook and quivered with blissful agitation and enjoyment as the ecstasy of delight came over him. He lay for a few minutes bathed in enjoyment, and then raising his head, thanked me most fervently for all the bliss I had conferred on him and expressed his hope that it had been accomplished without much suffering on my part. In answer I gently turned both him and myself on one side, too much delighted with its presence to allow his sword to escape from my scabbard, and made him look at the pillow on which my weapon had rested, and where a plenteous effusion of the balmy liquid plainly attested that I too had shared in the delights of his enjoyment. He expressed his great gratification at this, as he said the sole drawback to his enjoyment had been the fear that it had been attained at my expense. But he said that what he now saw emboldened him to make a new request, and as the difficulty had now been overcome, to ask whether I might be persuaded to allow him still to retain his present quarter and enjoy another victory. I readily agreed. I told him that the sensations produced upon me by the insertion of his weapon in so sensitive a place was so agreeable – that it was so was, indeed, very evident from the powerful manner in which it still affected mine – that he must allow it to remain quietly where it was for a time and let me enjoy the agreeable sensation of its presence there.

He said he could desire nothing better, and we lay for a considerable period thus pleasantly conjoined. During this time I purposely turned the conversation upon Laura and Frank. I began by joking him about what Laura would say if she saw us in such a situation defrauding her of her just rights. He replied that he did not know what she would say, but that he knew what she ought to say, or at least what he would say if he were to find her in a similar situation, and that was that as she could not assist in contributing to his happiness at present, she was very glad to find that he had been able to get somebody else who could.

'Then,' said I, 'you would not be offended, if she were to follow your example.'

'No, certainly not,' was his reply. 'I don't mean to say that I would not rather prefer that I should have her entirely to myself, but I am so fond of her that if I found it would contribute to her happiness to enjoy herself with another, I should not make the slightest objection, provided she would only allow me to contribute to her enjoyment as much as I could.' He went on to say that he was sadly afraid she would never allow him that pleasure, that he did once hope she might have been induced to accept him, but for the last few weeks, with the exception of the previous night, she had been colder than ever, and he was afraid to press her on the subject for fear of being at once rejected.

I ventured cautiously to express my opinion that he was too distrustful of his own merits, and that he stood higher in Laura's favour than he seemed to imagine.

He eagerly caught at my words, and asked on what grounds I thought so. He said he saw that from my old acquaintance with her as a boy, I was on more intimate terms with her than anyone else and more likely to understand her sentiments, and that he had often thought of speaking to me on the subject. Indeed, he said he would almost have been jealous of my influence with her had I been a few years older and had it not been that, instead of appearing to be annoyed at his attentions to her, I had rather given him every opportunity to pursue them.

As I felt he was watching me, I endeavoured to keep my countenance as well as I could, but I was aware that the blood mounting in my cheeks must to some extent betray the secret interest I took in the subject. I thought the best plan was to acknowledge that from our early intimacy, and the kindness she had always shown me, I did take a great interest in her, and that it was perhaps only my being sensible that she could neither look up to nor respect one so much younger than herself that prevented this feeling from ripening into a warmer attachment, but that I was old enough to be able to wish to promote her happiness even If I could not myself be the means of doing so, and that from what I had seen of her feelings towards him, I had always thought they might be happy together, and consequently had wished him success.

He pressed me very much regarding what she thought, or might have said of him.

I told him that of course it was not a subject on which I could have ventured to speak to her seriously, that sometimes a looker-on saw more of the game than the players, and that I thought she did like him and was only restrained from showing it more by his not urging his suit so much as he perhaps might have done. We had some further conversation on the subject, and I added that I knew she was of a reserved disposition as regarded her own feelings and did not like to have them noticed and commented on by strangers and that perhaps the idea of all the parade and show which he might think necessary at the celebration of his marriage and the discussion of the matter for months previously might annoy her, while she would probably have been more easily induced to consent had he been a person of less rank and consequence, when all this exhibition would have been avoided.

He said that if she had any difficulty on this ground, nothing could be easier than to obviate it, for as far as he was concerned it would give him the greatest satisfaction to dispense with all formalities, except necessary settlements which he would take care should not occupy much time, and they might be quietly married at their own church in the neighbourhood without making any fuss about it; that with the exception of his mother and sister he had no relations he cared anything about or whom he would wish to be present, so that Laura could have everything her own way.

Without attempting to urge too much, I gave him to understand that I thought he had better come to an explanation with her as soon as possible and make her aware of his ideas on these points. And I promised to endeavour to ascertain her wishes as far as I could and make him acquainted with them.

I had long felt by the unruliness of his member, which was deeply imbedded within me, how powerful an impression the discussion of this subject produced upon him. He very soon disregarded my injunctions to keep quiet – the delightful intruder would keep wandering up and down in the path of pleasure – and before our conversation was concluded, I felt the warm injection twice spouted into me. After this, he said he would not venture to trespass upon my kindness any further for the present, and urged me to take his place, which, excited as I was by his performances, I was very well disposed to do. He made every arrangement for my entering him in the most agreeable manner, inserting the weapon himself and tickling and playing with the appendages.

When fairly entered and enjoying myself to the utmost, I laughingly said that if he was going to run away with Laura I could not hope for any long continuance of our present agreeable amusement and I must try if I could persuade Frank to allow me to enjoy with him some of the pleasant pastimes he had been teaching me. He eagerly caught at the idea and urged me to do so, offering to leave with me all his books and pictures to show to him, and telling me to let him have any of them he liked, and at the same time begging me, if I succeeded, to allow him to join in our amusements, as the possession of one resembling Laura so much would be the next thing to enjoying herself. This was exactly what I wanted, for I felt satisfied that after having enjoyed the brother he could never complain of anything the sister might do. Having then brought my enterprise to a satisfactory termination, I made him leave me, and joined Laura and Frank.

Although they had been able to see everything, they had not heard all that passed. Coming to my bed, they proceeded to satisfy the burning desires which the scene they had just witnessed had lighted up in them. While thus agreeably employed, I joked Laura about the martyrdom I had undergone for her sake and what she was to look forward to suffer when she attempted to take in the stupendous instrument whose performances she had just seen. She did not appear to be much afraid of it, and said judging from the manner in which I had apparently enjoyed its presence within me there was not much reason for apprehension. But she eagerly asked what we had been talking about, as she had heard only so far as to make out that she was the subject of our discourse. She was quite delighted to find that the result had been so satisfactory, and it was at once resolved that, when Sir Charles pressed the matter, she would consent and that I should contrive to impress upon him the propriety of his urging the completion of the marriage and as little delay and ceremony as possible.

Frank and I made up a party to ride with them that forenoon, and we took care to let them have an opportunity for an explanation. Laura was in a gracious mood. Sir Charles acted on my advice, pressed his suit, was accepted, explained his own wish to have the marriage concluded as soon as possible, but at the same time saying that on that point as on every other he should wish to consult her feelings in every respect, and was given to understand that her sentiments coincided with his. Having obtained her consent, he spoke to her father as soon as we returned from our ride, and as the settlements he proposed were most satisfactory, it was at once arranged. And it was settled that the marriage should take place within a month.

When Sir Charles came to me the next morning, he was in ecstasies at the successful termination of his suit, which he asserted was in a great measure due to my good advice, and he urged me to attend him on the happy occasion. As this afforded a good excuse for my remaining at the Hall, and being on a good footing with Laura, I readily agreed. Laura having expressed a wish that they should be quiet during the few weeks she was to remain at home, it was arranged that the visits of some friends who were expected should be postponed. Her aunt, immediately on hearing of the marriage, returned to the Hall, but I made Laura give her mother a hint that, though she did not like to say so to her aunt herself, she would prefer being allowed to enjoy the privacy of an apartment by herself. Her mother thought this was quite reasonable, and another room was prepared for Miss Middleton. Frank was allowed to remain at home till after the marriage, and we thus secured another month of our delightful pastime to which we gave ourselves up without scruple or reserve. Sir Charles, though unwilling to tear himself away from the pleasure he was enjoying and anticipating, was obliged to go to town to make the necessary arrangements. I was desirous before he went to take a photographic view of him in the act of enjoying me, as I thought that in the event of Laura being obliged to have recourse to any compulsion upon him, her object would be better attained by making him aware she was in possession of such a picture than by any reference to me or explanation as to how she came to know anything on the subject. It was necessary for this purpose to bring Frank on the scene. As he was quite willing to join in the sport, having been greatly taken with what he had witnessed of Sir Charles' operations, I told the latter that by means of his pictures I had come to a good understanding with him and that he had agreed to comply with our wishes. Giving him to believe that there was a double maidenhead to be taken, I proposed that they should both be disposed of at the same time, and offered him his choice which he would prefer. He said that if it was left to him to decide he would prefer to make the attack in the rear, and we settled that he should come to me the next morning when I could get Frank to meet us.

Frank was in bed with me when Sir Charles arrived. I at once turned down the bed-clothes stripped off his shirt and exhibited him quite naked, his fiery little dart, standing erect and unhooded, exhibiting its proportions in the most splendid manner, and I asked if he had ever seen anything more beautiful. He threw himself on the charming boy and covered every part of him with kisses, while I undressed him and reduced him to a similar state of nakedness as ourselves. As soon as this was done, I prepared Frank for the sacrifice. I was apprehensive that there would be as much difficulty in introducing the magnificent weapon into his lovely, but narrow aperture as there had been in my own case, and I endeavoured to provide against the worst as satisfactorily as I could. I knelt down on the bed and made him place himself kneeling also so as to rest his belly on my back. Sir Charles then placed himself behind him and grasped him firmly round the loins, making his splendid weapon appear between his thighs, where I saw it rubbing fiercely against Frank's less mature organ. Taking hold of it and making it move back a little, I introduced my hand between Frank's thighs, and separating the lips of the delicious aperture between his lovely buttocks, I directed the point of the throbbing monster to the proper spot. Holding it firmly in the requisite position, I told Sir Charles to press it gently forwards. This he immediately did and to my great astonishment I felt it gradually advancing and slipping into the gulf of pleasure without difficulty, till I was obliged to withdraw the grasp my hand held on it. I had hardly done so when I saw the enormous pillar entirely swallowed up, and on turning my eyes to Frank's face, I could not discover on his countenance the slightest trace of pain or suffering. Satisfied that I need have no further apprehension on his account, I turned myself a little round, so as to take my part in the play, and placing myself directly before him, so as to bring my buttocks in contact with his warm soft belly, I insinuated Frank's charming little darling into my rear. While holding me fast with one arm round the middle, he grasped my stiffly erected standard with the other hand. Thinking that the power and weight of metal of Sir Charles' performer in the rear would prevent Frank from exerting himself much in the combat, I resolved to render any great exertion on his part unnecessary. For keeping time with Sir Charles' motions, I commenced a series of heaves by which, whenever Sir Charles' weapon was fully driven up to the hilt in his hinder quarter, his own was as fully and as pleasantly introduced within me. This delightful operation very soon produced such a state of ecstatic delirium that he could not refrain from giving vent to the most enthusiastic praises of our performances in such a loud tone that I was obliged to beg him to be quiet to prevent suspicion being aroused. The delight was too excessive to endure long, and before Sir Charles was ready to perform his part in the final scene, I felt dear Frank's discharge poured into me, as his head sank upon my back and his convulsive grasp of my throbbing instrument relaxed. I retained him in this position for a few seconds longer, while the fierce heaves of Sir Charles, driving his steed to and fro in the delicious field of battle, testified to the soul-stirring effect that had been produced upon him and soon relieved his high mettled charger of a portion of his superabundant fluid. Then withdrawing from Frank, he laid him down on the bed, and again renewed his caresses which very soon reanimated the slightly drooping head of his darling charmer.

We agreed, however, that it would be better to allow Frank to be passive in the next encounter, and accordingly I took the centre position, and entering Frank's delicious rear, I exposed my own to be breached by the enormous battering ram of Sir Charles. The assault, however, was not nearly so terrible, and with a little care I now contrived to take it all in, and speedily enjoyed the felicity of feeling its throbbing pulsation beating within me over the whole extent of the cavity which it so completely filled up. Frank's charming receptacle for my own heaving instrument was of that pleasing elasticity that I should not have discovered it had ever once been invaded by a larger weapon than my own, and the voluptuous sensations it produced upon my burning member as, excited to the highest pitch and swollen to the utmost extension, the fiery dart was plunged in and out of the burning furnace, were most exquisite. I felt, too, the full effect which Frank had already experienced of the greatly increased pleasure during the amorous encounter which resulted from the pressure in the interior of so large an instrument as that of Sir Charles. And much as I had enjoyed my former encounters with them both separately, most assuredly this one, in which they both combined their utmost efforts to produce the most lascivious sensations it is possible to conceive, far surpassed everything that had taken place previously.

Another scene of delicious toying succeeded. The darling objects which had already given us so much delight were again investigated and admired, and each new proof of the bliss they were capable of conferring upon us only made us more eager to offer up our worship to them. Another delicious combat succeeded. Sir Charles this time took the combat-position, and I again received his member within me. But my concern being now well saturated with the blissful libations that had been already poured into it, the monster slipped into me this time with very little difficulty. Frank, on the other hand, was delighted as well as surprised to discover that he had no easy task to force his way into the agreeable fortress he was about to storm in Sir Charles' rear. But the difficulty only enhanced the pleasure when the breach was fairly made, and the invader revelled in full and undisputed possession of the interior works. And if I might judge from the exclamations of delight, they both enjoyed themselves to their hearts' content when they had once gained admission to their respective destinations. So much so that after they had run one course they gave no signs of wishing to change their positions. I put my hand behind to ascertain the state of matters, and found both the heroes still in such an excited condition that I said if they were disposed to break another lance in the same lists I was quite willing to keep my place, provided Sir Charles would take my charger in hand and lead him on to participate in the pleasing conflict. This proposal was highly approved of and at once carried into effect, to the entire satisfaction of all parties. After this I made Sir Charles leave us, not wishing that we should be entirely worked out as I was quite aware poor Laura would be in a sad state if she found that we were unable to do anything in the way of appeasing her longings after the excitement she must have undergone while witnessing our voluptuous proceedings.

As soon as he was gone, Laura made her appearance and scolded us heartily for having wasted so much of our precious strength and enjoyed ourselves so completely without her. But as we each contrived to give her pretty satisfactory proof that we had not spent all our treasures, we soon put her in a good humour again; especially as Sir Charles was to leave on the next day, when she would have us all to herself again.

In the course of the day, I easily persuaded Sir Charles to allow me to take likenesses of us all three in the various attitudes of enjoying each other, one of which I took care should be sealed up and deposited where Laura would have it at command in the event of her finding it necessary to have recourse of it, even if I should not be at hand at the time. As Sir Charles was obliged after this to be almost constantly absent, we gave up to him the few nights he occasionally spent at the Hall, and the remainder were passed with Laura in a constant series of repetitions of delightful sports which, however agreeable to the actors, would involve a tiresome repetition were I to detail them.

The only variety was Frank's adventure with Betsy. Having been once accustomed to indulge his passions, he regretted sadly that the enjoyment would continue only for so short a period, as Laura and her Charles were to go abroad immediately on their marriage, and he began to look about him for some object to console him in her absence. He soon fixed upon Betsy, but he found it more difficult to obtain her consent than he had expected. When I joked her on the subject, she admitted that she liked the boy, but said she was afraid there was a great risk he might talk of it and get her into a scrape. Finding that Frank was very desirous to have her, I agreed to promote his wishes. I had endeavoured to conceal as much as possible from Betsy my intercourse with Laura, but she was too quick not to have discovered that there existed a good understanding between us, though I still pretended that although we were sometimes in the habit of amusing ourselves together after her old fashion she had not yet granted me the last favour. I now told her that Laura had discovered my intercourse with her, and that previous to her own marriage she wished to see us perform the conjugal rites that she might know how to conduct herself when it came to be her turn, and that I had therefore arranged, as Frank was to be out early the next morning, Laura was to come to my room where I had promised that Betsy and I should comply with her wishes. Frank got one of his sister's caps which concealed his hair, and a nightshirt which closed in front over his breast, and it was hardly possible for anyone to tell that it was not Laura herself. Indeed, the disguise was so complete that the next time Sir Charles came to enjoy himself with us, I made Frank dress up in the same manner and pretend to be asleep in bed with me, and it was only when I could not restrain a burst of laughter at his consternation that Sir Charles discovered the trick we had played on him. Nor do I think he was perfectly satisfied until the removal of Frank's shirt showed standing proof that it did not cover a woman's form.

Betsy's discovery was made in a different manner. When she came, Frank kept under the bedclothes until I had stripped her, and getting into bed with her performed the hymenial rites in due order. When we had finished, I slipped off her on the other side of the bed from Frank, leaving her lying on her back all exposed to his observation. He commenced a survey of every part of her, joking her on the beauties he discovered and on the manner in which she had enjoyed the operation that had just been performed, and wondering whether it would give her as much satisfaction. Gradually he began to embrace her, and at last got upon her, asking me if that was the way Sir Charles would do it to her.

'Yes that is it,' said I, as he got between her thighs and placed himself in the position in which I had lately been, 'only he would not have this stupid night-dress about him, and he will have something stiff between his legs to put into that pretty little hole you see before you, now try what you can do to imitate him.'

While Frank clasped her in his arms and pressed his mouth to hers, I raised his shirt, and pointing his weapon at the mark, he thrust himself forward, and it slipped into her in an instant. Betsy's consternation was extreme as she felt the warm flesh within her. She had on many occasions tried the effect of Laura's substitute, but her experience of the real article had been quite enough to satisfy her that this was something of a different description, and she exclaimed, 'Goodness gracious Miss Laura, what is the meaning of this?'

Frank replied, tearing off his cap and exhibiting his short curls instead of Laura's flowing ringlets, 'Well, I am glad I have got something to prove I am not a girl, for I was beginning to be afraid that the change of dress had effected a complete transformation.'

It was too late for any objection now. Nor did Betsy appear at all disposed to make any. On the contrary, the lascivious boy's motions were so lively and so well directed and his capacity for conferring pleasure so much greater than she had expected that she at once yielded herself up to the enjoyment, and joined in his amorous transports with hearty good will. And when he had given and drawn from her the first proof of their mutual satisfaction with each other and the young rogue still retained his position and proceeded to giver her a second dose of his prolific balm, she was quite transported with delight and exerted herself with so much vigour and set to second his endeavours that they very soon sank exhausted in each other's arms enjoying to the utmost the second proof of the completion of their mutual overwhelming bliss.

But these hours of happiness were too delightful to last long. The day appointed for the marriage came upon us before we could believe it possible. Though sorely against my will I thought it right to suggest to Laura whether it would not be prudent that she should pass the last night of her presumed virgin state without having her inmost recesses explored for fear of any traces being left. But though she at first agreed that this precaution would be advisable, she could not make up her mind to put it in practice. To our surprise and joy she came to us as usual as soon as she was left alone for the night. Unwilling to run the risk of her appearing fatigued and exhausted in the morning, we resolved to concentrate our forces upon her and take our farewell that night. Time after time we kept up the amorous combat, sometimes in succession and sometimes combining our forces for a joint attack both in front and rear, almost without intermission until we were fairly exhausted; and it was only when after repeated engagements even her fond caresses failed to revive our enervated champions that, taking an affectionate farewell, she retired to her own apartment. The exercise so far from injuring seemed to have a beneficial effect on her charms, and never had she looked more lovely than she appeared the next morning when she was transferred to the arms of the enraptured Sir Charles.

Most fortunately everything turned out eventually even more agreeably than we had ventured to hope. A few days afterwards I had the gratification of hearing from Laura that she had satisfactorily put in operation the device I had suggested, which, combined with the difficulty Sir Charles experienced from his great size in obtaining an entrance and the pain she pretended to experience when he forced his way within her supposed virgin sanctuary, completely prevented any suspicion on his part. And loving her as I did, I was pleased with her frank avowal that not only his general conduct and kindness left her nothing to wish for, but that in her nuptial intercourse with him she derived if possible even greater pleasure than she enjoyed with us. The symptoms which had alarmed us passed off without producing the dreaded consequence, and it was not till some weeks after the usual time had elapsed that she presented the delighted Sir Charles with a son who was soon followed by numerous successors.

Frank before long joined the army, and in the arms of others soon found consolation, though he never forgot the charms of his first instructress. When Laura and I met again, we could not refrain from renewing our old delights and comparing the changes which had taken place in each other's charms, but with the exception of one single occasion, I believe I am the only one she ever allowed to participate with her husband in the pleasures she was so well calculated to confer.

After the marriage I got alarmed about Betsy, and regretted that I had allowed her to know so much as she did. The only remedy I could devise was to persuade her to go to a distant country where she would have no temptation to speak on the subject. On sounding her, I found that, trusting to the influence she thought she had obtained over Frank and me, she was not disposed to be removed from us. I therefore had recourse to John and found him not only much more intelligent but also more sensible than his mistress. I had not much difficulty in convincing him that if he had the means of settling in Australia he was much more likely to prosper there than by continuing in service in this country.

As a further inducement, and a reason why I took an interest in them, I told him I had discovered that Frank had taken a fancy for Betsy and that, though there was no reason to suppose anything occurred, it would be better they should be separated. He was quite of the same opinion, and as the consequences of the operations of some one of us upon Betsy threatened in a short time to become apparent, he made it a condition of their marriage that she should emigrate with him. As I had a strong suspicion that I had at least dug out the foundation, if not laid the cornerstone, of the structure which Betsy was about to rear, I took care they should have the means to settle comfortably, and from his knowledge in horse breeding, John soon prospered there. Very soon after their arrival in the colony and precisely at the expiration of the usual period from my first entrance within her, she presented her husband with a son. She never had another child.

FLOSSIE:
A VENUS OF SIXTEEN

Preface

In presenting to a critical public this narrative of a delightful experience, I am conscious of an inability to do justice to the indescribable charm of my subject.

A true daughter of the Paphian goddess, Flossie added to the erotic allurements inherited from her immortal mother a sense of humour which is not traceable in any of the proceedings on Mount Ida or elsewhere. Those of my readers, who have had the rare good fortune to meet with the combination, will not gainsay my assertion that it is an incomparable incentive to deeds of love.

If some of those deeds, as here set down, should seem to appertain to a somewhat advanced school of amatory action, I beg objectors to remember that Flossie belongs to the end of the century, *when such things are done*, to the safety, comfort and delight of vast numbers of fair English girls, and to the unspeakable enjoyment of their adorers.

So, in the words of the City toastmaster:

'Pray silence, gentlemen, for your heroine, Flossie: a Venus of Sixteen.'

J.A.

Postscript – Flossie has herself revised this unpretending work, and has added a footnote here and there which she trusts may not be regarded as painful interruptions to a truthful tale.

All thine the new wine of desire
   The fruit of four lips as they clung
Till the hair and the eyelids took fire;
   The fan of a serpentine tongue,
The froth of the serpents of pleasure,
   More salt than the foam of the sea,
Now felt as a flame, not at leisure
   As wine-shed for me!

They were purple of rainment, and golden,
   Filled full of thee, fiery with wine,
Thy lovers, in haunts unbeholden,
   In marvellous chambers of thine.
They are fled and their footprints escape us
   Who appraise thee, adore, and abstain,
O daughter of Death and Priamus!
   Our Lady of Pain.

                            A.C. Swinburne

Chapter One

'My love, she's but a lassie yet'

Towards the end of a bright sunny afternoon in June, I was walking in one of the quieter streets of Piccadilly, when my eye was caught by two figures coming in my direction. One was that of a tall, finely-made woman about twenty-seven years of age, who would under other circumstances, have received something more than an approving glance. But it was her companion that rivetted my gaze of almost breathless admiration. This was a young girl of sixteen, of such astounding beauty of face and figure as I had never seen or dreamt of. Masses of bright, wavy, brown hair fell to her waist. Deep violet eyes looked out from under long curling lashes, and seemed to laugh in unison with the humorous curves of the full red lips. These and a thousand other charms I was to know by heart later on, but what struck me most at this view, was the extraordinary size and beauty of the girl's bust, shown to all possible advantage by her dress which, in the true artistic French style, crept in between her breasts, outlining their full and perfect form with loving fidelity. Tall and lithe, she moved like a young goddess, her short skirt shewing the action of a pair of exquisitely moulded legs, to which the tan-coloured open-work silk stockings were plainly designed to invite attention. Unable to take my eyes from this enchanting vision, I was approaching the pair, when to my astonishment, the elder lady suddenly spoke my name.

'You do not remember me, Captain Archer.' For a moment I was at a loss, but the voice gave me the clue.

'But I do,' I answered, 'you are Miss Letchford, who used to teach my sisters.'

'Quite right. But I have given up teaching, for which fortunately there is not longer any necessity. I am living in a flat with my dear little friend here. Let me introduce you, – Flossie Eversley – Captain Archer.'

The violet eyes laughed up at me; and the red lips parted in a merry smile. A dimple appeared at the corner of the mouth. I was done for! Yes; at thirty-five years of age, with more than my share of experiences in every phase of love, I went down before this lovely girl with her childish face smiling at me above the budding womanhood of her rounded breasts, and confessed myself defeated!

A moment or two later, I had passed from them with the address of the flat in my pocket, and under promise to go down to tea on the next day.

At midday I received the following letter:

Dear Captain Archer,

I am sorry to be obliged to be out when you come; and yet not altogether sorry, because I should like you to know Flossie very well. She is an orphan, without a relation in the world. She is just back from a Paris school. In years she is of course a child, but in tact and knowledge she is a woman; also in figure, as you can see for yourself! She is of an exceedingly warm and passionate nature, and a look that you gave her yesterday was not lost upon her. In fact, to be quite frank, she had fallen in love with you! You will find her a delightful companion. Use her *very* tenderly, and she will do anything in the world for you. Speak to her about life in the French school; she loves to talk of it. I want her to be happy, and I think you can help. Remember she is only just sixteen.

Yours sincerely,

Eva Letchford

I must decline any attempt to describe my feelings on receiving this remarkable communication. My first impulse was to give up the promised call at the flat. But the flower-like face, the soft red lips and the laughing eyes passed before my mind's eye, followed by an instant vision of the marvellous breasts and the delicate shapely legs in their brown silk stockings, and I knew that fate was too strong for me. For it was of course impossible to misunderstand the meaning of Eva Letchford's letter, and indeed, when I reached the flat, she herself opened the door to me, whispering as she passed out, 'Flossie is in there, waiting for you. You two can have the place to yourselves. One last word. You have been much in Paris, have you not? So has Flossie. She is *very* young – *and there are ways* – Goodbye.'

I passed into the next room. Flossie was curled up in a long chair, reading. Twisting her legs from under her petticoats, with a sudden movement that brought into full view her delicately embroidered drawers, she rose and came towards me, a rosy flush upon her cheeks, her eyes shining, her whole bearing instinct with an enchanting mixture of girlish coyness and anticipated pleasure. Her short white skirt swayed as she moved across the room, her breasts stood out firm and round under the close-fitting woven silk jersey; what man of mortal flesh and blood could withstand such allurements as these! Not I, for one! In a moment, she was folded in my arms. I rained kisses on her hair, her forehead, her eyes, her cheeks, and then, grasping her body closer and always closer to me, I glued my lips upon the scarlet mouth and revelled in a long and maddeningly delicious kiss – a kiss to be ever remembered – so well remembered now, indeed, that I must make some attempt to describe it. My hands were behind Flossie's head, buried in her long brown hair. Her arms were round my body, locked and clinging. At the first impact, her lips were closed, but a moment later they parted, and slowly, gently, almost as if in the performance of some solemn duty, the rosy tongue crept into my mouth, and bringing with it a flood of the scented juices from her throat, curled amorously round my own, whilst her hands dropped to my buttocks, and standing on tiptoe, she drew me to her with such extraordinary intimacy that it seemed our bodies were already in conjunction. Not a word was spoken on either side – indeed, under the circumstances, speech was impossible, for our tongues had twined together in a caress of unspeakable sweetness, which neither would be the first to forego. At last, the blood was coursing through my veins at a pace that became unbearable and I was compelled to unglue my mouth from hers. Still silent, but with love and longing in her eyes, she pressed me into a low chair, and seating herself on the arm, passed her hand behind my head, and looking full into my eyes, whispered my name in accents that were like the sound of a running stream. I kissed her open mouth again and again, and then, feeling that the time had come for some little explanation:

'How long will it be before your friend Eva comes back?' I asked.

'She has gone down into the country, and won't be here till late this evening.'

'Then I may stay with you, may I?'

'Yes, do, do, *do*, Jack. Do you know, I have got seats for an Ibsen play tonight, I was wondering . . . if . . . you would . . . take me!'

'Take *you* – to an Ibsen play – with your short frocks, and all that hair down your back! Why, I don't believe they'd let us in?'

'Oh, if *that's* all, wait a minute.'

She skipped out of the room with a whisk of her petticoats and a free display of brown silk legs. Almost before I had time to wonder what she was up to, she was back again. She had put on a long skirt of Eva's, her hair was coiled on the top of her head, she wore my 'billycock' hat and a pair of blue pincenez, and carrying a crutch-handled stick, she advanced upon me with a defiant air, and glaring down over the top of her glasses, she said in a deep masculine voice:

'Now, sir, if you're ready for Ibsen, *I* am. Or if your tastes are so *low* that you can't care about a play, I'll give you a skirt dance.'

As she said this, she tore off the long dress, threw my hat onto a sofa, let down her hair with a turn of the wrist, and motioning me to the piano, picked up her skirts and began to dance.

Enchanted as I was by the humour of her quick change to the 'Ibsen woman', words are vain to describe my feelings as I feebly tinkled a few bars on the piano and watched the dancer.

Every motion was the perfection of grace and yet no Indian Nautch-girl could have more skilfully expressed the idea of sexual allurement. Gazing at her in speechless admiration, I saw the violet eyes glow with passion, the full red lips part, the filmy petticoats were lifted higher and higher; the loose frilled drawers gleamed white. At last breathless and panting, she fell back upon a chair, her eyes closed, her legs parted, her breasts heaving. A mingled perfume came to my nostrils – half '*odor di faemina*, half the scent of white rose from her hair and clothes.

I flung myself upon her.

'Tell me, Flossie darling, what shall I do *first*?

The answer came, quick and short.

'Kiss me – *between my legs*!'

In an instant, I was kneeling before her. Her legs

fell widely apart. Sinking to a sitting posture, I plunged my head between her thighs. The petticoats incommoded me a little, but I soon managed to arrive at the desired spot. Somewhat to my surprise, instead of finding the lips closed and barricaded as is usual in the case of young girls, they were ripe, red and pouting, and as my mouth closed eagerly upon the delicious orifice and my tongue found and pressed upon the trembling clitoris, I knew that my qualms of conscience had been vain. My utmost powers were now called into play and I sought, by every means I possessed, to let Flossie know that I was no halfbaked lover. Passing my arms behind her, I extended my tongue to its utmost length and with rapid agile movements penetrated the scented recesses. Her hands locked themselves under my head, soft gasps of pleasure came from her lips, and as I delivered at last an effective attack upon the erect clitoris, her fingers clutched my neck, and with a sob of delight, she crossed her legs over my back, and pressing my head towards her, held me with a convulsive grasp, whilst the aromatic essence of her being flowed softly into my enchanted mouth.

As I rose to my feet, she covered her face with her hands and I saw a blue eye twinkle out between the fingers with an indescribable mixture of bashfulness and fun. Then, as if suddenly remembering herself, she sat up, dropped her petticoats over her knees, and looking up at me from under the curling lashes, said in a tone of profound melancholy.

'Jack, am I not a *disgraceful* child! All the same, I wouldn't have missed *that* for a million pounds.'

'Nor would I, little sweetheart; and whenever you would like to have it again—'

'No, no, it is your turn now.'

'What! Flossie; you don't mean to say—'

'But I *do* mean to say it, and to *do* it too. Lie down on that sofa at once, sir.'

'But, Flossie, I really—'

Without another word she leapt at me, threw her arms round my neck and fairly bore me down onto the divan. Falling on the top of me, she twined her silken legs round mine and gently pushing the whole of her tongue between my lips, began to work her body up and down with a wonderful sinuous motion which soon brought me to a state of excitement bordering on frenzy. Then, shaking a warning finger at me to keep still, she slowly slipped to her knees on the floor.

In another moment, I felt the delicate fingers round my straining yard. Carrying it to her mouth she touched it ever so softly with her tongue; then slowly parting her lips she pushed it gradually between them, keeping a grasp of the lower end with her hand which she moved gently up and down. Soon the tongue began to quicken its motion, and the brown head to work rapidly in a perpendicular direction. I buried my hands under the lovely hair, and clutched the white neck towards me, plunging the nut further and further into the delicious mouth until I seemed almost to touch the uvula. Her lips, tongue and hands now worked with redoubled ardour, and my sensations became momentarily more acute, until with a cry I besought her to let me withdraw. Shaking her head with great emphasis, she held my yard in a firmer grasp, and passing her disengaged hand behind me, drew me towards her face, and with an unspeakable clinging action of her mouth, carried out the delightful act of love to its logical conclusion, declining to remove her lips until, some minutes after, the last remaining evidences of the late crisis had completely disappeared.

Then and not till then, she stood up, and bending over me, as I lay, kissed me on the forehead, whispering:—

'There! Jack, now I love you twenty times more than ever.'*

I gazed into the lovely face in speechless adoration.

'Why don't you say something?' she cried. 'Is there anything else you want me to do?'

'Yes,' I answered, 'there is.'

'Out with it, then.'

'I am simply dying to see your breasts, naked.'

'Why, you darling, of course, you shall! Stay there a minute.'

Off she whisked again, and almost before I could realize she had gone, I looked up and she was before me. She had taken off everything but her chemise and stockings, the former lowered beneath her breasts.

Any attempt to describe the beauties thus laid bare to my adoring gaze must necessarily fall absurdly short of the reality. Her neck, throat and arms were full and exquisitely rounded, bearing no trace of juvenile immaturity.

Her breasts, however, were of course the objects of my special and immediate attention. Size, perfection of form and colour, I had never seen their equals, nor could the mind of man conceive anything so alluring as the coral nipples which stood out firm and erect, craving kisses. A wide space intervened between the two snowy hillocks which heaved a little with the haste of her late exertions. I gazed a moment in breathless delight and admiration, then rushing towards her, I buried my face in the enchanting valley, passed my burning lips over each of the neighbouring slopes and finally seized upon one after the other of the rosy nipples, which I sucked, mouthed and tongued with a frenzy of delight.

*This is a fact, as every girl knows who has ever gamahuched and been gamahuched by the man or boy she loves. As a *link*, it beats fucking out of the field. I've tried both and I *know*.   *Flossie*

The daring little girl lent herself eagerly to my every action, pushing her nipples into my mouth and eyes, pressing her breasts against my face, and clinging to my neck with her lovely naked arms.

Whilst we were thus amorously employed, my little lady had contrived dexterously to slip out of her chemise, and now stood before me naked but for her brown silk stockings and little shoes.

'There, Mr Jack, now you can see my breasts, and everything else that you like of mine. In future, this will be my full-dress costume for making love to you in. Stop, though; it wants just one touch.' And darting out of the room, she came back with a beautiful chain of pearls round her neck, finishing with a pendant of rubies which hung just low enough to nestle in the Valley of Delight, between the wonderful breasts.

'I am, now,' she said, 'The White Queen of the Gama Huchi Islands. My kingdom is bounded on this side by the piano, and on the other by the furthest edge of the bed in the next room. Any male person found wearing a *stitch* of clothing within those boundaries will be sentenced to lose his p . . . but soft! who comes here?'

Shading her eyes with her hand she gazed in my direction:—

'Aha! a stranger; and, unless these royal eyes deceive us, a man! He shall see what it is to defy our laws! What ho! within there! Take this person and remove his p . . .'

'Great Queen!' I said, in a voice of deep humility, 'if you will but grant me two minutes, I will make haste to comply with your laws.'

'And we, good fellow, will help you. (*Aside.*)

'Methinks he is somewhat comely*. (*Aloud.*)

---

*Don't believe I ever said anything of the sort, but if I did, 'methinks' I'd better take this opportunity of withdrawing the statement.   *Flossie*

'But first let us away with these garments, which are more than aught else a violation of our Gama Huchian Rules, Good! now the shirt. And what, pray, is *this*? We thank you, sir, but we are not requiring any *tent-poles* just now.'

'Then if your Majesty will deign to remove your royal fingers I will do my humble best to cause the offending pole to disappear. At present, with your Majesty's hand upon it—!'

'Silence, Sir! Your time is nearly up, and if the last garment be not removed in twenty seconds . . . So! you obey. Tis well! You shall see how we reward a faithful subject of our laws.' And thrusting my yard between her lips, the Great White Queen of the Gama Huchi Islands sucked in the whole column to the very root, and by dint of working her royal mouth up and down, and applying her royal fingers to the neighbouring appendages, soon drew into her throat a tribute to her greatness, which, from its volume and the time it took in the act of payment, plainly caused her Majesty the most exquisite enjoyment. Of my own pleasure I will only say that it was delirious, whilst in this, as in all other love sports in which we indulged, an added zest was given by the humour and fancy with which this adorable child-woman designed and carried out our amusements. In the present case, the personating of the Great White Queen appeared to afford her especial delight, and going on with the performance, she took a long branch of pampas-grass from its place and waving it over my head, she said:—

'The next ceremony to be performed by a visitor to these realms will, we fear, prove somewhat irksome, but it must be gone through. We shall now place our royal person on this lofty throne. You, sir, will sit upon this footstool before us. We shall then wave our sceptre three times. At the third wave, our knees will part and our guest will see before him the royal spot of love. This he will proceed to salute with a kiss which shall last until we are pleased to signify that we have had enough. Now, most noble guest, open your mouth, *don't* shut your eyes, and prepare! One, two, *three.*'

The pampas-grass waved, the legs parted, and nestling between the ivory thighs, I saw the scarlet lips open and show the erected clitoris peeping forth from its nest below the slight brown tuft which adorned the base of the adorable belly. I gazed and gazed in mute rapture, until a sharp strident voice above me said:

'Now then, there, move on, please; can't have you blocking up the road all day!' Then changing suddenly to her own voice:—

'Jack, if you don't kiss me at once I shall *die!*'

I pressed towards the delicious spot and taking the whole cunt into my mouth passed my tongue upwards along the perfumed lips until it met the clitoris, which trust itself amorously between my lips, imploring kisses. These I rained upon her with all the ardour I could command, clutching the rounded bottom with feverish fingers and drawing the naked belly closer and ever closer to my burning face, whilst my tongue plunged deep within the scented cunt and revelled in its divine odours and the contraction of its beloved lips.

The Great White Queen seemed to relish this particular form of homage, for it was many minutes before the satin thighs closed, and with the little hands under my chin, she raised my face and looking into my eyes with inexpressible love and sweetness shining from her own, she said simply:—

'Thank you, Jack. You're a darling!'—

By way of answer I covered her with kisses, omitting no single portion of the lovely naked body, the various beauties of which lent themselves with charming zest to my amorous doings. Upon the round and swelling breasts, I lavished renewed devotion, sucking the rosy nipples with a fury of delight, and relishing to the full the quick movements of rapture with which the lithe clinging form was constantly shaken, no less than the divine aroma passing to my nostrils as the soft thighs opened and met again, the rounded arms rose and fell, and with this, the faintly perfumed hair brushing my face and shoulders mingled its odour of tea-rose.

All this was fast exciting my senses to the point of madness, and there were moments when I felt that to postpone much longer the consummation of our ardour would be impossible.

I looked at the throbbing breasts, remembered the fragrant lips below that had pouted ripely to meet my kisses, the developed clitoris that told of joys long indulged in. And then . . . and then . . . the sweet girlish face looked up into mine, the violet eyes seemed to take on a pleading expression, and as if reading my thoughts, Flossie pushed me gently into a chair, seated herself on my knee, slipped an arm round my neck, and pressing her cheek to mine, whispered:—

'Poor, *poor* old thing! I know what it wants; and *I* want it too – badly, oh! so badly. But, Jack, you can't guess what a friend Eva has been to me, and I've promised her *not to*! You see I'm only just sixteen, and . . . *the consequences*! There! don't let us talk about it. Tell me all about yourself, and then I'll tell you about me. When you're tired of hearing me talk, you shall stop my mouth with – well, whatever you like. Now sir, begin!'

I gave her a short narrative of my career from boyhood upwards, dry and dull enough in all conscience!

'Yes, yes, that's all very nice and prim and proper,' she cried. 'But you haven't told me the principal thing of all – when you first began to be – naughty, and with whom?'

I invented some harmless fiction which, I saw, the

quickwitted girl did not believe, and begged her to tell me her own story, which she at once proceeded to do. I shall endeavour to transcribe it, though it is impossible to convey any idea of the humour with which it was delivered, still less of the irrepressible fun which flashed from her eyes at the recollection of her schoolgirl pranks and amourettes. There were, of course, many interruptions*, for most of which I was probably responsible; but, on the whole, in the following chapter will be found a fairly faithful transcript of Flossie's early experiences. Some at least of these I am sanguine, will be thought to have been of a sufficiently appetizing character.

*The first of these is a really serious one, but for this the impartial reader will see that the responsibility was divided.

Chapter Two

'How Flossie acquired the French tongue.'

'Before I begin, Jack, I should like to hold something nice and solid in my hand, to sort of give me confidence as I go on. Have you got anything about you that would do!'

I presented what seemed to me the most suitable article 'in stock' at the moment.

'Aha!' said Flossie in an affected voice, 'the very thing! How *very* fortunate that you should happen to have it ready!'

'Well, madam, you see it is an article we are constantly being asked for by our lady-customers. It is rather an expensive thing – seven pound ten—'

'Yes, it's rather stiff. Still, if you can assure me that it will always keep in its present condition, I shouldn't mind spending a good deal upon it.'

'You will find, madam, that anything you may spend upon it will be amply returned to you. Our ladies have always expressed the greatest satisfaction with it.'

'Do you mean that you find they come more than once? If so, I'll take it now.'

'Perhaps you would allow me to bring it myself—?'

'Thanks, but I think I can hold it quite well in my hand. It won't go off suddenly, will it?'

'Not if it is kept in a cool place, madam.'

'And it mustn't be shaken, I suppose, like *that*, for instance?' (Shaking it.)

'For goodness gracious sake, take your hand away, Flossie, or there'll be a catastrophe.'

'That is a good word, Jack! But do you suppose that if I saw a "catastrophe" coming I shouldn't know what to do with it?'

'*What* should you do?'

'Why, what *can* you do with a catastrophe of that sort but *swallow it*?'

The effect of this little interlude upon us both was magnetic. Instead of going on with her story, Flossie commanded me to lie upon my back on the divan, and having placed a couple of pillows under my neck, knelt astride of me with her face towards my feet. With one or two caressing movements of her bottom, she arranged herself so that the scarlet vulva rested just above my face. Then gently sinking down, she brought her delicious cunt full upon my mouth from which my tongue instantly darted to penetrate the adorable recess. At the same moment, I felt the brown hair fall upon my thighs, my straining prick plunged between her lips, and was engulfed in her velvet mouth to the very root, whilst her hands played with feverish energy amongst the surrounding parts, and the nipples of her breasts rubbed softly against my belly.

In a very few moments, I had received into my mouth her first tribute of love and was working with might and main to procure a second, whilst she in her turn, wild with pleasure my wandering tongue was causing her, grasped my yard tightly between her lips, passing them rapidly up and down its whole length, curling her tongue round the nut, and maintaining all the time an ineffable sucking action which very soon produced its natural result. As I poured a torrent into her eager mouth, I felt the soft lips which I was kissing contract for a moment upon my tongue and then part again to set free the aromatic flood to which the intensity of her sensations imparted additional volume and sweetness.

The pleasure, we were both experiencing from this the most entrancing of all the reciprocal acts of love, was too keen to be abandoned after one effort. Stretching my hands upwards to mould and press the swelling breasts and erected nipples, I seized the rosy clitoris anew between my lips, whilst Flossie resumed her charming operations upon my instrument which she gamahuched with ever increasing zest and delight, and even with a skill and variety of action which would have been marvellous in a woman of double her age and experience. Once again the fragrant dew was distilled upon my enchanted tongue, and once again the velvet mouth closed upon my yard to receive the results of its divinely pleasurable ministrations.

Raising herself slowly and almost reluctantly from her position, Flossie laid her naked body at full length upon mine, and after many kisses upon my mouth, eyes and cheeks said, 'Now you may go and refresh yourself with a bath while I dress for dinner.'

'But where are we going to dine?' I asked.

'You'll see presently. *Go* along, there's a good boy!'

I did as I was ordered and soon came back from the bath-room, much refreshed by my welcome ablutions.

Five minutes later Flossie joined me, looking lovelier than ever, in a short-sleeved pale blue muslin frock, cut excessively low in front, black openwork silk stockings and little embroidered shoes.

'Dinner is on the table,' she said, taking my arm and leading me into an adjoining room where an exquisite little cold meal was laid out, to which full justice was speedily done, followed by coffee made by my hostess, who produced some Benedictine and a box of excellent cigars.

'There, Jack, if you're quite comfy, I'll go on with my story. Shall I stay here, or come and sit on your knee?'

'Well, as far as getting on with the story goes, I think you are better in that chair, Flossie—'

'But I told you I must have something to hold.'

'Yes, you did, and the result was that we didn't get very far with the story, if you remember—'

'Remember! As if I was likely to forget. But look at this,' holding up a rounded arm bare to the shoulder. 'Am I to understand that you'd rather not have this round your neck?'

Needless to say she was to understand nothing of the sort, and a moment later she was perched upon my knee and having with deft penetrating fingers enough under her magic touch, began her narrative.

'I don't think there will be much to tell you until my school life at Paris begins. My father and mother both died when I was quite small; I had no brothers or sisters, and I don't believe I've got a relation in the world. You mustn't think I want to swagger, Jack, but I am rather rich. One of my two guardians died three years ago and the other is in India and doesn't care a scrap about me. Now and then, he writes and asks how I am getting on, and when he heard I was going to live with Eva (whom he knows quite well) he seemed perfectly satisfied. Two years ago he arranged for me to go to school in Paris.

'Now I must take great care not to shock you, but there's nothing for it but to tell you that about this time I began to have the most wonderful feelings all over me – a sort of desperate longing for something, I didn't know what – which used to become almost unbearable when I danced or played any game in which a boy or man was near me. At the Paris school was a very pretty girl, named Ylette de Vespertin, who, for some reason I never could understand, took a fancy to me. She was two years older than I, had several brothers and boy cousins at home, and being up to every sort of lark and mischief, was just the girl I wanted as confidante. Of course she had no difficulty in explaining the whole thing to me, and in the course of a day or two, I knew everything there was to know. On the third day of our talks Ylette slipped a note into my hand as I was going up to bed. Now, Jack, you must really go and look out of the window while I tell you what it said:

Chérie,
     Si tu veux te faire sucer la langue, les seins et le con, viens dans mon lit toute nue ce soir. C'est moi qui te ferai voir les anges.
Viens de suite à ton,

                                        Ylette

'I have rather a good memory, and even if I hadn't, I don't think I could ever forget the words of that note, for it was the beginning of a most delicious time for me.

'I suppose if I had been a well-regulated young person, I should have taken no notice of the invitation. As it was, I stripped myself naked in a brace of shakes, and flew to Ylette's bedroom which was next door to the one I occupied. I had not realized before what a beautifully made girl she was. Her last garment was just slipping from her as I came in, and I stared in blank admiration at her naked figure which was like a statue in the perfection of its lines. A furious longing to touch it seized me, and springing upon her, I passed my hands feverishly up and down her naked body, until grasping me round the waist, she half dragged, half carried me to the bed, laid me on the edge of it, and kneeling upon the soft rug, plunged her head between my legs, and bringing her lips to bear full upon the *other* lips before her, parted them with a peculiar action of the mouth and inserted her tongue with a sudden stroke which sent perfect waves of delight through my whole body, followed by still greater ecstasy when she went for the particular spot *you* know of, Jack – the one near the top, I mean – and twisting her tongue over it, under it, round it and across it, soon brought about the result she wanted, and in her own expressive phrase "me faisait voir les anges".

'Of course I had no experience, but I did my best to repay her for the pleasures she had given me, and as I happen to possess an extremely long and pointed tongue, and Ylette's cunt – oh Jack, *I've said it at last!* Go and look out of the window again; or better still, come and stop my naughty mouth with – I *meant* your tongue, but this will do better still. The wicked monster, what a size he is! Now put both your hands behind my head, and push him in till he touches my throat. Imagine he is *somewhere else*, work like a demon, and for your life, don't stop until the very end of all things Ah! the dear, darling, delicious thing! How he throbs with excitement! I believe he can *see* my mouth waiting for him. Come, Jack, my darling, my beloved, let me gamahuche you. I want to feel this heavenly prick of yours between my lips and against my tongue, so that I may suck it and drain every drop that comes from it into my mouth. Now, Jack now . . .'

The red lips closed hungrily upon the object of their desire, the rosy tongue stretched itself amorously along the palpitating yard, and twice, the tide of love poured freely forth to be received with every sign of delight into the velvet mouth.

Nothing in my experience had ever approached the pleasure which I derived from the intoxicating contact of this young girl's lips and tongue upon my most sensitive parts, enhanced as it was by my love for her, which grew apace, and by her own intense delight in the adorable pastime. So keen indeed were the sensations she procured me that I was almost able to forget the deprivation laid upon me by Flossie's promise to her friend. Indeed, when I reflected upon her youth, and the unmatched beauty of her girlish shape with its slender waist, smooth satin belly and firm rounded breasts, the whole seemed too perfect a work of nature to be marred – at least as yet – by the probable consequences of an act of coition carried to its logical conclusion by a pair of ardent lovers.

So I bent my head once more to its resting place between the snowy thighs, and again drew from my darling little mistress the fragrant treasures of love's sacred store house, lavished upon my clinging lips with gasps and sighs and all possible tokens of enjoyment in the giving.

After this it was time to part, and at Flossie's suggestion I undressed her, brushed our her silky hair and put her into bed. Lying on her white pillow, she looked so fair and like a child that I was for saying goodnight with just a single kiss upon her cheek. But this was not in accordance with her views on the subject. She sat up in bed, flung her arms round my neck, nestled her face against mine and whispered in my ear:

'I'll never give a promise again as long as I live.'

It was an awful moment and my resolution all but went down under the strain. But I just managed to resist, and after one prolonged embrace, during which Flossie's tongue went twining and twisting round my own with an indescribably lascivious motion, I planted a farewell kiss full upon the nipple of her left breast, sucked it for an instant and fled from the room.

On reaching my own quarters I lit a cigar and sat down to think over the extraordinary good fortune by which I had chanced upon this unique liaison. It was plain to me that in Flossie I had encountered probably the only specimen of her class. A girl of sixteen, with all the fresh charm of that beautiful age united to the fascination of a passionate and amorous woman. Add to these a finely-strung temperament, a keen sense of humour, and the true artist's striving after thoroughness in all she did, and it will be admitted that all these qualities meeting in a person of quite faultless beauty were enough to justify the self-congratulations with which I contemplated my present luck, and the rosy visions of pleasure to come which hung about my waking and sleeping senses till the morning.

About midday I called at the flat. The door was opened to me by Eva Letchford.

'I am so glad to see you,' she said. 'Flossie is out on her bicycle, and I can say what I want to.'

As she moved to the window to draw up the blind a little, I had a better opportunity of noticing what a really splendid-looking woman she had become. Observing my glances of frank admiration, she sat down in a low easy chair opposite to me, crossed her shapely legs, and looking over at me with a bright pleasant smile, said:

'Now, Jack – I may call you Jack, of course, because we are all three going to be great friends – you had my letter the other day. No doubt you thought it a strange document, but when we know one another better, you will easily understand how I came to write it.'

'My dear girl, I understand it already. You forget I have had several hours with Flossie. It was her happiness you wanted to secure, and I hope she will tell you our plan was successful.'

'Flossie and I have not secrets. She has told me everything that passed between you. She has also told me what did *not* pass between you, and how you did not even try to make her break her promise to me.'

'I should have been a brute if I had—'

'Then I am afraid nineteen men out of twenty are

brutes – but that's neither here nor there. What I want you to know is that I appreciate your nice feeling, and that some day soon I shall, with Flossie's consent, take an opportunity of showing that appreciation in a practical way.'

Here she crossed her right foot high over the left knee and very leisurely removed an imaginary speck of dust from the shotsilk stocking.

'Now I must go and change my dress. You'll stay and lunch with us in the coffee room, won't you? – that's right. This is my bedroom. I'll leave the door open so that we can talk till Flossie comes. She promised to be in by one o'clock.'

We chatted away on indifferent subjects whilst I watched with much satisfaction the operations of the toilette in the next room.

Presently a little cry of dismay reached me:

'Oh dear, oh dear! do come here a minute, Jack. I have pinched one of my breasts with my stays and made a little red mark. Look! *Do* you think it will show in evening dress?'

I examined the injury with all possible care and deliberation.

'My professional opinion is, madam, that as the mark is only an inch above the nipple we may fairly hope—'

'*Above* the nipple! then I'm afraid it will be a near thing,' said Eva with a merry laugh.

'Perhaps a little judicious stroking by an experienced hand might—'

'Naow then there, naow then!' suddenly came from the door in a hoarse cockney accent.

'You jest let the lydy be, or oi'll give yer somethink to tyke 'ome to yer dinner, see if oi don't!'

'Who is this person?' I asked of Eva, placing my hands upon her two breasts as if to shield them from the intruder's eye.

'Person yerself!' said the voice, 'fust thing *you've*

a-got ter do is ter leave 'old of my donah's breasties and then oi'll *tork* to yer!'

'But the lady has hurt herself, sir, and was consulting me professionally.'

There was a moment's pause, during which I had time to examine my opponent whom I found to be wearing a red tam-o'-shanter cap, a close-fitting knitted silk blouse, a short white flannel skirt, and scarlet stockings. This charming figure threw itself upon me open-armed and open-mouthed and kissed me with delightful abandon.

After a hearty laugh over the success of Flossie's latest 'impersonation', Eva pushed us both out of the room, saying: 'Take her away, Jack, and see if *she* has got any marks. Those bicycle saddles are rather trying sometimes. We will lunch in a quarter of an hour.'

I bore my darling little mistress away to her room, and having helped her to strip off her clothes, I inspected on my knees the region where the saddle might have been expected to gall her, but found nothing but a fair expanse of firm white bottom which I saluted with many lustful kisses upon every spot within reach of my tongue. Then I took her naked to the bathroom, and sponged her from neck to ankles, dried her thoroughly, just plunged my tongue once into her cunt, carried her back to her room, dressed her and presented her to Eva within twenty minutes of our leaving the latter's bedroom.

Below in the coffee-room, a capitally served luncheon awaited us. The table was laid in a sort of little annexe to the principal room, and I was glad of the retirement, since we were able to enjoy to the full the constant flow of fun and mimicry with which Flossie brought tears of laughter to our eyes throughout the meal. Eva, too, was gifted with a fine sense of the ridiculous, and as I myself was at least an appreciative audience, the ball was kept rolling with plenty of spirit.

After lunch Eva announced her intention of going to a concert in Piccadilly, and a few minutes later Flossie and I were once more alone.

'Jack,' she said. 'I feel thoroughly and hopelessly naughty this afternoon. If you like I will go on with my story while you lie on the sofa and smoke a cigar.'

This exactly suited my views and I said so.

'Very well, then. First give me a great big kiss with all the tongue you've got about you. Ah! that was good! Now I'm going to sit on this footstool beside you, and I *think* one or two of these buttons might be unfastened, so that I can feel whether the story is producing any effect upon you. Good gracious! why, it's as hard and stiff as a poker already. I really *must* frig it a little—'

'Quite gently and slowly then, *please* Flossie, or—'

'Yes, quite, *quite* gently and slowly, so – is that nice, Jack?'

'Nice is not the word, darling!'

'Talking of words, Jack, I am afraid I shall hardly be able to finish my adventures without occasionally using a word or two which you don't hear at a Sunday School Class. Do you mind, very much? Of course you can always go and look out of the window, can't you!'

'My dearest little sweetheart, when we are alone together like this, and both feeling extremely naughty, as we do now, any and every word that comes from your dear lips sounds sweet and utterly void of offence to me.'

'Very well, then; that makes it ever so much easier to tell my story, and if I *should* become too shocking – well, you know how I love you to stop my mouth, don't you Jack!'

A responsive throb from my imprisoned member gave her all the answer she required.

'Let me see,' she began, 'where was I? Oh, I remember, in Ylette's bed.'

'Yes, she had gamahuched you, and you were just performing the same friendly office for her.'

'Of course: I was telling you how the length of my tongue made up for the shortness of my experience, or so Ylette was kind enough to say. I think she meant it too; at any rate she spent several times before I gave up my position between her legs. After this we tried the double gamahuche, which proved a great success because, although she was, as I have told you, older than I, we were almost exactly of a height, so that as she knelt over me, her cunt came quite naturally upon my mouth, and her mouth upon my cunt, and in this position we were able to give each other an enormous amount of pleasure.'

At this point I was obliged to beg Flossie to remove her right hand from the situation it was occupying.

'What I cannot understand about it,' she went on, 'is that there are any number of girls in France, and a good many in England too, who after they have once been gamahuched by another girl don't care about anything else. Perhaps it means that they have never been really in love with a man, because to *me* one touch of your lips in that particular neighbourhood is worth ten thousand kisses from anybody else, male or female and when I have got your dear, darling, delicious prick in my mouth, I want nothing else in the whole wide world, except to give you the greatest possible amount of pleasure and to make you spend down my throat in the quickest possible time—'

'If you really want to beat the record, Flossie, I think there's a good chance now—'

Almost before the words had passed my lips the member in question was between *hers*, where it soon throbbed to the crisis in response to the indescribable sucking action of mouth and tongue of which she possessed the secret.

On my telling her how exquisite were the sensations she procured me by this means she replied:

'Oh, you have to thank Ylette for that! Just before we became friends she had gone for the long holidays to a country house belonging to a young couple who were great friends of hers. There was a very handsome boy of eighteen or so staying in the house. He fell desperately in love with Ylette and she with him, and he taught her exactly how to gamahuche him so as to produce the utmost amount of pleasure. As she told me afterwards, "Every day, every night, almost ever hour, he would bury his prick in my mouth, frig it against my tongue, and fill my throat with a divine flood. With a charming amiability, he worked incessantly to show me every kind of gamahuching, all the possible ways of sucking a man's prick. Nothing, said he, should be left to the imagination, which, he explained, can never produce such good results as a few practical lessons given in detail upon a real standing prick, plunged to the very root in the mouth of the girl pupil, to whom one can thus describe on the spot the various suckings, hard, soft, slow or quick, of which sit is essential she should know the precise effect in order to obtain the quickest and most copious flow of the perfumed liquor which she desires to draw from her lover."

"I suppose," Ylette went on, "that one invariably likes what one can do well. Anyhow, my greatest pleasure in life is to suck a good-looking boy's prick. If he likes to slip his tongue into my cunt at the same time, *tant mieux*."

'Unfortunately this delightful boy could only stay a fortnight, but as there were several other young men of the party, and as her lover was wise enough to know that after his recent lessons in the art of love, Ylette could not be expected to be an abstainer, he begged her to enjoy herself in his absence, with the result, as she said that "au bout d'une semaine il n'y avait pas un vit dans la maison qui ne m'avait tripoté la luette, ni une langue qui n'était l'amie intime de mon con."

'Every one of these instructions Ylette passed on to

me, with practical illustrations upon my second finger standing as substitute for the real thing, which, of course, was not to be had in the school – at least not just then.

'She must have been an excellent teacher, for I have never had any other lessons than hers, and yours is the first and only staff of love that I have ever had the honour of gamahuching. However, I mean to make up now for lost time, for I would have you to know, my darling, that I am madly in love with every bit of your body, and that most of all do I adore your angel prick with its coral head that I so love to suck and plunge into my mouth. Come, Jack, come! Let us have one more double gamahuche. One moment! There! Now I am naked. I am going to kneel over your face with my legs wide apart and my cunt kissing your mouth. Drive the whole of your tongue into it, won't you, Jack, and make it curl round my clitoris. Yes! that's it – just like that. Lovely! Now I can't talk any more, because I am going to fill my mouth with the whole of your darling prick; push; push it down my throat, Jack, and when the time comes, spend your very longest and most. I'm going to frig you a little first and rub you under your balls. Goodness! how the dear thing is standing. In he goes now . . . m . . . m . . . m . . . m . . . m . . . m . . .!

A few inarticulate gasps and groans of pleasure were the only sounds audible for some minutes during which each strove to render the sensations of the other as acute as possible. I can answer for it that Flossie's success was complete, and by the convulsive movements of her bottom and the difficulty I experienced in keeping the position of my tongue upon her palpitating clitoris, I gathered that operations had not altogether failed in their object. In this I was confirmed by the copious and protracted discharge which the beloved cunt delivered into my throat at the same instant as the incomparable mouth received my yard to the very root, and a perfect torrent rewarded her delicious efforts for my enjoyment.

'Ah, Jack! that was just heavenly,' she sighed, as she rose from her charming position. '*How* you did spend, that time, you darling old boy, and so did I, eh, Jack?'

'My little angel, I thought you would never have finished,' I replied.

'Do you know, Jack, I believe you really did get a little way down my throat, then! At any rate you managed the "tripotage de luette" that Ylette's friend recommended so strongly!'

'And I don't think I ever got quite so far into your cunt, Flossie.'

'That's quite true; I felt your tongue touch a spot it had never reached before. And just wasn't it lovely when you got there! It almost makes me spend again to think of it! But I am not going to be naughty any more. And to show you how truly virtuous I am feeling, I'll continue my story if you like. I want to get on with it, because I know you must be wondering all the time how a person of my age can have come to be so . . . what shall we say, Jack?'

'Larky,' I suggested.

'Yes, "larky" will do. Of course I have always been "older than my age" as the saying goes, and my friendship with Ylette and all the lovely things she used to do to me made me "come on" much faster than most girls. I ought to tell you that I got to be rather a favourite at school, and after it came to be known that Ylette and I were on gamahuching terms, I used to get little notes from lots of other girls in the school imploring me to sleep with them. One dear thing even went so far as to give me the measurements of her tongue, which she had taken with a piece of string.'

'Oh, I say, Flossie, *come now* – I can swallow a good deal but—'

'You can indeed, Jack, as I have good reason to know! But all the same it's absolutely true. You can't have any conception what French schoolgirls of sixteen are like. There is nothing they won't do to get themselves gamahuched, and if a girl is pretty or fascinating or has particularly good legs, or specially large breasts, she may, if she likes, have a fresh admirer's head under her petticoats every day of the week. Of course, it's all very wrong and dreadful, I know, but what else can you expect? In France gamahuching between grown-up men and women is a recognized thing—'

'Not only in France, *nowadays*,' I put in.

'So I have heard. But at any rate in France everybody does it. Girls at school naturally know this, as they know most things. At that time of life - at *my* time of life, if you like - a girl thinks and dreams of nothing else. She cannot, except by some extraordinary luck, find herself alone with a boy or man. One day her girl chum at school pops her head under her petticoats and gamahuches her deliciously. How can you wonder if from that moment she is ready to go through fire and water to obtain the same pleasure?'

'Go on, Flossie. You are simply delicious today!'

'Don't laugh, Jack. I am very serious about it. I don't care how much a girl of (say) my age longs for a boy to be naughty with - it's perfectly right and natural. What I think is bad is that she should *begin* by having a liking for a girl's tongue inculcated into her. I should like to see boys and girls turned loose upon one another once a week or so at authorized gamahuching parties, which should be attended by masters and governesses (who would have to see that the *other* thing was not indulged in, of course). Then the girls would grow up with a good healthy taste for the other sex, and even if they did do a little gamahuching amongst themselves between whiles, it would only be to keep themselves going till the next "party". By my plan a boy's prick would be the central object of their desires, as it ought to be. Now *I* think that's a very fine scheme, Jack, and as soon as I am a little older, I shall go to Paris and put it before the Minister of Education!'

'But why wait, Flossie? Why not go now?'

'Well, you see, if the old gentleman (I suppose he is old, isn't he, or he wouldn't be a minister?) – if he saw a girl in short frocks, he would think she had got some private object to serve in regard to the gamahuching parties. Whereas a grown-up person who had plainly left school might be supposed to be doing it unselfishly for the good of the rising generation.'

'Yes, I understand that. But when you *do* go, Flossie, please take me or some other respectable person with you, because I don't altogether trust that Minister of Education and whatever the length of your frocks might happen to be at the time, I feel certain that, old or young, the moment you had explained your noble scheme, he would be wanting some practical illustrations on the office armchair!'

'How dare you suggest such a thing, Jack! You are to understand, sir, that from henceforth my mouth is reserved for three purposes, to eat with, to talk with, and to kiss you with on whatever part of your person I may happen to fancy at the moment. By the way, you won't mind my making just one exception in favour of Eva, will you? She loves me to make her nipples stand with my tongue; occasionally, too, we perform the "*soixant neuf*".'

'When the next performance takes place, may I be there to see?' I ejaculated fervently.

'Oh, Jack, how shocking!'

'Does it shock you, Flossie? Very well, then I withdraw it, and apologize.'

'You cannot withdraw it now. You have distinctly stated that you would like to be there when Eva and I have our next gamahuche.'

'Well, I suppose I *did* say.'

'Silence, sir,' said Flossie in a voice of thunder, and shaking her brown head at me with inexpressible ferocity. 'You have made a proposal of the most indecent character, and the sentence of the Court is that, at the first possible opportunity, you shall be *held to that proposal*! Meanwhile the Court condemns you to receive 250 kisses on various parts of your body, which it will at once proceed to administer. Now, sir, off with your clothes!'

'Mayn't I keep my . . .'

'No, sir, you may *not*!'

The sentence of the Court was accordingly carried out to the letter, somewhere about three-fourths of the kisses being applied upon one and the same part of the prisoner to which the Court attached its mouth with extraordinary gusto.

Chapter Three

Nox Ambrosiana

My intercourse with the tenants of the flat became daily more intimate and more frequent. My love for Flossie grew intensely deep and strong as opportunities increased for observing the rare sweetness and amiability of her character, and the charm which breathed like a spell over everything she said and did. At one moment, so great was her tact and so keen her judgment, I would find myself consulting her on a knotty point with the certainty of getting sound advice; at another the child in her would suddenly break out and she would romp and play about like the veriest kitten. Then there would be yet another reaction, and without a word of warning, she would become amorous and caressing and seizing upon her favourite plaything, would push it into her mouth and suck it in a perfect frenzy of erotic passion. It is hardly necessary to say that these contrasts of mood lent an infinite zest to our liaison and I had almost ceased to long for its more perfect consummation. But one warm June evening, allusion was again made to the subject by Flossie, who repeated her sorrow for the deprivation she declared I must be feeling so greatly.

I assured her that it was not so.

'Well, Jack, if you aren't, *I* am,' she cried. 'And what is more there is someone else who is "considerably likewise" as our old gardener used to say.'

'What *do* you mean, child?'

She darted into the next room and came back almost directly.

'Sit down there and listen to me. In that room, lying asleep on her bed, is the person whom, after you, I love best in the world. There is nothing I wouldn't do for her, and I'm sure you'll believe this when I tell you that I am going to beg you on my knees, to go in there and do to Eva what my promise to her prevents me from letting you do to me. Now, Jack, I know you love me and you know *dearly* I love you. Nothing can alter *that*. Well, Jack, if you will go into Eva, gamahuche her well and let her gamahuche you (she *adores* it), and then have her thoroughly and in all positions – I shall simply love you a thousand times better than ever.'

'But Flossie, my darling, Eva doesn't—'

'Oh, doesn't she! Wait till you get between her legs, and see! Come along; I'll just put you inside the room and then leave you. She is lying outside her bed for coolness – on her side. Lie down quietly *behind* her. She will be almost sure to think it's me, and perhaps you will hear – something interesting. Quick's the word! Come!'

The sight which met my eyes on entering Eva's bedroom was enough to take one's breath away. She lay on her side, with her face towards the door, stark naked, and fast asleep. I crept noiselessly towards her and gazed upon her glorious nudity in speechless delight. Her dark hair fell in a cloud about her white shoulders. Her fine face was slightly flushed, the full red lips a little parted. Below, the gleaming breasts caught the light from the shaded lamp at her bedside, the pink nipples rising and falling to the time of her quiet breathing. One fair round arm was behind her head, the other lay along the exquisitely turned thigh. The good St Anthony might have been pardoned for owning himself defeated by such a picture!

As is usual with a sleeping person who is being looked at, Eva stirred a little, and her lips opened as if to speak. I moved on tiptoe to the other side of the bed, and stripping myself naked, lay down beside her.

Then, without turning round, a sleepy voice said, 'Ah, Flossie, are you there? What have you done with Jack? (*a pause*). When are you going to lend him to me for a night, Flossie? I wish I'd got him here now, between my legs – betwe-e-e-n m-y-y-y le-egs! Oh dear! how randy I do feel tonight. When I *do* have Jack for a night, Flossie, may I take his prick in my mouth before we do the other thing? Flossie – Floss*ee* – why don't you answer? Little darling! I expect she's tired out, and no wonder! Well, I suppose I'd better put something on me and go to sleep too!'

As she raised herself from the pillow, her hand came in contact with my person.

'Angels and Ministers of Grace defend us! What's this? *You*, Jack! *And you've heard what I've been saying?*'

'I'm afraid I have, Eva.'

'Well, it doesn't matter; I meant it all, and more besides! Now before I do anything else I simply must run in and kiss that darling Floss for sending you to me. It is just like her, and I can't say anything stronger than *that*!'

'Jack,' she said on coming back to the room. 'I warn you that you are going to have a stormy night. In the matter of love, I've gone starving for many months. Tonight I'm fairly roused, and when in that state, I believe I am about the most erotic bedfellow to be found anywhere. Flossie has given me leave to *say* and *do* anything and everything to you, and I mean to use the permission for all its worth. Flossie tells me that you are an absolutely perfect gamahucher. Now I adore being gamahuched. Will you do that for me, Jack?'

'My dear girl, I should rather think so!'

'Good! But it is not to be all on one side. I shall gamahuche you, too, and you will have to own that I know something of the art. Another thing you may perhaps like to try is what the French call "*fouterie aux seins*".'

'I know all about it, and if I may insert Monsieur Jacques between those magnificent breasts of yours, I shall die of the pleasure.'

'Good again. Now we come to the legitimate drama, from which you and Floss have so nobly abstained. I desire to be thoroughly and comprehensively fucked tonight – sorry to have to use the word, Jack, but it is the only one that expresses my meaning.'

'Don't apologize, dear. Under present circumstances all words are allowable.'

'Glad to hear you say that, because it makes conversation so much easier. Now let me take hold of your prick, and frig it a little, so that I may judge what size it attains in full erection. So! he's a fine boy, and I think he will fit my cunt to a turn. I must kiss his pretty head, it looks so tempting. Ah! delicious! See here Jack, I will lie back with my head on the pillow, and you shall just come and kneel over me and have me in the mouth. Push away gaily, just as if you were fucking me, and when you are going to spend, slip one hand under my neck and drive your prick down my throat, and do not *dare* to withdraw it until I have received all you have to give me. Sit upon my chest first for a minute and let me tickle your prick with the nipples of my breasts. Is that nice? Ah! I knew you would like it! *Now* kneel up to my face, and I will suck you.'

With eagerly pouting lips and clutching fingers, she seized upon my straining hard, and pressed it into her soft mouth. Arrived there, it was saluted by the velvet tongue which twined itself about the nut in a thousand lascivious motions.

Mindful of Eva's instructions, I began to work the instrument as if it was in another place. At once she laid her hands upon my buttocks and regulated the time of my movements, assisting them by a corresponding action of her head. Once, owing to carelessness on my part, her lips lost their hold altogether; with a little cry, she caught my prick in her fingers and in an instant, it was again between her lips and revelling in the adorable pleasure of their sucking.

A moment later and my hands were under her neck, for the signal, and my very soul seemed to be exhaled from me in response to the clinging of her mouth as she felt my prick throb with the passage of love's torrent.

After a minute's rest, and a word of gratitude for the transcendent pleasure she had given me, I began a tour of kisses over the enchanting regions which lay between her neck and her knees, ending with a protracted sojourn in the last, she said:

'Please to begin by passing your tongue slowly round the edges of the lips, then thrust it into the lower part at full length and keep it there working it in and out for a little. Then move it gradually up to the top and when there, press your tongue firmly against my clitoris for a minute or so. Next take the clitoris between your lips and suck it *furiously*, bite it gently, and slip the point of your tongue underneath it. When I have spent twice, which I am sure to do in the first three minutes, get up and lie between my legs, drive the whole of your tongue into my mouth and the whole of your prick into my cunt, and fuck me with all your might and main!'

I could not resist a smile at the naiveté of these circumstantial directions. My amusement was not lost upon Eva, who hastened to explain, by reminding me again that it was 'ages' since she had been touched by a man. 'In gamahuching,' she said, 'the *details* are everything. In copulation they are not so important, since the principal things that increase one's enjoyment – such as the quickening of the stroke towards the end by the man, and the knowing exactly how and when to applying the *nipping* action of the cunt by the woman – come more or less naturally, especially with practice. But now, Jack, I want to be gamahuched, please.'

'And I'm longing to be at you, dear. Come and kneel astride of me, and let me kiss your cunt without any more delay.'

Eva was pleased to approve of this position and in another moment, I was slipping my tongue into the delicious cavity which opened wider and wider to receive its caresses, and to enable it to plunge further and further into the perfumed depths. My attentions were next turned to the finely developed clitoris which I found to be extraordinarily sensitive. In fact, Eva's own time limit of three minutes had not been reached, when the second effusion escaped her, and a third was easily obtained by a very few more strokes of the tongue. After this, she laid herself upon her back, drew me towards her and, taking hold of my prick, placed it tenderly between her breasts, and pressing them together with her hands, urged me to enjoy myself in this enchanting position. The length and stiffness imported to my member by the warmth and softness of her breasts delighted her beyond measure, and she implored me to fuck her without any further delay. I was never more ready or better furnished than at that moment, and after she had once more taken my prick into her mouth for a moment, I slipped down to the desired position between her thighs which she had already parted to their uttermost to receive me. In an instant she had guided the staff of love to the exact spot, and with a heave of her bottom, aided by an answering thrust from me, had buried it to the root within the soft down of its natural covering.

Eva's description of herself as an erotic bedfellow had hardly prepared me for the joys I was to experience in her arms. From the moment the nut of my yard touched her womb, she became as one possessed. Her eyes were turned heavenwards, her tongue twined round my own in rapture, her hands played about my body, now clasping my neck, now working feverishly up and down my back, and ever and again, creeping down to her lower parts where her first and second finger would rest compass-shaped upon the two edges of her cunt, pressing themselves upon my prick as it glided in and out and adding still further to the maddening pleasure I was undergoing. Her breath came in short quick gasps, the calves of her legs sometimes lay upon my own but more often were locked over my loins or buttocks, thus enabling her to time to a nicety the strokes of my body, and to respond with accurately judged thrusts from her own splendid bottom. At last a low musical cry came from her parted lips, she strained me to her naked body with redoubled fury and driving the whole length of her tongue into my mouth, she spent long and deliciously, whilst I flooded her clinging cunt with a torrent of unparalleled volume and duration.

'Jack,' she whispered, 'I have never enjoyed anything half so much in my life before. I hope you liked it too?'

'I don't think you can expect anyone to say that he "liked" fucking *you*, Eva! One might "like" kissing your hand, or helping you on with an opera cloak or some minor pleasure of that sort. But to lie between a pair of legs like yours, cushioned on a pair of breasts like yours, with a tongue like yours down one's throat, and one's prick held in the soft grip of a cunt like yours, is to undergo a series of sensations such as don't come twice in a lifetime.'

Eva's eyes flashed as she gathered me closer in her naked arms and said:

'*Don't* they, though! In this particular instance I am going to see that they come twice *within half an hour*!'

'Well, I've come twice in less than half an hour and—'

'Oh! I know what you are going to say, but we'll soon put that all right.'

A careful examination of the state of affairs was then made by Eva who bent her pretty head for the purpose, kneeling on the bed in a position which enabled me to gaze at my leisure upon all her secret charms.

Her operations meanwhile were causing me exquisite delight. With an indescribable tenderness of action, soft and caressing as that of a young mother tending her sick child, she slipped the fingers of her left hand under my balls while the other hand wandered luxuriously over the surrounding country and finally came to an anchor upon my prick, which not unnaturally began to show signs of returning vigour. Pleased at the patient's improved state of health, she passed her delicious velvet tongue up and down and round and into a standing position! This sudden and satisfactory result of her ministrations so excited her that, without letting go of her prisoner, she cleverly passed one leg over me as I lay, and behold us in the traditional attitude of the *gamahuche a deux*! I now, for the first time, looked upon Eva's cunt in its full beauty, and I gladly devoted a moment to the inspection before plunging my tongue between the rich red lips which seemed to kiss my mouth as it clung in ecstasy in their luscious folds. I may say here that in point of colour, proportion and beauty of outline, Eva Letchford's cunt was the most perfect I had ever seen or gamahuched, though in after years my darling little Flossie's displayed equal faultlessness, and, as being the cunt of my beloved little sweetheart, whom I adored, it was entitled to and received from me a degree of homage never accorded to any other before or since.

The particular part of my person to which Eva was paying attention soon attained in her mouth a size and hardness which did the highest credit to her skill. With my tongue revelling in its enchanted resting-place, and my prick occupying what a house-agent might truthfully describe as 'this most desirable site', I was personally content to remain as we were, whilst Eva, entirely abandoning herself to her charming occupation, had apparently forgotten the object with which she had originally undertaken it. Fearing therefore lest the clinging mouth and delicately twining tongue should bring about the crisis which Eva had designed should take place elsewhere, I reluctantly took my lips from the clitoris they were enclosing at the moment, and called to its owner to stop.

'But Jack, you're just going to spend!' was the plaintive reply.

'Exactly, dear! And how about the "twice in half an hour".'

'Oh! of course. You were going to fuck me again, weren't you! Well, you'll find Massa Johnson in pretty good trim for the fray,' and she laughingly held up my prick, which was really of enormous dimensions, and plunging it downwards let it rebound with a loud report against my belly.

This appeared to delight her, for she repeated it several times. Each time the elasticity seemed to increase and the force of the recoil to become greater.

'The darling!' she cried, as she kissed the coral head. 'He is going to his own chosen abiding place. Come! Come! Come! blessed, *blessed* prick. Bury yourself in this loving cunt which longs for you; frig yourself deliciously against the lips which wait to kiss you; plunge into the womb which yearns to receive your life-giving seed; pause as you go by to press the

clitoris that loves you. Come, divine, adorable prick!
Fuck me, fuck me, fuck me! fuck me long and hard:
fuck and spare not! – Jack, you are into me, my cunt
clings to your prick, do you feel how it nips you?
Push, Jack, further; now your balls are kissing my
bottom. That's lovely! Crush my breasts with your
chest, cr-r-r-r-ush them, Jack. Now go slowly a
moment, and let your prick gently rub my clitoris. So
. . . o . . . o . . . Now faster and harder . . . faster
still – now your tongue in my mouth, and dig your
nails into my bottom. I'm going to spend: fuck, Jack,
fuck me, fuck me, fu-u-u-uck me! Heavens! what
bliss it is! Ah you're spending too. Bo . . . o . . . o . . .
oth together, both toge . . . e . . . e . . . ther. Pour it
into me, Jack! Flood me, drown me, fill my womb.
God! What rapture. Don't stop. Your prick is still
hard and long. Drive it into me – touch my navel. Let
me get my hand down to frig you as you go in and out.
The sweet prick! He's stiffer than ever. How splendid
of him! Fuck me again, Jack, Ah! fuck me till tomorrow, fuck me till I die.'

I fear that this language in the cold form of print
may seem more than a little crude. Yet those who have
experience of a beautiful and refined woman, abandoning herself in moments of passion to similar freedom of speech, will own the stimulus thus given to the
sexual powers. In the present instance its effect,
joined to the lascivious touches and never ceasing
efforts to arouse and increase desire of this deliciously
lustful girl, was to impart an unprecedented stiffness
to my member which throbbed almost to bursting
within the enclosing cunt and pursued its triumphant
career to such lengths, that even the resources of the
insatiable Eva gave out at last, and she lay panting in
my arms, where soon afterwards she passed into a
quiet sleep. Drawing a silken coverlet over her, I rose
with great caution, slipped on my clothes, and in five
minutes was on my way home.

Chapter Four

More of Flossie's school-life; and other matters

'Good morning, Captain Archer, I trust that you have slept well?' said Flossie on my presenting myself at the flat early the next day. 'My friend Miss Letchford,' she went on, in a prim middle-aged tone of voice, 'has not yet left her apartment. She complains of having passed a somewhat disturbed night owing to – ahem!'

'Rats in the wainscot?' I suggested.

'No, my friend attributes her sleepless condition to a severe irritation in the – forgive the immodesty of my words – lower part of her person, followed by a prolonged pricking in the same region. She is still feeling the effects, and I found her violently clasping a pillow between her – ahem! – legs, with which she was apparently endeavouring to soothe her feelings.'

'Dear me! Miss Eversley, do you think I could be of any assistance?' (*stepping towards Eva's door*).

'You are *most* kind, Captain Archer, but I have already done what I could in the way of friction and – other little attentions, which left the poor sufferer somewhat calmer. Now, Jack, you wretch! you haven't kissed me yet . . . That's better! You will not be surprised to hear that Eva has given me a full and detailed description of her sleepless night, in her own language, which I have no doubt you have discovered, is just a bit *graphic* at times.'

'Well, my little darling, I did my best, as I knew you would wish me to do. It wasn't difficult with such a bed-fellow as Eva. But charming and amorous as she is, I couldn't help feeling all the time "if it were only my little Flossie lying under me now!" By the way, how utterly lovely you are this morning, Floss.'

She was dressed in a short sprigged cotton frock, falling very little below her knees, shot pink and black stockings, and low patent leather shoes with silver buckles. Her long wavy brown hair gleamed gold in the morning light, and the deep blue eyes glowed with health and love, and now and again flashed with merriment. I gazed upon her in rapture at her beauty.

'Do you like my frock, Jack? I'm glad. It's the first time I've had it on. It's part of my trousseau.'

'Your *what*, Flossie?' I shouted.

'I said my trousseau,' she repeated quietly, but with sparks of fun dancing in her sweet eyes. 'The fact is, Jack, Eva declared the other day that though I am not married to you, you and I are really on a sort of honeymoon. So, as I have just had a good lot of money from the lawyers, she made me go with her and buy everything new. Look here,' (*unfastening her bodice*) 'new stays, new chemise, new stockings and oh! Jack, *look*! such *lovely* new drawers – none of your horrid vulgar knickerbockers, trimmings and lovely little tucks all the way up, and quite wide open in front for . . . ventilation I suppose! Feel what soft stuff they are made of! Eva was awfully particular about these drawers. She is always so practical, you know.'

'Practical!' I interrupted.

'Yes. What she said was that you would often be wanting to kiss me between my legs when there wasn't time to undress and be naked together, so that I must have drawers made of the finest and most delicate stuff to please you, and with the opening cut extra wide so as not to get in the way of your tongue! Now don't you call that practical?'

'I do indeed! Blessed Eva, that's another good turn I owe her!'

'Well, for instance, there isn't time to undress *now*, Jack and—'

She threw herself back in her chair and in an instant, I had plunged under the short rose-scented petticoats and had my mouth glued to the beloved cunt once more. In the midst of the delicious operation, I fancied I heard a slight sound from the direction of Eva's door and just then, Flossie locked her hands behind my head and pressed me to her with even more than her usual ardour; a moment later deluging my throat with the perfumed essence of her being.

'You darling old boy, how you *did* make me spend that time! I really think your tongue is longer than it was. Perhaps the warmth of Eva's interior has made it grow! Now I must be off to the dressmaker's for an hour or so. By the way, she wants to make my frocks longer. She declares people can see my drawers when I run upstairs.'

'Don't you let her do it, Floss.'

'*Rather not!* What's the use of buying expensive drawers like mine if you can't show them to a pal! *Good* morning, Captain! Sorry I can't stop. While I'm gone you might just step in and see how my lydy friend's gettin' on. Fust door on the right. *Good* morning!'

For a minute or two, I lay back in my chair and wondered whether I would not take my hat and go. But a moment's further reflection told me that I must do as Flossie directed me. To this decision, I must own, the memory of last night's pleasure and the present demands of a most surprising erection contributed in no small degree. Accordingly, I tapped at Eva's bedroom door.

She had just come from her bath and wore only a peignoir and her stockings. On seeing me, she at once let fall her garment and stood before me in radiant nakedness.

'Look at this,' she said, holding out a half-sheet of notepaper. 'I found it on my pillow when I woke an hour ago.'

If Jack comes this morning I shall send him in to see you while I go to Virginie's. Let him – *anything beginning with "f" or "s" that rhymes with* luck – you. "A hair of the dog" etc., will do you both good. My time will come. Ha! Ha!

Floss

'Now I ask you, Jack, was there ever such an adorable little darling?'

My answer need not be recorded.

Eva came close to me and thrust her hand inside my clothes.

'Ah! I see you are of the same way of thinking as myself,' she said taking hold of my fingers and carrying them onto her cunt, which pouted hungrily. 'So let us have one good royal fuck and then you can stay here with me while I dress, and I'll tell you anything that Flossie may have left out about her school-life in Paris. Will that meet your views?'

'Exactly,' I replied.

'Very well then. As we are going to limit ourselves to *one*, would you mind fucking me *en levrette*?'

'Any way you like, most puissant and fucksome of ladies!'

I stripped off my clothes in a twinkling and Eva placed herself in position, standing on the rug and bending forwards with her elbows on the bed. I reverently saluted the charms thus presented to my lips, omitting none, and then rising from my knees, advanced, weapon in hand, to storm the breach. As I approached, Eva opened her legs to their widest extent, and I drove my straining prick into the mellow cunt, fucking it with unprecedented vigour and delight, as the lips alternately parted and contracted, nipping me with an extraordinary force in response to the pressure of my right forefinger upon the clitoris and of my left upon the nipples of the heaving breasts. Keen as was the enjoyment we were both experiencing, the fuck – as invariably the case with a morning performance – was of very protracted duration, and several minutes had elapsed before I dropped my arms to Eva's thighs and, with my belly glued against her bottom and my face nestling between her shoulder blades, felt the rapturous throbbing of my prick as it discharged an avalanche into the innermost recesses of her womb.

'Don't move, Jack, for Heaven's sake,' she cried.

'Don't want to, Eva, I'm quite happy where I am, thank you!'

Moving an inch or two further out from the bed so as to give herself more 'play', she started an incredibly provoking motion of her bottom, so skilfully executed that it produced the impression of being almost *spiral*. The action is difficult to describe, but her bottom rose and fell, moved backward and forward, and from side to side in quick alternation, the result being that my member was constantly in contact with, as it were, some fresh portion of the embracing cunt, the soft folds of which seemed by their varied and tender caresses to be pleading to him to emerge from his present state of partial apathy and resume the proud condition he had displayed before.

'Will he come up this way, Jack, or shall I take the dear little man in my mouth and suck him into an erection?'

'I think he'll be all right as he is, dear. Just keep on nipping him with your cunt and push your bottom a little closer to me so that I may feel your naked flesh against mine . . . *that's* it.'

'Ah! the darling prick, he's beginning to swell! He's going to fuck me directly, I know he is! Your finger on my cunt in front, please Jack, and the other hand on my nipples. So! *that's* nice. Oh dear! How I *do* want your tongue in my mouth, but that can't be. Now begin and fuck me slowly at first. Your *second* finger on my clitoris, please, and frig me in time to the motion of your body. Now fuck faster a little, and deeper into me. Push, dear, push like a demon. Pinch my nipple; a little faster on the clitoris. I'm spending! I'm dying of delight! Fuck me, Jack, keep on fucking me. Don't be afraid. Strike against my bottom with all your strength, harder still, harder! Now put your hands down to my thighs and *drag* me on to you. Lovely! grip the flesh of my thighs with your fingers and fuck me to the very womb.'

'Eva, look out! I'm going to spend!'

'So am I, Jack. Ah! how your prick throbs against my cunt! Fuck me, Jack, to the last moment, spend your last drop, as I'm doing. One last push up to the hilt – there, keep him in like that and let me have a deluge from you. How exquisite! how adorable to spend together! *One* moment more before you take him out, and let me kiss him with my cunt before I say goodbye.'

'What a nip that was, Eva, it felt more like a hand on me than a—'

'Yes,' she interrupted, turning round and facing me with her eyes languorous and velvety with lust, 'that is my only accomplishment, and I must say I think it's a valuable one! In Paris I had a friend – but no matter I'm not going to talk about myself, but about Flossie. Sit down in that chair, and have a cigarette while I talk to you. I'm going to stay naked if you don't mind. It's so hot. Now if you're quite comfy, I'll begin.'

She seated herself opposite to me, her splendid naked body full in the light from the window near her.

'There is a part of Flossie's school story,' began Eva, 'which she has rather shrunk from telling you, and so I propose to relate the incident, in which I am sure you will be sufficiently interested. For the first twelve months of her school days in Paris, nothing very special occurred beyond the cementing of her friendship with Ylette Vespertin. Flossie was a tremendous favourite with the other girls on account of her sweet nature and her extraordinary beauty, and there is no doubt that a great many curly heads were popped under her petticoats at one time and another. All these heads, however, belonged to her own sex, and no great harm was done. But at last there arrived at the convent a certain Camille de Losgrain, who, though by no means averse to the delights of gamahuche, nursed a strong preference for male, as against female charms. Camille speedily struck up an alliance with a handsome boy of seventeen who lived in the house next door. This youth had often seen Flossie and greatly desired her acquaintance. It seems that his bedroom window was on the same level as that of the room occupied by Flossie, Camille and three other girls, all of whom knew him by sight and had severally expressed a desire to have him between their legs. So it was arranged one night that he was to climb onto a buttress below his room, and the girls would manage to haul him into theirs. All this had to be done in darkness, as of course no light could be shown. The young gentleman duly arrived on the scene in safety – the two eldest girls divested him of his clothes, and then, according to previous agreement, the five damsels sat naked on the edge of the bed in the pitch dark room, and Master Don Juan was to decide, by passing his hands over their bodies, which of the five should be favoured with his attentions. No one was to speak, to touch his person or to make any sign of interest. Twice the youth essayed this novel kind of ordeal by touch, and after a moment's profound silence he said, "J'ai choisi, c'est la troisieme." "La troisieme" was no other than Flossie, the size of whose breasts had at once attracted him as well as given a clue to her identity. And now, Jack, I hope the sequel will not distress you. The other girls accepted the decision most loyally, having no doubt anticipated it. They laid Flossie tenderly on the bed and lavished every kind of caress upon her, gamahuching her with especial tenderness, so as to open the road as far as possible to the invader. It fortunately turned out to be the case that the boy's prick was not by any means of abnormal size, and as the dear little maidenhead had been already subjected to very considerable wear and tear of fingers and tongues the entrance was, as she told me herself, effected with a minimum of pain and discomfort, hardly felt indeed in the midst of the frantic kisses upon mouth, eyes, nipples, breasts and buttocks which the four excited girls rained upon her throughout the operation. As for the boy, his enjoyment knew no bounds, and when his allotted time was up could hardly be persuaded to make the return voyage to his room. This, however, was at last accomplished, and the four virgins hastened to hear from their ravished friend the full true and particular account of her sensations. For several nights after this, the boy made his appearance in the room, where he fucked all the other four in succession, and pined openly for Flossie, who, however, regarded him as belonging to Camille and declined anything beyond the occasional service of his tongue which she greatly relished and which he, of course, as gladly put at her disposal.

'All this happened just before my time and was related to me afterwards by Flossie herself. Then I was engaged to teach English at the convent. Like everyone else who is brought in contact with her, I at once fell in love with Flossie and we quickly became the greatest of friends. Six months ago, came a change of fortune for me, an old bachelor uncle dying suddenly and leaving me a competence. By this time, the attachment between Flossie and myself had become so deep that the child could not bear the thought of parting from me. I too was glad enough of the excuse thus given for writing to Flossie's guardian – who has never taken more than a casual interest in her – to propose her returning to England with me and the establishment of a joint menage. My "references" being satisfactory, and Flossie having declared herself to be most anxious for the plan, the guardian made no objection and in short – here we are!'

'Well, that's a very interesting story, Eva. Only – *confound* that French boy and his buttress!'

'Yes, you would naturally feel like that about it, and I don't blame you. Only you must remember that if it hadn't been for the size of Flossie's breasts, and its being done in the dark, and . . .'

'But Eva, you don't mean to tell me the young brute wouldn't have chosen her out of the five if there had been a *light*, do you!'

'No, of course not. What I *do* mean is that it was all a sort of fluke, and that Flossie is really, to all intents and purposes . . .'

'Yes, yes, I know what you would like to say, and I entirely and absolutely agree with you. I *love* Flossie with all my heart and soul and . . . well, that French boy can go to the devil!'

'Miss Eva! Miss Eva!' came a voice outside the door.

'Well, what is it?'

'Oh, if you please, Miss, there's a young man downstairs called for his little account. Says 'e's the coals, Miss. I *towld* him you was engaged, Miss.'

'Did you – and what did he say?'

' "Ow!" 'e sez, "engyged, *is* she," 'e sez – "well, you tell 'er from me confidential-like, as it's 'igh time she was *married*," 'e sez!'

Our shouts of laughter brought Flossie scampering into the room, evidently in the wildest spirits.

'Horful scandal in 'igh life,' she shouted. 'A genl'man dish-covered in a lydy's aportments! 'arrowin' details. Speshul! Pyper! Speshul! – Now then, you two, what have you been doing while I've been gone? Suppose you tell me exactly what you've done and I'll tell you exactly what *I've* done' – then in a tone of cheap melodrama – 'Aha! 'ave I surproised yer guilty secret? She winceth! Likewise 'e winceth! in fact they both winceth! Thus h'am I avenged upon the pair!' And kneeling down between us, she pushed a dainty finger softly between the lips of Eva's cunt, and with her other hand took hold of my yard and tenderly frigged it, looking up into our faces all the time with inexpressible love and sweetness shining from her eyes.

'You *dears*!' she said. 'It *is* nice to have you two naked together like this!'

A single glance passed between Eva and me, and getting up from our seats we flung ourselves upon the darling and smothered her with kisses. Then Eva, with infinite gentleness and many loving touches, proceeded to undress her, handing the dainty garments to me one by one to be laid on the bed near me. As the fair white breasts came forth from the corset, Eva gave a little cry of delight, and pushing the lace-edged chemise below the swelling globes, took one erect and rosy nipple into her mouth, and putting her hand behind my neck, motioned me to take the other. Shivers of delight coursed up and down the shapely body over which our fingers roamed in all directions. Flossie's remaining garments were soon allowed to fall by a deft touch from Eva, and the beautiful girl stood before us in all her radiant nakedness. We paused a moment to gaze upon the spectacle of loveliness. The fair face flushed with love and desire; the violet eyes shone; the full rounded breasts put forth their coral nipples as if craving to be kissed again; below the smooth satin belly appeared the silken tuft that shaded without concealing the red lips of the adorable cunt; the polished thighs gained added whiteness by contrast with the dark stockings which clung amorously to the finely moulded legs.

'Now, Jack, *both together*,' said Eva, suddenly.

I divined what she meant and arranging a couple of large cushions on the wide divan, I took Flossie in my arms and laid her upon them, her feet upon the floor. Her legs opened instinctively and thrusting my head between her thighs, I plunged my tongue into the lower part of the cunt, whilst Eva, kneeling over her, upon the divan, attacked the developed clitoris. Our mouths thus met upon the exchanted spot and our tongues filled every corner and crevice of it. My own, I must admit, occasionally wandered downwards to the adjacent regions, and explored the valley of delight in that direction. But wherever we went and whatever we did, the lithe young body beneath continued to quiver from head to foot with excess of pleasure, shedding its treasures now in Eva's mouth, now in mine and sometimes in both at once! But vivid as were the delights she was experiencing, they were of a passive kind only, and Flossie was already artist enough to know that the keenest enjoyment is only obtained when giving and receiving are equally shared. Accordingly I was not surprised to hear her say:

'Jack, could you come up here to me now, please?'

Signalling to me to kneel astride her face, she seized my yard, guided it to her lips and then locking her hands over my loins, she alternately tightened and relaxed her grasp, signifying that I was to use the delicious mouth freely as a substitute for the interdicted opening below. The peculiar sucking action of her lips, of which I have spoken before, bore a pleasant resemblance to the nipping of an accomplished cunt, whilst the never-resting tongue, against whose soft folds M Jacques frigged himself luxuriously in his passage between the lips and throat, added a provocation to the lascivious sport not to be enjoyed in the ordinary act of coition. Meanwhile Eva had taken my place between Flossie's legs and was gamahuching the beloved cunt with incredible ardour. A sloping mirror on the wall above enabled me to survey the charming scene at my leisure, and to observe the spasms of delight which, from time to time, shook both the lovely naked forms below me. At last my own time arrived, and Flossie, alert as usual for the signs of approaching crisis, clutched my bottom with convulsive fingers and held me close pressed against her face, whilst I flooded her mouth with the stream of love that she adored. At the same moment the glass told me that Eva's lips were pushing far into the vulva to receive the result of their amorous labours, the passage of which from cunt to mouth was accompanied by every token of intense enjoyment from both the excited girls.

Rest and refreshment were needed by all three after the strain of our morning revels, and so the party broke up for the day after Flossie had mysteriously announced that she was designing something 'extra special', for the morrow.

Chapter Five

Birthday Festivities

The next morning there was a note from Flossie asking me to come as soon as possible after receiving it.

I hurried to the flat and found Flossie awaiting me, and in one of her most enchanting moods. It was Eva's birthday, as I was now informed for the first time, and to do honour to the occasion, Flossie had put on a costume in which she was to sell flowers at a fancy bazaar a few days later. It consisted of a white tam-o'-shanter cap with a straight upstanding feather – a shirt of the thinnest and gauziest white silk falling open at the throat and having a wide sailor collar – a broad lemon-coloured sash, a very short muslin skirt, lemon-coloured silk stockings and high-heeled brown shoes. At the opening of the shirt, a bunch of flame-coloured roses nestled between the glorious breasts, to the outlines of which all possible prominence was given by the softly clinging material. As she stood waiting to hear my verdict, her red lips slightly parted, a rosy flush upon her cheeks, and love and laughter beaming from the radiant eyes, the magic of her youth and beauty seemed to weave a fresh spell around my heart, and a torrent of passionate words burst from my lips as I strained the lithe young form to my breast and rained kisses upon her hair, her eyes, her cheeks and mouth.

She took my hand in her hand and quietly led me to

my favourite chair, and then seating herself on my knee, nestled her face against my cheek and said:

'Oh, Jack, Jack, my darling boy, how can you possibly love me like that!' The sweet voice trembled and a tear or two dropped softly from the violet eyes whilst an arm stole round my neck and red lips were pressed in a long intoxicating kiss upon my mouth.

We sat thus for some time when Flossie jumped from my knee, and said:

'We are forgetting all about Eva. Come in to her room and see what I have done.'

We went hand in hand into the bedroom and found Eva still asleep. On the chairs were laid her dainty garments, to which Flossie silently drew my attention. All along the upper edge of the chemise and corset, round the frills of the drawers and the hem of the petticoat, Flossie had sewn a narrow chain of tiny pink and white rosebuds, as a birthday surprise for her friend. I laughed noiselessly, and kissed her hand in token of my appreciation of the charming fancy.

'Now for Eva's birthday treat,' whispered Flossie in my ear. 'Go over into that corner and undress yourself as quietly as you can. I will help you.'

Flossie's 'help' consisted chiefly in the use of sundry wiles to induce an erection. As these included the slow frigging in which she was such an adept, as well as the application of her rosy mouth and active tongue to every part of my prick, the desired result was rapidly obtained.

'Now, Jack, you are going to have Eva whilst I look on. Some day, my turn will come, and I want to see exactly how to give you the greatest possible amount of pleasure. Come and stand here by me, and we'll wake her up.'

We passed round the bed and stood in front of Eva, who still slept on unconscious.

'Ahem!' from Flossie.

The sleeping figure turned lazily. The eyes unclosed

and fell upon the picture of Flossie in her flower-girl's dress, standing a little behind me and, with her right hand passed in front of me, vigorously frigging my erected yard, whilst the fingers of the other glided with a softly caressing motion over and under the attendant balls.

Eva jumped up, flung off her nightdress and crying to Flossie, *'Don't leave go!'* fell on her knees, seized my prick in her mouth and thrust her hand under Flossie's petticoats. The latter, obeying Eva's cry, continued to frig me deliciously from behind, whilst Eva furiously sucked the nut and upper part, and passing her disengaged hand round my bottom, caused me a new and exquisite enjoyment by inserting a dainty finger into the aperture thus brought within her reach. Flossie now drew close up to me and I could feel the swelling breasts in their thin silken covering pressed against my naked back, whilst her hand quickened its maddeningly provoking motion upon my prick and Eva's tongue pursued its enchanted course with increasing ardour and many luscious convolutions. Feeling I was about to spend, Flossie slipped her hand further down towards the root so as to give room for Eva's mouth to engulf almost the whole yard, a hint which the latter was quick to take, for her lips at once pressed close down to Flossie's fingers and with my hands behind my fair gama-hucher's neck, I poured my very soul into her waiting and willing throat.

During the interval which followed, I offered my congratulations to Eva and told her how sorry I was not to have known of her birthday before, so that I might have presented a humble gift of some sort. She hastened to assure me that nothing in the world, that I could have brought, would be more welcome than what I had just given her!

Eva had not yet seen her decorated underclothes and these were now displayed by Flossie with

countless merry jokes and quaint remarks. The pretty
thought was highly appreciated and nothing would do
but our dressing Eva in the flowery garments. When
this was done, Flossie suggested a can-can, and the
three of us danced a wild *pas-de-trois* until the breath
was almost out of our bodies. As we lay panting in
various unstudied attitudes of exhaustion, a ring was
heard at the door and Flossie, who was the only pre-
sentable one of the party went out to answer the
summons. She came back in a minute with an enormous basket of Neapolitan violets. Upon our
exclaiming at this extravagance Flossie gravely delivered herself of the following statement:

'Though not in a position for the moment to furnish chapter and verse, I am able to state with convic-
tion that in periods from which we are only separated
by some twenty centuries or so, it was customary for
ladies and gentlemen of the time to meet and discuss
the business of pleasure of the hour without the
encumberance of clothes upon their bodies. The
absence of *arrière-pensée* shown by this commendable practice might lead the superficial to conclude
that these discussions led to no practical results.
Nothing could be further from the truth. The interviews were invariably held upon a Bank of Violets (so
the old writers tell us), and at a certain point in the
proceedings, the lady would fall back upon this bank
with her legs spread open at the then equivalent to an
angle of forty-five. The gentleman would thereupon
take in his right (or dexter) hand the instrument which
our modern brevity of speech has taught us to call his
prick. This, with some trifling assistance on her part,
he would introduce into what the same latter-day
rage for conciseness of expression leaves us powerless
to describe otherwise than as her cunt. On my right we
have the modern type of the lady, on my left, that of
the gentleman. In the middle, the next best thing to a
bank of violets. Ha! you take me at last! Now I'm

going to put them all over the bed, and when I'm ready, you, Eva, will kindly oblige by depositing your snowy bottom in the middle, opening your legs and admitting Mr Jack to the proper position between them.'

While delivering this amazing oration, Flossie had gradually stripped herself entirely naked. We both watched her movements in silent admiration as she strewed the bed from end to end with the fragrant blossoms, which filled the room with their delightful perfume. When all was ready, she beckoned to Eva to lay herself on the bed, whispering to her, though not so low but that I could hear.

'Imagine you are Danae. I'll trouble you for the size of Jupiter's prick! Just look at it!' – then much lower, but still audibly – 'You're going to be fucked, Eva darling, jolly well fucked! And I'm going to *see* you – *Lovely!*'

The rose-edged chemise and drawers were once more laid aside and the heroine of the day stretched herself voluptuously on the heaped-up flowers, which sent forth fresh streams of fragrance in response to the pressure of the girl's naked body.

'Ah, a happy thought!' cried Flossie. 'If you would lie *across* the bed with your legs hanging down, and Jack wouldn't mind standing up to his work, I think I could be of some assistance to you both.'

The change was quickly made, a couple of pillows were slipped under Eva's head, and Flossie, kneeling across the other's face, submitted her cunt to be gamahuched by her friend's tongue which at once darted amorously to its place within the vulva. Flossie returned the salutation for a moment and then resting her chin upon the point just above Eva's clitoris, called me to 'come on'. I placed myself in position and was about to storm the breach when Flossie found the near proximity of my yard to be too much for her feelings and begged to be allowed to gamahuche me for a minute.

'After that, I'll be quite good,' she added to Eva, 'and will only *watch*.'

Needless to say I made no objection. The result, as was the case with most of Flossie's actions, was increased pleasure to everybody concerned and to Eva as much as anyone inasmuch as the divine sucking of Flossie's rosy lips and lustful tongue produced a sensible hardening and lengthening of my excited member.

After performing this delightful service, she was for moving away, but sounds of dissent were heard from Eva, who flung her arms round Flossie's thighs and drew her cunt down in closer contact with the caressing mouth.

From my exalted position, I could see all that was going on and this added enormously to the sensations I began to experience when Flossie, handling my yard with deft fingers, dropped a final kiss upon the nut, and then guided it to the now impatient goal. With eyes lit up with interest and delight, she watched it disappear with the soft red lips whose movements she was near enough to follow closely. Under these conditions, I found myself fucking Eva with unusual vigour and penetration, whilst she, on her part, returned my strokes with powerful thrusts of her bottom and exquisitely pleasurable contractions of her cunt upon my prick.

Flossie, taking in all this with eager eyes, became madly excited, and at last sprang from her kneeling position on the bed, and taking advantage of an *outward* motion of my body, bent down between us, and pushing the point of her tongue under Eva's clitoris, insisted on my finishing the performance with this charming incentive added. Its effect upon both Eva and myself was electric, and as her clitoris and my prick shared equally in the contact of the tongue, we were not long in bringing the entertainment to an eminently satisfactory conclusion.

The next item in the birthday programme was the exhibition of half a dozen cleverly executed pen and ink sketches – Flossie's gift to Eva – showing the three of us in attitudes not to be found in the illustrations of the 'Young Ladies Journal'. A discussion arose as to whether Flossie had not been somewhat flattering to the longitudinal dimensions of the present writer's member. She declared that the proportions were 'according to *Cocker*' – obviously, as she wittily said, the highest authority on the question.

'Anyhow, I'm going to take measurements and then you'll see I'm right! In the picture the length of Jack's prick is exactly one-third of the distance from his chin to his navel. Now measuring the real article – Hello! I *say*, Evie, what *have* you done to him!'

In point of fact, the object under discussion was feeling the effects of his recent exercise and had dropped to a partially recumbent attitude.

Eva, who was watching the proceedings with an air of intense amusement called out:

'Take it between your breasts, Flossie; you will see the difference then!'

The mere prospect of such a lodging imparted a certain amount of vigour to Monsieur Jacques, who was thereupon introduced into the delicious cleft of Flossie's adorable bosom, and in rapture at the touch of the soft flesh on either side of him, at once began to assume more satisfactory proportions.

'But he's not up to his full height yet,' said Flossie. 'Come and help me, Evie dear; stand behind Jack and frig him whilst I gamahuche him in front. *That's* the way to get him up to concert pitch! When I feel him long and stiff enough in my mouth, I'll get up and take his measure.'

The success of Flossie's plan was immediate and complete, and when the measurements were made, the proportions were found to be exactly twenty-one and seven inches respectively, whilst in the drawing they were three inches to one inch. Flossie proceeded to execute a wild war-dance of triumph over this signal vindication of her accuracy, winding up by insisting on my carrying her pick-a-back round the flat. Her enjoyment of this ride was unbounded, as also was mine, for besides the pleasure arising from the close contact of her charming body, she contrived to administer a delicious friction to my member with the calves of her naked legs.

On our return to the bedroom, Eva was sitting on the edge of the low divan.

'Bring her to me here,' she cried.

I easily divined what was wanted, and carrying my precious burden across the room, I faced round with my back to Eva. In the sloping glass to the left, I could see her face disappear between the white rounded buttocks, at the same moment that her right hand moved in front of me and grasped my yard which it frigged with incomparable tenderness and skill. This operation was eagerly watched by Flossie over my shoulder, while she clung to me with arms and legs and rubbed herself against my loins with soft undulating motions like an amorous kitten, the parting lips of her cunt kissing my back and her every action testifying to the delight with which she was receiving the attentions of Eva's tongue upon the neighbouring spot.

My feelings were now rapidly passing beyond my control, and I had to implore Eva to remove her hand, whereupon Flossie, realizing the state of affairs, jumped down from her perch, and burying my prick in her sweet mouth, sucked and frigged me in such a frenzy of desire that she had very soon drawn from me the last drop I had to give her.

A short period of calm ensued after this last ebullition, but Flossie was in too mad a mood today to remain long quiescent.

'Eva,' she suddenly cried, 'I believe I am as tall as

you nowadays, and I am *quite sure* my breasts are as large as yours. I'm going to measure and see!'

After Eva's height had been found to be only a short inch above Flossie's, the latter proceeded to take the most careful and scientific measurements of the breasts. First came the circumference, then the diameter *over* the nipples, then the diameter omitting the nipples, then the distance from the nipple to the upper and lower edges of the hemispheres, and so on. No dry as dust old savant, staking his reputation upon an absolutely accurate calculation of the earth's surface, could have carried out his task with more ineffable solemnity than did this merry child who, one knew, was all the time secretly bubbling over with the fun of her quaint conceit.

The result was admitted to be what Flossie called it – 'a moral victory' for herself, inasmuch as half a square inch, or as Flossie declared, 'fifteen thirty-*two*-*ths*', was all the superiority of area that Eva could boast.

'There's one other measurement I *should* like to have taken,' said Eva, 'because in spite of my ten years *de plus* and the fact that my cunt is not altogether a stranger to the joys of being fucked, I believe that Flossie would win *that* race, and I should like her to have one out of three!'

'*Lovely!*' cried Flossie. 'But Jack must be the judge. Here's the tape, Jack: fire away. Now, Evie, come and lie beside me on the edge of the bed, open your legs, and swear to abide by the verdict!'

After a few minutes fumbling with the tape and close inspection of the parts in dispute, I retired to a table and wrote down the following, which I pinned against the window curtain.

'Letchford v. Eversley

Mesdames,

In compliance with your instructions I have this day surveyed the private premises belonging to the above parties, and have now the honour to submit the following report, plan, and measurements.

As will be seen from the plan, Miss Letchford's cunt is exactly $3\frac{1}{16}$ inches from the underside of clitoris to the base of vulva. Miss Eversley's cunt, adopting the same line of measurement, gives $3\frac{5}{8}$ inches.

I may add that the premises appear to me to be thoroughly desirable in both cases, and to a good, upright and painstaking tenant would afford equally pleasant accommodation in spring, summer, autumn or winter.

A small but well-wooded covert is attached to each, whilst an admirable dairy is in convenient proximity.

With reference to the Eversley property, I am informed that it has not yet been occupied, but in view of its size and beauty, and the undoubted charms of the surrounding country, I confidently anticipate that a permanent and satisfactory tenant (such as I have ventured to describe above), will very shortly be found for it. My opinion of its advantages as a place of residence may, indeed, be gathered from the fact that I am greatly disposed to make an offer in my own person.

Yours faithfully,
J Archer

As the two girls stood with their hands behind their backs reading my ultimatum, Flossie laughed uproariously, but I noticed that Eva looked grave and thoughtful.

Had I written anything that annoyed her? I could hardly think so, but while I was meditating on the possibility, half resolved to put it to the test by a simple question, Eva took Flossie and myself by the hand, led us to the sofa and sitting down between us, said:

'Listen to me, you two dears! You, Flossie, are my chosen darling, and most beloved little friend. You, Jack, are Flossie's lover, and for her sake as well as for your own, I have the greatest affection for you. You both know all this. Well, I have not the heart to keep you from one another any longer. Flossie, dear, I hereby absolve you from your promise to me. Jack, you have behaved like a brick, as you are. Come here tomorrow at your usual time and I think we shall be able to agree upon *"a tenant for the Eversley property"*.'

This is not a novel of sentiment, and a description of what followed would therefore be out of place. Enough to say that after one wild irrepressible shriek of joy and gratitude from Flossie, the conversation took a sober and serious turn, and soon afterwards we parted for the day.

Chapter Six

The tenant in possession

The next morning's post brought me letters from both Eva and Flossie.

My dear Jack, (wrote the former)

Tomorrow will be a red letter day for you two! And I want you both to get the utmost of delight from it. So let no sort of scruple or compunction spoil your pleasure. Flossie is, in point of physical development, a woman. As such, she longs to be fucked by the man she loves. Fuck her therefore with all and more than all the same skill and determination you displayed in fucking me. She can think and talk of nothing else. Come early tomorrow and bring your admirable prick in its highest state of efficiency and stiffness!

Yours,
Eva

Flossie wrote:

I cannot sleep a wink for thinking of what is coming to me tomorrow. All the time I keep turning over in my mind how best to make it nice for you. I am practising Eva's "nip". I *feel* as if I could do it, but nipping *nothing* is not really practice, is it, Jack? My beloved, I kiss your prick, in imagination. Tomorrow I will do it in the flesh, for I warn you that nothing will ever induce me to give up *that*, nor will even the seven inches which I yearn to have in my cunt ever bring me to consent to being deprived of the sensation of your dear tongue when it curls between the lips and pays polite attentions to my clitoris! But you shall have me as you like tomorrow, and all days to follow. I am to be in the future. . .

Yours body and soul,
Flossie

When I arrived at the flat I found Flossie had put on the costume in which I had seen her the first day of our acquaintance. The lovely little face wore an expression of gravity, as though to show me she was not forgetting the importance of the occasion. I am not above confessing that, for my part, I was profoundly moved.

We sat beside one another, hardly exchanging a word. Presently Flossie said:

'Whenever you are *ready*, Jack, I'll go to my room and undress.'

The characteristic naiveté of this remark somewhat broke the spell that was upon us, and I kissed her with effusion.

'Shall it be . . . *quite* naked, Jack?'

'Yes, darling, if *you* don't mind.'

'All right. When I am ready I'll call to you.'

Five minutes later, I heard the welcome summons.

From the moment I found myself in her room, all sense of restraint vanished at a breath. She flew at me in a perfect fury of desire, pushed me by sheer force upon my back on the bed, and lying at full length upon me with her face close to mine, she said:

'Because I was a girl and not a woman, Jack, you have never fucked me. But you are going to fuck me now, and I shall be a woman. But first, I want to be a girl to you still for a few minutes only. I want to have your dear prick in my mouth again; I want you to kiss my cunt in the old delicious way; I want to lock my naked arms round your naked body; and hold you to my face, whilst I wind my tongue round your prick until you spend. Let me do all this, Jack, and then you shall fuck me till the skies fall.'

Without giving me time to reply to this frenzied little oration, Flossie had whisked round and was in position for the double gamahuche she desired. Parting her legs to their widest extent on each side of my face, she sank gently down until her cunt came full upon my open mouth. At the same moment I felt my prick seized and plunged deep into her mouth with which she at once commenced the delicious sucking action I knew so well. I responded by driving my tongue to the root into the rosy depths of her perfumed cunt, which I sucked with ever increasing zest and enjoyment, drawing fresh treasures from its inner recesses at every third or fourth stroke of my tongue. Words fail me to describe the unparalleled vigour of her sustained attack upon my erected prick, which she sucked, licked, tongued and frigged with such a furious *abandon* and at the same time with such a subtle skill and knowledge of the sublime art of gamahuching, that the end came with unusual rapidity, and wave after wave of the sea of love broke in ecstasy upon the 'coral strand' of her adorable mouth. For a minute or two more, her lips retained their hold and then, leaving her position, she came and lay down beside me, nestling her naked body against mine, and softly chafing the lower portion of my prick whilst she said:

'Now Jack darling, I am going to talk to you about the different ways of fucking, because of course you will want to fuck me, and I shall want to be fucked, in every possible position, and in every single part of my body where a respectable young woman may reasonably *ask* to be fucked.'

The conversation which followed agreeably filled the intervening time before the delicate touches which Flossie kept constantly applying to my prick caused it to raise its head to a considerable altitude, exhibiting a hardness and rigidity which gave high promise for the success of the coming encounter.

'Good gracious!' cried Flossie. 'Do you think I shall ever find room for all that, Jack?'

'For that, and more also, sweetheart,' I replied.

'*More!* Why, *what* more are you going to put into me?'

'This is the only article I propose to introduce at present, Floss. But I mean that when Monsieur Jacques finds himself for the first time with his head buried between the delicious cushions in *there*' (*touching her belly*) 'he will most likely beat his own record in the matter of length and stiffness.'

'Do you mean, Jack, that he will be bigger with me than he was with Eva?' said Flossie with a merry twinkle.

'Certainly I mean it,' was my reply. 'To fuck a beautiful girl like Eva must always be immensely enjoyable, but to fuck a young Venus of sixteen, who besides being the perfection of mortal loveliness, is also one's own chosen and adorable little sweetheart – *that* belongs to a different order of pleasure altogether.'

'And I suppose, Jack, that when the sixteen-year-old is simply dying to be fucked by her lover, as I am at this moment, the chances are that she may be able to make it rather nice for him, as well as absolutely heavenly for herself. Now I can wait no longer. "First position" at once, please, Jack. Give me your prick in my hand and I will direct his wandering footsteps.'

'He's at the door, Flossie; shall he enter?'

'Yes. Push him in slowly and fuck gently at first, so

that I may find out by degrees how much he's going to hurt me. A little further, Jack. Why, he's more than halfway in already! Now you keep still and I'll thrust a little with my bottom.'

'Why, Floss, you darling, you're nipping me deliciously!'

'Can you feel me, Jack? How lovely! Fuck me a little more, Jack, and get in deeper, that's it! Now faster and harder. What glorious pleasure it is!'

'And no pain, darling?'

'Not a scrap. One more good push and he'll be in up to the hilt, won't he? Eva told me to put my legs over your back. Is that right?'

'Quite right, and if you're sure I'm not hurting you, Floss, I'll really begin now and fuck you in earnest.'

'That's what I'm here for, sir,' she replied with a touch of her never-absent fun even in this supreme moment.

'Here goes, then!' I answered. Having once made up her mind that she had nothing to dread, Flossie abandoned herself with enthusiasm to the pleasures of the moment. Locking her arms round my neck and her legs round my buttocks, she cried to me to fuck her with all my might.

'Drive your prick into me again and again, Jack. Let me feel your belly against mine. Did you feel my cunt nip you then? Ah! how you are fucking me now! – fucking me, fu . . . u . . . ucking me!'

Her lovely eyes turned to heaven, her breath came in quick short gasps, her fingers wandered feverishly about my body. At last, with a cry, she plunged her tongue into my mouth and, with convulsive undulations of her little body, let loose the floods of her being to join the deluge which, with sensations of exquisite delight, I poured into her burning cunt.

The wild joy of this our first act of coition was followed by a slight reaction and, with a deep sigh of contentment Flossie fell asleep in my arms, leaving my prick still buried in its natural resting place. Before long, my own eyelids closed and, for an hour or more, we lay thus gaining from blessed sleep fresh strength to enter upon new transports of pleasure.

Flossie was the first to awake, stirred no doubt by the unaccustomed sensations of a swelling prick within her. I awoke to find her dear eyes resting upon my face, her naked arms round my neck an her cunt enfolding my yard with a soft and clinging embrace.

Her bottom heaved gently, and accepting the invitation thus tacitly given, I turned my little sweetheart on her back and, lying luxuriously between her widely parted legs, once more drove my prick deep into her cunt and fucked her with slow lingering strokes, directed upwards so as to bring all possible contact to bear upon the clitoris.

This particular motion afforded her evident delight and the answering thrusts of her bottom were delivered with ever increasing vigour and precision, each of us relishing to the full the efforts of the other to augment the pleasure of the encounter. With sighs and gasps and little cries of rapture, Flossie strained me to her naked breasts, and twisting her legs tightly round my own, cried out that she was spending and implored me to let her feel my emission mix with hers. By dint of clutching her bottom with my hands, driving the whole length of my tongue into her mouth I was just able to manage the simultaneous discharge she coveted, and once more I lay upon her in a speechless ecstasy of consummated passion.

Any one of my readers who has had the supreme good fortune to fuck the girl of his heart will bear me out in saying that the lassitude following upon such a meeting is greater and more lasting than the mere weariness resulting from an ordinary act of copulation 'where love is not'.

Being well aware of this fact, I resolved that my beloved little Flossie's powers should not be taxed any further for the moment, and told her so.

'But Jack,' she cried, almost in tears, 'we've only done it *one* way, and Eva says there are at least *six*! And oh, I do *love* it so!'

'And so do I, little darling. But also, I love *you*, and I'm not going to begin by giving you and that delicious little caressing cunt of yours more work than is good for you both.'

'Oh, dear! I suppose you're right, Jack.'

'Of course I'm right, darling. Tomorrow I shall come and fuck you again, and the next day, and the next, and many days after that. It will be odd if we don't find ourselves in Eva's six different positions before we've done!'

At this moment Eva herself entered the room.

'Well, Flossie . . . ?' she said.

'Ask Jack!' replied Flossie.

'Well Jack, then . . . ?' said Eva.

'Ask Flossie!' I retorted, and fled from the room.

The adventures I have, with many conscious imperfections, related in the foregoing pages, were full of interest to me, and were, I am disposed to think, not without their moments of attraction for my fellow actors in the scenes depicted.

It by no means necessarily follows that they will produce a corresponding effect upon the reading public who, in my descriptions of Floss and her ways, may find only an ineffectual attempt to set forth the charms of what appears to me an absolutely unique temperament. If haply it should prove to be otherwise, I should be glad to have the opportunity of continuing a veritable labour of love by recounting certain further experiences of Eva, Floss and

Yours faithfully,
Jack

EROTIC CLASSICS FROM
CARROLL & GRAF

☐ Anonymous/AUTOBIOGRAPHY OF A FLEA		$3.95
☐ Anonymous/CAPTURED		$4.50
☐ Anonymous/CONFESSIONS OF AN ENGLISH MAID		$4.50
☐ Anonymous/THE CONSUMMATE EVELINE		$4.95
☐ Anonymous/THE EDUCATION OF A MAIDEN		$4.50
☐ Anonymous/THE EROTIC READER		$4.50
☐ Anonymous/THE EROTIC READER II		$3.95
☐ Anonymous/THE EROTIC READER III		$4.50
☐ Anonymous/THE EROTIC READER IV		$4.95
☐ Anonymous/THE EROTIC READER V		$4.95
☐ Anonymous/FALLEN WOMAN		$4.50
☐ John Cleland/FANNY HILL		$4.95
☐ Anonymous/FANNY HILL'S DAUGHTER		$3.95
☐ Anonymous/FORBIDDEN PLEASURES		$4.95
☐ Anonymous/HAREM NIGHTS		$4.95
☐ Anonymous/INDISCREET MEMOIRS		$4.50
☐ Anonymous/A LADY OF QUALITY		$3.95
☐ Anonymous/LAY OF THE LAND		$4.50
☐ Anonymous/LEDA IN BLACK ON WHITE		$4.95
☐ Anonymous/MAID AND MISTRESS		$4.50
☐ Anonymous/THE MERRY MENAGE		$4.50
☐ Anonymous/SATANIC VENUS		$4.50
☐ Anonymous/SWEET CONFESSIONS		$4.50
☐ Anonymous/TROPIC OF LUST		$4.50
☐ Anonymous/VENUS IN INDIA		$3.95
☐ Anonymous/WHITE THIGHS		$4.50

Available from fine bookstores everywhere or use this coupon for ordering.

Carroll & Graf Publishers, Inc., 260 Fifth Avenue, N.Y., N.Y. 10001

Please send me the books I have checked above. I am enclosing $_____ (please add $1.25 per title to cover postage and handling.) Send check drawn on a U.S. bank or money order—no cash or C.O.D.'s please. N.Y. residents please add 8¼% sales tax.

Mr/Mrs/Ms _____

Address _____

City _____ State/Zip _____

Please allow four to six weeks for delivery.